WITHDRAWN
FOR SALE

CYBER-KILLERS

CYBER-KILLERS

Edited by Ric Alexander
Introduced by Peter F. Hamilton

> **ERRATA**
> The acknowledgement for
> THE STATE OF THE ART
> *should read:*
> copyright © Iain M Banks
> *subsequently published in*
>
> THE STATE OF THE ART
>
> © Iain M Banks 1991.
> *Reproduced by permission of
> the author and Mic Cheetham
> Literary Agency*

ORION

Copyright © Edited by Ric Alexander 1997
Introduction: Copyright © Peter F. Hamilton 1997
All rights reserved

The right of Ric Alexander to be identified as the
editor of this work has been asserted by him in accordance with
the Copyright, Designs and Patents Act 1988.

First published in Great Britain in 1997 by
Orion
An imprint of Orion Books Ltd
Orion House, 5 Upper St Martin's Lane, London WC2H 9EA

A CIP catalogue record for this book is available
from the British Library

ISBN 0 75280 783 8 (hardcover)

ISBN 0 75280 980 6 (trade paperback)

Typeset by Deltatype Ltd, Birkenhead, Merseyside
Printed in Great Britain by
Clays Ltd, St Ives plc

LINCOLNSHIRE
COUNTY COUNCIL

MENU

Introduction *Peter F. Hamilton*

ONE NETWORK TERRORISTS

ifdefDEBUG+'world/enough'+'time' *Terry Pratchett* 3
Blood Music *Greg Bear* 15
Sam Hall *Poul Anderson* 37
Blood Sisters *Joe Haldeman* 65
Crime on Mars *Arthur C. Clarke* 79
The Pardoner's Tale *Robert Silverberg* 85
A Gift from the Culture *Iain M. Banks* 105
Murder Will In *Frank Herbert* 121

TWO ROBOT CRIME

The Undercity *Dean Koontz* 151
Imposter *Philip K. Dick* 163
Fondly Fahrenheit *Alfred Bester* 177
Comfort Me, My Robot *Robert Bloch* 195
Home is the Hangman *Roger Zelazny* 207
Watchbird *Robert Sheckley* 261
From Fanaticism, or for Reward *Harry Harrison* 281
Adventure of the Metal Murderer *Fred Saberhagen* 293

THREE VIRTUAL MURDER

A Kind of Murder *Larry Niven* 303
Zone of Terror *J. G. Ballard* 317
Tricentennial *John Shirley* 333
Johnny Mnemonic *William Gibson* 341
Angel *Pat Cadigan* 357
Dreamers *Kim Newman* 373
Virtually Lucid Lucy *Ian Watson* 385
Virtually Alive *Peter James* 403

ACKNOWLEDGEMENTS

The editor is grateful to the following authors, agents and publishers for permission to include copyright stories in this collection: Colin Smythe Ltd on behalf of Terry Pratchett for his story, #ifdefDEBUG+'world/enough'+'time', Victor Gollancz Ltd for 'Blood Music' by Greg Bear, 'Imposter' by Philip K. Dick, 'Johnny Mnemonic' by William Gibson and 'Virtually Lucid Lucy' by Ian Watson; Scott Meredith Literary Agency for 'Sam Hall' by Poul Anderson and 'Crime on Mars' by Arthur C. Clarke; Penguin Group for 'Blood Sisters' by Joe Haldeman; *Playboy* Inc and the author for 'The Pardoner's Tale' by Robert Silverberg; Little Brown Publishers & Orbit Books for 'A Gift From the Culture' by Iain M. Banks; Headline Publishing Group for 'Murder Will In' by Frank Herbert; International Scripts and the author for 'The Undercity' by Dean Koontz; Fantasy House Inc for 'Fondly Fahrenheit' by Alfred Bester; the author for 'Comfort Me, My Robot' by Robert Bloch; Conde Nast Publications Inc for 'Home is the Hangman' by Roger Zelazny, 'Watchbird' by Robert Sheckley and 'A Kind of Murder' by Larry Niven; Abner Stein Literary Agency for 'From Fanaticism, or for Reward' by Harry Harrison; *Omni* Publications for 'Adventure of the Metal Murderer' by Fred Saberhagen; Random Publishing Group and Jonathan Cape Ltd for 'Zone of Terror' by J. G. Ballard; the author and Eyeball Books for 'Tricentennial' by John Shirley; Davis Publications Inc for 'Angel' by Pat Cadigan; the author for 'Dreamers' by Kim Newman; the *Daily Telegraph* and the author for 'Virtually Alive' by Peter James. While every effort has been made to contact the copyright holders of material used in this collection, in the case of any accidental infringement, concerned parties are asked to contact the editor in care of the publishers.

INTRODUCTION

Like a software virus silently downloading from the very technology it prefixes, the word *cyber* has successfully infiltrated and contaminated modern culture. By doing so, by multiplying and attaching itself to new media genres as they are born, it has developed beyond single definition.

Today it acts as the universal symbol for a streetwise tomorrow. Include it in a book title, and the publishing house's science fiction imprint logo printed on the spine becomes an irrelevance. Scour the straight-to-video section of your local rental shop, and you'll find it describing a dozen *Terminator* rip-offs where androids in mirror shades clunk over back-lot sandpits toting huge black guns (and chasing women whose dress sense hasn't evolved much from fifties pulp magazine covers). Read the blurb for software games, and there it sits as a subliminal trigger for the image of implant-boosted marines pre-loaded behind your eyes. You *know* what you're getting.

The product has become its own label.

Unfortunately, this process has meant it falling prey to modern imagery, living in danger of becoming its own cliché. Total cyber-pap. Bio-electronic synthesis seemingly always threatens to bite the human race on its collective arse, those shiny chrome and plastic systems forever glitching into second-rate James Bond villainy.

The stories Ric Alexander has chosen for this anthology will, I hope, go a long way to righting such a flawed perception. Examined properly, cybernetic applications can tell us a lot about ourselves.

When I read through this book I was surprised at how old some of the stories were. Ye gods, there's even talk of tape spools and tubes. Some mistake here, surely? Cybernetics and androids might have been mentioned in the Fifties, but the true components of our contemporary cyber-culture have only been available since the mid-Seventies at the earliest, when processors started cropping up in mundane domestic gadgets and Steve Austin first ran across our TV screens in his wonderfully paradoxical slow motion.

As we all know, nothing dates science fiction like technological development. The ongoing computer revolution proves that. We're in the era of essential six-monthly upgrades if you merely want to stay level with the competition; and as for racing ahead of them, forget it. The future of the Fifties didn't come and go in a flurry of moonshots and nuclear power plant construction; it never existed, not as a viable entity. The smarter writers from that age circumvented the problem of obsolescence with a decent narrative drive, each of them proffering an original idea of how people will cope with strange circumstances. Which is why they're being reprinted now, the validity of their stories firmly intact.

So forget the odd anachronism they throw up, overlook their lack of global webs and nanonic synapse junctions, and discover the essentially human theme they relate.

At its root function, cybernetics is about the fusion of the biological and the mechanical/electronic. Exactly how that fusion can be achieved provides the diversity which makes the subject so engrossing – a diversity well represented by the A-list authors in *Cyber-killers*. It is through the nature of the interface itself that our essence is thrown into sharp relief. Interfaces that vary from Poul Anderson's 'Sam Hall', in which the protagonist is little more than a computer operator, to Peter James's 'Virtually Alive' where people can be transferred into programs. How they react to their circumstances is what counts; the technology is merely a stage on which their emotional performance can unfold.

Fine, we learn about ourselves from studying the possible problems an advanced technological society could present us with. But why cyber-*killers*? Hasn't this brought us full circle back to my original complaint? Doesn't this perpetuate the myth of a fast-track evolutionary successor devoting itself to wiping us out because its mighty positronic brain considers us nothing more than irritating insects?

No, in these pages, as in life, the technology itself isn't evil. Like the saying goes, guns don't kill people, people kill people. True, but then, guns are designed specifically to kill; communication networks and household droids are not. At least, not at first. People, however, are eternally ingenious in their ability to subvert the ordinary. All of us have a dark side capable of doing this; the most fascinating and frightening aspect of our character, and the most revealing. We try desperately to hold it in check, some of us for our entire lives. Others succumb to temptation.

Here then, is a selection of new temptations. Read and be wary.

Peter F. Hamilton
Rutland, December 1996

ONE
NETWORK TERRORISTS

INTERFACE:/
The crime of the future will be that of outwitting the computer. It is already being done. By stealing a code, or by multifarious fakery that the dumb computer can't see through, numbers are so manipulated by the computer's incredible innocence as to sluice money into unauthorised hands. Naturally, the computer can always be redesigned so as to prevent whatever fiddle is discovered. But then it will be up to human beings to invent a new and more subtle, or more elaborate, scam. And no doubt they will.

Isaac Asimov
Crime Up To Date (1983)

ONLINE: **ONE/1** *Subject*: Darren Thompson, computer sleuth

ifdefDEBUG+'world/enough'+'time'

Terry Pratchett

INFO: Now crime is targeting the computer it takes a special kind of investigator to solve cases. Men like Darren Thompson: Internet-wise, clued up on virtual reality and possessing a nice line in sardonic wit. Just the sort of sleuth, in fact, to help the law discover precisely *why* people are dying at their Seagems.

Terry Pratchett, the creator of the 'Discworld' novels, needs very little introduction. He's just about the biggest-selling author of fantasy novels in the world today. Terry actually began writing while he was still at school in Beaconsfield, England, and created his first short story, 'The Hades Business', at thirteen. It appeared in *Science Fantasy* in 1965. He used the money to buy a typewriter – but now he's rarely seen without a laptop or his trademark fedora hat. Terry says he was introduced to high-tech during his time as press officer for the Central Electricity Generating Board – which happened to coincide with the Three Mile Island disaster in America. 'It was my job to say, "Radioactivity? What radioactivity? Oh, *that* radioactivity!"' he recalls. One of his comic novels, *Only You Can Save Mankind* (1992), is about a computer game in which an alien battle fleet wants to negotiate for peace – the problem is that games don't work that way; it's kill or be killed. The problem for Darren Thompson in this story which Terry wrote for *Digital Dreams* in 1990 is, though, rather more complex ... and certainly more deadly.

Never could stand the idea of machines in people. It's not proper. People say, hey, what about pacemakers and them artificial kidneys and that, but they're still machines no matter what.

Some of them have nuclear batteries. Don't tell me that's right.

I tried this implant once, it was supposed to flash the time at the bottom left-hand corner of your eyeball once a second, in little red numbers. It was for the busy exec, they said, who always needs to know, you know, *subliminally* what the time is. Only mine kept resetting to Tuesday, 1 January 1980 every time I blinked, so I took it back, and the salesman tried to sell me one that could show the time in twelve different capitals plus stock market reports and that. All kinds of other stuff, too. It's getting so you can get these new units and you go to have a slash, excuse my French, and all these little red numbers scroll up with range and position details and a vector-graphics lavvy swims across your vision, *beepbeepbeep*, lock-on, fire …

She's around somewhere. You might of even seen her. Or him. It's like immortality.

Can't abide machines in people. Never could, never will.

I mention this because, when I got to the flat, the copper on the door had that panicky look in his eye they have when they're listening to their internal radio.

I mean, probably it looked a great idea on paper. Whole banks of crime statistics and that, delivered straight to the inside of your head. Only they get headaches from all the noise. And what good is it, every time a cab goes by, they get this impulse to pick up a fare from Flat 27, Rushdie Road? My joke.

I went in and there was this smell.

Not from the body, though. They'd got rid of that smell, first thing.

No. This smell, it was just staleness. The kind of smell old plastic makes. It was the kind of smell a place gets that *ought* to be dirty, only there's not enough dirt around, so what you get is ground-in cleanness. When you leave home, say, and your mum keeps the room just like it was for ten years, that's the kind of smell you get. The whole flat was like that, although there were no aeroplanes hanging from the ceiling.

So I get called into the main room and immediately I spot the Seagem, because I'm trained, you notice things like that. It was a series Five, which in my opinion were a big mistake. The Fours were pretty near ideal, so why tinker? It's like saying, hey, we've invented the perfect bicycle so, next thing we'll do, we'll put thirteen more wheels on it – like, for example, they replaced the S-2030s with the S-4060, not a good move in my opinion.

This one was dead. I mean, the power light was on and it was warm, but if it was operating you'd expect to see lights moving on the panel. Also, there was this really big 4711 unit on top, which you don't expect to see in a private house. It's a lab tool. It was a dual model, too. Smell *and* taste. I could see by the model number it was one of the ones you use a tongue glove with, which is actually quite OK. Never could understand the spray-on polymers. People say, hey, isn't it like having a condom in your mouth, but it's better than having to scrape gunk off your tongue at bed-time.

Lots of other stuff had been hooked in, too, and half a dozen phone lines into a patch unit. There was a 1MT memory sink, big as a freezer.

Someone who knew what they wanted to buy had really been spending some money here.

And, oh yes, in the middle of it, like they'd told me on the phone, the old guy. He was dead, too. Sitting on a chair. They weren't going to do anything to him until I'd been, they said.

Because of viruses, you see. People get funny ideas about viruses.

They'd taken his helmet off and you could see the calluses where the nose plugs had been. And his face was white, I mean, *yes*, he was dead and everything, but it had been like something under a stone even before, and his hair was all long and crinkly and horrible where it had been growing under the helmet. And he didn't have a beard, what he had was just long, long chin hair, never had a blade to it in years. He looked like God would look if he was on really serious drugs. And dead, of course.

Actually, he was not that old at all. Thirty-eight. Younger than me. Of course, I jog.

This other copper was standing by the window, trying to pick up HQ through the microwave mush. He looked bored. All the first-wave scene-of-crime types had long been and gone. He just nodded to the Seagem and said, 'You know how to fix these things?'

That was just to establish, you know, that there was them and us, and I was a them. But they always call me in. Reliable, see. Dependable. You can't trust the big boys, they're all dealers and agents for the afer companies, they're locked in. Me, I could go back to repairing micro-swatch players tomorrow. Darren Thompson, Artificial Realities repaired, washing-machine motors rewound. I can do it, too. Ask kids today even to repair a TV, they'll laugh at you, they'll say you're out of the Ark.

I said, 'Sometimes. If they're fixable. What's the problem?'

'That's what we'd like you to find out,' he says, more or less suggesting, if we can't pin something on him we'll pin it on you, chum. 'Can you get a shock off these things?'

'No way. You see, the interfaces –'

'All right, all right. But you know what's being said about 'em. Maybe he was using it for weird kicks.' Coppers think everyone uses them for weird kicks.

'I object most strongly to that,' said this other voice. 'I object most strongly, and I shall make a note of it. There's absolutely no evidence.'

There was this other man. In a suit. Neat. He was sitting by one of these little portable office terminals. I hadn't noticed him before because he was one of these people you wouldn't notice if he was with you in a wardrobe.

He smiled the sort of smile you have to learn and stuck out his hand. Can't remember his face. He had a warm, friendly handshake, the kind where you want to have a wash afterwards.

'Pleased to meet you, Mr Thompson,' he said. 'I'm Carney. Paul Carney. Seagem public affairs department. Here to see that you are allowed to carry out your work. *Without* interference.' He looked at the copper, who was definitely not happy. 'And any pressure,' he added.

Of course, they've always wanted to nail Seagem, I know that. So I suppose they have to watch business. But I've done thirty, forty visits where afers have died, and men in suits don't turn up, so this was special. All the money in the equipment should've told me that.

Life can get very complicated for men in overalls who have problems with men in suits.

'Look,' I said. 'I know my way around these things OK, but if you want some really detailed testing then I would have thought your people'll –'

'Seagem's technical people are staying *right* out of this,' snapped the copper. 'This is a straight in-situ report, you understand. For the coroner. Mr Carney is not allowed to give you any instructions at all.'

Uniforms, too. They can give you grief.

So I took the covers off, opened the toolbox, and stuck in. That's my world. They might think they're big men, but when I've got the back of something and its innards all over the floor, it's me that's the boss …

Of course, they're all called Seagems, even the ones made by Hitachi or Sony or Amstrad. It's like Hoovers and hoovers. In a way, they aren't difficult. Nine times out of ten, if you're in trouble, you're talking loose boards, unseated panels, maybe a burnout somewhere. The other one time it's probably something you can only cure by taking the sealed units into the hypercleanroom and tapping them with a lump hammer, style of thing.

People say, hey, bet you got an armful of degrees and that. Not me. Basically, if you can repair a washing machine you can do everything to a

ifdef DEBUG+'world/enough'+'time'

Seagem that you *can* do outside a lab. So long as you can remember where you put the screws down, it's not taxing. That's if it's a *hardware* problem, of course. Software can be a pain. You got to be a special type of person to handle the software. Like me. No imagination, and proud of it.

'Kids use these things, you know,' said the copper, when I was kneeling on the floor with the interface boards stacked around me.

(I always call them coppers, because of tradition. Did you know that 'copper' as slang for policeman comes from the verb 'to cop', first reliably noted in 1859? No, you don't, because, after all that big thing ten years ago about the trees and that, the university put loads of stuff into those big old read/write optical units, and some kid managed to get a McLint virus into the one in the wossname department. You know? Words? History of words. This was before I specialized in Seagems, only in those days they were still called Computer Generated Environments. And they called me in and all I could haul out of 5kT of garbage was half a screenful which I read before it wiped. This guy was crying. 'The whole history of English philology is up the swanee,' he said, and I said, would it help if I told him the word 'copper' was first reliably noted in 1859, and he didn't even make a note of it. He should of. They could, you know, start again. I mean, it wouldn't be much, but it would be a start. Often wondered what 'up the swanee' really means. Don't suppose I'll ever know, now.)

'Kids use them,' he said. You could tell he wanted to use a word like 'bastards', but not with the suit around.

Not ones like these they don't, I thought. This stuff is top of the range. You couldn't get it in the shops.

'If I caught my lad with one, I'd tan his hide. We used to play healthy games when I was a kid. Elite, Space Invaders, that stuff.'

'Yeah.' Let's see, attach probes *here* and *here* ...

'Please allow Mr Thompson to get on with his work,' said the suit.

'I think,' said the copper nastily, 'we ought to tell him who this man *is*.' Then they started to argue about it.

I suppose I'd assumed he was just some old guy who'd hooked into one porno afer too many. Not a bad way to go, by the way. People say, hey, what you mean? Dying of an overdose of artificial sex is OK? And I say, compared to about a million other ways, yes. Realities can't kill you unless you want to go. The normal feedback devices can't raise a bruise, whatever the horror stories say, although between you and me I've heard of, you know, *things*, exoskeletons, the army used 'em but they've turned up elsewhere. They can let your dreams kick the shit out of you.

'He's Michael Dever,' said the copper. 'Mr Thompson should know that. He invented half this stuff. He's a *big* man at Seagem. Hasn't been into the office for five years, apparently. Works from home. Worked,' he corrected himself. 'Top man in development. Lives like this. Lived. Sends all his stuff in over the link. No one bothered about it, see, because he's a genius. Then he missed an important deadline yesterday.'

That explained about the suit, then. Heard about Dever, of course, but all the pix in the mags showed this guy in a T-shirt and a grin. Old pix, then. A big man, yes. So maybe important stuff in the machine. Or he was testing something. Or they thought, maybe someone had slipped him a virus. After all, there were enough lines into the unit.

Nothing soiled though, I thought. Some people who are gone on afer will live in shit, but you do get the thorough ones, who work it all out beforehand – fridge stacked with TV dinners, bills paid direct by the bank, half an hour out from under every day for housework and aerobics, and then off they go for a holiday in their heads.

'Better than most I've seen,' I said. 'Neat. No trouble to anyone. I've been called into ones because of the smell even when they *weren't* dead.'

'Why's he got those pipes hooked up to the helmet?' said the copper.

He really didn't know. I supposed he hadn't had much to do with afers, not really. A lot of the brighter coppers keep away from them, because you can get really depressed. What we had here was Entonox mixture, the intelligent afer's friend. Little tubes to your nose plugs, then a little program on the machine which brings you out of your reality just enough every day for e.g. a go on the exercise bike, a meal, visit the bathroom.

'If you're going to drop out of your own reality, you need all the help you can get,' I explained. 'So the machine trickles you some gas and fades the program gradually. Gives you enough of a high to come out of it without screaming.'

'What if the valves stick?' asked the suit.

'Can't. There's all kinds of fail-safes, and it monitors your –'

'We believe the valves may have stuck,' said the suit firmly.

Well. Good thinking. Seagem don't make valves. The little gas units are definitely third-party add-ons. So if some major employee dies under the helmet, it's nice to blame valves. Only I've never heard of a valve sticking, and there really *are* a load of fail-safes. The only way it'd work is if the machine held some things off and some things on, and that's *purpose*, and machines don't have that.

Only it's not my place to say things like that.

'Poor guy,' I said.

The copper unfolded at high speed and grabbed my shoulder and towed me out and into a bedroom, just like that. 'Just you come and look at this,' he kept saying. 'Just you come and *look*. This isn't one of your bloody electronic things. Poor guy? Poor guy? This is *real*.'

There was this other dead body next door, see.

He thought I was going to be shocked. Well, I wasn't.

You see worse things in pictures of Ancient Egypt. You see worse things on TV. *I* see them for real, sometimes. *Nearly* fresh corpses can be upsetting, believe me, but this wasn't because it'd been years. Plenty of time for the air to clear. Of course, I only saw the head, I wouldn't have liked to have been there when they pulled the sheets back.

She might have been quite good-looking, although of course it was hard to be sure. There were coroner's stickers over everything.

'Know what she died of?' asked the copper. 'Forensic think she was pregnant and something went wrong. She bled to death. And her just *lying* there, and him in the next room in his little porno world. Name was Suzannah. Of course, all the neighbours are suddenly concerned that they never saw her around for years. Kept themselves to themselves,' he mimicked shrilly. 'Half of 'em afers too, you bet.

'He left her for five years. Just left her there.'

He was wrong. Listen, I've been called in before when an afer's died, and like I said it's the smell every time. Like rotting food, you know. But Dever or someone had sealed the room nicely, and put her in a body-bag thing.

Anyway, let's face it, most people these days smell via a Seagem of some sort. Keeps you from smelling what you don't want to smell.

It began with the Dataglove, and then there were these whole body suits, and along with them were the goggles – later the helmets – where the computer projected the images. So you could walk into the screen, you could watch your hands move inside the images, you could *feel* them. All dead primitive stuff now, like Edison's first television or whatever. No smell, not much colour, hardly any sensory feedback. Took ages to crack smell.

Everyone said, hey, this is *it*, like your accountant can wear a whole reality suit and stroll around *inside* your finances. And chemists can manipulate computer simulations of molecules and that. Artificial realities would push back the boundaries of, you know, man's thirst for wossname.

Well, yeah. My dad said once, 'Know where I first saw a microchip? Inside a ping-pong game.'

So prob'ly those thirsty for pushing back boundaries pushed 'em back all right, but where you *really* started seeing reality units was on supermarket checkout girls and in sports shops, because you could have a whole golf course in your home and stuff like that. If you were really rich. Really very rich. But then Seagem marketed a cut-down version, and then Amstrad, and then everything went mad.

You see people in the streets every day with reality units. Mostly they're just changing a few little things. You know. Maybe they edit out black men, or slogans, or add a few trees. Just tinkering a bit, just helping themselves get through the day.

Well *sure*, I know what some afers do. I know kids who think you can switch the wires so you taste sound and smell vision. What you really do is, you get a blinding headache if you're lucky. And there's the people who, like I said, can't afford a rollafloor so they go hiking through the Venusian jungles or whatever in a room eight feet square and fall out the window. And afers have burned alive and turned into couch crisps. You've seen it all on the box. At least, you have if you're not an afer. They don't watch much.

Odd, really. Government is against it. Well, it's a drug. One you can't tax. And they say, freedom is the birthright of every individual, but you start being free, they get upset. Coppers seem to be offended, too. But ... well. Take rape. I mean, you don't hear about it these days. Not when you can pick up *Dark Alley Cruiser* down the rental shop. Not that I've watched it, you understand, but I'm told the girl's very good, does all that's expected of her, which you don't have to be an Eisenstein to work out isn't what it'd be like for real, if you catch my drift. And there's other stuff, I won't even mention the titles. I don't need to, do I? It's not all remakes of *Rambo XXIV* with you in the title role is what I mean.

I reckon what the coppers don't like is *there's all this crime going on in your head and they can't touch you for it.*

There's all that stuff on the TV about how it corrupts people. All these earnest professors sitting round in leather chairs – of course *they* never use *their* machines for anything except the nature programmes or high-toned stuff like *Madam Ovary*. Probably does corrupt people but, I don't know, everything's been corrupting people since the, you know, dawn of thingy, but with afers it stays inside. They aren't about to go and knock over some thin little girl in cotton underwear coming back from the all-night chippy, not after *Dark Alley Cruiser*. Probably can't, anyway. And it's cheap so you don't have to steal for it. A lot of them forget to feed themselves. Afers are the kind of problems that come with the solutions built in.

I like a good book, me.

They watched me very hard when I checked the gas-feed controls. The add-on stuff was pretty good. You could see where it was hooked into everything else. I bet if I had time to really run over it on the bench you'd find he had a little daydream every day. Probably didn't even properly come out from under. Funny thing, that, about artificial realities. You know how you can be dreaming and the buzzer goes and the dream sort of incorporates the buzzer into the plot? Probably it was like that.

It had been well-maintained. Cleaned regularly and everything. You can get into trouble otherwise, you get build-ups of gunk on connectors and things. That's why all my customers, I tell them, you take out a little insurance, I'll be round every six months regular, you can give me the key, I've even got a bypass box so if you're, you know, *busy* I can do a quick service and be away and you won't know I've been. This is personal service. They trust me.

I switched off the power to the alarms, cleaned a few boards for the look of it, reseated everything, switched it back on. Et wolla.

The copper leaned over my shoulder.

'How did you *do* that?' he said.

'Well,' I said, 'there was no negative bias voltage on the sub-logic multiplexer,' which shut him up.

Thing is, there wasn't anything wrong. It wasn't that I couldn't find a fault, there was nothing to say that a fault existed. It was as if it'd just been told to shut down everything. Including him.

Valve stuck ... that meant too much nitrous oxide. The scene of crime people prob'ly had to get the smile off his face with a crowbar.

The lights came on, there were all the little whirrs and gurgles you get when these things boot up, the memory sinks started to hum, we were cooking with gas.

They got excited about all this.

And then, of course, I had to get out my own helmet.

Viruses, that's the thing. Started off as a joke. Some kid'd hack into someone else's reality, scrawl messages on the walls. A joke, like the McLints. Only, instead of scrambling the wage bill or wiping out English literature, you turned their brain to cheese. Frighten them to death, or whatever. Scares the hell out of some people, the thought that you can kill people that way. They act illogical. You find someone dead under an afer unit, you call in someone like me. Someone with no imagination.

You'd be amazed, the things I've seen.

You're right.

You're clever. You've had an education.

You're saying, hey, I know what you saw. You saw the flat, right, and it was just like it was really, only maybe cleaner, and she was still alive in it, and maybe there was a kid's voice in the next room, the kid they never had, because, right, he'd sat there maybe five years ago maybe while she was still warm and done the reality creation job of a lifetime. And he was living in it, just sane enough to make sure he *kept* on living in it. An artificial reality just like reality ought to have been.

Right. You're right. You knew it. I should've held something back, but that's not like me.

Don't ask me to describe it. Why ask me to describe it? It was *his*.

I told the other two and the PR man said firmly, 'Well, all right. And then a valve stuck.'

'Look,' I said, 'I'll just make a report, OK? About what I've found. I'm a wire man, I don't mess around with pipes. But I wouldn't mind asking you a question.'

That got them. That got them. People like me don't normally ask questions, apart from 'Where's the main switch?'

'Well?' said the suit.

'See,' I said, 'it's a funny old world. I mean, you can hide a body from *people* these days, it's easy. But there's a lot more to it in the real world. I mean, there's banks and credit companies, right? And medical checks and polls and stuff. There's this big electric shadow everyone's got. If you die –'

They were both looking at me in this funny way. Then the suit shrugged and the uniform handed me this print-out from the terminal. I read it, while the memory sink whirred and whirred and whirred …

She visited the doctor last year.

The girl who runs the supermarket checkouts swears she sees her regularly.

She writes stories for kids. She's done three in the last five years. Quite good, apparently. Very much like the stuff she used to do before she was dead. One of them got an award.

She's still alive. Out there.

It's like I've always said. Most of the conversations you have with most people are just to reassure one another that you're alive, so you don't need a very complex paragorithm. And Dever could do some *really* complex stuff.

She's been getting everywhere. She was on that flight to Norway that got blown up last year. The stewardess saw her. Of course, the girl was wearing environment gear, all aircrew do, it stops them having to look at ugly passengers. Mrs Dever still had a nice time in Oslo. Spent some money there.

She was in Florida, too. At the same time.

She's a virus. The first ever self-replicating reality virus.

She's everywhere.

Anyway, you won't of heard about it, because it all got hushed up because Seagem are bigger than you thought. They buried him and what was left of her. In a way.

I heard from, you know, contacts that at one point the police were considering calling it murder, but what was the point? The way they saw it, all the evidence of her still being alive was just something he'd arranged, sort of to cover things up. I don't think so because I like happy endings, me.

And it really went on for a long time, the memory sink. Like I said, the flat had more data lines running into it than usual, because he needed them for his work.

I reckon *he's* gone out there, now.

You walk down the street, you've got your reality visor on, who knows if who you're seeing is really there? I mean, maybe it isn't like being alive, but perhaps it isn't like being dead.

I've got photos of both of them. Went through old back issues of the Seagem house magazine, they were both at some long-service presentation. She *was* quite good-looking. You could tell they liked one another.

Makes sense they'll look just like that now. Every time I switch a visor on, I wonder if I'll spot them. Wouldn't mind knowing how they did it, might like to be a virus myself one day, could be an expert at it.

He owes me, anyway. I got the machine going again and I never told them what she *said* to me, when I saw her in his reality. She said, 'Tell him to hurry.'

Romantic, really. Like that play ... what was it ... with the good dance numbers, supposed to be in New York. Oh, yeah. *Romeo and Juliet.*

People in machines, I can live with that.

People say to me, hey, this what the human race meant for? I say, buggered if I know; who knows? We never went back to the Moon, or that other place, the red one, but we didn't spend the money down here on Earth either. So people just curl up and live inside their heads.

Until now, anyway.

They could be anywhere. Of course, it's not like life but prob'ly it isn't death either. I wonder what compiler he used? I'd of loved to have had a look at it before he shut the machine down. When I re-booted it, I sort of initialized him and sent him out. Sort of like a godfather, me.

And anyway, I heard somewhere there's this god, he dreams the whole universe, so is it real or what? Begins with a 'b'. Buddha, I think. Maybe some other god comes round every six million years to service the machinery.

But me, I prefer to settle down of an evening with a good book. People don't read books these days. Don't seem to do anything, much. You go down any street, it's all dead, all these people living in their own realities.

I mean, when I was a kid, we thought the future would be all crowded and cool and rainy with big glowing Japanese adverts everywhere and people eating noodles in the street. At least you'd be communicating, if only to ask the other guy to pass the soy sauce. My joke. But what we got, we got this Information Revolution, what it means is no bugger knows anything and doesn't know they don't know, and they just give up.

You shouldn't turn in on yourself. It's not what being human means. You got to reach out.

For example, I'm really enjoying *Elements of OSCF Bandpass Design in Computer Generated Environments.*

Man who wrote it seems to think you can set your S-2030s without isolating your cascade interfaces.

Try that in the real world and see what happens.

ONLINE: **ONE/2** *Subject:* Vergil Ulam, biochip scientist

Blood Music

Greg Bear

INFO: Vergil Ulam is working in the experimental field of MABs – Medically Applicable Biochips. They are microscopic logic circuits which can be injected into the human body to troubleshoot. But they can also be unstoppable instruments of death ...

Greg Bear has been hailed as a potential successor to Arthur C. Clarke in the realms of ambitious and imaginative hard sf, and as if in recognition of this has already won several Hugo and Nebula awards to confirm his status as a major writer. A fan turned author, Greg has combined crime and sf in a number of his short stories: in 'The Wind from a Burning Woman' (1983) and 'Tangents' (1989), but perhaps most notably in 'Queen of Angels' (1990), a detective story set in an overcrowded, computer-run, futuristic Los Angeles, told from the viewpoint of a biotransformed female cop. It also deals with the use of virtual reality as a means of entrapment.

'Blood Music', written for *Analog* in 1983, had an interesting gestation. 'The idea for the story occurred to me within ten minutes of reading an article in *New Scientist*,' Greg explains. 'It was all about biochips: theoretical organic computers that might be as small as a single cell.' (Greg later turned the idea into the basis of a novel also called *Blood Music* (1985), but which departs substantially from the short story.)

There is a principle in nature I don't think anyone has pointed out before. Each hour, a myriad of trillions of little live things – bacteria, microbes, 'animalcules' – are born and die, not counting for much except in the bulk of their existence and the accumulation of their tiny effects. They do not perceive deeply. They do not suffer much. A hundred billion, dying, would not begin to have the same importance as a single human death.

Within the ranks of magnitude of all creatures, small as microbes or great as humans, there is an equality of 'elan', just as the branches of a tall tree, gathered together, equal the bulk of the limbs below, and all the limbs equal the bulk of the trunk.

That, at least, is the principle. I believe Vergil Ulam was the first to violate it.

It had been two years since I'd last seen Vergil. My memory of him hardly matched the tan, smiling, well-dressed gentleman standing before me. We had made a lunch appointment over the phone the day before, and now faced each other in the wide double doors of the employees' cafeteria at the Mount Freedom Medical Center.

'Vergil?' I asked. 'My God, Vergil!'

'Good to see you, Edward.' He shook my hand firmly. He had lost ten or twelve kilos and what remained seemed tighter, better proportioned. At university, Vergil had been the pudgy, shock-haired, snaggle-toothed whiz kid who hot-wired doorknobs, gave us punch that turned our piss blue, and never got a date except with Eileen Termagent, who shared many of his physical characteristics.

'You look fantastic,' I said. 'Spend a summer in Cabo San Lucas?'

We stood in line at the counter and chose our food. 'The tan,' he said, picking out a carton of chocolate milk, 'is from spending three months under a sunlamp. My teeth were straightened just after I last saw you. I'll explain the rest, but we need a place to talk where no one will listen close.'

I steered him to the smokers' corner, where three diehard puffers were scattered among six tables.

'Listen, I mean it,' I said as we unloaded our trays. 'You've changed. You're looking good.'

'I've changed more than you know.' His tone was motion-picture ominous, and he delivered the line with a theatrical lift of his brows. 'How's Gail?'

Gail was doing well, I told him, teaching nursery school. We'd married the year before. His gaze shifted down to his food – pineapple slice and cottage cheese, piece of banana cream pie – and he said, his voice almost cracking, 'Notice something else?'

I squinted in concentration. 'Uh.'

'Look closer.'

'I'm not sure. Well, yes, you're not wearing glasses. Contacts?'

'No. I don't need them any more.'

'And you're a snappy dresser. Who's dressing you now? I hope she's as sexy as she is tasteful.'

'Candice isn't – wasn't responsible for the improvement in my clothes,' he said. 'I just got a better job, more money to throw around. My taste in clothes is better than my taste in food, as it happens.' He grinned the old Vergil self-deprecating grin, but ended it with a peculiar leer. 'At any rate, she's left me, I've been fired from my job, I'm living on savings.'

'Hold it,' I said. 'That's a bit crowded. Why not do a linear breakdown? You got a job. Where?'

'Genetron Corp.,' he said. 'Sixteen months ago.'

'I haven't heard of them.'

'You will. They're putting out common stock in the next month. It'll shoot off the board. They've broken through with MABs. Medical –'

'I know what MABs are,' I interrupted. 'At least in theory. Medically Applicable Biochips.'

'They have some that work.'

'What?' It was my turn to lift my brows.

'Microscopic logic circuits. You inject them into the human body, they set up shop where they're told and troubleshoot. With Dr Michael Bernard's approval.'

That was quite impressive. Bernard's reputation was spotless. Not only was he associated with the genetic engineering biggies, but he had made news at least once a year in his practice as a neurosurgeon before retiring. Covers on *Time, Mega, Rolling Stone*.

'That's supposed to be secret – stock, breakthrough, Bernard, everything.' He looked around and lowered his voice. 'But you do whatever the hell you want. I'm through with the bastards.'

I whistled. 'Make me rich, huh?'

'If that's what you want. Or you can spend some time with me before rushing off to your broker.'

'Of course.' He hadn't touched the cottage cheese or pie. He had, however, eaten the pineapple slice and drunk the chocolate milk. 'So tell me more.'

'Well, in med school I was training for lab work. Biochemical research.

I've always had a bent for computers, too. So I put myself through my last two years –'

'By selling software packages to Westinghouse,' I said.

'It's good my friends remember. That's how I got involved with Genetron, just when they were starting out. They had big money backers, all the lab facilities I thought anyone would ever need. They hired me, and I advanced rapidly.

'Four months and I was doing my own work. I made some breakthroughs –' he tossed his hand nonchalantly – 'then I went off on tangents they thought were premature. I persisted and they took away my lab, handed it over to a certifiable flatworm. I managed to save part of the experiment before they fired me. But I haven't exactly been cautious ... or judicious. So now it's going on outside the lab.'

I'd always regarded Vergil as ambitious, a trifle cracked, and not terribly sensitive. His relations with authority figures had never been smooth. Science, for him, was like the woman you couldn't possibly have, who suddenly opens her arms to you, long before you're ready for mature love – leaving you afraid you'll forever blow the chance, lose the prize. Apparently, he did. 'Outside the lab? I don't get you.'

'Edward, I want you to examine me. Give me a thorough physical. Maybe a cancer diagnostic. Then I'll explain more.'

'You want a five-thousand-dollar exam?'

'Whatever you can do. Ultrasound, NMR, thermogram, everything.'

'I don't know if I can get access to all that equipment. NMR full-scan has only been here a month or two. Hell, you couldn't pick a more expensive way –'

'Then ultrasound. That's all you'll need.'

'Vergil, I'm an obstetrician, not a glamour-boy lab-tech. OB-GYN, butt of all jokes. If you're turning into a woman, maybe I can help you.'

He leaned forward, almost putting his elbow into the pie, but swinging wide at the last instant by scant millimeters. The old Vergil would have hit it square. 'Examine me closely and you'll ...' He narrowed his eyes. 'Just examine me.'

'So I make an appointment for ultrasound. Who's going to pay?'

'I'm on Blue Shield.' He smiled and held up a medical credit card. 'I messed with the personnel files at Genetron. Anything up to a hundred thousand dollars medical, they'll never check, never suspect.'

He wanted secrecy, so I made arrangements. I filled out his forms myself. As long as everything was billed properly, most of the examination could take place without official notice. I didn't charge for my services. After all, Vergil had turned my piss blue. We were friends.

He came in late at night. I wasn't normally on duty then, but I stayed late, waiting for him on the third floor of what the nurses called the Frankenstein wing. I sat on an orange plastic chair. He arrived, looking olive-colored under the fluorescent lights.

He stripped, and I arranged him on the table. I noticed, first off, that his ankles looked swollen. But they weren't puffy. I felt them several times. They seemed healthy but looked odd. 'Hm,' I said.

I ran the paddles over him, picking up areas difficult for the big unit to hit, and programmed the data into the imaging system. Then I swung the table around and inserted it into the enameled orifice of the ultrasound diagnostic unit, the hum-hole, so-called by the nurses.

I integrated the data from the hum-hole with that from the paddle sweeps and rolled Vergil out, then set up a video frame. The image took a second to integrate, then flowed into a pattern showing Vergil's skeleton. My jaw fell.

Three seconds of that and it switched to his thoracic organs, then his musculature, and, finally, vascular system and skin.

'How long since the accident?' I asked, trying to take the quiver out of my voice.

'I haven't been in an accident,' he said. 'It was deliberate.'

'Jesus, they beat you to keep secrets?'

'You don't understand me, Edward. Look at the images again. I'm not damaged.'

'Look, there's thickening here –' I indicated the ankles – 'and your ribs – that crazy zigzag pattern of interlocks. Broken sometime, obviously. And –'

'Look at my spine,' he said. I rotated the image in the video frame.

Buckminster Fuller, I thought. It was fantastic. A cage of triangular projections, all interlocking in ways I couldn't begin to follow, much less understand. I reached around and tried to feel his spine with my fingers. He lifted his arms and looked off at the ceiling.

'I can't find it,' I said. 'It's all smooth back there.' I let go of him and looked at his chest, then prodded his ribs. They were sheathed in something tough and flexible. The harder I pressed, the tougher it became. Then I noticed another change.

'Hey,' I said. 'You don't have any nipples.' There were tiny pigment patches, but no nipple formations at all.

'See?' Vergil asked, shrugging on the white robe. 'I'm being rebuilt from the inside out.'

In my reconstruction of those hours, I fancy myself saying, 'So tell me about it.' Perhaps mercifully, I don't remember what I actually said.

He explained with his characteristic circumlocutions. Listening was like trying to get to the meat of a newspaper article through a forest of sidebars and graphic embellishments.

I simplify and condense.

Genetron had assigned him to manufacturing prototype biochips, tiny circuits made out of protein molecules. Some were hooked up to silicon chips little more than a micrometer in size, then sent through rat arteries to chemically keyed locations, to make connections with the rat tissue and attempt to monitor and even control lab-induced pathologies.

'*That* was something,' he said.

'We recovered the most complex microchip by sacrificing the rat, then debriefed it – hooked the silicon portion up to an imaging system. The computer gave us bar graphs, then a diagram of the chemical characteristics of about eleven centimeters of blood vessel ... then put it all together to make a picture. We zoomed down eleven centimeters of rat artery. You never saw so many scientists jumping up and down, hugging each other, drinking buckets of bug juice.' Bug juice was lab ethanol mixed with Dr Pepper.

Eventually, the silicon elements were eliminated completely in favor of nucleoproteins. He seemed reluctant to explain in detail, but I gathered they found ways to make huge molecules – as large as DNA, and even more complex – into electrochemical computers, using ribosome-like structures as 'encoders' and 'readers' and RNA as 'tape'. Vergil was able to mimic reproductive separation and reassembly in his nucleoproteins, incorporating program changes at key points by switching nucleotide pairs. 'Genetron wanted me to switch over to supergene engineering, since that was the coming thing everywhere else. Make all kinds of critters, some out of our imagination. But I had different ideas.' He twiddled his finger around his ear and made theremin sounds. 'Mad scientist time, right?' He laughed, then sobered. 'I injected my best nucleoproteins into bacteria to make duplication and compounding easier. Then I started to leave them inside, so the circuits could interact with the cells. They were heuristically programmed; they taught themselves. The cells fed chemically coded information to the computers, the computers processed it and made decisions, the cells became smart. I mean, smart as planaria, for starters. Imagine an *E. coli* as smart as a planarian worm!'

I nodded. 'I'm imagining.'

'Then I really went off on my own. We had the equipment, the techniques; and I knew the molecular language. I could make really dense, really complicated biochips by compounding the nucleoproteins, making them into little brains. I did some research into how far I could go, theoretically. Sticking with bacteria, I could make a biochip with the computing capacity of a sparrow's brain. Imagine how jazzed I was! Then I saw a way to increase the complexity a thousandfold, by using something we regarded as a nuisance – quantum chit-chat between the fixed elements of the circuits. Down that small, even the slightest change could bomb a biochip. But I developed a program that actually predicted and took advantage of electron tunneling. Emphasized the heuristic aspects of the computer, used the chit-chat as a method of increasing complexity.'

'You're losing me,' I said.

'I took advantage of randomness. The circuits could repair themselves, compare memories, and correct faulty elements. I gave them basic instructions: Go forth and multiply. Improve. By God, you should have seen some of the cultures a week later! It was amazing. They were evolving all on their own, like little cities. I destroyed them all. I think one of the petri dishes would have grown legs and walked out of the incubator if I'd kept feeding it.'

'You're kidding.' I looked at him. 'You're not kidding.'

'Man, they *knew* what it was like to improve! They knew where they had to go, but they were just so limited, being in bacteria bodies, with so few resources.'

'How smart were they?'

'I couldn't be sure. They were associating in clusters of a hundred to two hundred cells, each cluster behaving like an autonomous unit. Each cluster might have been as smart as a rhesus monkey. They exchanged information through their pili, passed on bits of memory, and compared notes. Their organization was obviously different from a group of monkeys. Their world was so much simpler, for one thing. With their abilities, they were masters of the petri dishes. I put phages in with them; the phages didn't have a chance. They used every option available to change and grow.'

'How is that possible?'

'What?' He seemed surprised I wasn't accepting everything at face value.

'Cramming so much into so little. A rhesus monkey is not your simple little calculator, Vergil.'

'I haven't made myself clear,' he said, obviously irritated. 'I was using nucleoprotein computers. They're like DNA, but all the information can interact. Do you know how many nucleotide pairs there are in the DNA of a single bacteria?'

It had been a long time since my last biochemistry lesson. I shook my head.

'About two million. Add in the modified ribosome structures – fifteen thousand of them, each with a molecular weight of about three million – and consider the combinations and permutations. The RNA is arranged like a continuous loop paper tape, surrounded by ribosomes ticking off instructions and manufacturing protein chains ...' His eyes were bright and slightly moist. 'Besides, I'm not saying every cell was a distinct entity. They cooperated.'

'How many bacteria in the dishes you destroyed?'

'Billions. I don't know.' He smirked. 'You got it, Edward. Whole planetsful of *E. coli*.'

'But Genetron didn't fire you then?'

'No. They didn't know what was going on, for one thing. I kept compounding the molecules, increasing their size and complexity. When bacteria were too limited, I took blood from myself, separated out white cells, and injected them with the new biochips. I watched them, put them through mazes and little chemical problems. They were whizzes. Time is a lot faster at that level – so little distance for the messages to cross, and the environment is much simpler. Then I forgot to store a file under my secret code in the lab computers. Some managers found it and guessed what I was up to. Everybody panicked. They thought we'd have every social watchdog in the country on our backs because of what I'd done. They started to destroy my work and wipe my programs. Ordered me to sterilize my white cells. Christ.' He pulled the white robe off and started to get dressed. 'I only had a day or two. I separated out the most complex cells –'

'How complex?'

'They were clustering in hundred-cell groups, like the bacteria. Each group as smart as a four-year-old kid, maybe.' He studied my face for a moment. 'Still doubting? Want me to run through how many nucleotide pairs there are in a mammalian cell? I tailored my computers to take advantage of the white cells' capacity. Four billion nucleotide pairs, Edward. And they don't have a huge body to worry about, taking up most of their thinking time.'

'Okay,' I said. 'I'm convinced. What did you do?'

'I mixed the cells back into a cylinder of whole blood and injected myself with it.' He buttoned the top of his shirt and smiled thinly at me. 'I'd programmed them with every drive I could, talked as high a level as I could using just enzymes and such. After that, they were on their own.'

'You programmed them to go forth and multiply, improve?' I repeated.

'I think they developed some characteristics picked up by the biochips in their *E. coli* phases. The white cells could talk to each other with extruded memories. They found ways to ingest other types of cells and alter them without killing them.'

'You're crazy.'

'You can see the screen! Edward, I haven't been sick since. I used to get colds all the time. I've never felt better.'

'They're inside you, finding things, changing them.'
'And by now, each cluster is as smart as you or I.'
'You're absolutely nuts.'

He shrugged. 'Genetron fired me. They thought I was going to take revenge for what they did to my work. They ordered me out of the labs, and I haven't had a real chance to see what's been going on inside me until now. Three months.'

'So ...' My mind was racing. 'You lost weight because they improved your fat metabolism. Your bones are stronger, your spine has been completely rebuilt –'

'No more backaches even if I sleep on my old mattress.'

'Your heart looks different.'

'I didn't know about the heart,' he said, examining the frame image more closely. 'As for the fat – I was thinking about that. They could increase my brown cells, fix up the metabolism. I haven't been as hungry lately. I haven't changed my eating habits that much – I still want the same old junk – but somehow I get around to eating only what I need. I don't think they know what my brain is yet. Sure, they've got all the glandular stuff – but they don't have the *big* picture, if you see what I mean. They don't know *I'm* in here. But boy, they sure did figure out what my reproductive organs are.'

I glanced at the image and shifted my eyes away.

'Oh, they look pretty normal,' he said, hefting his scrotum obscenely. He snickered. 'But how else do you think I'd land a real looker like Candice? She was just after a one-night stand with a techie. I looked okay then, no tan but trim, with good clothes. She'd never screwed a techie before. Joke time, right? But my little geniuses kept us up half the night. I think they made improvements each time. I felt like I had a goddamned fever.'

His smile vanished. 'But then one night my skin started to crawl. It really scared me. I thought things were getting out of hand. I wondered what they'd do when they crossed the blood-brain barrier and found out about *me* – about the brain's real function. So I began a campaign to keep them under control. I figured, the reason they wanted to get into the skin was the simplicity of running circuits across a surface. Much easier than trying to maintain chains of communication in and around muscles, organs, vessels. The skin was much more direct. So I bought a quartz lamp.' He caught my puzzled expression. 'In the lab, we'd break down the protein in biochip cells by exposing them to ultraviolet light. I alternated sunlamp with quartz treatments. Keeps them out of my skin and gives me a nice tan.'

'Give you skin cancer, too,' I commented.

'They'll probably take care of that. Like police.'

'Okay. I've examined you, you've told me a story I still find hard to believe ... what do you want me to do?'

'I'm not as nonchalant as I act, Edward. I'm worried. I'd like to find some way to control them before they find out about my brain. I mean, think of it, they're in the trillions by now, each one smart. They're cooperating to some extent. I'm probably the smartest thing on the planet, and they haven't even begun to get their act together. I don't really want them to take over.' He laughed unpleasantly. 'Steal my soul, you know? So think of some treatment to block them. Maybe we can starve the little buggers. Just think on it.' He buttoned his shirt. 'Give me a call.' He handed me a slip of paper with his address and phone number. Then he went to the keyboard and erased the image on the frame, dumping the memory of the examination. 'Just you,' he said. 'Nobody else for now. And please ... hurry.'

It was three o'clock in the morning when Vergil walked out of the examination room. He'd allowed me to take blood samples, then shaken my hand – his palm was damp, nervous – and cautioned me against ingesting anything from the specimens.

Before I went home, I put the blood through a series of tests. The results were ready the next day.

I picked them up during my lunch break in the afternoon, then destroyed all of the samples. I did it like a robot. It took me five days and nearly sleepless nights to accept what I'd seen. His blood was normal enough, though the machines diagnosed the patient as having an infection. High levels of leukocytes – white blood cells – and histamines. On the fifth day, I believed.

Gail came home before I did, but it was my turn to fix dinner. She slipped one of the school's disks into the home system and showed me video art her nursery kids had been creating. I watched quietly, ate with her in silence.

I had two dreams, part of my final acceptance. In the first, that evening, I witnessed the destruction of the planet Krypton, Superman's home world. Billions of superhuman geniuses went screaming off in walls of fire. I related the destruction to my sterilizing the samples of Vergil's blood.

The second dream was worse. I dreamed that New York City was raping a woman. By the end of the dream, she gave birth to little embryo cities, all wrapped up in translucent sacs, soaked with blood from the difficult labor.

I called him on the morning of the sixth day. He answered on the fourth ring. 'I have some results,' I said. 'Nothing conclusive. But I want to talk with you. In person.'

'Sure,' he said. 'I'm staying inside for the time being.' His voice was strained; he sounded tired.

Vergil's apartment was in a fancy high-rise near the lake shore. I took the elevator up, listening to little advertising jingles and watching dancing holograms display products, empty apartments for rent, the building's hostess discussing social activities for the week.

Vergil opened the door and motioned me in. He wore a checked robe with long sleeves and carpet slippers. He clutched an unlit pipe in one hand, his fingers twisting it back and forth as he walked away from me and sat down, saying nothing.

'You have an infection,' I said.

'Oh?'

'That's all the blood analyses tell me. I don't have access to the electron microscopes.'

'I don't think it's really an infection,' he said. 'After all, they're my own cells. Probably something else ... some sign of their presence, of the change. We can't expect to understand everything that's happening.'

I removed my coat. 'Listen,' I said, 'you really have me worried now.' The expression on his face stopped me: a kind of frantic beatitude. He squinted at the ceiling and pursed his lips.

'Are you stoned?' I asked.

He shook his head, then nodded once, very slowly. 'Listening,' he said.

'To what?'

'I don't know. Not sounds ... exactly. Like music. The heart, all the blood vessels, friction of blood along the arteries, veins. Activity. Music in the blood.' He looked at me plaintively. 'Why aren't you at work?'

'My day off. Gail's working.'

'Can you stay?'

I shrugged. 'I suppose.' I sounded suspicious. I glanced around the apartment, looking for ashtrays, packs of papers.

'I'm not stoned, Edward,' he said. 'I may be wrong, but I think something big is happening. I think they're finding out who I am.'

I sat down across from Vergil, staring at him intently. He didn't seem to notice. Some inner process involved him. When I asked for a cup of coffee, he motioned to the kitchen. I boiled a pot of water and took a jar of instant from the cabinet. With cup in hand, I returned to my seat. He twisted his head back and forth, eyes open. 'You always knew what you wanted to be, didn't you?' he asked.

'More or less.'

'A gynecologist. Smart moves. Never false moves. I was different. I had goals, but no direction. Like a map without roads, just places to be. I didn't give a shit for anything, anyone but myself. Even science. Just a means. I'm surprised I got so far. I even hated my folks.'

He gripped his chair arms.

'Something wrong?' I asked.

'They're talking to me,' he said. He shut his eyes.

For an hour he seemed to be asleep. I checked his pulse, which was strong and steady, felt his forehead – slightly cool – and made myself more coffee. I was looking through a magazine, at a loss what to do, when he opened his eyes again. 'Hard to figure exactly what time is like for them,' he said. 'It's taken them maybe three, four days to figure out language, key human concepts. Now they're on to it. On to me. Right now.'

'How's that?'

He claimed there were thousands of researchers hooked up to his neurons. He couldn't give details. 'They're damned efficient, you know,' he said. 'They haven't screwed me up yet.'

'We should get you into the hospital now.'

'What in hell could other doctors do? Did *you* figure out any way to control them? I mean, they're my own cells.'

'I've been thinking. We could starve them. Find out what metabolic differences –'

'I'm not sure I want to be rid of them,' Vergil said. 'They're not doing any harm.'

'How do you know?'

He shook his head and held up one finger. 'Wait. They're trying to figure out what space is. That's tough for them: they break distances down into concentrations of chemicals. For them, space is like intensity of taste.'

'Vergil –'

'Listen! Think, Edward!' His tone was excited but even. 'Something big is happening inside me. They talk to each other across the fluid, through membranes. They tailor something – viruses? – to carry data stored in nucleic acid chains. I think they're saying "RNA". That makes sense. That's one way I programmed them. But plasmidlike structures, too. Maybe that's what your machines think is a sign of infection – all their chattering in my blood, packets of data. Tastes of other individuals. Peers. Superiors. Subordinates.'

'Vergil, I still think you should be in a hospital.'

'This is my show, Edward,' he said. 'I'm their universe. They're amazed by the new scale.' He was quiet again for a time. I squatted by his chair and pulled up the sleeve to his robe. His arm was crisscrossed with white lines. I was about to go to the phone when he stood and stretched. 'Do you realize,' he said, 'how many body cells we kill each time we move?'

'I'm going to call for an ambulance,' I said.

'No, you aren't.' His tone stopped me. 'I told you, I'm not sick, this is my show. Do you know what they'd do to me in a hospital? They'd be like cavemen trying to fix a computer. It would be a farce.'

'Then what the hell am I doing here?' I asked, getting angry. 'I can't do anything. I'm one of those cavemen.'

'You're a friend,' Vergil said, fixing his eyes on me. I had the impression I was being watched by more than just Vergil. 'I want you here to keep me company.' He laughed. 'But I'm not exactly alone.'

He walked around the apartment for two hours, fingering things, looking out windows, slowly and methodically fixing himself lunch. 'You know, they can actually feel their own thoughts,' he said about noon. 'I mean, the cytoplasm seems to have a will of its own, a kind of subconscious life counter to the rationality they've only recently acquired. They hear the chemical "noise" of the molecules fitting and unfitting inside.'

At two o'clock, I called Gail to tell her I would be late. I was almost sick with tension, but I tried to keep my voice level. 'Remember Vergil Ulam? I'm talking with him right now.'

'Everything okay?' she asked.

Was it? Decidedly not. 'Fine,' I said.

'Culture!' Vergil said, peering around the kitchen wall at me. I said goodbye and hung up the phone. 'They're always swimming in that bath of information. Contributing to it. It's a kind of gestalt thing. The hierarchy is absolute. They send tailored phages after cells that don't interact properly. Viruses specified to individuals or groups. No escape. A rogue cell gets pierced by the virus, the cell blebs outward, it explodes and dissolves. But it's not just a dictatorship. I think they effectively have more freedom than in a democracy. I mean, they vary so differently from individual to individual. Does that make sense? They vary in different ways than we do.'

'Hold it,' I said, gripping his shoulders. 'Vergil, you're pushing me to the edge. I can't take this much longer. I don't understand, I'm not sure I believe –'

'Not even now?'

'Okay, let's say you're giving me the right interpretation. Giving it to me straight. Have you bothered to figure out the consequences yet? What all this means, where it might lead?'

He walked into the kitchen and drew a glass of water from the tap then returned and stood next to me. His expression had changed from childish absorption to sober concern. 'I've never been very good at that.'

'Are you afraid?'

'I was. Now, I'm not sure.' He fingered the tie of his robe. 'Look, I don't want you to think I went around you, over your head or something. But I met with Michael Bernard yesterday. He put me through his private clinic, took specimens. Told me to quit the lamp treatments. He called this morning, just before you did. He says it all checks out. And he asked me not to tell anybody.' He paused and his expression became dreamy again. 'Cities of cells,' he continued. 'Edward, they push tubes through the tissues, spread information –'

'Stop it!' I shouted. 'Checks out? What checks out?'

'As Bernard puts it, I have "severely enlarged macrophages" throughout my system. And he concurs on the anatomical changes.'

'What does he plan to do?'

'I don't know. I think he'll probably convince Genetron to reopen the lab.'

'Is that what you want?'

'It's not just having the lab again. I want to show you. Since I stopped the lamp treatments, I'm still changing.' He undid his robe and let it slide to the floor. All over his body, his skin was crisscrossed with white lines. Along his back, the lines were starting to form ridges.

'My God,' I said.

'I'm not going to be much good anywhere else but the lab soon. I won't be able to go out in public. Hospitals wouldn't know what to do, as I said.'

'You're ... you can talk to them, tell them to slow down,' I said, aware how ridiculous that sounded.

'Yes, indeed I can, but they don't necessarily listen.'

'I thought you were their god or something.'

'The ones hooked up to my neurons aren't the big wheels. They're researchers, or at least serve the same function. They know I'm here, what I am, but that doesn't mean they've convinced the upper levels of the hierarchy.'

'They're disputing?'

'Something like that. It's not all that bad, anyway. If the lab is reopened, I have a home, a place to work.' He glanced out the window, as if looking for someone. 'I don't have anything left but them. They aren't afraid, Edward. I've never felt so close to anything before.' The beatific smile again. 'I'm responsible for them. Mother to them all.'

'You have no way of knowing what they're going to do.'

He shook his head.

'No, I mean it. You say they're like a civilization –'

'Like a thousand civilizations.'

'Yes, and civilizations have been known to screw up. Warfare, the environment –'

I was grasping at straws, trying to restrain a growing panic. I wasn't competent to handle the enormity of what was happening. Neither was Vergil. He was the last person I would have called insightful and wise about large issues.

'But I'm the only one at risk.'

'You don't know that. Jesus, Vergil, look what they're *doing* to you!'

'To me, all to me!' he said. 'Nobody else.'

I shook my head and held up my hands in a gesture of defeat. 'Okay, so Bernard gets them to reopen the lab, you move in, become a guinea pig. What then?'

'They treat me right. I'm more than just good old Vergil Ulam now. I'm a goddamned galaxy, a super-mother.'

'Super-host, you mean.' He conceded the point with a shrug.

I couldn't take any more. I made my exit with a few flimsy excuses, then sat in the lobby of the apartment building, trying to calm down. Somebody had to talk some sense into him. Who would he listen to? He had gone to Bernard ...

And it sounded as if Bernard was not only convinced, but very interested. People of Bernard's stature didn't coax the Vergil Ulams of the world along unless they felt it was to their advantage.

I had a hunch, and I decided to play it. I went to a pay phone, slipped in my credit card, and called Genetron.

'I'd like you to page Dr Michael Bernard,' I told the receptionist.

'Who's calling, please?'

'This is his answering service. We have an emergency call and his beeper doesn't seem to be working.'

A few anxious minutes later, Bernard came on the line. 'Who the hell is this?' he asked. 'I don't have an answering service.'

'My name is Edward Milligan. I'm a friend of Vergil Ulam's. I think we have some problems to discuss.'

We made an appointment to talk the next morning.

I went home and tried to think of excuses to keep me off the next day's hospital shift. I couldn't concentrate on medicine, couldn't give my patients anywhere near the attention they deserved.

Guilty, angry, afraid.

That was how Gail found me. I slipped on a mask of calm and we fixed dinner together. After eating, holding on to each other, we watched the city lights come on in late twilight through the bayside window. Winter starlings pecked at the yellow lawn in the last few minutes of light, then flew away with a rising wind which made the windows rattle.

'Something's wrong,' Gail said softly. 'Are you going to tell me, or just act like everything's normal?'

'It's just me,' I said. 'Nervous. Work at the hospital.'

'Oh, lord,' she said, sitting up. 'You're going to divorce me for that Baker woman.' Mrs Baker weighed three hundred and sixty pounds and hadn't known she was pregnant until her fifth month.

'No,' I said, listless.

'Rapturous relief,' Gail said, touching my forehead lightly. 'You know this kind of introspection drives me crazy.'

'Well, it's nothing I can talk about yet, so …' I patted her hand.

'That's disgustingly patronizing,' she said, getting up. 'I'm going to make some tea. Want some?' Now she was miffed, and I was tense with not telling.

Why not just reveal all? I asked myself. An old friend was turning himself into a galaxy.

I cleared away the table instead. That night, unable to sleep, I looked down on Gail in bed from my sitting position, pillow against the wall, and tried to determine what I knew was real, and what wasn't.

I'm a doctor, I told myself. A technical, scientific profession. I'm supposed to be immune to things like future shock.

Vergil Ulam was turning into a galaxy.

How would it feel to be topped off with a trillion Chinese? I grinned in the dark and almost cried at the same time. What Vergil had inside him was unimaginably stranger than Chinese. Stranger than anything I – or Vergil – could easily understand. Perhaps ever understand.

But I knew what was real. The bedroom, the city lights faint through gauze curtains. Gail sleeping. Very important. Gail in bed, sleeping.

The dream returned. This time the city came in through the window and attacked Gail. It was a great, spiky lighted-up prowler, and it growled in a language I couldn't understand, made up of auto horns, crowd noises, construction bedlam. I tried to fight it off, but it got to her – and turned into a drift of stars, sprinkling all over the bed, all over everything. I jerked awake and stayed up until dawn, dressed with Gail, kissed her, savored the reality of her human, unviolated lips.

I went to meet with Bernard. He had been loaned a suite in a big downtown hospital; I rode the elevator to the sixth floor, and saw what fame and fortune could mean.

The suite was tastefully furnished, fine serigraphs on wood-paneled walls, chrome and glass furniture, cream-colored carpet, Chinese brass, and wormwood-grain cabinets and tables.

He offered me a cup of coffee, and I accepted. He took a seat in the breakfast nook, and I sat across from him, cradling my cup in moist palms. He wore a dapper gray suit and had graying hair and a sharp profile. He was in his mid sixties and he looked quite a bit like Leonard Bernstein.

'About our mutual acquaintance,' he said. 'Mr Ulam. Brilliant. And, I won't hesitate to say, courageous.'

'He's my friend. I'm worried about him.'

Bernard held up one finger. 'Courageous – and a bloody damned fool. What's happening to him should never have been allowed. He may have done it under duress, but that's no excuse. Still, what's done is done. He's talked to you, I take it.'

I nodded. 'He wants to return to Genetron.'

'Of course. That's where all his equipment is. Where his home probably will be while we sort this out.'

'Sort it out – how? Why?' I wasn't thinking too clearly. I had a slight headache.

'I can think of a large number of uses for small, superdense computer elements with a biological base. Can't you? Genetron has already made breakthroughs, but this is something else again.'

'What do you envision?'

Bernard smiled. 'I'm not really at liberty to say. It'll be revolutionary. We'll have to get him in lab conditions. Animal experiments have to be conducted. We'll start from scratch, of course. Vergil's ... um ... colonies can't be transferred. They're based on his own white blood cells. So we have to develop colonies that won't trigger immune reactions in other animals.'

'Like an infection?' I asked.

'I suppose there are comparisons. But Vergil is not infected.'

'My tests indicate he is.'

'That's probably the bits of data floating around in his blood, don't you think?'

'I don't know.'

'Listen, I'd like you to come down to the lab after Vergil is settled in. Your expertise might be useful to us.'

Us. He was working with Genetron hand in glove. Could he be objective? 'How will you benefit from all this?'

'Edward, I have always been at the forefront of my profession. I see no reason why I shouldn't be helping here. With my knowledge of brain and nerve functions, and the research I've been conducting in neurophysiology –'

'You could help Genetron hold off an investigation by the government,' I said.

'That's being very blunt. Too blunt, and unfair.'

'Perhaps. Anyway, yes: I'd like to visit the lab when Vergil's settled in. If I'm still welcome, bluntness and all.' He looked at me sharply. I wouldn't be playing on *his* team; for a moment, his thoughts were almost nakedly apparent.

'Of course,' Bernard said, rising with me. He reached out to shake my hand. His palm was damp. He was as nervous as I was, even if he didn't look it.

I returned to my apartment and stayed there until noon, reading, trying to sort things out. Reach a decision. What was real, what I needed to protect.

There is only so much change anyone can stand: innovation, yes, but slow application. Don't force. Everyone has the right to stay the same until they decide otherwise.

The greatest thing in science since …

And Bernard would force it. Genetron would force it. I couldn't handle the thought. 'Neo-Luddite,' I said to myself. A filthy accusation.

When I pressed Vergil's number on the building security panel, Vergil answered almost immediately. 'Yeah,' he said. He sounded exhilarated. 'Come on up. I'll be in the bathroom. Door's unlocked.'

I entered his apartment and walked through the hallway to the bathroom. Vergil lay in the tub, up to his neck in pinkish water. He smiled vaguely and splashed his hands. 'Looks like I slit my wrists, doesn't it?' he said softly. 'Don't worry. Everything's fine now. Genetron's going to take me back. Bernard just called.' He pointed to the bathroom phone and intercom.

I sat on the toilet and noticed the sunlamp fixture standing unplugged next to the linen cabinets. The bulbs sat in a row on the edge of the sink counter. 'You're sure that's what you want?' I said, my shoulders slumping.

'Yeah, I think so,' he said. 'They can take better care of me. I'm getting cleaned up, going over there this evening. Bernard's picking me up in his limo. Style. From here on in, everything's style.'

The pinkish color in the water didn't look like soap. 'Is that bubble bath?' I asked. Some of it came to me in a rush then and I felt a little weaker; what had occurred to me was just one more obvious and necessary insanity.

'No,' Vergil said. I knew that already.

'No,' he repeated, 'it's coming from my skin. They're not telling me everything, but I think they're sending out scouts. Astronauts.' He looked at me with an expression that didn't quite equal concern; more like curiosity as to how I'd take it.

The confirmation made my stomach muscles tighten as if waiting for a punch. I had never even considered the possibility until now, perhaps because I had been concentrating on other aspects. 'Is this the first time?' I asked.

'Yeah,' he said. He laughed. 'I've half a mind to let the little buggers down the drain. Let them find out what the world's really about.'

'They'd go everywhere,' I said.

'Sure enough.'

'How ... how are you feeling?'

'I'm feeling pretty good now. Must be billions of them.' More splashing with his hands. 'What do you think? Should I let the buggers out?'

Quickly, hardly thinking, I knelt down beside the tub. My fingers went for the cord on the sunlamp and I plugged it in. He had hot-wired doorknobs, turned my piss blue, played a thousand dumb practical jokes and never grown up, never grown mature enough to understand that he was sufficiently brilliant to transform the world; he would never learn caution.

He reached for the drain knob. 'You know, Edward, I –'

He never finished. I picked up the fixture and dropped it into the tub, jumping back at the flash of steam and sparks. Vergil screamed and thrashed and jerked and then everything was still, except for the low, steady sizzle and the smoke wafting from his hair.

I lifted the toilet lid and vomited. Then I clenched my nose and went into the living room. My legs went out from under me and I sat abruptly on the couch.

After an hour, I searched through Vergil's kitchen and found bleach, ammonia, and a bottle of Jack Daniel's. I returned to the bathroom, keeping the center of my gaze away from Vergil. I poured first the booze, then the bleach, then the ammonia into the water. Chlorine started bubbling up and I left closing the door behind me.

The phone was ringing when I got home. I didn't answer. It could have been the hospital. It could have been Bernard. Or the police. I could envision having to explain everything to the police. Genetron would stonewall; Bernard would be unavailable.

I was exhausted, all my muscles knotted with tension and whatever name one can give to the feelings one has after –

Committing genocide?

That certainly didn't seem real. I could not believe I had just murdered a hundred trillion intelligent beings. Snuffed a galaxy. It was laughable. But I didn't laugh.

It was easy to believe that I had just killed one human being, a friend. The smoke, the melted lamp rods, the drooping electrical outlet and smoking cord.

Vergil.

I had dunked the lamp into the tub with Vergil.

I felt sick. Dreams, cities raping Gail (and what about his girlfriend, Candice?). Letting the water filled with them out. Galaxies sprinkling over us all. What horror. Then again, what potential beauty – a new kind of life, symbiosis and transformation.

Had I been thorough enough to kill them all? I had a moment of panic. Tomorrow, I thought, I will sterilize his apartment. Somehow, I didn't even think of Bernard.

When Gail came in the door, I was asleep on the couch. I came to, groggy, and she looked down at me.

'You feeling okay?' she asked, perching on the edge of the couch. I nodded.

'What are you planning for dinner?' My mouth didn't work properly. The words were mushy. She felt my forehead.

'Edward, you have a fever,' she said. 'A very high fever.'

I stumbled into the bathroom and looked in the mirror. Gail was close behind me. 'What is it?' she asked.

There were lines under my collar, around my neck. White lines, like freeways. They had already been in me a long time, days.

'Damp palms,' I said. So obvious.

I think we nearly died. I struggled at first, but in minutes I was too weak to move. Gail was just as sick within an hour.

I lay on the carpet in the living room, drenched in sweat. Gail lay on the couch, her face the color of talcum, eyes closed, like a corpse in an embalming parlor. For a time I thought she was dead. Sick as I was, I raged – hated, felt tremendous guilt at my weakness, my slowness to understand all the possibilities. Then I no longer cared. I was too weak to blink, so I closed my eyes and waited.

There was a rhythm in my arms, my legs. With each pulse of blood, a kind of sound welled up within me, like an orchestra thousands strong, but not playing in unison; playing whole seasons of symphonies at once. Music in the blood. The sound became harsher, but more coordinated, wave-trains finally canceling into silence, then separating into harmonic beats.

The beats seemed to melt into me, into the sound of my own heart.

First, they subdued our immune responses. The war – and it was a war, on a scale never before known on Earth, with trillions of combatants – lasted perhaps two days.

By the time I regained enough strength to get to the kitchen faucet, I could feel them working on my brain, trying to crack the code and find the god within the protoplasm. I drank until I was sick, then drank more moderately and took a glass to Gail. She sipped at it. Her lips were cracked, her eyes blood-shot and ringed with yellowish crumbs. There was some color in her skin. Minutes later, we were eating feebly in the kitchen.

'What in hell is happening?' was the first thing she asked. I didn't have the strength to explain. I peeled an orange and shared it with her. 'We should call a doctor,' she said. But I knew we wouldn't. I was already receiving messages; it was becoming apparent that any sensation of freedom we experienced was illusory.

The messages were simple at first. Memories of commands, rather than the commands themselves, manifested themselves in my thoughts. We were not to leave the apartment – a concept which seemed quite abstract to those in control, even if undesirable – and we were not to have contact with others. We would be allowed to eat certain foods and drink tap water for the time being.

With the subsidence of the fevers, the transformations were quick and drastic. Almost simultaneously, Gail and I were immobilized. She was sitting at the table, I was kneeling on the floor. I was able barely to see her in the corner of my eye.

Her arm developed pronounced ridges.

They had learned inside Vergil; their tactics within the two of us were very different. I itched all over for about two hours – two hours in hell – before they made the breakthrough and found me. The effort of ages on their timescale paid off and they communicated smoothly and directly with this great, clumsy intelligence who had once controlled their universe.

They were not cruel. When the concept of discomfort and its undesirability was made clear, they worked to alleviate it. They worked too effectively. For another hour, I was in a sea of bliss, out of all contact with them.

With dawn the next day, they gave us freedom to move again; specifically, to go to the bathroom. There were certain waste products they could not deal with. I voided those – my urine was purple – and Gail followed suit. We looked at each other vacantly in the bathroom. Then she managed a slight smile. 'Are they talking to you?' she asked. I nodded. 'Then I'm not crazy.'

For the next twelve hours, control seemed to loosen on some levels. I suspect there was another kind of war going on in me. Gail was capable of limited motion, but no more.

When full control resumed, we were instructed to hold each other. We did not hesitate.

'Eddie ...' she whispered. My name was the last sound I ever heard from outside.

Standing, we grew together. In hours, our legs expanded and spread out. Then extensions grew to the windows to take in sunlight, and to the kitchen to take water from the sink. Filaments soon reached to all corners of the room, stripping paint and plaster from the walls, fabric and stuffing from the furniture.

By the next dawn, the transformation was complete.

I no longer have any clear view of what we look like. I suspect we resemble cells – large, flat, and filamented cells, draped purposefully across most of the apartment. The great shall mimic the small.

Our intelligence fluctuates daily as we are absorbed into the minds within. Each day, our individuality declines. We are, indeed, great clumsy dinosaurs. Our memories have been taken over by billions of them, and our personalities have been spread through the transformed blood.

Soon there will be no need for centralization.

Already the plumbing has been invaded. People throughout the building are undergoing transformation.

Within the old time frame of weeks, we will reach the lakes, rivers, and seas in force.

I can barely begin to guess the results. Every square inch of the planet will teem with thought. Years from now, perhaps much sooner, they will subdue their own individuality – what there is of it.

New creatures will come, then. The immensity of their capacity for thought will be inconceivable.

All my hatred and fear is gone now.

I leave them – us – with only one question.

How many times has this happened, elsewhere? Travelers never came through space to visit the Earth. They had no need.

They had found universes in grains of sand.

ONLINE: **ONE/3** *Subject:* Sam Hall, network terrorist

Sam Hall

Poul Anderson

INFO: Just *who* is Sam Hall? When his name first turns up on the police computer files, he's a small-time crook. But then he turns killer, is labelled Public Enemy No.1 and still remains just as elusive. So now it's a case of where does fact end and fiction begin?

Poul Anderson combines the ability to write great sf and fantasy fiction and has scooped his fair share of Hugo and Nebula awards. Born in Pennsylvania of Scandinavian parents, he studied at the University of Minnesota where he gained a degree in physics that has enabled him to give much of his work a distinct sense of authenticity. Poul is widely admired for his multi-faceted 'Technic History' series featuring law and order agent Dominic Flandry and his battle against crime and corruption in the Galaxy. A similar series, the 'Psychotechnic League', is about the use of computers in furthering the exploration of the solar system. 'Sam Hall', which Poul wrote for *Astounding* in 1953, is, though, a more down-to-earth tale which demonstrates how a little cunning and a lot of computer power can make almost any crime *seem* possible.

Click. Bzzzz. Whrrr.

Citizen Blank Blank, Anytown, Somewhere, USA, approaches the hotel desk. 'Single with bath.'

'Sorry, sir, our fuel ration doesn't permit individual baths. One can be drawn for you; that will be twenty-five dollars extra.'

'Oh, is that all? Okay.'

Citizen Blank Blank reaches into his pocket with an automatic gesture and withdraws his punched card and gives it to the registry machine. Aluminium jaws close on it, copper teeth feel for the holes, electronic tongue tastes the life of Citizen Blank.

Place and date of birth. Parents. Race. Religion. Educational, military, and civilian service records. Marital status. Occupations, up to and including current one. Affiliations. Physical measurements, fingerprints, retinals, blood type. Basic psychotype. Loyalty rating. Loyalty index as a function of time to moment of last checkup. Click, click. Bzzz.

'Why are you here, sir?'

'Salesman. I expect to be in New Pittsburg tomorrow night.'

The clerk (32 yrs, married, two children; NB, confidential: Jewish. To be kept out of key occupations) punches the buttons.

Click, click. The machine returns the card. Citizen Blank puts it back in his wallet.

'Front!'

The bellboy (19 yrs, unmarried; NB, confidential: Catholic. To be kept out of key occupations) takes the guest's trunk. The elevator creaks upstairs. The clerk resumes his reading. The article is entitled 'Has Britain Betrayed Us?' Other articles in the magazine include 'New Indoctrination Program for the Armed Forces', 'Labor Hunting on Mars', 'I Was a Union Man for the Security Police', 'New Plans for YOUR Future'.

The machine talks to itself. Click, click. A tube winks at its neighbor as if they shared a private joke. The total signal goes out over the wires.

With a thousand other signals, it shoots down the last cable and into the sorter unit of Central Records. Click, click. Bzzz. Whrrr. Wink and glow. A scanner sweeps through the memory circuits. The distorted molecules of one spool show the pattern of Citizen Blank Blank, and this is sent back. It enters the comparison unit, to which the incoming signal corresponding to Citizen Blank Blank has also been shunted. The two are perfectly in phase; nothing wrong. Citizen Blank Blank is staying in the town where, last night, he said he would, so he has not had to file a correction.

The new information is added to the record of Citizen Blank Blank. The whole of his life returns to the memory bank. It is wiped from the scanner and comparison units, so that these may be free for the next arriving signal.

The machine has swallowed and digested another day. It is content.

Thornberg came into his office at the usual time. His secretary glanced up to say 'Good morning,' and looked closer. She had been with him for enough years to read the nuances in his carefully controlled face. 'Anything wrong, chief?'

'No.' He spoke it harshly, which was also peculiar. 'No, nothing wrong. I feel a bit under the weather, maybe.'

'Oh.' The secretary nodded. You learned discretion in the government. 'Well, I hope you get better soon.'

'Thanks. It's nothing.' Thornberg limped over to his desk, sat down, and took out a pack of cigarettes. He held one for a moment in nicotine-yellowed fingers before lighting it, and there was an emptiness in his eyes. Then he puffed ferociously and turned to his mail. As chief technician of Central Records, he received a generous tobacco ration and used all of it.

The office was not large – a windowless cubicle, furnished with gaunt orderliness, its only decoration a picture of his son and one of his late wife. Thornberg seemed too big for it. He was tall and lean, with thin, straight features and neatly brushed graying hair. He wore a plain version of the Security uniform, with his insignia of Technical Division and major's rank but no other decoration, none of the ribbons to which he was entitled. The priesthood of Matilda the Machine were a pretty informal lot for these days.

He chain-smoked his way through the mail. Routine stuff, most of it having to do with the necessary change-overs for installing the new identification system. 'Come on, June,' he said to his secretary. Irrationally, he preferred dictating to her rather than to a recorder. 'Let's get this out of the way fast, I've got work to do.'

He held one letter before him. 'To Senator E. W. Harmison, SOB, New Washington. Dear Sir: In re your communication of the 14th inst., requesting my personal opinion of the new ID system, may I say that it is not a technician's business to express opinions. The directive ordering that every citizen shall have one number applying to all his papers and functions – birth certificate, education, rations, social security, service, etc. – has obvious long-range advantages, but naturally entails a good deal of work in reconverting all our electronic records. The President having decided that the gain in the long run justifies the present difficulties, it behoves all citizens to obey. Yours, and so forth.' He smiled with a certain coldness. 'There, that'll fix *him*! I don't know what good Congress is anyway, except to plague honest bureaucrats.'

Privately, June decided to modify the letter. Maybe a senator was only a rubber stamp, but you couldn't brush him off so curtly. It is part of a secretary's job to keep the boss out of trouble.

'Okay, let's get to the next,' said Thornberg. 'To Colonel M. R. Hubert, Director of Liaison Division, Central Records Agency, Security Police, etc. Dear Sir: In re your memorandum of the 14th inst., requiring a definite date for completion of the ID conversion, may I respectfully state that it is impossible for me honestly to set one. It is necessary for us to develop a memory-modification unit which will make the change-over in all our records without our having to take out and alter each of the three hundred million or so spools in the machine. You realize that one cannot predict the exact time needed to complete such a project. However, research is progressing satisfactorily (refer him to my last report, will you?), and I can confidently say that conversion will be finished and all citizens notified of their numbers within two months at the latest. Respectfully, and so on. Put that in a nice form, June.'

She nodded. Thornberg went on through his mail, throwing most of it into a basket for her to answer alone. When he was done he yawned and lit another cigarette. 'Praise Allah that's over. Now I can get down to the lab.'

'You have some afternoon appointments,' she reminded him.

'I'll be back after lunch. See you.' He got up and went out of the office.

Down an escalator to a still lower subterranean level, along a corridor, returning the salutes of passing technicians without thinking about it. His face was immobile, and perhaps only the stiff swinging of his arms said anything.

Jimmy, he thought. *Jimmy, kid.*

He entered the guard chamber, pressing hand and eye to the scanners in the farther door. Finger and retinal patterns were his pass; no alarm sounded; the door opened for him and he walked into the temple of Matilda.

She crouched hugely before him, tier upon tier of control panels, instruments, blinking lights, like an Aztec pyramid. The gods murmured within her and winked red eyes at the tiny man who crawled over her monstrous flanks. Thornberg stood for a moment regarding the spectacle. Then he smiled, a tired smile creasing his face along one side. A sardonic memory came back to him, bootlegged stuff from the forties and fifties of the last century which he had read: French, German, British, Italian. The intellectuals had been all hot and bothered about the Americanization of Europe, the crumbling of old culture before the mechanized barbarism of soft drinks, advertising, chrome-plated automobiles (dollar grins, the Danes had called them), chewing gum, plastics ... None of them had protested the simultaneous Europeanization of America: government control, a military caste, light-years of bureaucratic records and red tape, censors, secret police, nationalism, and racialism.

Oh, well.

But, Jimmy, boy, where are you now, what are they doing to you?

Thornberg went over to the bench where his best engineer, Rodney, was testing a unit. 'How's it coming?' he asked.

'Pretty good, chief,' said Rodney. He didn't bother to salute; Thornberg had, in fact, forbidden it in the labs as a waste of time. 'A few bugs yet, but we're getting them out.'

You had to have a gimmick which would change numbers without altering anything else. Not too easy a task, when the memory banks depended on individual magnetic domains. 'Okay,' said Thornberg. 'Look, I'm going up to the main controls. Going to run a few tests myself – some of the tubes have been acting funny over in Section Thirteen.'

'Want an assistant?'

'No, thanks. I just want not to be bothered.'

Thornberg resumed his way across the floor, its hardness echoing dully under his shoes. The main controls were in a special armored booth nestling against the great pyramid, and he had to be scanned again before the door opened for him. Not many were allowed in here.

The complete archives of the nation were too valuable to take chances with.

Thornberg's loyalty rating was AAB-2 – not absolutely perfect, but the best available among men of his professional caliber. His last drugged checkup had revealed certain doubts and reservations about government policy, but there was no question of disobedience. *Prima facie*, he was certainly bound to be loyal. He had served with distinction in the war against Brazil, losing a leg in action; his wife had been killed in the abortive Chinese rocket raids ten years ago; his son was a rising young Space Guard officer on Venus. He had read and listened to forbidden stuff, blacklisted books, underground and foreign propaganda, but then every intellectual dabbled with that; it was not a serious offense if your record was otherwise good and if you laughed off what the prohibited things said.

He sat for a moment regarding the control board inside the booth. Its complexity would have baffled most engineers, but he had been with Matilda so long that he didn't even need the reference tables.

Well –

It took nerve, this. A hypnoquiz was sure to reveal what he was about to do. But such raids were, necessarily, in a random pattern; it was unlikely that he would be called up again for years, especially with his rating. By the time he was found out, Jack should have risen far enough in the Guard ranks to be safe.

In the privacy of the booth Thornberg permitted himself a harsh grin. 'This,' he murmured to the machine, 'will hurt me worse than it does you.'

He began punching buttons.

There were circuits installed which could alter the records – take out an entire one and write whatever was desired in the magnetic fields. Thornberg had done the job a few times for high officials. Now he was doing it for himself.

Jimmy Obrenowicz, son of his second cousin, hustled off at night by Security police on suspicion of treason. The records showed what no private citizen was supposed to know: Jimmy was in Camp Fieldstone. Those who returned from there were very quiet and said nothing about where they had been; sometimes they were incapable of speech.

It wouldn't do for the chief of Central Records to have a relative in Fieldstone. Thornberg punched buttons for half an hour, erasing, changing. It was a tough job – he had to go back several generations, altering lines of descent. But when he was through, Jimmy Obrenowicz was no relation whatever to the Thornbergs.

And I thought the world of that kid. But I'm not doing it for myself, Jimmy. It's for Jack. When the cops go through your file, later today no doubt, I can't let them find out you're related to Captain Thornberg on Venus and a friend of his father.

He slapped the switch that returned the spool to its place in the memory bank. *With this act do I disown thee.*

After that he sat for a while, relishing the quiet of the booth and the clean impersonality of the instruments. He didn't even want to smoke.

So now they were going to give every citizen a number, tattooed on him, no doubt. One number for everything. Thornberg foresaw popular slang referring to the numbers as 'brands', and Security cracking down on those who used the term. Disloyal language.

Well, the underground was dangerous. It was supported by foreign countries who didn't like an American-dominated world – at least, not one dominated by today's kind of America, though once 'USA' had meant 'Hope'. The rebels were said to have their own base out in space somewhere and to have honeycombed the country with their agents. It could be. Their propaganda was subtle: we don't want to overthrow the nation; we only want to liberate it; we want to restore the Bill of Rights. It could attract a lot of unstable souls. But Security's spy hunt was bound to drag in any number of citizens who had never meditated treason. Like Jimmy – or had Jimmy been an undergrounder after all? You never knew. Nobody ever told you.

There was a sour taste in Thornberg's mouth. He grimaced. A line of a song came back to him. '*I hate you one and all.*' How had it gone? They used to sing it in his college days. Something about a very bitter character who'd committed a murder.

Oh, yes. 'Sam Hall'. How did it go, now? You needed a gravelly bass to sing it properly.

> *Oh, my name it is Sam Hall, it is Sam Hall.*
> *Yes, my name it is Sam Hall, it is Sam Hall.*
> *Oh, my name it is Sam Hall,*
> *And I hate you one and all,*
> *Yes, I hate you one and all, God damn your eyes.*

That was it. And Sam Hall was about to swing for murder. He remembered now. He felt like Sam Hall himself. He looked at the machine and wondered how many Sam Halls were in it.

Idly, postponing his return to work, he punched for the file – name, Samuel Hall, no other specifications. The machine mumbled to itself. Presently it spewed out a file of papers, microprinted on the spot from the memory banks. Complete dossier on every Sam Hall, living and dead, from the time the records began to be kept. To hell with it. Thornberg chucked the papers down the incinerator slot.

'*Oh, I killed a man, they say, so they say –*'

The impulse was blinding in its savagery. They were dealing with Jimmy at this moment, probably pounding him over the kidneys, and he, Thornberg, sat here waiting for the cops to requisition Jimmy's file, and there was nothing he could do. His hands were empty.

By God, he thought. *I'll give them Sam Hall!*

His fingers began to race; he lost his nausea in the intricate technical problem. Slipping a fake spool into Matilda – it wasn't easy. You couldn't duplicate numbers, and every citizen had a lot of them. You had to account for every day of his life.

Well, some of that could be simplified. The machine had only existed for twenty-five years; before then the files had been kept on paper in a dozen different offices. Let's make Sam Hall a resident of New York, his dossier there lost in the bombing thirty years ago. Such of his papers as were on file in New Washington had also been lost, in the Chinese attack.

That meant he simply reported as much detail as he could remember, which needn't be a lot.

Let's see. 'Sam Hall' was an English song, so Sam Hall should be British himself. Came over with his parents, oh, thirty-eight years ago, when he was only three, and naturalized with them; that was before the total ban on immigration. Grew up on New York's lower East Side, a tough kid, a slum kid. School records lost in the bombing, but he claimed to have gone through the tenth grade. No living relatives. No family. No definite occupation, just a series of unskilled jobs. Loyalty rating BBA-O, which meant that purely routine questions showed him to have no political opinions at all that mattered.

Too colorless. Give him some violence in his background. Thornberg punched for information on New York police stations and civilian police officers destroyed in the last raids. He used them as the source of records that Sam Hall had been continually in trouble – drunkenness, disorderly conduct, brawls, a suspicion of holdups and burglary, but not strong enough to warrant calling in Security's hypnotechnicians for quizzing him.

Hmmm. Better make him 4-F, no military service. Reason? Well, a slight drug addiction; men weren't so badly needed nowadays that hopheads had to be cured. Neocoke – that didn't impair the faculties too much; indeed the addict was abnormally fast and strong under the influence, though there was a tough reaction afterwards.

Then he would have had to put in a term in civilian service. Let's see. He spent his three years as a common laborer on the Colorado Dam project; so many men had been involved there that no one would remember him, or at least it would be hard finding a supervisor who did.

Now to fill in. Thornberg used a number of automatic machines to help him. Every day in twenty-five years had to be accounted for; but of course the majority would show no travel or change of residence. Thornberg punched for cheap hotels housing many at a time – no record would be kept there, everything being filed in Matilda; and no one would remember a shabby individual patron. Sam Hall's present address was given as the Triton, a glorified flophouse on the East Side not far from the craters. At present unemployed, doubtless living off past savings. Oh, blast! It was necessary to file income-tax returns. Thornberg did so.

Hmmm – physical ID. Make him of average height, stock, black-haired and black-eyed, a bent nose, and a scar on his forehead – tough-looking, but not enough so as to make him especially memorable. Thornberg filled in the precise measurements. It wasn't hard to fake fingerprints and retinal patterns; he threw in a censor circuit so he wouldn't accidentally duplicate anyone else.

When he was done, Thornberg leaned back and sighed. There were plenty of holes yet in the record, but he could fill them in at his leisure. It had been a couple of hours' hard, concentrated work – utterly pointless, except that he had blown off steam. He felt a lot better.

He glanced at his watch. *Time to get back on the job, son.* For a rebellious moment he wished no one had ever invented clocks. They had made possible the science he loved, but they had then proceeded to mechanize man. Oh, well, too late now. He got up and went out of the booth. The door closed itself behind him.

It was about a month later that Sam Hall committed his first murder.

The night before, Thornberg had been at home. His rank entitled him to good housing even if he did live alone – two rooms and bath on the ninety-eighth floor of a unit in town, not far from the camouflaged entrance to Matilda's underground domain. The fact that he was in Security, even if he didn't belong to the man-hunting branch, gave him so much added deference that he often felt lonely. The superintendent had even offered him his daughter once – 'Only twenty-three, sir, just released by a gentleman of marshal's rank, and looking for a nice patron, sir.' Thornberg had refused, trying not to be prissy about it. *Autres temps, autres moeurs* – but still, she wouldn't have had any choice about getting client status, the first time anyway. And Thornberg's marriage had been a long and happy one.

He had been looking through his bookshelves for something to read. The Literary Bureau had lately been trumpeting Whitman as an early example of Americanism, but though Thornberg had always liked the poet, his hands strayed perversely to the dogeared volume of Marlowe. Was that escapism? The LB was very down on escapism. Oh, well, these were tough times. It wasn't easy to belong to the nation which was enforcing peace on a sullen world – you had to be realistic and energetic and all the rest, no doubt.

The phone buzzed. He went over and clicked on the receiver. Martha Obrenowicz's plain plump face showed in the screen; her gray hair was wild and her voice a harsh croak.

'Uh – hello,' he said uneasily. He hadn't called her since the news of her son's arrest. 'How are you?'

'Jimmy is dead,' she told him.

He stood for a long while. His skull felt hollow.

'I got word today that he died in camp,' said Martha. 'I thought you'd want to know.'

Thornberg shook his head, back and forth, very slowly. 'That isn't news I ever wanted, Martha,' he said.

'It isn't *right*!' she shrieked. 'Jimmy wasn't a traitor. I knew my own son. Who ought to know him better? He had some friends I was kind of doubtful of, but Jimmy, he wouldn't ever –'

Something cold formed in Thornberg's breast. You never knew when calls were being tapped.

'I'm sorry, Martha,' he said without tone. 'But the police are very careful about these things. They wouldn't act till they were sure. Justice is one of our traditions.'

She looked at him for a long time. Her eyes held a hard glitter. 'You too,' she said at last.

'Be careful, Martha,' he warned her. 'I know it's a blow to you, but don't say anything you might regret later. After all, Jimmy may have died accidentally. Those things happen.'

'I – forgot,' she said jerkily. 'You ... are ... in Security ... yourself.'

'Be calm,' he said. 'Think of it as a sacrifice for the national interest.'

She switched off on him. He knew she wouldn't call him again. And it wouldn't be safe to see her.

'Goodbye, Martha,' he said aloud. It was like a stranger speaking.

He turned back to the bookshelf. *Not for me*, he told himself thinly. *For Jack*. He touched the binding of *Leaves of Grass*. *Oh, Whitman, old rebel*, he thought, with a curious dry laughter in him, *are they calling you Whirling Walt now?*

That night he took an extra sleeping pill. His head still felt fuzzy when he reported for work, and after a while he gave up trying to answer the mail and went down to the lab.

While he was engaged with Rodney, and making a poor job of understanding the technical problem under discussion, his eyes strayed to Matilda. Suddenly he realized what he needed for a cathartic. He broke off as soon as possible and went into the main control booth.

For a moment he paused at the keyboard. The day-by-day creation of Sam Hall had been an odd experience. He, quiet and introverted, had shaped a rowdy life and painted a rugged personality. Sam Hall was more real to him than many of his associates. *Well, I'm a schizoid type myself. Maybe I should have been a writer*. No, that would have meant too many restrictions, too much fear of offending the censor. He had done exactly as he pleased with Sam Hall.

He drew a deep breath and punched for unsolved murders of Security officers, New York City area, within the last month. They were surprisingly common. Could it be that dissatisfaction was more general than the government admitted? But when the bulk of a nation harbors thoughts labeled treasonous, does the label still apply?

He found what he wanted. Sergeant Brady had incautiously entered the

Crater district after dark on the 27th of last month, on a routine checkup mission; he had worn the black uniform, presumably to give himself the full weight of authority. The next morning he had been found in an alley with his head bashed in.

> *Oh, I killed a man, they say, so they say.*
> *Yes, I killed a man, they say, so they say.*
>   *I beat him on the head*
>   *And I left him there for dead,*
> *Yes, I left him there for dead, God damn his eyes.*

Newspapers had no doubt deplored this brutality perpetrated by the traitorous agents of enemy powers. ('*Oh, the parson, he did come, he did come.*') A number of suspects had been rounded up at once and given a stiff quizzing. ('*And the sheriff, he came too, he came too.*') There had been nothing proven as yet, though one Joe Nikolsky (fifth generation American, mechanic, married, four children, underground pamphlets found in his room) had been arrested yesterday on suspicion.

Thornberg sighed. He knew enough of Security methods to be sure they would get somebody for such a killing. They couldn't allow their reputation for infallibility to be smirched by a lack of conclusive evidence. Maybe Nikolsky had done the crime – he couldn't *prove* he had simply been out for a walk that evening – and maybe he hadn't. But hell's fire, why not give him a break? He had four kids. With such a black mark, their mother could find work only in a recreation house.

Thornberg scratched his head. This had to be done carefully. Let's see. Brady's body would have been cremated by now, but of course there had been a thorough study first. Thornberg withdrew the dead man's file from the machine and microprinted a replica of the evidence – nothing. Erasing that, he inserted the statement that a blurred thumbprint had been found on the victim's collar and referred to ID labs for reconstruction. In the ID file he inserted the report of such a job, finished only yesterday due to a great press of work. (True enough – they had been busy lately on material sent from Mars, seized in a raid on a rebel meeting place.) The probable pattern of the whorls was – and here he inserted Sam Hall's right thumb.

He returned the spools and leaned back in his chair. It was risky; if anyone thought to check with the ID lab, he was done for. But that was unlikely; the chances were that New York would accept the findings with a routine acknowledgement which some clerk at the lab would file without studying. The more obvious dangers were not too great either: a busy police force would not stop to ask if any of their fingerprint men had actually developed that smudge; and as for hypnoquizzing showing

Nikolsky really was the murderer, well, then the print would be assumed that of a passer-by who had found the body without reporting it.

So now Sam Hall had killed a Security officer – grabbed him by the neck and smashed his skull with a weighted club. Thornberg felt a lot better.

New York Security shot a request to Central Records for any new material on the Brady case. An automaton received it, compared the codes, and saw that fresh information had been added. The message flashed back, together with the dossier on Sam Hall and two others – for the reconstruction could not be absolutely accurate.

The other two men were safe enough, as it turned out. Both had alibis. The squad that stormed into the Triton Hotel and demanded Sam Hall were met with blank stares. No such person was registered. No one of the description was known there. A thorough quizzing corroborated this. So – Sam Hall had managed to fake an address. He could have done that easily enough by punching the buttons on the hotel register when no one was looking. Sam Hall could be anywhere!

Joe Nikolsky, having been hypnoed and found harmless, was released. The fine for possessing subversive literature would put him in debt for the next few years – he had no influential friends to get it suspended – but he'd stay out of trouble if he watched his step. Security sent out an alarm for Sam Hall.

Thornberg derived a sardonic amusement from watching the progress of the hunt as it came to Matilda. No one with the ID card had bought tickets on any public transportation. That proved nothing. Of the hundreds who vanished every year, some at least must have been murdered for their ID cards, and their bodies disposed of. Matilda was set to give the alarm when the ID of a disappeared person showed up somewhere. Thornberg faked a few such reports, just to give the police something to do.

He slept more poorly each night, and his work suffered. Once he met Martha Obrenowicz on the street – passed by hastily without greeting her – and couldn't sleep at all, even with maximum permissible drugging.

The new ID system was completed. Machines sent notices to every citizen, with orders to have their numbers tattooed on the right shoulder blade within six weeks. As each tattoo center reported that such-and-such person had had the job done, Matilda's robots changed the record appropriately. Sam Hall, AX-428-399-075, did not report for his tattoo. Thornberg chuckled at the AX symbol.

Then the telecasts flashed a story that made the nation sit up and listen. Bandits had held up the First National Bank in America-town, Idaho (formerly Moscow), making off with a good five million dollars in assorted bills. From their discipline and equipment it was assumed that they were rebel agents, possibly having come in a spaceship from their unknown interplanetary base, and that the raid was intended to help finance their nefarious activities. Security was cooperating with the Armed Forces to track down the evidence, and arrests were expected hourly, etc., etc.

Thornberg went to Matilda for a complete account. It had been a bold job. The robbers had apparently worn plastic face masks and light body armor under ordinary clothes. In the scuffle of the getaway one man's mask had slipped aside – only for a moment, but a clerk who happened to see it had, with the aid of hypnosis, given a fairly good description. A brown-haired, heavy-set fellow, Roman nose, thin lips, toothbrush mustache.

Thornberg hesitated. A joke was a joke; and helping poor Nikolsky was perhaps morally defensible; but aiding and abetting a felony which was in all likelihood an act of treason –

He grinned to himself, without much humor. It was too much fun playing God. Swiftly he changed the record. The crook had been of medium height, dark, scar-faced, broken-nosed – he sat for a while wondering how sane he was. How sane anybody was.

Security Central asked for the complete file on the holdup, with any correlations the machine could make. It was sent to them. The description given could have been that of many men, but the scanners eliminated all but one possibility. *Sam Hall*.

The hounds bayed forth again. That night Thornberg slept well.

Dear Dad,
Sorry I haven't written before, but we've been kept pretty busy here. As you know, I've been with a patrol in Gorbuvashtar for the past several weeks – desolate country, like all this blasted planet. Sometimes I wonder if I'll ever see the sun again. And lakes and forests and – who wrote that line about the green hills of earth? We can't get much to read out here, and sometimes my mind feels rusty. Not that I'm complaining, of course. This is a necessary job, and somebody has to do it.

We'd hardly gotten back from the patrol when we were called out on special duty, bundled into rockets, and tossed halfway around the planet through the worst gale I've ever seen, even on Venus. If I hadn't been an officer and therefore presumably a gentleman, I'd have upchucked. A lot of the boys did, and we were a pretty sorry crew when we landed. But we had to go into action right away. There was a strike in the thorium mines and the local men couldn't break it. We had to use guns before we could bring them to reason. Dad, I felt sorry for the poor devils, I don't mind admitting it. Rocks and hammers and sluice hoses against machine guns! And conditions in the mines are pretty rugged. They DELETED BY CENSOR someone has to do that job too, and if no one will volunteer, for any kind of pay, they have to assign civilian-service men arbitrarily. It's for the state.

Otherwise nothing new. Life is pretty monotonous. Don't believe the adventure stories – adventure is weeks of boredom punctuated by moments of being scared gutless. Sorry to be so brief, but I want to get this on the outbound rocket. Won't be another for a couple of months. Everything well, really. I hope the same for you and live for the day we'll meet again. Thanks a million for the cookies – you know you can't afford to pay the freight, you old spendthrift! Martha baked them, didn't she? I recognized the Obrenowicz touch. Say hello to her and Jim for me. And most of all, my kindest thoughts go to you.

As ever,
Jack.

The telecasts carried 'Wanted' messages for Sam Hall. No photographs of him were available, but an artist could draw an accurate likeness from Matilda's precise description, and his truculent face began to adorn public places. Not long thereafter, the Security offices in Denver were blown up by a grenade tossed from a speeding car that vanished into traffic. A witness said he had glimpsed the thrower, and the fragmentary picture given under hypnosis was not unlike Sam Hall's. Thornberg doctored the record a bit to make it still more similar. The tampering was risky, of course; if Security ever became suspicious, they could easily check back with their witnesses. But it was not too big a chance to take, for a scientifically quizzed man told everything germane to the subject which his memory, conscious, subconscious, and cellular, held. There was never any reason to repeat such an interrogation.

Thornberg often tried to analyze his own motives. Plainly enough, he disliked the government. He must have contained that hate all his life, carefully suppressed from awareness, and only recently had it been forced into his conscious mind; not even his subconscious could have formulated it earlier, or he would have been caught by the loyalty probes. The hate derived from a lifetime of doubts (had there been any real reason to fight Brazil other than to obtain those bases and mining concessions? Had the Chinese attack perhaps been provoked – or even faked, for their government had denied it?) and the million petty frustrations of the garrison state. Still – the strength of it! The violence!

By creating Sam Hall he had struck back, but it was an ineffectual blow, a timid gesture. Most likely his basic motive was simply to find a halfway safe release; in Sam Hall he lived vicariously all the things that the beast within him wanted to do. Several times he had intended to discontinue his sabotage, but it was like a drug: Sam Hall was becoming necessary to his own stability.

The thought was alarming. He ought to see a psychiatrist – but no, the doctor would be bound to report his tale, he would go to camp, and Jack, if not exactly ruined, would be under a cloud for the rest of his life. Thornberg had no desire to go to camp, anyway. His own existence had compensations – interesting work, a few good friends, art and music and literature, decent wine, sunsets and mountains, memories. He had started this game on impulse, but now it was too late to stop it.

For Sam Hall had been promoted to Public Enemy Number One.

Winter came, and the slopes of the Rockies under which Matilda lay were white beneath a cold greenish sky. Air traffic around the nearby town was lost in that hugeness: brief hurtling meteors against infinity; ground traffic could not be seen at all from the Records entrance. Thornberg took the special tubeway to work every morning, but he often walked the five miles back, and his Sundays were usually spent in long hikes over the slippery trails. That was a foolish thing to do alone in winter, but he felt reckless.

He was working in his office shortly before Christmas when the intercom said: 'Major Sorensen to see you, sir. From Investigation.'

Thornberg felt his stomach tie itself into a cold knot. 'All right,' he answered in a voice whose levelness surprised him. 'Cancel any other appointments.' Security Investigation took priority over everything.

Sorensen walked in with a hard, military clack of boots. He was a big blond man, heavy-shouldered, his face expressionless and his eyes as pale and cold and remote as the winter sky. The black uniform fitted him like another skin; the lightning badge of his service glittered against it like a frosty star. He stood stiffly before the desk, and Thornberg rose to give him an awkward salute.

'Please sit down, Major Sorensen. What can I do for you?'

'Thanks.' The cop's voice was crisp and harsh. He lowered his bulk into a chair and drilled Thornberg with his eyes. 'I've come about the Sam Hall case.'

'Oh – the rebel?' Thornberg's skin prickled. It was all he could do to meet those eyes.

'How do you know he's a rebel?' asked Sorensen. 'It's never been proved officially.'

'Why – I assumed – the bank raid – and then the posters say he's believed to be in the underground –'

Sorensen inclined his cropped head ever so slightly. When he spoke again it was in a relaxed tone, almost casual: 'Tell me, Major Thornberg, have you followed the Hall dossier in detail?'

Thornberg hesitated. He wasn't supposed to do so unless ordered; he only kept the machine running. A memory came back to him, something he had read once: 'When suspected of a major sin, admit the minor ones frankly. It disarms suspicion.' Something like that.

'As a matter of fact, I have,' he said. 'I know it's against regs, but I was interested and – well, I couldn't see any harm in it. I've not discussed it with anyone, of course.'

'No matter.' Sorensen waved a muscular hand. 'If you hadn't done so, I'd have ordered you to. I want your opinion on this.'

'Why – I'm not a detective –'

'You know more about Records, though, than anyone else. I'll be frank with you – under the rose, naturally.' Sorensen seemed almost friendly now. *Was it a trick to put his prey off guard?* 'You see, there are some puzzling features about this case.'

Thornberg kept silent. He wondered if Sorensen could hear the thudding of his heart.

'Sam Hall is a shadow,' said the cop. 'The most careful checkups eliminate any chance of his being identical with anyone else of that name. In fact, we've learned that the name occurs in a violent old drinking song – is it coincidence, or did the song suggest crime to Sam Hall, or did he by some incredible process get that alias into his record instead of his real name? Whatever the answer there, we know that he's ostensibly without military training, yet he's pulled off some beautiful pieces of precision attack. His IQ is only 110, but he evades all our traps. He has no politics, yet he turns on Security without warning. We have not been able to find one person who remembers him – not one, and believe me, we have been thorough. Oh, there are a few subconscious memories which might be of him, but probably aren't – and so aggressive a personality should be remembered consciously. No undergrounder or foreign agent we've caught had any knowledge of him, which defies probability. The whole business seems impossible.'

Thornberg licked his lips. Sorensen, the hunter of men, must know he was frightened; but would he assume it to be the normal nervousness of a man in the presence of a Security officer?

Sorensen's face broke into a hard smile. 'As Sherlock Holmes once remarked,' he said, 'when you have eliminated every other hypothesis, then the one which remains, however improbable, must be the right one.'

Despite himself, Thornberg was jolted. Sorensen hadn't struck him as a reader.

'Well,' he asked slowly, 'what is your remaining hypothesis?'

The other man watched him for a long time, it seemed for ever, before replying. 'The underground is more powerful and widespread than people realize. They've had some seventy years to prepare, and there are many good brains in their ranks. They carry on scientific research of their own. It's top secret, but we know they have perfected a type of weapon we cannot duplicate yet. It seems to be a hand gun throwing bolts of energy – a blaster, you might call it – of immense power. Sooner or later they're going to wage open war against the government.

'Now, could they have done something comparable in psychology? Could they have found a way to erase or cover up memories selectively, even on the cellular level? Could they know how to fool a personality tester, how to disguise the mind itself? If so, there may be any number of Sam Halls in our very midst, undetectable until the moment comes for them to strike.'

Thornberg felt almost boneless. He couldn't help gasping his relief, and hoped Sorensen would take it for a sign of alarm.

'The possibility is frightening, isn't it?' The blond man laughed harshly. 'You can imagine what is being felt in high official circles. We've put all the psychological researchers we could get to work on the problem – bah! Fools! They go by the book; they're afraid to be original even when the state tells them to.

'It may just be a wild fancy, of course. I hope it is. But we have to *know*. That's why I approached you personally, instead of sending the usual requisition. I want you to make a search of the records – everything pertaining to the subject, every man, every discovery, every hypothesis. You have a broad technical background and, from your psychorecord, an unusual amount of creative imagination. I want you to do what you can to correlate all your data. Co-opt anybody you need. Submit to my office a report on the possibility – or should I say probability – of this notion, and if there is any likelihood of it being true, sketch out a research program which will enable us to duplicate the results and counteract them.'

Thornberg fumbled for words. 'I'll try,' he said lamely. 'I'll do my best.'

'Good. It's for the state.'

Sorensen had finished his official business, but he didn't go at once. 'Rebel propaganda is subtle stuff,' he said quietly, after a pause. 'It's dangerous because it uses our own slogans, with a twisted meaning. Liberty, equality, justice, peace. Too many people can't appreciate that times have changed and the meanings of words have necessarily changed with them.'

'I suppose not,' said Thornberg. He added the lie: 'I never thought much about it.'

'You should,' said Sorensen. 'Study your history. When we lost World War III we had to militarize to win World War IV, and after that, for our own safety, we had to mount guard on the whole human race. The people demanded it at the time.'

The people, thought Thornberg, *never appreciated freedom till they'd lost it. They were always willing to sell their birthright. Or was it merely that, being untrained in thinking, they couldn't see through demagoguery, couldn't visualize the ultimate consequences of their wishes?* He was vaguely shocked at the thought; wasn't he able to control his own mind any longer?

'The rebels,' said Sorensen, 'claim that conditions have changed, that militarization is no longer necessary – if it ever was – and that America would be safe enough in a union of free countries. It's devilishly clever propaganda, Major Thornberg. Watch out for it.'

He got up and took his leave. Thornberg sat for a long time staring after the door. Sorensen's last words were – odd, to say the least. Was it a hint – or was it bait in a trap?

The next day Matilda received a news item whose details were carefully censored for the public channels. A rebel force had landed in the stockade of Camp Jackson, in Utah, gunned down the guards, and taken away the prisoners. The camp doctor had been spared, and related that the leader of the raid, a stocky man in a mask, had ironically said to him: 'Tell your friends I'll call again. My name is Sam Hall.'

Space Guard ship blown up on Mesa Verde Field. On a fragment of metal someone has scrawled: 'Compliments of Sam Hall.'

Army quartermaster depot robbed of a million dollars. Bandit chief says, before disappearing, that he is Sam Hall.

Squad of Security police, raiding a suspected underground hideout in New Pittsburgh, cut down by machine-gun fire. Voice over hidden loudspeaker cries: 'My name it is Sam Hall!'

Dr Matthew Thomson, chemist in Seattle, suspected of underground connections, is gone when his home is raided. Note left on desk says: 'Off to visit Sam Hall. Back for liberation. MT.'

Defense plant producing important robomb parts blown up near Miami by small atomic bomb, after being warned over the phone that the bomb has been planted and they have half an hour to get their workers out. The caller, masked, styles himself Sam Hall.

Army laboratory in Houston given similar warning by Sam Hall. A fake, but a day's valuable work is lost in the alarm and the search.

Scribbled on walls from New York to San Diego, from Duluth to El Paso, Sam Hall, Sam Hall, Sam Hall.

Obviously, thought Thornberg, the underground had seized on the invisible and invincible man of legend and turned him to their own purposes. Reports of him poured in from all over the country, hundreds every day – Sam Hall seen here, Sam Hall seen there. Ninety-nine per cent could be dismissed as hoaxes, hallucinations, mistakes; it was another national craze, fruit of a jittery time, like the sixteenth- and seventeenth-century witch hunts or the twentieth-century flying saucers. But Security and civilian police had to check on every one.

Thornberg planted a number of them himself.

Mostly, though, he was busy with his assignment. He could understand what it meant to the government. Life in the garrison state was inevitably founded on fear and mistrust, every man's eye on his neighbor; but at least psychotyping and hypnoquizzing had given a degree of surety. Now, with that staff knocked out from under them –

His preliminary studies indicated that a discovery such as Sorensen had hypothesized, while not impossible, was too far beyond the scope of modern science for the rebels to have perfected. Such research carried on nowadays would, from the standpoint of practicality if not of knowledge, be a waste of time and trained men.

He spent a good many sleepless hours and used up a month's cigarette ration before he could decide what to do. All right, he'd aided insurrection in a small way, and he shouldn't boggle at the next step. Still – nevertheless – did he want to?

Jack – the boy had a career lined out for himself. He loved the big deeps beyond the sky as he would love a woman. If things changed, what then of Jack's career?

Well, what was it now? Stuck on a dreary planet as guardsman and executioner of homesick starvelings poisoned by radioactivity – never even seeing the sun. Come the day, Jack could surely wangle a berth on a real spacer; they'd need bold men to explore beyond Saturn. Jack was too honest to make a good rebel, but Thornberg felt that after the initial shock he would welcome a new government.

But treason! Oaths!

When in the course of human events—

It was a small thing that decided Thornberg. He passed a shop downtown and noticed a group of the Youth Guard smashing in its windows and spattering yellow paint over the goods: O, Moses, Jesus, Mendelssohn, Hertz, and Einstein! Once he had taken this path, a curious serenity possessed him. He stole a vial of prussic acid from a chemist friend and carried it in his pocket; and as for Jack, the boy would have to take his chances too.

The work was demanding and dangerous. He had to alter recorded facts which were available elsewhere, in books and journals and the minds of men. Nothing could be done with the basic theory, of course, but quantitative results could be juggled a little so that the overall picture was subtly askew. He would co-opt carefully chosen experts, men whose psychotypes indicated they would take the easy course of relying on Matilda instead of checking the original sources. And the correlation and integration of innumerable data, the empirical equations and extrapolations thereof, could be tampered with.

He turned his regular job over to Rodney and devoted himself entirely to the new one. He grew thin and testy; when Sorensen called up trying to hurry him, he snapped back: 'Do you want speed or quality?' and wasn't too surprised at himself afterward. He got little sleep, but his mind seemed unnaturally clear.

Winter faded into spring while Thornberg and his experts labored and while the nation shook, psychically and physically, with the growing violence of Sam Hall. The report Thornberg submitted in May was so voluminous and detailed that he didn't think the government researchers would bother referring to any other source. Its conclusion: Yes, given a brilliant man applying Belloni matrices to cybernetic formulas and using some unknown kind of colloidal probe, a psychological masking technique was plausible.

The government yanked every man it could find into research. Thornberg knew it was only a matter of time before they realized they had been had. How much time, he couldn't say. But when they were sure –

> *Now up the rope I go, up I go.*
> *Now up the rope I go, up I go.*
>   *And the bastards down below,*
>   *They say: 'Sam, we told you so.'*
>   *They say: 'Sam, we told you so', God damn their eyes.*

REBELS ATTACK
SPACESHIPS LAND UNDER COVER OF RAINSTORM, SEIZE POINTS NEAR N. DETROIT
FLAME WEAPONS USED AGAINST ARMY BY REBELS

'The infamous legions of the traitors have taken key points throughout the nation, but already our gallant forces have hurled them back. They have come out in early summer like toadstools, and will wither as fast – WHEEEEEE-OOOOOO!' Silence.

'All citizens are directed to keep calm, remain loyal to their country, and stay at their usual tasks until otherwise ordered. Civilians will report to their local defense commanders. All military reservists will report immediately for active duty.'

'Hello, Hawaii! Are you there? Come in, Hawaii! Calling Hawaii!'

'CQ, Mars GHQ calling ... buzz, wheeee ... seized Syrtis Major Colony and ... whoooo ... help needed ...'

'The Lunar rocket bases are assaulted and carried. The commander blows them up rather than surrender. A pinpoint flash on the moon's face, a new crater; what will they name it?'

'So they've got Seattle, have they? Send a robomb flight. Blow the place off the map. ... Citizens? To hell with citizens! This is war!'

'... in New York. Secretly drilled rebels emerged from the notorious Crater district and stormed ...'

'... assassins were shot down. The new President has already been sworn in and ...'

BRITAIN, CANADA, AUSTRALIA, REFUSE ASSISTANCE TO GOV'T

'... no, sir. The bombs reached Seattle all right. But they were all stopped before they hit – some kind of energy gun ...'

'COMECO to all Army commanders in Florida and Georgia: Enemy action has made Florida and the Keys temporarily untenable. Army units will withdraw as follows ...'

'Today a rebel force engaging an Army convoy in Donner Pass was annihilated by a well-placed tactical atomic bomb. Though our own men suffered losses on this account ...'

'COMECO to all Army commanders in California: The mutiny of units stationed near San Francisco poses a grave problem ...'

SP RAID REBEL HIDEOUT, BAG FIVE OFFICERS

'All right, so the enemy is about to capture Boston. We *can't* issue weapons to the citizens. They might turn them on us!'

SPACE GUARD UNITS EXPECTED FROM VENUS

Jack, Jack, Jack!

It was strange, living in the midst of a war. Thornberg had never thought it would be like this. Drawn faces, furtive eyes, utter confusion in the telecast news and the irregularly arriving panic when a rebel jet whistled overhead – but nothing else. No gunfire, no bombs, no battles at all except the unreal ones you heard about. The only casualty lists here were due to Security – people kept disappearing, and nobody spoke about them.

But then, why should the enemy bother with this unimportant mountain town? The Army of Liberation, as it styled itself, was grabbing key points of industry, transportation, communication; was fighting military units, sabotaging buildings and machines, assassinating important men in the government. By its very purpose, it couldn't wage total war, couldn't annihilate the folk it wanted to free. Rumor had it that the defenders were not so finicky.

Most citizens were passive. They always are. It is doubtful if more than one-fourth of the population was ever near a combat during the Third American Revolution. City dwellers might see fire in the sky, hear the whistle and crack of artillery, scramble out of the way of soldiers and armored vehicles, cower in shelters when the rockets thundered overhead – but the battle was fought outside town. If it came to street fighting, the rebels wouldn't push in; they would either withdraw and wait or they would rely on agents inside the city. Then one might hear the crack of rifles and grenades, rattle of machine guns, sharp discharge of energy beams, and see corpses in the street. But it ended with a return of official military government or with the rebels marching in and setting up their own provisional councils. (They were rarely greeted with cheers and flowers. Nobody knew how the war would end. But there were words whispered to them, and they usually got good service.) As nearly as possible, the average American continued his average life.

Thornberg went on in his own way. Matilda, as the information center, was working at full blast. If the rebels ever learned where she was –

Or did they know?

He could not spare much time for his private sabotage, but he planned it carefully and made every second tell when he was alone in the control booth. Sam Hall reports, of course – Sam Hall here, Sam Hall there, pulling off this or that incredible stunt. But what did one man, even a superman, count for in these gigantic days? Something else was needed.

Radio and newspapers announced jubilantly that Venus had finally been contacted. The Moon and Mars had fallen, there was only silence from the Jovian satellites, but everything seemed in order on Venus – a few feeble uprisings had been quickly smashed. The powerful Guard units there would be on their way to Earth at once. Troop transports had to orbit most of the way, so it would take a good six weeks before they could arrive, but when they did they would be a powerful reinforcement.

'Looks like you might see your boy soon, chief,' said Rodney.

'Yes,' said Thornberg, 'I might.'

'Tough fighting.' Rodney shook his head. 'I'd sure as hell hate to be in it.'

If Jack is killed by a rebel gun, when I have aided the rebel's cause –

Sam Hall, reflected Thornberg, had lived a hard life, all violence and enmity and suspicion. Even his wife hadn't trusted him.

> *And my Nellie dressed in blue*
> *Says: 'Your trifling days are through.*
> *Now I know that you'll be true,*
> *God damn your eyes.'*

Poor Sam Hall. It was no wonder he had killed a man.

Suspicion!

Thornberg stood for a taut moment while an eerie tingle went through him. The police state was founded on suspicion. Nobody could trust anyone else. And with the new fear of psychomasking, and research on that project suspended during the crisis –

Steady, boy, steady. Can't rush into this. Have to plan it out very carefully.

Thornberg punched for the dossiers of key men in the administration, in the military, in Security. He did it in the presence of two assistants, for he thought that his own frequent sessions alone in the control booth were beginning to look funny.

'This is top secret,' he warned them, pleased with his own cool manner. He was becoming a regular Machiavelli. 'You'll be skinned alive if you mention it to anyone.'

Rodney gave him a shrewd glance. 'So they're not even sure of their own top men now, are they?' he murmured.

'I've been told to make some checks,' snapped Thornberg. 'That's all you need to know.'

He studied the files for many hours before coming to a decision. Secret observations were, of course, made of everyone from time to time. A cross check with Matilda showed that the cop who had filed the last report on Lindahl had been killed the next day in a spontaneous and abortive uprising. The report was innocuous: Lindahl had stayed at home, studying some papers; he had been alone in the house except for a bodyguard who had been in another room and not seen him. And Lindahl was Undersecretary of Defense.

Thornberg changed the record. A masked man – stocky, black-haired – had come in and talked for three hours with Lindahl. They had spoken low, so that the cop's ears, outside the window, couldn't catch what was said. The visitor had gone away then, and Lindahl had retired. The cop went back in great excitement and made out his report and gave it to the signalman, who had sent it on to Matilda.

Tough on the signalman, thought Thornberg. *They'll want to know why he didn't tell this to his chief in New Washington, if the observer was killed before doing so. He'll deny every such report, and they'll hypnoquiz him – but they don't trust that method any more!*

His sympathy didn't last long. What counted was having the war over before Jack got home. He refiled the altered spool and did a little backtracking, shifting the last report of Sam Hall from Salt Lake City to Philadelphia. Make it more plausible. Then, as opportunity permitted, he did some work on other men's records.

He had to wait two haggard days before the next requisition came from

Security for a fresh cross check on Sam Hall. The scanners swept in an intricate pattern, cog turned over, a tube glowed. Circuits were activated elsewhere, the spool LINDAHL was unrolled before the microprinter inside the machine. Cross references to that spool ramified in all directions. Thornberg sent the preliminary report back with a query: This matter looked interesting; did they want more information?

They did!

Next day the telecast announced a drastic shakeup in the Department of Defense. Lindahl was not heard from again.

And I, thought Thornberg grimly, *have grabbed a very large tiger by the tail. Now they'll have to check everybody – and I'm one man, trying to keep ahead of the whole Security police!*

Lindahl is a traitor. How did his chief ever let him get on the board? Secretary Hoheimer was pretty good friends with Lindahl, too. Get Records to cross check Hoheimer.

What's this? Hoheimer himself! Five years ago, yes, but even so – the records show that he lived in an apartment unit where *Sam Hall* was janitor! Grab Hoheimer! Who'll take his place? General Halliburton? That stupid old bastard? Well, at least his dossier is clean. Can't trust those slick characters.

Hoheimer has a brother in Security, general's rank, good detection record. A blind? Who knows? Slap the brother in jail, at least for the duration. Better check his staff ... Central Records shows that his chief field agent, Jones, has five days unaccounted for a year ago; he claimed Security secrecy at the time, but a double cross check shows it wasn't so. Shoot Jones! He has a nephew in the Army, a captain. Pull that unit out of the firing line till we can study it man by man! We've had too many mutinies already.

Lindahl was also a close friend of Benson, in charge of the Tennessee Atomic Ordnance Works. Haul Benson in!

The first Hoheimer's son is an industrialist, he owns a petroleum-synthesis plant in Texas. Nab him! His wife is a sister of Leslie, head of the War Production Coordination Board. Get Leslie too. Sure, he's doing a good job, but he may be sending information to the enemy. Or he may just be waiting for the signal to sabotage the whole works. We can't trust *anybody*, I tell you!

What's this? Records relays an Intelligence report that the mayor of Tampa was in cahoots with the rebels. It's marked 'Unreliable, Rumor' – but Tampa *did* surrender without a fight. The mayor's business partner is Gale, who has a cousin in the Army, commanding a robomb base in New Mexico. Check both the Gales, Records ... So the cousin was absent four days without filing his whereabouts, was he? Military privileges or not, arrest him and find out where he was!

– Attention, Records, attention, Records, urgent Brigadier John Harmsworth Gale, etc., etc., refused to divulge information required by Security officers, claiming to have been at his base all the time. Can this be an error on your part?

– Records to Security Central, ref: etc., etc. No possibility of error exists except in information received.

– to Records, ref: etc., etc. Gale's story corroborated by three of his officers.

Put that whole damned base under arrest! Recheck those reports. Who sent them in, anyway?

– to Records, ref: etc., etc. On attempt to arrest entire personnel, Robomb Base 37-J fired on Security detachment and repulsed it. At last reports Gale was calling for rebel forces fifty miles off to assist him. Details will follow for the files as soon as possible.

So Gale was a traitor – or was he driven to it by fear? Have Records find out who filed that information about him in the first place. *We can't trust anybody!*

Thornberg was not much surprised when his door was kicked open and the Security squad entered. He had been expecting it for days now. One man can't keep ahead of the game for ever. No doubt the accumulated inconsistencies had finally drawn suspicion his way; or perhaps, ironically, the chains of accusation he had forged had by chance led to him; or perhaps Rodney or another person here had decided something was amiss with the chief and lodged a tip.

He felt no blame for whoever it was, if that had been the case. The tragedy of civil war was that it turned brother against brother; millions of good and decent men were with the government because they had pledged themselves to be. Mostly, he felt tired.

He looked down the barrel of the gun and then raised weary eyes to the hard face behind it. 'I take it I'm under arrest?' he asked tonelessly.

'Get up!' The face was flat and brutal, there was sadism in the heavy mouth. A typical blackcoat.

June whimpered. The man who held her was twisting her arm behind her back. 'Don't do that,' said Thornberg. 'She's innocent.'

'Get up, I said!' The gun thrust closer.

'Don't come near me, either.' Thornberg lifted his right hand. It was clenched around a little ball. 'See this? It's a gimmick I made. No, not a bomb, just a small radio control. If my hand relaxes, the rubber will expand and pull a switch shut.'

The men recoiled a little.

'Let the girl go, I said,' repeated Thornberg patiently.

'You surrender first!'

June screamed as the cop twisted harder.

'No,' said Thornberg. 'This is more important than any one of us. I was prepared, you see. I expect to die. So if I let go of this ball, the radio signal closes a relay and a powerful magnetic field is generated in Matilda – in the Records machine. Every record the government has will be wiped clean. I hate to think what your fellows will do to you if you let that happen.'

Slowly, the cop released June. She slumped to the floor, crying.

'It's a bluff!' said the man with the gun. There was sweat on his face.

'Try it and find out.' Thornberg forced a smile. 'I don't care.'

'You traitor!'

'And a very effective one, wasn't I? I've got the government turned end for end and upside down. The Army's in an uproar, officers deserting right and left for fear they'll be arrested next. Administration is hogtied and trembling. Security is chasing its own tail around half a continent. Assassination and betrayal are daily occurrences. Men go over to the rebels in droves. The Army of Liberation is sweeping a demoralized and ineffectual resistance before it everywhere. I predict that New Washington will capitulate within a week.'

'And your doing!' Finger tense on the trigger.

'Oh, no. No single man can change history. But I was a rather important factor, yes. Or let's say – Sam Hall was.'

'What are you going to do?'

'That depends on you, my friend. If you shoot me, gas me, knock me out, or anything of that sort, my hand will naturally relax. Otherwise we'll just wait till one side or the other gets tired.'

'You're bluffing!' snapped the squad leader.

'You could, of course, have the technicians here check Matilda and see if I'm telling the truth,' said Thornberg. 'And if I am, you could have them disconnect my electromagnet. Only I warn you, at the first sign of any such operation on your part I'll let go this ball. Look in my mouth.' He opened it. 'A glass vial, full of poison. After I let the ball go, I'll close my teeth together hard. So you see I have nothing to fear from you.'

Bafflement and rage flitted over the faces that watched him. They weren't used to thinking, those men.

'Of course,' said Thornberg, 'there is one other possibility for you. At last reports, a rebel jet squadron was based not a hundred miles from here. We could call it and have them come and take this place over. That might be to your own advantage too. There is going to be a day of reckoning with you blackcoats, and my influence could shield you, however little you deserve it.'

They stared at each other. After a very long while the squad leader shook his head. 'No!'

The man behind him pulled out a gun and shot him in the back.

Thornberg smiled.

'As a matter of fact,' he told Sorensen, 'I *was* bluffing. All I had was a tennis ball with a few small electrical parts glued on it. Not that it made much difference at that stage, except to me.'

'Matilda will be handy for us in mopping up,' said Sorensen. 'Want to stay on?'

'Sure, at least till my son arrives. That'll be next week.'

'You'll be glad to hear we've finally contacted the Guard in space: just a short radio message, but the commander has agreed to obey whatever government is in power when he arrives. That'll be us, so your boy won't have to do any fighting.'

There were no words for that. Instead Thornberg said, with a hard-held casualness, 'You know, I'm surprised that *you* should have been an undergrounder.'

'There were a few of us even in Security,' said Sorensen. 'We were organized in small cells, spotted throughout the nation, and wangled things so we could hypnoquiz each other.' He grimaced. 'It wasn't a pleasant job, though. Some of the things I had to do – Well, that's over with now.'

He leaned back in his chair, putting his booted feet on the desk. A Liberation uniform was usually pretty sloppy; they didn't worry about spit-and-polish, but he had managed to be immaculate. 'There was a certain amount of suspicion about Sam Hall at first,' he said. 'The song, you know, and other items. My bosses weren't stupid. I got myself detailed to investigate you; a close checkup gave me grounds to suspect you of revolutionary thoughts, so naturally I gave you a clean bill of health. Later on I cooked up this fantasy of the psychological mask and got several high-ranking men worried about it. When you followed my lead on that, I was sure you were on our side.' He grinned. 'So naturally our army never attacked Matilda!'

'You must have joined your forces quite recently.'

'Yeah, I had to scram out of Security during the uproar and witch hunt you started. You damn near cost me my life, Thorny, know that? Well worth it, though, just to see those cockroaches busily stepping on each other.'

Thornberg leaned gravely over his desk. 'I always had to assume you rebels were sincere,' he said. 'I've never been sure. But now I can check up. Do you intend to destroy Matilda?'

Sorensen nodded. 'After we've used her to help us find some people we want rather badly, and to get reorganized – of course. She's too powerful an instrument. It's time to loosen the strings of government.'

'Thank you,' whispered Thornberg.

He chuckled after a moment. 'And that will be the end of Sam Hall,' he said. 'He'll go to whatever Valhalla is reserved for the great characters of fiction. I can see him squabbling with Sherlock Holmes and shocking the hell out of King Arthur and striking up a beautiful friendship with Long John Silver. You know how the ballad ends?' He sang softly: *'Now up in heaven I dwell, in heaven I dwell –'*

Unfortunately, the conclusion is pretty rugged. Sam Hall never was satisfied.

ONLINE: **ONE/4** *Subject*: Jack Loomis, private eye

Blood Sisters

Joe Haldeman

INFO: Jack Loomis doubles as a computer sleuth and private eye. When luscious Ghentlee Arden, class one hooker, saunters into his office and lays the news on Jack that she needs protection from some guy who's bothering her, he soon finds himself up to his neck in human and not so human dangers.

Joe Haldeman says he used to read the crime novels of Raymond Chandler, Mickey Spillane and the other writers of pulp detective stories. One day he began to wonder how the gumshoes of the future might deal with crime. 'So I groped around in the science fiction bag of tricks,' he says, 'and came up with some clones and computers and enough weaponry to take over a small Central American nation.' The result is 'Blood Sisters', which gives a whole new meaning to the term 'hard-boiled fiction'. Joe started out as a brilliant student of physics, astronomy and computer science at the University of Maryland and then served as a combat engineer in Vietnam between 1967–9 where he was badly wounded and awarded a Purple Star for bravery. No surprise, then, that war and combat should have featured in several of his novels including *The Forever War* (1975), which has been widely compared to Robert Heinlein's classic *Starship Troopers* (1959). Indeed, among Joe's many admirers is Stephen King, who said of him recently that he is 'the only writer of science fiction I've been comfortable with since the heyday of Robert Heinlein'. Joe's interest in computers can be seen in stories like his technothriller *Tools of the Trade* (1987), and especially 'Blood Sisters', which he wrote for *Playboy* in 1985.

So I used to carry two different business cards: J. Michael Loomis, Data Concentration, and Jack Loomis, Private Investigator. They mean the same thing, nine cases out of ten. You have to size up a potential customer, decide whether he'd feel better hiring a shamus or a clerk.

Some people still have these romantic notions about private detectives and get into a happy sweat at the thought of using one. But it *is* the twenty-first century and, endless Bogart reruns notwithstanding, most of my work consisted of sitting at my office console and using it to subvert the privacy laws of various states and countries – finding out embarrassing things about people, so other people can divorce them or fire them or get a piece of the slickery.

Not to say I didn't go out on the street sometimes; not to say I didn't have a gun and a ticket for it. There are Forces of Evil out there, friends, although most of them would probably rather be thought of as businessmen who use the law rather than fear it. Same as me. I was always happy, though, to stay on this side of murder, treason, kidnapping – any lobo offense. This brain may not be much, but it's all I have.

I should have used it when the woman walked into my office. She had a funny way of saying hello:

'Are you licensed to carry a gun?'

Various retorts came to mind, most of them having to do with her expulsion, but after a period of silence I said yes and asked who had referred her to me. Asked politely, too, to make up for staring. She was a little more beautiful than anyone I'd ever seen before.

'My lawyer,' she said. 'Don't ask who he is.'

With that, I was pretty sure this was some sort of elaborate joke. Story detectives always have beautiful mysterious customers. My female customers tend to be dowdy and too talkative, and much more interested in alimony than romance.

'What's your name, then? Or am I not supposed to ask that either?'

She hesitated. 'Ghentlee Arden.'

I turned the console on and typed in her name, then a seven-digit code. 'Your legal firm is Lee, Chu, and Rosenstein. And your real name is Maribelle Four Ghentlee: fourth clone of Maribelle Ghentlee.'

'Arden is my professional name. I dance.' She had a nice blush.

I typed in another string of digits. Sometimes this sort of thing would lose a customer. 'Says here you're a registered hooker.'

'Call girl,' she said frostily. 'Class One courtesan. I was getting to that.'

I'm a liberal-minded man; I don't have anything against hookers *or* clones. But I like my customers to be frank with me. Again, I should have shown her the door – then followed her through it.

Instead: 'So. You have a problem?'

'Some men are bothering me, one man in particular. I need some protection.'

That gave me pause. 'Your union has a Pinkerton contract for that sort of thing.'

'*My* union.' Her face trembled a little. 'They don't let clones in the union. I'm an associate, for classification. No protection, no medical, no *anything*.'

'Sorry, I didn't know that. Pretty old-fashioned.' I could see the reasoning, though. Dump a thousand Maribelle Ghentlees on the market, and a merely ravishing girl wouldn't have a chance.

'Sit down.' She was on the verge of tears. 'Let me explain to you what I can't do.

'I can't hurt anyone physically. I can't trace this cod down and wave a gun on his face, tell him to back off.'

'I know,' she sobbed. I took a box of Kleenex out of my drawer, passed it over.

'Listen, there are laws about harassment. If he's really bothering you, the cops'll be glad to freeze him.'

'I can't go to the police.' She blew her nose. 'I'm not a citizen.'

I turned off the console. 'Let me see if I can fill in some blanks without using the machine. You're an unauthorized clone.'

She nodded.

'With bought papers.'

'Of course I have papers. I wouldn't be in your *machine* if I didn't.'

Well, she wasn't dumb, either. 'This cod. He isn't just a disgruntled customer.'

'No.' She didn't elaborate.

'One more guess,' I said, 'and then you do the talking for a while. He knows you're not legal.'

'He should. He's the one who pulled me.'

'Your own daddy. Any other surprises?'

She looked at the floor. 'Mafia.'

'Not the legal one, I assume.'

'Both.'

The desk drawer was still open; the sight of my own gun gave me a bad chill. 'There are two reasonable courses open to me. I could handcuff you to the doorknob and call the police. Or I could knock you over the head and call the Mafia. That would probably be safer.'

She reached into her purse; my hand was halfway to the gun when she took out a credit flash, thumbed it, and passed it over the desk. She easily had five times as much money as I make in a good year, and I'm in a comfortable seventy per cent bracket.

'You must have one hell of a case of bedsores.'

'Don't be stupid,' she said, suddenly hard. 'You can't make that kind of money on your back. If you take me on as a client, I'll explain.'

I erased the flash and gave it back to her. 'Miz Ghentlee. You've already told me a great deal more than I want to know. I don't want the police to put me in jail, I don't want the courts to scramble my brains with a spoon. I don't want the Mafia to take bolt cutters to my appendages.'

'I could make it worth your while.'

'I've got all the money I can use. I'm only in this profession because I'm a snoopy bastard.' It suddenly occurred to me that was more or less true.

'That wasn't completely what I meant.'

'I assumed that. And you tempt me, as much as any woman's beauty has ever tempted me.'

She turned on the waterworks again.

'Christ. Go ahead and tell your story. But I don't think you can convince me to do anything for you.'

'My real clone-mother wasn't named Maribelle Ghentlee.'

'I could have guessed that.'

'She was Maxine Kraus.' She paused. 'Maxine … Kraus.'

'Is that supposed to mean something to me?'

'Maybe not. What about *Werner* Kraus?'

'Yeah.' Swiss industrialist, probably the richest man in Europe. 'Some relation?'

'She's his daughter and only heir.'

I whistled. 'Why would she want to be cloned, then?'

'She didn't know she was being cloned. She thought she was having a Pap test.' She smiled a little. 'Ironic posture.'

'And they pulled you from the scraping.'

She nodded. 'The Mafia bought her physician. Then killed him.'

'You mean the real Mafia?' I said.

'That depends on what you call real. Mafia Incorporated comes into it too, in a more or less legitimate way. I was supposedly one of six Maribelle Ghentlee clones that they had purchased to set up as courtesans in New Orleans, to provoke a test case. They claimed that the Sisterhood's prohibition against clone prostitutes constituted unfair restraint of trade.'

'Never heard of the case. I guess they lost.'

'Of course. They wouldn't have done it in the South if they'd wanted to win.'

'Wait a minute. Jumping ahead. Obviously, they plan ultimately to use you as a substitute for the real Maxine Kraus.'

'When the old man dies, which will be soon.'

'Then why would they parade you around in public?'

'Just to give me an interim identity. They chose Ghentlee as a clone-mother because she was the closest one available to Maxine Kraus's physical appearance. I had good make-up; none of the real Ghentlee clones suspected I wasn't one of them.'

'Still ... what happens if you run into someone who knows what the real Kraus looks like? With your face and figure, she must be all over the gossip sheets in Europe.'

'You're sweet.' Her smile could make me do almost anything. Short of taking on the Mafia. 'She's a total recluse, though, for fear of kidnappers. She probably hasn't seen twenty people in her entire life.

'And she isn't beautiful, though she has the raw materials for it. Her mother died when she was still a baby – killed by kidnappers.'

'I remember that.'

'So she's never had a woman around to model herself after. No one ever taught her how to do her hair properly, or use make-up. A man buys all her clothes. She doesn't have anyone to be beautiful *for*.'

'You feel sorry for her.'

'More than that.' She looked at me with an expression that somehow held both defiance and hopelessness. 'Can you understand? She's my mother. I was force-grown so we're the same apparent age, but she's still my only parent. I love her. I won't be part of a plan to kill her.'

'You'd rather die?' I said softly. She was going to.

'Yes. But that wouldn't accomplish anything, not if the Mafia does it. They'd take a few cells and make another clone. Or a dozen, or a hundred, until one came along with a personality to go along with matricide.'

'Once they know you feel this way –'

'They do know. I'm running.'

That galvanized me. 'They know who your lawyer is?'

'My lawyer?' She gasped when I took the gun out of the drawer. People who only see guns on the cube are usually surprised at how solid and heavy they actually look.

'Could they trace you here, is what I mean.' I crossed the room and slid open the door. No one in the corridor. I twisted a knob and twelve heavy magnetic bolts slammed home.

'I don't think so. The lawyers gave me a list of names, and I just picked one I liked.'

I wondered whether it was Jack or J. Michael. I pushed a button on the wall and steel shutters rolled down over the view of Central Park. 'Did you take a cab here?'

'No, subway. And I went up to One hundred and twenty-fifth and back.'

'Smart.' She was staring at the gun. 'It's a .48 Magnum Recoilless. Biggest handgun a civilian can buy.'

'You need one so big?'

'Yes.' I used to carry a .25 Beretta, small enough to conceal in a bathing suit. I used to have a partner, too. It was a long story, and I didn't like to tell it. 'Look,' I said. 'I have a deal with the Mafia. They don't do divorce work and I don't drop bodies into the East River. Understand?' I put the gun back in the drawer and slammed it shut.

'I don't blame you for being afraid –'

'Afraid? Miz Four Ghentlee, I'm not afraid. I'm *terrified*! How old do you think I am?'

'Call me Belle. You're thirty-five, maybe forty. Why?'

'You're kind – and I'm rich. Rich enough to buy youth: I've been in this *business* almost forty years. I take lots of vitamins and try not to fuck with the Mafia.'

She smiled and then was suddenly somber. Like a baby. 'Try to understand me. You've lived sixty years?'

I nodded. 'Next year.'

'Well, I've been alive barely sixty *days*. After four years in a tank, growing and learning.

'Learning isn't *being*, though. Everything is new to me. When I walk down a street, the sights and sounds and smells, it's ... it's like a great flower opening to the sun. Just to sit alone in the dark –'

Her voice broke.

'You can't even *know* how much I want to live – and that's not condescending; it's a statement of fact. Yet I want you to kill me.'

I could only shake my head.

'If you can't hide me you have to kill me.' She was crying now, and wiped the tears savagely from her cheeks. 'Kill me and make sure every cell in my body is destroyed.'

She took out her credit card flash and set it on the desk.

'You can have all my money, whether you save me or kill me.'

She started walking around the desk. Along the way she did something with a clasp and her dress slithered to the floor. The sudden naked beauty was like an electric shock.

'If you save me, you can have me. Friend, lover, wife ... slave. For ever.' She held a posture of supplication for a moment, then eased toward me.

Watching the muscles of her body work made my mouth go dry. She reached down and started unbuttoning my shirt.

I cleared my throat. 'I didn't know clones had navels.'

'Only special ones. I have other special qualities.'

Idiot, something reminded me, every woman you've ever loved has sucked you dry and left you for dead. I clasped her hips with my big hands and drew her warmth to me. Close up, the navel wasn't very convincing; nobody's perfect.

I'd done drycleaning jobs before, but never so cautiously or thoroughly. That she was a clone made the business a little more delicate than usual, since clones' lives are more rigidly supervised by the government than ours are. But the fact that her identity was false to begin with made it easier; I could second-guess the people who had originally drycleaned her.

I hated to meddle with her beauty, and that beauty made plastic surgery out of the question. Any legitimate doctor would be suspicious, and going to an underworld doctor would be suicidal. So we dyed her hair black and bobbed it. She stopped wearing make-up and bought some truly froppy clothes. She kept a length of tape stuck across her buttocks to give her a virgin-schoolgirl kind of walk. For everyone but me.

The Mafia had given her a small fortune – birdseed to them – both to ensure her loyalty and to accustom her to having money, for impersonating Kraus. We used about half of it for the drycleaning.

A month or so later there was a terrible accident on a city bus. Most of the bodies were burned beyond recognition; I did some routine bribery, and two of them were identified as the clone Maribelle Four Ghentlee and John Michael Loomis, private eye. When we learned the supposed clone's body had disappeared from the morgue, we packed up our money – long since converted into currency – and a couple of toothbrushes and pulled out.

I had a funny twinge when I closed the door on that console. There couldn't be more than a half-dozen people in the world who were my equals at using that instrument to fish information out of the System. But I had to either give it up or send Belle off on her own.

We flew to the West Indies and looked around. Decided to settle on the island of St Thomas. I'd been sailing all my life, so we bought a fifty-foot boat and set up a charter service for tourists. Some days we took parties out to skin-dive or fish. Other days we anchored in a quiet cove and made love like happy animals.

After about a year, we read in the little St Thomas paper that Werner Kraus had died. They mentioned Maxine but didn't print a picture of her. Neither did the San Juan paper. We watched all the news programs for a couple of days (had to check into a hotel to get access to a video cube) and collected magazines for a month. No pictures, to our relief, and the news stories remarked that Fraulein Kraus went to great pains to stay out of the public eye.

Sooner or later, we figured, some *paparazzo* would find her, and there would be pictures. But by then it shouldn't make any difference. Belle had let her hair grow out to its natural chestnut, but we kept it cropped boyishly short. The sun and wind had darkened her skin and roughened it, and a year of fighting the big boat's rigging had put visible muscle under her sleekness.

The marina office was about two broom closets wide. It was a beautiful spring morning, and I'd come in to put my name on the list of boats available for charter. I was reading the weather printout when Belle sidled through the door and squeezed in next to me at the counter. I patted her on the fanny. 'With you in a second, honey.'

A vise grabbed my shoulder and spun me around.

He was over two meters tall and so wide at the shoulders that he literally couldn't get through the door without turning sideways. Long white hair and pale blue eyes. White sport coat with a familiar cut: tailored to de-emphasize the bulge of a shoulder holster.

'You don't do that, friend,' he said with a German accent.

I looked at the woman, who was regarding me with aristocratic amusement. I felt the blood drain from my face and damned near said my name out loud.

She frowned. 'Helmuth,' she said to the guard, '*Sie sind ihm erschrocken.* I'm sorry,' she said to me, 'but my friend has quite a temper.' She had a perfect North Atlantic accent, and her voice sent a shiver of recognition down my back.

'I am sorry,' he said heavily. Sorry he hadn't had a chance to throw me into the water, he was.

'I must look like someone you know,' she said. 'Someone you know rather well.'

'My wife. The similarity is ... quite remarkable.'

'Really? I should like to meet her.' She turned to the woman behind the counter. 'We'd like to charter a sailing boat for the day.'

The clerk pointed at me. 'He has a nice fifty-foot one.'

'That's fine! Will your wife be aboard?'

'Yes ... yes, she helps me. But you'll have to pay the full rate,' I said rapidly. 'The boat normally takes six passengers.'

'No matter. Besides, we have two others.'

'And you'll have to help me with the rigging.'

'I should hope so. We love to sail.' That was pretty obvious. We had been wrong about the wind and sun, thinking that Maxine would have led a sheltered life; she was almost as weathered as Belle. Her hair was probably long, but she had it rolled up in a bun and tied back with a handkerchief.

We exchanged false names: Jack Jackson and Lisa von Hollerin. The bodyguard's name was Helmuth Zwei Kastor. She paid the clerk and called her friends at the marina hotel, telling them to meet her at the *Abora*, slip thirty-nine.

I didn't have any chance to warn Belle. She came up from the galley as we were swinging aboard. She stared open-mouthed and staggered, almost fainting. I took her by the arm and made introductions, everybody staring.

After a few moments of strange silence, Helmuth Two whispered, '*Du bist ein Klon.*'

'She can't be a clone, silly man,' Lisa said. 'When did you ever see a clone with a navel?' Belle was wearing shorts and a halter. 'But we could be twin sisters. That *is* remarkable.'

Helmuth Two shook his head solemnly. Belle had told me that a clone can always recognize a fellow clone, by the eyes. Never be fooled by a man-made navel.

The other two came aboard. Helmuth One was, of course, a Xerox of Helmuth Two. Lisa introduced Maria Salamanca as her lover: a small olive-skinned Basque woman, no stunning beauty, but having an attractive air of friendly mystery about her.

Before we cast off, Lisa came to me and apologized. 'We are a passing strange group of people. You deserve something extra for putting up with us.' She pressed a gold Krugerrand into my palm – worth at least triple the charter fare – and I tried to act suitably impressed. We had over a thousand of them in the keel, for ballast.

The *Abora* didn't have an engine; getting it in and out of the crowded marina was something of an accomplishment. Belle and Lisa handled the sails expertly, while I manned the wheel. They kept looking at each other, then touching. When we were in the harbor, they sat together at the prow, holding hands. Once we were in the open water, they went below together. Maria went into a sulk, but the two clones jollied her out of it.

I couldn't be jealous of her. An angel can't sin. But I did wonder what you would call what they were doing. Was it a weird kind of incest? Transcendental masturbation? I only hoped Belle would keep her mouth shut, at least figuratively.

After about an hour, Lisa came up and sat beside me at the wheel. Her hair was long and full, and flowed like dark liquid in the wind, and she was naked. I tentatively rested my hand on her thigh. She had been crying.

'She told me. She had to tell me.' Lisa shook her head in wonder. 'Maxine One Kraus. She had to stay below for a while. Said she couldn't trust her legs.' She squeezed my hand and moved it back to the wheel.

'Later, maybe,' she said. 'And don't worry; your secret is safe with us.' She went forward and put an arm around Maria, speaking rapid German to her and the two Helmuths. One of the guards laughed and they took off their incongruous jackets, then carefully wrapped up their weapons and holsters. The sight of a .48 Magnum Recoilless didn't arouse any nostalgia in me. Maria slipped out of her clothes and stretched happily. The guards did the same. They didn't have navels but were otherwise adequately punctuated.

Belle came up then, clothed and flushed, and sat quietly next to me. She stroked my bicep and I ruffled her hair. Then I heard Lisa's throaty laugh and suddenly turned cold.

'Hold on a second,' I whispered. 'We haven't been using our heads.'

'Speak for yourself.' She giggled.

'Oh, be serious. This stinks of coincidence. That she should turn up here, that she should wander into the office just as –'

'Don't worry about it.'

'Listen. She's no more Maxine Kraus than you are. They've found us. She's another clone, one that's going to –'

'She's Maxine. If she were a clone, I could tell immediately.'

'Spare me the mystical claptrap and take the wheel. I'm going below.' In the otherwise empty engine compartment, I'd stored an interesting assortment of weapons and ammunition.

She grabbed my arm and pulled me back down to the seat. 'You spare *me* the private eye claptrap and listen – you're right, it's no coincidence. Remember that old foreigner who came by last week?'

'No.'

'You were up on the stern, folding sail. He was just at the slip, for a second, to ask directions. He seemed flustered –'

'I remember. Frenchman.'

'I thought so too. He was Swiss, though.'

'And that was no coincidence, either.'

'No, it wasn't. He's on the board of directors of one of the banks we used to liquify our credit. When the annual audit came up, they'd managed to put together all our separate transactions –'

'Bullshit. That's impossible.'

She shook her head and laughed. 'You're good, but they're good, too. They were curious about what we were trying to hide, using their money, and traced us here. Found we'd started a business with only one per cent of our capital.

'Nothing wrong with that, but they were curious. This director was headed for a Caribbean vacation anyhow; he said he'd come by and poke around.'

I didn't know how much of this to believe. I gauged the distance between where the Helmuths were sunning and the prow, where they had carefully stowed their guns against the boat's heeling.

'He'd been a lifelong friend of Werner Kraus. That's why he was so rattled. One look at me and he had to rush to the phone.'

'And we're supposed to believe,' I said, 'that the wealthiest woman in the world would come down to see what sort of innocent game we were playing. With only two bodyguards.'

'Five. There are two other Helmuths, and Maria is ... versatile.'

'Still can't believe it. After a lifetime of being protected from her own shadow –'

'That's just it. She's tired of it. She turned twenty-five last month, and came into full control of the fortune. Now she wants to take control of her own life.'

'Damned foolish. If it were me, I would've sent my giants down alone.' I had to admit that I essentially did believe the tale. We'd been alone in open water for more than an hour, and would've long been shark bait if that had been their intent. Getting sloppy in your old age, Loomis.

'I probably would have too,' Belle said. 'Maxine and I are the same woman in some ways, but you and the Mafia taught me caution. She's been in a cage all her life, and just wanted out. Wanted to sail someplace besides her own lake, too.'

'It was still a crazy chance to take.'

'So she's a little crazy. Romantic, too, in case you haven't noticed.'

'Really? When I peeked in you were playing checkers.'

'Bastard.' She knew the one place I was ticklish. Trying to get away, I jerked the wheel and nearly tipped us all into the drink.

We anchored in a small cove where I knew there was a good reef. Helmuth One stayed aboard to guard while the rest of us went diving.

The fish and coral were beautiful as ever, but I could only watch Maxine and Belle. They swam slowly hand-in-hand, kicking with unconscious synchrony, totally absorbed. Though the breathers kept their hair wrapped up identically, it was easy to tell them apart, since Maxine had an all-over tan. Still, it was an eerie kind of ballet, like a mirror that didn't quite work. Maria and Helmuth Two were also hypnotized by the sight.

I went aboard early, to start lunch. I'd just finished slicing ham when I heard the drone of a boat, rather far away. Large siphon-jet, by the rushing sound of it.

The guard shouted, 'Zwei – *komm' herauf!*'

Hoisted myself up out of the galley. The boat was about two kilometers away, and coming roughly in our direction, fast.

'Trouble coming?' I asked him.

'Cannot tell yet, sir. I suggest you remain below.' He had a gun in each hand, behind his back.

Below, good idea. I slid the hatch off the engine compartment and tipped over the cases of beer that hid the weaponry. Fished out two heavy plastic bags, left the others in place for the time being. It was all up-to-date American Coast Guard issue, and had cost more than the boat.

I had rehearsed this a thousand times in my mind, but I hadn't realized the bags would be slippery with condensation and oil and be impossible to tear with your hands. I stood up to get a knife from the galley, and it was almost the last thing I ever did.

I looked up at a loud succession of splintering sounds and saw a line of holes marching toward me from the bow, letting in blue light and lead. I dropped and heard bullets hissing over my head; heard the regular cough-cough-cough of Helmuth One's return fire. At the stern there was a cry of pain and then a splash; they must have caught the other guard coming up the ladder.

Also not in the rehearsals was the effect of absolute death-panic on bladder control; some formal corner of my mind was glad I hadn't yet dressed. I controlled my trembling well enough to cut open the bag that held the small-caliber spitter, and it only took three tries to get the cassette of ammunition fastened to the receiver. I jerked back the arming lever and hurried back to the galley hatch, carrying an armload of cassettes.

The spitter was made for sinking boats, quickly. It fired small flechettes, the size of old-fashioned metal stereo needles, fifty rounds per second. The flechettes moved at supersonic speed and each carried a small explosive charge. In ten seconds, they could do more damage to a boat than a man with a chainsaw could, with determination and leisure.

I resisted the urge to blast away and get back under cover (not that the hull afforded much real protection). We had clamped traversing mounts for the gun on three sides of the galley hatch – nautically inclined customers usually asked what they were; I always shrugged and said they'd come with the boat – because the spitter is most effective if you can hold the point of aim precisely on the waterline.

They were concentrating fire on the bow, most of it going high. Helmuth One was evidently shooting from a prone position, difficult target. I slid the spitter on to its mount and cranked up its scope to maximum power.

When I looked through the scope, a lifetime of target-shooting reflexes took over: deep breath, half let out, do the Zen thing. Their boat moved toward the center of the scope's field, and I waited. It was a Whaler Unsinkable. One man crouched at the bow, firing what looked like a .20 mm recoilless, clamped on the rail above a steel plate. They were less than a hundred meters away.

The Whaler executed a sharp starboard turn, evidently to give the gunner a better angle on our bow. Good boatmanship, good tactics, but bad luck. Their prow touched on the junction of my crosshairs right at the waterline, and I didn't even have to track. I just pressed the trigger and watched a cloud of black smoke and steam zip from prow to stern. Not even an Unsinkable can stay upright with its keel sliced off. The boat slewed sideways into the water, spilling people, and turned turtle. Didn't sink, though.

I snapped a fresh cassette into place and tried to remember where the hydrogen tank was on that model. Second burst found it, and the boat dutifully exploded. The force of the blast was enough to ram the scope's eyepiece back into my eye, painfully.

Helmuth One peered down at me. 'What is that?'

'Coast Guard weapon, a spitter.'

'May I try it?'

'Sure.' I traded places with him, glad to be up in the breeze. My boat was a mess. The mainmast had been shattered by a direct hit, waist high. The starboard rail was splinters, forward, and near misses had gouged up my nice teak foredeck. My eye throbbed, and for some reason my ears were ringing.

I remembered why the next second, as Helmuth fired. The spitter makes a sound like a cat dying, but louder. I had been too preoccupied to hear it.

I unshipped a pair of binoculars to check his marksmanship. He was shooting at the floating bodies. What a spitter did to one was terrible to see.

'Jesus, Helmuth …'

'Some of them may yet live,' he said apologetically.

At least one did. Wearing a life jacket, she had been floating face down but suddenly began treading water. She was holding an automatic pistol in both hands. She looked exactly like Belle and Maxine.

I couldn't say anything; couldn't take my eyes off her. She fired two rounds, and I felt them slap into the hull beneath me. I heard Helmuth curse, and suddenly her shoulders dissolved in a spray of meat and bone and her head fell into the water.

My gorge rose and I didn't quite make it to the railing. Deck was a mess anyhow.

*

Helmuth Two, it turned out, had been hit in the side of the neck, but it was a big neck and he survived. Maxine called a helicopter, which came out piloted by Helmuth Three.

After an hour or so, Helmuth Four joined us in a large speedboat loaded down with gasoline, thermite, and shark chum. By that time, we had transferred the gold and a few more important things from my boat on to the helicopter. We chummed the area thoroughly and, as sharks began to gather, towed both hulks out to deep water, where they burned brightly and sank.

The Helmuths spent the next day sprinkling the island with money and threats, while Maxine got to know Belle and me better, behind the heavily guarded door of the honeymoon suite of the quaint old Sheraton that overlooked the marina. She made us a job offer – a life offer, actually – and we accepted without hesitation. That was six years ago.

Sometimes I do miss our old life – the sea, the freedom, the friendly island, the lazy idylls with Belle. Sometimes I even miss New York's hustle and excitement, and the fierce independence of my life there.

We do travel on occasion, but with extreme caution. The clone that Helmuth killed in that lovely cove might have been Belle's sister, pulled from Maxine, or Belle's own daughter, since the Mafia had had plenty of opportunities to collect cells from her body. It's immaterial. What's important is that if they could make one, they could make an army of them.

Like our private army of Helmuths and Lamberts and Delias. I'm chief of security, and the work is interesting, most of it at a console as good as the one I had in Manhattan. No violence since that one afternoon six years ago, not yet. I did have to learn German, though, which was an outrage to a brain as old as mine.

We haven't made any secret of the fact that Belle is Maxine's clone. The official story is that Fraulein Kraus had a clone made of herself, for 'companionship'. This started a fad among the wealthy, being the first new sexual wrinkle since the invention of the vibrator.

Belle and Maxine take pains to dress alike and speak alike and even have unconsciously assimilated one another's mannerisms. Most of the non-clone employees can't tell which is which, and even I sometimes confuse them, at a distance.

Close up, which happens with gratifying frequency, there's no problem. Belle has a way of looking at me that Maxine could never duplicate. And Maxine is literally a trifle prettier: you can't beat a real navel.

ONLINE: **ONE/5** *Subject*: DI Rawlings, Mars Cop

Crime on Mars

Arthur C. Clarke

INFO: On Mars, where people live inside protective shields against the freezing, near-vacuum atmosphere, law enforcement is reckoned to be easy. But there is an ingenious criminal about with his eye on a priceless artefact. However, even on the Red Planet, the best laid crimes do not always go according to plan.

Arthur C. Clarke inspired the most famous of all fictional computers, HAL 900, the neurotic, humanoid machine that appeared in the movie *2001: A Space Odyssey* (1968), based on his short story 'The Sentinel' which he adapted for the screen with the director, Stanley Kubrick. At his home in Sri Lanka, Arthur has his own smaller version, 'HAL Junior' (actually an HP9100A), on which he has written several stories that focus on the threat computers can pose to mankind, including 'Into The Comet', 'The Nine Billion Names of Godd' and 'Dial F For Frankenstein'.

Born in Minehead, England, Clarke became fascinated by technology as a schoolboy and, after working as a radar instructor in the RAF during World War Two, studied for a BSc in physics and mathematics at King's College, London. He began writing science fiction in the late 1940s and since then has risen to a position of pre-eminence in the genre, receiving numerous honours including a Nebula Grand Master in 1986. 'Crime on Mars', which Arthur wrote for *Fantasy and Science Fiction* in 1960, is his only detective story and given the recent missions by the Russians and Americans to land there is highly topical. Commenting on the tale, Arthur said recently, 'The problem it deals with is not, perhaps, the most serious obstacle to the colonisation of Mars. But it exists – and there's not a thing anyone can do about it.'

'We don't have much crime on Mars,' said Detective-Inspector Rawlings, a little sadly. 'In fact, that's the chief reason I'm going back to the Yard. If I stayed here much longer, I'd get completely out of practice.'

We were sitting in the main observation lounge of the Phobos Spaceport, looking out across the jagged sun-drenched crags of the tiny moon. The ferry rocket that had brought us up from Mars had left ten minutes ago and was now beginning the long fall back to the ochre-tinted globe hanging there against the stars. In half an hour we would be boarding the liner for Earth – a world on which most of the passengers had never set foot, but still called 'home'.

'At the same time,' continued the Inspector, 'now and then there's a case that makes life interesting. You're an art dealer, Mr Maccar; I'm sure you heard about that spot of bother at Meridian City a couple of months ago.'

'I don't think so,' replied the plump, olive-skinned little man I'd taken for just another returning tourist. Presumably the Inspector had already checked through the passenger list; I wondered how much he knew about me, and tried to reassure myself that my conscience was – well, reasonably clear. After all, everybody took *something* out through Martian customs –

'It's been rather well hushed up,' said the Inspector, 'but you can't keep these things quiet for long. Anyway, a jewel thief from Earth tried to steal Meridian Museum's greatest treasure – the Siren Goddess.'

'But that's absurd!' I objected. 'It's priceless, of course – but it's only a lump of sandstone. You might just as well steal the *Mona Lisa*.'

The Inspector grinned, rather mirthlessly. '*That's* happened too,' he said. 'Maybe the motive was the same. There are collectors who would give a fortune for such an object, even if they could only look at it themselves. Don't you agree, Mr Maccar?'

'That's perfectly true,' said the art dealer. 'In my business you meet all sorts of crazy people.'

'Well, this chappie – name's Danny Weaver – had been well paid by one of them. And if it hadn't been for a piece of fantastically bad luck, he might have brought it off.'

The Spaceport PA system apologized for a further slight delay owing to final fuel checks, and asked a number of passengers to report to Information. While we were waiting for the announcement to finish, I recalled what little I knew about the Siren Goddess. Although I'd never seen the original, like most other departing tourists I had a replica in my baggage. It bore the certificate of the Mars Bureau of Antiquities, guaranteeing that 'this full-scale reproduction is an exact copy of the so-called Siren Goddess, discovered in the Mare Sirenium by the Third Expedition, AD 2012 (AM 23).'

It's quite a tiny thing to have caused so much controversy. Only eight or nine inches high – you wouldn't look at it twice if you saw it in a museum on Earth. The head of a young woman, with slightly oriental features, elongated earlobes, hair curled in tight ringlets close to the scalp, lips half parted in an expression of pleasure or surprise – and that's all.

But it's an enigma so baffling that it has inspired a hundred religious sects, and driven quite a few archeologists out of their minds. For a perfectly human head has no right whatsoever to be found on Mars, whose only intelligent inhabitants were crustaceans – 'educated lobsters', as the newspapers are fond of calling them. The aboriginal Martians never came near to achieving space-flight, and in any event their civilization died before men existed on Earth.

No wonder the Goddess is the Solar System's Number One mystery. I don't suppose we'll find the answer in my lifetime – if we ever do.

'Danny's plan was beautifully simple,' continued the Inspector. 'You know how absolutely dead a Martian city gets on Sunday, when everything closes down and the colonists stay home to watch the TV from Earth. Danny was counting on this when he checked into the hotel in Meridian West, late Friday afternoon. He'd have Saturday for reconnoitering the Museum, an undisturbed Sunday for the job itself, and on Monday morning he'd be just another tourist leaving town.

'Early Saturday he strolled through the little park and crossed over into Meridian East, where the Museum stands. In case you don't know, the city gets it name because it's exactly on longitude 180 degrees; there's a big stone slab in the park with the Prime Meridian engraved on it, so that visitors can get themselves photographed standing in two hemispheres at once. Amazing what simple things amuse some people.

'Danny spent the day going over the Museum, exactly like any other tourist determined to get his money's worth. But at closing time he didn't leave; he'd holed up in one of the galleries not open to the public, where the Museum had been arranging a Late Canal Period reconstruction but had run out of money before the job could be finished. He stayed there until about midnight, just in case there were any enthusiastic researchers still in the building. Then he emerged and got to work.'

'Just a minute,' I interrupted. 'What about the night watchman?'

'My dear chap! They don't have such luxuries on Mars. There weren't even any burglar alarms, for who would bother to steal lumps of stone? True, the Goddess was sealed up neatly in a strong glass and metal cabinet, just in case some souvenir hunter took a fancy to her. But even if she were stolen, there was nowhere the thief could hide, and of course all outgoing traffic would be searched as soon as the statue was missed.'

That was true enough. I'd been thinking in terms of Earth, forgetting that every city on Mars is a closed little world of its own beneath the force-field that protects it from the freezing near-vacuum. Beyond those electronic shields is the utterly hostile emptiness of the Martian Outback, where a man will die in seconds without protection. That makes law enforcement very easy.

'Danny had a beautiful set of tools, as specialized as a watch-maker's. The main item was a microsaw no bigger than a soldering iron; it had a wafer-thin blade, driven at a million cycles a second by an ultrasonic power-pack. It would go through glass or metal like butter – and leave a cut only about as thick as a hair. Which was very important for Danny, as he could not leave any traces of his handiwork.

'I suppose you've guessed how he intended to operate. He was going to cut through the base of the cabinet and substitute one of those souvenir replicas for the genuine Goddess. It might be a couple of years before some inquisitive expert discovered the awful truth, and long before then the original would have been taken to Earth, perfectly disguised as a copy of itself, with a genuine certificate of authenticity. Pretty neat, eh?

'It must have been a weird business, working in that darkened gallery with all those million-year-old carvings and unexplainable artefacts around him. A museum on Earth is bad enough at night, but at least it's – well, *human*. And Gallery Three, which houses the Goddess, is particularly unsettling. It's full of bas-reliefs showing quite incredible animals fighting each other; they look rather like giant beetles, and most paleontologists flatly deny that they could ever have existed. But imaginary or not, they belonged to this world, and they didn't disturb Danny as much as the Goddess, staring at him across the ages and defying him to explain her presence here. She gave him the creeps. How do I know? He told me.

'Danny set to work on that cabinet as carefully as any diamond-cutter preparing to cleave a gem. It took most of the night to slice out the trap door, and it was nearly dawn when he relaxed and put down the saw. There was still a lot of work to do, but the hardest part was over. Putting the replica into the case, checking its appearance against the photos he'd thoughtfully brought with him, and covering up his traces might take a good part of Sunday, but that didn't worry him in the least. He had another twenty-four hours, and would welcome Monday's first visitors so that he could mingle with them and make his exit.

'It was a perfectly horrible shock to his nervous system, therefore, when the main doors were noisily unbarred at eight-thirty and the museum staff – all six of them – started to open up for the day. Danny bolted for the emergency exit, leaving everything behind – tools, Goddesses, the lot.

'He had another big surprise when he found himself in the street: it should have been completely deserted at this time of day, with everyone at home reading the Sunday papers. But here were the citizens of Meridian East, as large as life, heading for plant or office on what was obviously a normal working day.

'By the time poor Danny got back to his hotel we were waiting for him. We couldn't claim much credit for deducing that only a visitor from Earth – and a very recent one at that – could have overlooked Meridian City's chief claim to fame. And I presume you know what *that* is.'

'Frankly, I don't,' I answered. 'You can't see much of Mars in six weeks, and I never went east of the Syrtis Major.'

'Well it's absurdly simple, but we shouldn't be too hard on Danny – even the locals occasionally fall into the same trap. It's something that doesn't bother us on Earth, where we've been able to dump the problem in the Pacific Ocean. But Mars, of course, is all dry land; and that means that *somebody* is forced to live with the International Date Line ...

'Danny, you see, had planned the job from Meridian West. It was Sunday over there all right – and it was still Sunday there when we picked him up at the hotel. But over in Meridian East, half a mile away, it was only Saturday. That little trip across the park had made all the difference! I told you it was rotten luck.'

There was a long moment of silent sympathy, then I asked, 'What did he get?'

'Three years,' said Inspector Rawlings.

'That doesn't seem very much.'

'Mars years – that makes it almost six of ours. And a whopping fine which, by an odd coincidence, came to exactly the refund value of his return ticket to Earth. He isn't in jail, of course – Mars can't afford that kind of nonproductive luxury. Danny has to work for a living, under discreet surveillance. I told you that the Meridian Museum couldn't afford a night watchman. Well, it has one now. Guess who?'

'All passengers prepare to board in ten minutes! Please collect your hand-baggage!' ordered the loudspeakers.

As we started to move toward the airlock, I couldn't help asking one more question.

'What about the people who put Danny up to it? There must have been a lot of money behind him. Did you get them?'

'Not yet; they'd covered their tracks pretty thoroughly, and I believe

Danny was telling the truth when he said he couldn't give us a lead. Still, it's not my case. As I told you, I'm going back to my old job at the Yard. But a policeman always keeps his eyes open – like an art dealer, eh, Mr Maccar? Why, you look a bit green about the gills. Have one of my space-sickness tablets.'

'No thank you,' answered Mr Maccar. 'I'm quite all right.'

His tone was distinctly unfriendly; the social temperature seemed to have dropped below zero in the last few minutes. I looked at Mr Maccar, and I looked at the Inspector. And suddenly I realized that we were going to have a very interesting trip.

ONLINE: **ONE/6** *Subject*: John Doe, hacker

The Pardoner's Tale

Robert Silverberg

INFO: John Doe is a criminal hacker with the golden touch – a man who has learned every trick to outsmart the law in a Los Angeles of the future. He's turned his skill into a financial bonanza by selling pardons to people under sentence by the authorities. And everything is going just fine for Joe until the day he meets up with an even smarter operator.

In almost half a century of prolific output, Robert Silverberg has written every kind of story from pulp sf to Nebula award-winning novels. Take, for example, *To Open the Sky* (1967) about the fad-dominated world of tomorrow; *The Stochastic Man* (1975) in which men have developed the power of foreseeing the future; and especially the 'New Springtime' series dealing with the repopulation of the Earth following a global disaster by various alien races.

Bob was born in New York and began to write at Columbia University while studying for a BA. Aside from his many contributions to magazines as varied as *Amazing Stories* and *Omni*, he has also collaborated on books with other major writers including Randall Garrett and Isaac Asimov. He wrote 'The Pardoner's Tale' for *Playboy* in 1987.

'Hey Sixteen, Housing Omicron Kappa, aleph sub-one,' I said to the software on duty at the Alhambra gate of the Los Angeles Wall.

Software isn't generally suspicious. This wasn't even very smart software. It was working off some great biochips – I could feel them jigging and pulsing as the electron stream flowed through them – but the software itself was just a kludge. Typical gatekeeper stuff.

I stood waiting as the picoseconds went ticking away by the millions.

'Name, please,' the gatekeeper said finally.

'John Doe. Beta Pi Upsilon 104324x.'

The gate opened. I walked into Los Angeles.

As easy as Beta Pi.

The wall that encircles LA is a hundred, a hundred fifty feet thick. Its gates are more like tunnels. When you consider that the wall runs completely around the LA basin from the San Gabriel Valley to the San Fernando Valley and then over the mountains and down the coast and back, the far side past Long Beach, and that it's at least sixty feet high and all that distance deep, you can begin to appreciate the mass of it. Think of the phenomenal expenditure of human energy that went into building it – muscle and sweat, sweat and muscle. I think about that a lot.

I suppose the walls around our cities were put there mostly as symbols. They highlight the distinction between city and countryside, between citizen and uncitizen, between control and chaos, just as city walls did five thousand years ago. But mainly they serve to remind us that we are all slaves nowadays. You can't ignore the walls. You can't pretend they aren't there. *We made you build them*, is what they say, and *don't you ever forget that*. All the same, Chicago doesn't have a wall sixty feet high and a hundred fifty feet deep. Houston doesn't. Phoenix doesn't. They make do with less. But LA is the main city. I suppose the Los Angeles wall is a statement: *I am the Big Cheese. I am the Ham What Am.*

The walls aren't there because the Entities are afraid of attack. They know how invulnerable they are. We know it, too. They just wanted to decorate their capital with something a little special. What the hell, it isn't *their* sweat that goes into building the walls. It's ours. Not mine personally, of course. But ours.

I saw a few Entities walking around just inside the wall, preoccupied as usual with God knows what and paying no attention to the humans in the vicinity. These were low-caste ones, the kind with the luminous orange spots along their sides. I gave them plenty of room. They have a way sometimes of picking a human up with those long elastic tongues, like a frog snapping up a fly, and letting him dangle in midair while they study him with those saucer-sized yellow eyes. I don't care for that. You don't get hurt, but it isn't agreeable to be dangled in midair by something that looks like a fifteen-foot-high purple squid standing on the tips of its tentacles. Happened to me once in St Louis, long ago, and I'm in no hurry to have it happen again.

The first thing I did when I was inside LA was find me a car. On Valley Boulevard about two blocks in from the wall I saw a '31 Toshiba El Dorado that looked good to me, and I matched frequencies with its lock and slipped inside and took about ninety seconds to reprogram its drive control to my personal metabolic cues. The previous owner must have been fat as a hippo and probably diabetic: her glycogen index was absurd and her phosphenes were wild.

Not a bad car, a little slow in the shift but what can you expect, considering the last time any cars were manufactured on this planet was the year 2034.

'Pershing Square,' I told it.

It had nice capacity, maybe sixty megabytes. It turned south right away and found the old freeway and drove off toward downtown. I figured I'd set up shop in the middle of things, work two or three pardons to keep my edge sharp, get myself a hotel room, a meal, maybe hire some companionship. And then think about the next move. It was winter, a nice time to be in LA. That golden sun, those warm breezes coming down the canyons.

I hadn't been out on the Coast in years. Working Florida mainly, Texas, sometimes Arizona. I hate the cold. I hadn't been in LA since '36. A long time to stay away, but maybe I'd been staying away deliberately. I wasn't sure. That last LA trip had left bad-tasting memories. There had been a woman who wanted a pardon, and I sold her a stiff. You have to stiff the customers now and then or else you start looking too good, which can be dangerous; but she was young and pretty and full of hope and I could have stiffed the next one instead of her, only I didn't. Sometimes I've felt bad, thinking back over that. Maybe that's what had kept me away from LA all this time.

A couple of miles east of the big downtown interchange, traffic began backing up. Maybe an accident ahead, maybe a roadblock. I told the Toshiba to get off the freeway.

Slipping through roadblocks is scary and calls for a lot of hard work. I knew that I probably could fool any kind of software at a roadblock and certainly any human cop, but why bother if you don't have to?

I asked the car where I was.

The screen lit up. Alameda near Banning, it said. A long walk to Pershing Square, looked like. I had the car drop me at Spring Street and went the rest of the way on foot. 'Pick me up at 1830 hours,' I told it. 'Corner of – umm – Sixth and Hill.' It went away to park itself and I headed for the Square to peddle some pardons.

It isn't hard for a good pardoner to find buyers. You can see it in their eyes: the tightly controlled anger, the smoldering resentment. And something else, something intangible, a certain sense of having a shred or two of inner integrity left, that tells you right away, here's somebody willing to risk a lot to regain some measure of freedom. I was in business within fifteen minutes.

The first one was an aging surfer sort, barrel chest and that sun-bleached look. The Entities haven't allowed surfing for ten, fifteen years – they've got their plankton seines just offshore from Santa Barbara to San Diego, gulping in the marine nutrients they have to have, and any beach boy who tried to take a whack at the waves out there would be chewed right up. But this guy must have been one hell of a performer in his day. The way he moved through the park, making little balancing moves as if he needed to compensate for the regularities of the earth's rotation, you could see how he would have been in the water. Sat down next to me, began working on his lunch. Thick forearms, gnarled hands. A wall laborer. Muscles knotting in his cheeks: the anger, forever simmering just below boil.

I got him talking after a while. A surfer, yes. Lost in the faraway and gone. He began sighing to me about legendary beaches where the waves were tubes and they came pumping end to end. 'Trestle Beach,' he murmured. 'That's north of San Onofre. You had to sneak through Camp Pendleton. Sometimes the Marines would open fire, just warning shots. Or Hollister Ranch, up by Santa Barbara.' His blue eyes got misty. 'Huntington Beach. Oxnard. I got everywhere, man.' He flexed his huge fingers. 'Now these fucking Entity hodads own the shore. Can you believe it? They *own* it. And I'm pulling wall, my second time around, seven days a week next ten years.'

'Ten?' I said. 'That's a shitty deal.'

'You know anyone who doesn't have a shitty deal?'

'Some,' I said. 'They buy out.'

'Yeah.'

'It can be done.'

A careful look. You never know who might be a borgmann. Those stinking collaborators are everywhere.

'Can it?'

'All it takes is money,' I said.

'And a pardoner.'

'That's right.'

'One you can trust.'

I shrugged. 'You've got to go on faith, man.'

'Yeah,' he said. Then, after a while: 'I heard of a guy, he bought a three-year pardon and wall passage thrown in. Went up north, caught a krill trawler, wound up in Australia, on the Reef. Nobody's ever going to find him there. He's out of the system. Right out of the fucking system. What do you think that cost?'

'About twenty grand,' I said.

'Hey, that's a sharp guess!'

'No guess.'

'Oh?' Another careful look. 'You don't sound local.'

'I'm not. Just visiting.'

'That's still the price? Twenty grand?'

'I can't do anything about supplying krill trawlers. You'd be on your own once you were outside the wall.'

'Twenty grand just to get through the wall?'

'And a seven-year labor exemption.'

'I pulled ten,' he said.

'I can't get you ten. It's not in the configuration, you follow? But seven would work. You could get so far, in seven, that they'd lose you. You could goddamned *swim* to Australia. Come in low, below Sydney, no seines there.'

'You know a hell of a lot.'

'My business to know,' I said. 'You want me to run an asset check on you?'

'I'm worth seventeen five. Fifteen hundred real, the rest collat. What can I get for seventeen five?'

'Just what I said. Through the wall, and seven years' exemption.'

'A bargain rate, hey?'

'I take what I can get,' I said. 'Give me your wrist. And don't worry. This part is read-only.'

I keyed his data implant and patched mine in. He had fifteen hundred in the bank and a collateral rating of sixteen thou, exactly as he claimed. We eyed each other very carefully now. As I said, you never know who the borgmanns are.

'You can do it right here in the park?' he asked.

'You bet. Lean back, close your eyes, make like you're snoozing in the sun. The deal is that I take a thousand of the cash now and you transfer five thou of the collateral bucks to me, straight labor-debenture deal. When you get through the wall I get the other five hundred cash and five thou more on sweat security. The rest you pay off at three thou a year plus interest, wherever you are, quarterly key-ins. I'll program the whole thing, including beep reminders on payment dates. It's up to you to make your travel arrangements, remember. I can do pardons and wall transits, but I'm not a goddamned travel agent. Are we on?'

He put his head back and closed his eyes.

'Go ahead,' he said.

It was fingertip stuff, straight circuit emulation, my standard hack. I picked up all his identification codes, carried them into central, found his records. He seemed real, nothing more or less than he had claimed. Sure enough, he had drawn a lulu of a labor tax, ten years on the wall. I wrote him a pardon good for the first seven of that. Had to leave the final three on the books, purely technical reasons, but the computers weren't going to be able to find him by then. I gave him a wall-transit pass, too, which meant writing in a new skills class for him, programmer third grade. He didn't think like a programmer and he didn't look like a programmer, but the wall software wasn't going to figure that out. Now I had made him a member of the human elite, the relative handful of us who are free to go in and out of the walled cities as we wish. In return for these little favors I signed over his entire life savings to various accounts of mine, payable as arranged, part now, part later. He wasn't worth a nickel any more, but he was a free man. That's not such a terrible trade-off.

Oh, and the pardon was a valid one. I had decided not to write any stiffs while I was in Los Angeles. A kind of sentimental atonement, you might say, for the job I had done on that woman all those years back.

You absolutely have to write stiffs once in a while, you understand. So that you don't look too good, so that you don't give the Entities reason to hunt you down. Just as you have to ration the number of pardons you do. I didn't have to be writing pardons at all, of course. I could have just authorized the system to pay me so much a year, fifty thou, a hundred, and taken it easy for ever. But where's the challenge in that?

So I write pardons, but no more than I need to cover my expenses, and I deliberately fudge some of them up, making myself look as incompetent as the rest so the Entities don't have a reason to begin trying to track the identifying marks of my work. My conscience hasn't been too sore about that. It's a matter of survival, after all. And most other pardoners are out-and-out frauds, you know. At least with me you stand a better-than-even chance of getting what you're paying for.

The next one was a tiny Japanese woman, the classic style, sleek, fragile, doll-like. Crying in big wild gulps that I thought might break her in half, while a gray-haired older man in a shabby business suit – her grandfather, you'd guess – was trying to comfort her. Public crying is a good indicator of Entity trouble. 'Maybe I can help,' I said, and they were both so distraught that they didn't even bother to be suspicious.

He was her father-in-law, not her grandfather. The husband was dead, killed by burglars the year before. There were two small kids. Now she had received her new labor-tax ticket. She had been afraid they were going to send her out to work on the wall, which of course wasn't likely to happen: the assignments are pretty random, but they usually aren't crazy, and what use would a ninety-pound girl be in hauling stone blocks around? The father-in-law had some friends who were in the know, and they managed to bring up the hidden encoding on her ticket. The computers hadn't sent her to the wall, no. They had sent her to Area Five. And they had given her a TTD classification.

'The wall would have been better,' the old man said. 'They'd see, right away, she wasn't strong enough for heavy work, and they'd find something else, something she could do. But Area Five? Who ever comes back from that?'

'You know what Area Five is?' I said.

'The medical experiment place. And this mark here, TTD. I know what that stands for, too.'

She began to moan again. I couldn't blame her. TTD means Test To Destruction. The Entities want to find out how much work we can really do, and they feel that the only reliable way to discover that is to put us through tests that show where the physical limits are.

'I will die,' she wailed. 'My babies! My babies!'

'Do you know what a pardoner is?' I asked the father-in-law.

A quick excited response: sharp intake of breath, eyes going bright, head nodding vehemently. Just as quickly the excitement faded, giving way to bleakness, helplessness, despair.

'They all cheat you,' he said.

'Not all.'

'Who can say? They take your money, they give you nothing.'

'You know that isn't true. Everybody can tell you stories of pardons that came through.'

'Maybe. Maybe,' the old man said. The woman sobbed quietly. 'You know of such a person?'

'For three thousand dollars,' I said, 'I can take the TTD off her ticket. For five I can write an exemption from service good until her children are in high school.'

Sentimental me. A fifty per cent discount, and I hadn't even run an asset check. For all I knew, the father-in-law was a millionaire. But no, he'd have been off cutting a pardon for her, then, and not sitting around like this in Pershing Square.

He gave me a long, deep, appraising look. Peasant shrewdness coming to the surface.

'How can we be sure of that?' he asked.

I might have told him that I was the king of my profession, the best of all pardoners, a genius hacker with the truly magic touch, who could slip into any computer ever designed and make it dance to my tune. Which would have been nothing more than the truth. But all I said was that he'd have to make up his own mind, that I couldn't offer any affidavits or guarantees, that I was available if he wanted me and otherwise it was all the same to me if she preferred to stick with her TTD ticket. They went off and conferred for a couple of minutes. When they came back, he silently rolled up his sleeve and presented his implant to me. I keyed his credit balance: thirty thou or so, not bad. I transferred eight of it to my accounts, half to Seattle, the rest to Los Angeles. Then I took her wrist, which was about two of my fingers thick, and got into her implant and wrote her the pardon that would save her life. Just to be certain, I ran a double validation check on it. It's always possible to stiff a customer unintentionally, though I've never done it. But I didn't want this particular one to be my first.

'Go on,' I said. 'Home. Your kids are waiting for their lunch.'

Her eyes glowed. 'If I could only thank you somehow –'

'I've already banked my fee. Go. If you ever see me again, don't say hello.'

'This will work?' the old man asked.

'You say you have friends who know things. Wait seven days, then tell the data bank that she's lost her ticket. When you get the new one, ask your pals to decode it for you. You'll see. It'll be all right.'

I don't think he believed me. I think he was more than half sure I had swindled him out of one-fourth of his life's savings, and I could see the hatred in his eyes. But that was his problem. In a week he'd find out that I really had saved his daughter-in-law's life, and then he'd rush down to the Square to tell me how sorry he was that he had had such terrible feelings toward me. Only by then I'd be somewhere else, far away.

They shuffled out the east side of the park, pausing a couple of times to peer over their shoulders at me as if they thought I was going to transform them into pillars of salt the moment their backs were turned. Then they were gone.

I'd earned enough now to get me through the week I planned to spend in LA. But I stuck around anyway, hoping for a little more. My mistake.

This one was Mr Invisible, the sort of man you'd never notice in a crowd, gray on gray, thinning hair, mild bland apologetic smile. But his eyes had a shine. I forget whether he started talking first to me, or me to him, but pretty soon we were jockeying around trying to find out things about each other. He told me he was from Silver Lake. I gave him a blank look. How in hell am I supposed to know all the zillion LA neighborhoods? Said that he had come down here to see someone at the big government HQ on Figueroa Street. All right: probably an appeals case. I sensed a customer.

Then he wanted to know where I was from. Santa Monica? West LA? Something in my accent, I guess. 'I'm a traveling man,' I said. 'Hate to stay in one place.' True enough. I need to hack or I go crazy; if I did all my hacking in just one city I'd be virtually begging them to slap a trace on me sooner or later, and that would be the end. I didn't tell him any of that. 'Came in from Utah last night. Wyoming before that.' Not true, either one. 'Maybe on to New York, next.' He looked at me as if I'd said I was planning a voyage to the moon. People out here, they don't go east a lot. These days most people don't go anywhere.

Now he knew that I had wall-transit clearance, or else that I had some way of getting it when I wanted it. That was what he was looking to find out. In no time at all we were down to basics.

He said he had drawn a new ticket, six years at the salt-field reclamation site out back of Mono Lake. People die like mayflies out there. What he wanted was a transfer to something softer, like Operations & Maintenance, and it had to be within the walls, preferably in one of the districts out by the ocean where the air is cool and clear. I quoted him a price and he accepted without a quiver.

'Let's have your wrist,' I said.

He held out his right hand, palm upward. His implant access was a pale-yellow plaque, mounted in the usual place but rounder than the standard kind and of a slightly smoother texture. I didn't see any great significance in that. As I had done maybe a thousand times before, I put my own arm over his, wrist to wrist, access to access. Our biocomputers made contact, and instantly I knew that I was in trouble.

Human beings have been carrying biochip-based computers in their bodies for the last forty or fifty years or so – long before the Entity invasion, anyway – but for most people it's just something they take for granted, like the vaccination mark on their thighs. They use them for the things they're meant to be used for, and don't give them a thought beyond that. The biocomputer's just a commonplace tool for them, like a fork, like a shovel. You have to have the hacker sort of mentality to be willing to turn your biocomputer into something more. That's why, when the Entities came and took us over and made us build walls around our cities, most people reacted just like sheep, letting themselves be herded inside and politely staying there. The only ones who can move around freely now – because we know how to manipulate the mainframes through which the Entities rule us – are the hackers. And there aren't many of us. I could tell right away that I had hooked myself on to one now.

The moment we were in contact, he came at me like a storm.

The strength of his signal let me know I was up against something special, and that I'd been hustled. He hadn't been trying to buy a pardon at all. What he was looking for was a duel. Mr Macho behind the bland smile, out to show the new boy in town a few of his tricks.

No hacker had ever mastered me in a one-on-one anywhere. Not ever. I felt sorry for him, but not much.

He shot me a bunch of stuff, cryptic but easy, just by way of finding out my parameters. I caught it and stored it and laid an interrupt on him and took over the dialog. My turn to test him. I wanted him to begin to see who he was fooling around with. But just as I began to execute, he put an interrupt on *me*. That was a new experience. I stared at him with some respect.

Usually any hacker anywhere will recognize my signal in the first thirty seconds, and that'll be enough to finish the interchange. He'll know that there's no point in continuing. But this guy either wasn't able to identify me or just didn't care, and he came right back with his interrupt. Amazing. So was the stuff he began laying on me next.

He went right to work, really trying to scramble my architecture. Reams of stuff came flying at me up in the heavy-megabyte zone.

– *jspike. dbltag. nslice. dzcnt.*

I gave it right back to him, twice as hard.

– *maxfrq. minpau. spktot. jspike.*

He didn't mind at all.

– *maxdz. spktim. falter. nslice.*

– *frqsum. eburst.*

– *iburst.*

– *prebst.*

– *nobrst.*

Mexican standoff. He was still smiling. Not even a trace of sweat on his forehead. Something eerie about him, something new and strange. This is some kind of borgmann hacker, I realized suddenly. He must be working for the Entities, roving the city, looking to make trouble for freelancers like me. Good as he was, and he was plenty good, I despised him. A hacker who had become a borgmann – now, that was truly disgusting. I wanted to short him. I wanted to burn him out, now. I had never hated anyone so much in my life.

I couldn't do a thing with him.

I was baffled. I was the Data King, I was the Megabyte Monster. All my life I had floated back and forth across a world in chains, picking every lock I came across. And now this nobody was tying me in knots. Whatever I gave him, he parried; and what came back from him was getting increasingly bizarre. He was working with an algorithm I had never seen before and was having serious trouble solving. After a little while I couldn't even figure out what he was doing to me, let alone what I was going to do to cancel it. It was getting so I could barely execute. He was forcing me inexorably toward a wetware crash.

'Who are you?' I yelled.

He laughed in my face.

And kept pouring it on. He was threatening the integrity of my implant, going at me down on the microcosmic level, attacking the molecules themselves. Fiddling around with electron shells, reversing charges and mucking up valences, clogging my gates, turning my circuits to soup. The computer that is implanted in my brain is nothing but a lot of organic chemistry, after all. So is my brain. If he kept this up the computer would go and the brain would follow, and I'd spend the rest of my life in the bibble-bibble academy.

This wasn't a sporting contest. This was murder.

I reached for the reserves, throwing up all the defensive blockages I could invent. Things I had never had to use in my life, but they were there when I needed them, and they did slow him down. For a moment I was able to halt his ballbreaking onslaught and even push him back. And give myself the breathing space to set up a few offensive combinations of my own. But before I could get them running, he shut me down once more and started to drive me toward crashville all over again. He was unbelievable.

I blocked him. He came back again. I hit him hard and he threw the punch into some other neural channel altogether and it went fizzling away.

I hit him again. Again he blocked it.

Then he hit me and I went reeling and staggering, and managed to get myself together when I was about three nanoseconds from the edge of the abyss.

I began to set up a new combination. But even as I did it, I was reading the tone of his data, and what I was getting was absolute cool confidence.

He was waiting for me. He was ready for anything I could throw. He was in that realm beyond mere self-confidence into utter certainty.

What it was coming down to was this. I was able to keep him from ruining me, but only just barely, and I wasn't able to lay a glove on him at all. And he seemed to have infinite resources behind him. I didn't worry him. He was tireless. He didn't appear to degrade at all. He just took all I could give and kept throwing new stuff at me, coming at me from six sides at once.

Now I understood for the first time what it must have felt like for all the hackers I had beaten. Some of them must have felt pretty cocky, I suppose, until they ran into me. It costs more to lose when you think you're good. When you *know* you're good. People like that, when they lose, they have to reprogram their whole sense of their relation to the universe.

I had two choices. I could go on fighting until he wore me down and crashed me. Or I could give up right now. In the end everything comes down to yes or no, on or off, one or zero, doesn't it?

I took a deep breath. I was staring straight into chaos.

'All right,' I said. 'I'm beaten. I quit.'

I wrenched my wrist free of his, trembled, swayed, went toppling down on the ground.

A minute later five cops jumped me and trussed me up like a turkey and hauled me away, with my implant arm sticking out of the package and a security lock wrapped around my wrist, as if they were afraid I was going to start pulling data right out of the air.

Where they took me was Figueroa Street, the big black marble ninety-story job that is the home of the puppet city government. I didn't give a damn. I was numb. They could have put me in the sewer and I wouldn't have cared. I wasn't damaged – the automatic circuit check was still running and it came up green – but the humiliation was so intense that I felt crashed. I felt destroyed. The only thing I wanted to know was the name of the hacker who had done it to me.

The Figueroa Street building has ceilings about twenty feet high everywhere, so that there'll be room for Entities to move around. Voices reverberate in those vast open spaces like echoes in a cavern. The cops sat me down in a hallway, still all wrapped up, and kept me there for a long time. Blurred sounds went lalloping up and down the passage. I wanted to hide from them. My brain felt raw. I had taken one hell of a pounding.

Now and then a couple of towering Entities would come rumbling through the hall, tiptoeing on their tentacles in that weirdly dainty way of theirs. With them came a little entourage of humans whom they ignored entirely, as they always do. They know that we're intelligent, but they just don't care to talk to us. They let their computers do that, via the Borgmann interface, and may his signal degrade for ever for having sold us out. Not that they wouldn't have conquered us anyway, but Borgmann made it ever so much easier for them to push us around by showing them how to connect our little biocomputers to their huge mainframes. I bet he was very proud of himself, too: just wanted to see if his gadget would work, and to hell with the fact that he was selling us into eternal bondage.

Nobody has ever figured out why the Entities are here or what they want from us. They simply came, that's all. Saw. Conquered. Rearranged us. Put us to work doing god-awful unfathomable tasks. Like a bad dream.

And there wasn't any way we could defend ourselves against them. Didn't seem that way to us at first – we were cocky, we were going to wage guerrilla war and wipe them out – but we learned fast how wrong we were, and we are theirs for keeps. There's nobody left with anything close to freedom except the handful of hackers like me; and, as I've explained, we're not dopey enough to try any serious sort of counterattack. It's a big enough triumph for us just to be able to dodge around from one city to another without having to get authorization.

Looked like all that was finished for me now. Right then I didn't give a damn. I was still trying to integrate the notion that I had been beaten; I didn't have capacity left over to work on a program for the new life I would be leading now.

'Is this the pardoner, over here?' someone said.

'That one, yeah.'

'She wants to see him now.'

'You think we should fix him up a little first?'

'She said now.'

A hand at my shoulder, rocking me gently. 'Up, fellow. It's interview time. Don't make a mess or you'll get hurt.'

I let them shuffle me down the hall and through a gigantic doorway and into an immense office with a ceiling high enough to give an Entity all the room it would want. I didn't say a word. There weren't any Entities in the office, just a woman in a black robe, sitting behind a wide desk at the far end. It looked like a toy desk in that colossal room. She looked like a toy woman. The cops left me alone with her. Trussed up like that, I wasn't any risk.

'Are you John Doe?' she asked.

I was halfway across the room, studying my shoes. 'What do you think?' I said.

'That's the name you gave upon entry to the city.'

'I give lots of names. John Smith, Richard Roe, Joe Blow. It doesn't matter much to the gate software what name I give.'

'Because you've gimmicked the gate?' She paused. 'I should tell you, this is a court of inquiry.'

'You already know everything I could tell you. Your borgmann hacker's been swimming around in my brain.'

'Please,' she said. 'This'll be easier if you cooperate. The accusation is illegal entry, illegal seizure of a vehicle, and illegal interfacing activity, specifically, selling pardons. Do you have a statement?'

'No.'

'You deny that you're a pardoner?'

'I don't deny, I don't affirm. What's the goddamned use.'

'Look up at me,' she said.

'That's a lot of effort.'

'Look up,' she said. There was an odd edge on her voice. 'Whether you're a pardoner or not isn't the issue. We know you're a pardoner. *I* know you're a pardoner.' And she called me by a name I hadn't used in a very long time. Not since '36, as a matter of fact.

I looked at her. Stared. Had trouble believing I was seeing what I saw. Felt a rush of memories come flooding up. Did some mental editing work on her face, taking out some lines here, subtracting a little flesh in a few places, adding some in others. Stripping away the years.

'Yes,' she said. 'I'm who you think I am.'

I gaped. This was worse than what the hacker had done to me. But there was no way to run from it.

'You work for them?' I asked.

'The pardon you sold me wasn't any good. You knew that, didn't you? I had someone waiting for me in San Diego, but when I tried to get through the wall they stopped me just like that, and dragged me away screaming. I could have killed you. I would have gone to San Diego and then we would have tried to make it to Hawaii in his boat.'

'I didn't know about the guy in San Diego,' I said.

'Why should you? It wasn't your business. You took my money, you were supposed to get me my pardon. That was the deal.'

Her eyes were gray with golden sparkles in them. I had trouble looking into them.

'You still want to kill me?' I asked. 'Are you planning to kill me now?'

'No and no.' She used my old name again. 'I can't tell you how astounded I was, when they brought you in here. A pardoner, they said. John Doe. Pardoners, that's my department. They bring all of them to me. I used to wonder years ago if they'd ever bring *you* in, but after a while I figured, no, not a chance, he's probably a million miles away, he'll never come back this way again. And then they brought in this John Doe, and I saw your face.'

'Do you think you could manage to believe,' I said, 'that I've felt guilty for what I did to you ever since? You don't have to believe it. But it's the truth.'

'I'm sure it's been unending agony for you.'

'I mean it. Please. I've stiffed a lot of people, yes, and sometimes I've regretted it and sometimes I haven't, but you were one that I regretted. You're the one I've regretted most. This is the absolute truth.'

She considered that. I couldn't tell whether she believed it even for a fraction of a second, but I could see that she was considering it.

'Why did you do it?' she asked after a bit.

'I stiff people because I don't want to seem too perfect,' I told her. 'You deliver a pardon every single time, word gets around, people start talking, you start to become legendary. And then you're known everywhere and sooner or later the Entities get hold of you, and that's that. So I always make sure to write a lot of stiffs. I tell people I'll do my best, but there aren't any guarantees, and sometimes it doesn't work.'

'You deliberately cheated me.'

'Yes.'

'I thought you did. You seemed so cool, so professional. So perfect. I was sure the pardon would be valid. I couldn't see how it would miss. And then I got to the wall and they grabbed me. So I thought, That bastard sold me out. He was too good just to have flubbed it up.' Her tone was calm, but the anger was still in her eyes. 'Couldn't you have stiffed the next one? Why did it have to be me?'

I looked at her for a long time.

'Because I loved you,' I said.

'Shit,' she said. 'You didn't even know me. I was just some stranger who had hired you.'

'That's just it. There I was full of all kinds of crazy instant lunatic fantasies about you, all of a sudden ready to turn my nice orderly life upside down for you, and all you could see was somebody you had hired to do a job. I didn't know about the guy from San Diego. All I knew was I saw you and I wanted you. You don't think that's love? Well, call it something else, then, whatever you want. I never let myself feel it before. It isn't smart, I thought, it ties you down, the risks are too big. And then I saw you and I talked to you a little and I thought something could be happening between us and things started to change inside me, and I thought, Yeah, yeah, go with it this time, let it happen, this may make everything different. And you stood there not seeing it, not even beginning to notice, just jabbering on and on about how important the pardon was for you. So I stiffed you. And afterwards I thought, Jesus, I ruined that girl's life and it was just because I got myself into a snit, and that was a fucking petty thing to have done. So I've been sorry ever since. You don't have to believe that. I didn't know about San Diego. That makes it even worse for me.' She didn't say anything all this time, and the silence felt enormous. So after a moment I said, 'Tell me one thing, at least. That guy who wrecked me in Pershing Square: who was he?'

'He wasn't anybody,' she said.

'What does that mean?'

'He isn't a who. He's a *what*. It's an android, a mobile antipardoner unit, plugged right into the big Entity mainframe in Culver City. Something new that we have going around town.'

'Oh,' I said. 'Oh.'

'The report is that you gave it one hell of a workout.'

'It gave me one, too. Turned my brain half to mush.'

'You were trying to drink the sea through a straw. For a while it looked like you were really going to do it, too. You're one goddamned hacker, you know that?'

'Why did you go to work for them?' I said.

She shrugged. 'Everybody works for them. Except people like you. You took everything I had and didn't give me my pardon. So what was I supposed to do?'

'I see.'

'It's not such a bad job. At least I'm not out there on the wall. Or being sent off for TTD.'

'No,' I said. 'It's probably not so bad. If you don't mind working in a room with such a high ceiling. Is that what's going to happen to me? Sent off for TTD?'

'Don't be stupid. You're too valuable.'

'To whom?'

'The system always needs upgrading. You know it better than anyone alive. You'll work for us.'

'You think I'm going to turn borgmann?' I said, amazed.

'It beats TTD,' she said.

I fell silent again. I was thinking that she couldn't possibly be serious, that they'd be fools to trust me in any kind of responsible position. And even bigger fools to let me near their computer.

'All right,' I said. 'I'll do it. On one condition.'

'You really have balls, don't you?'

'Let me have a rematch with that android of yours. I need to check something out. And afterward we can discuss what kind of work I'd be best suited for here. Okay?'

'You know you aren't in any position to lay down conditions.'

'Sure I am. What I do with computers is a unique art. You can't make me do it against my will. You can't make me do anything against my will.'

She thought about that. 'What good is a rematch?'

'Nobody ever beat me before. I want a second try.'

'You know it'll be worse for you than before.'

'Let me find that out.'

'But what's the point?'

'Get me your android and I'll show you the point,' I said.

She went along with it. Maybe it was curiosity, maybe it was something else, but she patched herself into the computer net and pretty soon they brought in the android I had encountered in the park, or maybe another one with the same face. It looked me over pleasantly, without the slightest sign of interest.

Someone came in and took the security lock off my wrist and left again. She gave the android its instructions and it held out its wrist to me and we made contact. And I jumped right in.

I was raw and wobbly and pretty damned battered, still, but I knew what I needed to do and I knew I had to do it fast. The thing was to ignore the android completely – it was just a terminal, it was just a unit – and go for what lay behind it. So I bypassed the android's own identity program, which was clever but shallow. I went right around it while the android was still setting up its combinations, dived underneath, got myself instantly from the unit level to the mainframe level and gave the master Culver City computer a hearty handshake.

Jesus, that felt good!

All that power, all those millions of megabytes squatting there, and I was plugged right into it. Of course, I felt like a mouse hitchhiking on the back of an elephant. That was all right. I might be a mouse, but that mouse was getting a tremendous ride. I hung on tight and went soaring along on the hurricane winds of that colossal machine.

And as I soared, I ripped out chunks of it by the double handful and tossed them to the breeze.

It didn't even notice for a good tenth of a second. That's how big it was. There I was, tearing great blocks of data out of its gut, joyously ripping and rending. And it didn't even know it, because even the most magnificent computer ever assembled is still stuck with operating at the speed of light, and when the best you can do is 186,000 miles a second it can take quite a while for the alarm to travel the full distance down all your neural channels. That thing was *huge*. Mouse riding on elephant, did I say? Amoeba piggybacking on brontosaurus, was more like it.

God knows how much damage I was able to do. But of course the alarm circuitry did cut in eventually. Internal gates came clanging down and all sensitive areas were sealed away and I was shrugged off with the greatest of ease. There was no sense staying around waiting to get trapped, so I pulled myself free.

I had found out what I needed to know. Where the defenses were, how they worked. This time the computer had kicked me out, but it wouldn't be able to, the next. Whenever I wanted, I could go in there and smash whatever I felt like.

The android crumpled to the carpet. It was nothing but an empty husk now.

Lights were flashing on the office wall.

She looked at me, appalled. 'What did you do?'

'I beat your android,' I said. 'It wasn't all that hard, once I knew the scoop.'

'You damaged the main computer.'

'Not really. Not much. I just gave it a little tickle. It was surprised, seeing me get access in there, that's all.'

'I think you really damaged it.'

'Why would I want to do that?'

'The question ought to be why you haven't done it already. Why you haven't gone in there and crashed the hell out of their programs.'

'You think I could do something like that?'

She studied me. 'I think maybe you could, yes.'

'Well, maybe so. Or maybe not. But I'm not a crusader, you know. I like my life the way it is. I move around, I do as I please. It's a quiet life. I don't start revolutions. When I need to gimmick things, I gimmick them just enough, and no more. And the Entities don't even know I exist. If I stick my finger in their eye, they'll cut my finger off. So I haven't done it.'

'But now you might,' she said.

I began to get uncomfortable. 'I don't follow you,' I said, although I was beginning to think that I did.

'You don't like risk. You don't like being conspicuous. But if we take your freedom away, if we tie you down in LA and put you to work, what the hell would you have to lose? You'd go right in there. You'd gimmick things but good.' She was silent for a time. 'Yes,' she said. 'You really would. I see it now, that you have the capability and that you could be put in a position where you'd be willing to use it. And then you'd screw everything up for all of us, wouldn't you?'

'What?'

'You'd fix the Entities, sure. You'd do such a job on their computer that they'd have to scrap it and start all over again. Isn't that so?'

She was on to me, all right.

'But I'm not going to give you the chance. I'm not crazy. There isn't going to be any revolution and I'm not going to be its heroine and you aren't the type to be a hero. I understand you now. It isn't safe to fool around with you. Because if anybody did, you'd take your little revenge, and you wouldn't care what you brought down on everybody else's head. You could ruin their computer, but then they'd come down on us and they'd make things twice as hard for us as they already are, and you wouldn't care. We'd all suffer, but you wouldn't care. No. My life isn't so terrible that I need you to turn it upside down for me. You've already done it to me once. I don't need it again.'

She looked at me steadily and all the anger seemed to be gone from her and there was only contempt left.

After a little she said, 'Can you go in there again and gimmick things so that there's no record of your arrest today?'

'Yeah. Yeah, I could do that.'

'Do it, then. And then get going. Get the hell out of here, fast.'

'Are you serious?'

'You think I'm not?'

I shook my head. I understood. And I knew that I had won and I had lost, both at the same time.

She made an impatient gesture, a shoofly gesture.

I nodded. I felt very very small.

'I just want to say – all that stuff about how much I regretted the thing I did to you back then – it was true. Every word of it.'

'It probably was,' she said. 'Look, do your gimmicking and edit yourself out and then I want you to start moving. Out of the building. Out of the city. Okay? Do it real fast.'

I hunted around for something else to say and couldn't find it. Quit while you're ahead, I thought. She gave me her wrist and I did the interface with her. As my implant access touched hers, she shuddered a little. It wasn't much of a shudder, but I noticed it. I felt it, all right. I think I'm going to feel it every time I stiff anyone, ever again. Any time I even think of stiffing anyone.

I went in and found the John Doe arrest entry and got rid of it, and then I searched out her civil service file and promoted her up two grades and doubled her pay. Not much of an atonement. But what the hell, there wasn't much I could do. Then I cleaned up my traces behind me and exited the program.

'All right,' I said. 'It's done.'

'Fine,' she said, and rang for her cops.

They apologized for the case of mistaken identity and let me out of the building and turned me loose on Figueroa Street. It was late afternoon and the street was getting dark and the air was cool. Even in Los Angeles winter is winter, of a sort. I went to a street access and summoned the Toshiba from wherever it had parked itself and it came driving up, five or ten minutes later, and I told it to take me north. The going was slow, rush-hour stuff, but that was okay. We came to the wall at the Sylmar gate, fifty miles or so out of town. The gate asked me my name. 'Richard Roe,' I said. 'Beta Pi Upsilon 104324x. Destination San Francisco.'

It rains a lot in San Francisco in the winter. Still, it's a pretty town. I would have preferred Los Angeles that time of year, but what the hell. Nobody gets all his first choices all the time. The gate opened and the Toshiba went through. Easy as Beta Pi.

ONLINE: **ONE/7** *Subject*: Wrobik Sennkil, gambler

A Gift from the Culture

Iain M. Banks

INFO: Wrobik Sennkil lives in the far-future society known as 'The Culture'. He's a gambler with bad debts and he's in trouble with the mob. But out of the night come two hoods who thrust a deadly computerised Light Plasma Projector into his hands and make him an offer he can't refuse ...

Iain M. Banks is the Scottish-born writer who has achieved phenomenal popularity in just over a decade. Following his controversial first book *The Wasp Factory* (1984), a horrific study of madness and surrealism, Iain tried sf with *Consider Phlebas* (1987) which launched what has proved to be a continuing series of complex novels about the Culture: a sophisticated, utopian, inter-galactic civilisation around nine millennia in the future where people can change sex, go into mental storage or dwell in a virtual paradise. There are, however, those who oppose the Culture, including renegades, criminals, and the tentacled Affronters living in ultraspace. The interplay between these factions and the civilisation's oppressive police force in novels such as *Use of Weapons* (1990) and *Excession* (1996) has helped to win Iain the accolade of being probably the leading – and certainly best-selling – young UK writer of the moment. 'A Gift from the Culture', written for *Interzone* in 1987, is one of his very few short stories about the unique society.

Money is a sign of poverty. This is an old Culture saying I remember every now and again, especially when I'm being tempted to do something I know I shouldn't, and there's money involved (when is there not?).

I looked at the gun, lying small and precise in Cruizell's broad, scarred hand, and the first thing I thought – after: Where the hell did they get one of *those*? – was: Money is a sign of poverty. However appropriate the thought might have been, it wasn't much help.

I was standing outside a no-credit gambling club in Vreccis Low City in the small hours of a wet weeknight, looking at a pretty, toy-like handgun while two large people I owed a lot of money to asked me to do something extremely dangerous and worse than illegal. I was weighing up the relative attractions of trying to run away (they'd shoot me), refusing (they'd beat me up; probably I'd spend the next few weeks developing a serious medical bill), and doing what Kaddus and Cruizell asked me to do, knowing that while there was a chance I'd get away with it – uninjured, and solvent again – the most likely outcome was a messy and probably slow death while assisting the security services with their enquiries.

Kaddus and Cruizell were offering me all my markers back, plus – once the thing was done – a tidy sum on top, just to show there were no hard feelings.

I suspected they didn't anticipate having to pay the final instalment of the deal.

So, I knew that logically what I ought to do was tell them where to shove their fancy designer pistol, and accept a theoretically painful but probably not terminal beating. Hell, I could switch the pain off (having a Culture background does have some advantages), but what about that hospital bill?

I was up to my scalp in debt already.

'What's the matter, Wrobik?' Cruizell drawled, taking a step nearer, under the shelter of the club's dripping eaves. Me with my back against the warm wall, the smell of wet pavements in my nose and a taste like metal in my mouth. Kaddus and Cruizell's limousine idled at the kerb; I could see the driver inside, watching us through an open window. Nobody passed on the street outside the narrow alley. A police cruiser flew over, high up, lights flashing through the rain and illuminating the underside of the rain clouds over the city. Kaddus looked up briefly, then ignored the passing craft. Cruizell shoved the gun towards me. I tried to shrink back.

'Take the gun, Wrobik,' Kaddus said tiredly. I licked my lips, stared down at the pistol.

'I can't,' I said. I stuck my hands in my coat pockets.

'Sure you can,' Cruizell said. Kaddus shook his head.

'Wrobik, don't make things difficult for yourself; take the gun. Just touch it first, see if our information is correct. Go on; take it.' I stared, transfixed, at the small pistol. 'Take the gun, Wrobik. Just remember to point it at the ground, not at us; the driver's got a laser on you and he might think you meant to use the gun on us ... come on; take it, touch it.'

I couldn't move, I couldn't think. I just stood, hypnotized. Kaddus took hold of my right wrist and pulled my hand from my pocket. Cruizell held the gun up near my nose; Kaddus forced my hand on to the pistol. My hand closed round the grip like something lifeless.

The gun came to life; a couple of lights blinked dully, and the small screen above the grip glowed, flickering round the edges. Cruizell dropped his hand, leaving me holding the pistol; Kaddus smiled thinly.

'There, that wasn't difficult, now was it?' Kaddus said. I held the gun and tried to imagine using it on the two men, but I knew I couldn't, whether the driver had me covered or not.

'Kaddus,' I said, 'I can't do this. Something else; I'll do anything else, but I'm not a hit-man; I can't –'

'You don't have to be an expert, Wrobik,' Kaddus said quietly. 'All you have to be is ... whatever the hell you are. After that, you just point and squirt: like you do with your boyfriend.' He grinned and winked at Cruizell, who bared some teeth. I shook my head.

'This is crazy, Kaddus. Just because the thing switches on for me –'

'Yeah; isn't that funny.' Kaddus turned to Cruizell, looking up to the taller man's face and smiling. 'Isn't that funny, Wrobik here being an alien? And him looking just like us.'

'An alien *and* queer,' Cruizell rumbled, scowling. 'Shit.'

'Look,' I said, staring at the pistol, 'it ... this thing, it ... it might not work,' I finished lamely. Kaddus smiled.

'It'll work. A ship's a big target. You won't miss.' He smiled again.

'But I thought they had protection against –'

'Lasers and kinetics they can deal with, Wrobik; this is something different. I don't know the technical details; I just know our radical friends paid a lot of money for this thing. That's enough for me.'

Our radical friends. This was funny, coming from Kaddus. Probably he meant the Bright Path. People he'd always considered bad for business, just terrorists. I'd have imagined he'd sell them to the police on general principles, even if they did offer him lots of money. Was he starting to hedge his bets, or just being greedy? They have a saying here: Crime whispers; money talks.

'But there'll be people on the ship, not just –'

'You won't be able to see them. Anyway; they'll be some of the Guard, Naval brass, some Administration flunkeys, Secret Service agents ... What do you care about them?' Kaddus patted my damp shoulder. 'You can do it.'

I looked away from his tired grey eyes, down at the gun, quiet in my fist, small screen glowing faintly. Betrayed by my own skin, my own touch. I thought about that hospital bill again. I felt like crying, but that wasn't the done thing amongst the men here, and what could I say? *I was a woman. I was Culture.* But I had renounced these things, and now I am a man, and now I am here in the Free City of Vreccis, where nothing is free.

'All right,' I said, a bitterness in my mouth, 'I'll do it.'

Cruizell looked disappointed. Kaddus nodded. 'Good. The ship arrives Ninthday; you know what it looks like?' I nodded. 'So you won't have any problems,' Kaddus smiled thinly. 'You'll be able to see it from almost anywhere in the City.' He pulled out some cash and stuffed it into my coat pocket. 'Get yourself a taxi. The underground's risky these days.' He patted me lightly on the cheek; his hand smelt of expensive scents. 'Hey, Wrobik; cheer up, yeah? You're going to shoot down a fucking starship. It'll be 'an experience.'' Kaddus laughed, looking at me and then at Cruizell, who laughed too, dutifully.

They went back to the car; it hummed into the night, tyres ripping at the rain-filled streets. I was left to watch the puddles grow, the gun hanging in my hand like guilt.

'I am a Light Plasma Projector, model LPP 91, series two, constructed in A/ 4882.4 at Manufactury Six in the Spanshacht-Trouferre Orbital, Ørvolöus Cluster. Serial number 3685706. Brain value point one. AM battery powered, rating: indefinite. Maximum power on single-bolt: 3.1×8^{10} joules, recycle time 14 seconds. Maximum rate of fire: 260 RPS. Use limited to Culture genofixed individuals only through epidermal gene analysis. To use with gloves or light armour, access "modes" store via command buttons. Unauthorized use is both prohibited and punishable. Skill requirement 12–75%C. Full instructions follow; use command buttons and screen to replay, search, pause or stop ...

'Instructions, part one: Introduction. The LPP 91 is an operationally intricate general-purpose "peace"-rated weapon not suitable for full battle use; its design and performance parameters are based on the recommendations of –'

The gun sat on the table, telling me all about itself in a high, tinny voice while I lay slumped in a lounger, staring out over a busy street in Vreccis Low City. Underground freight trains shook the rickety apartment block every few minutes, traffic buzzed at street level, rich people and police moved through the skies in fliers and cruisers, and above them all the starships sailed.

I felt trapped between these strata of purposeful movements.

Far in the distance over the city, I could just see the slender, shining tower of the city's Lev tube, rising straight towards and through the clouds, on its way to space. Why couldn't the Admiral use the Lev instead of making a big show of returning from the stars in his own ship? Maybe he thought a glorified elevator was too undignified. Vainglorious bastards, all of them. They deserved to die (if you wanted to take that attitude), but why did I have to be the one to kill them? Goddamned phallic starships.

Not that the Lev was any less prick-like, and anyway, no doubt if the Admiral had been coming down by the tube Kaddus and Cruizell would have told me to shoot *it* down; holy shit. I shook my head.

I was holding a long glass of jahl – Vreccis City's cheapest strong booze. It was my second glass, but I wasn't enjoying it. The gun chattered on, speaking to the sparsely furnished main room of our apartment. I was waiting for Maust, missing him even more than usual. I looked at the terminal on my wrist; according to the time display he should be back any moment now. I looked out into the weak, watery light of dawn. I hadn't slept yet.

The gun talked on. It used Marain, of course; the Culture's language. I hadn't heard that spoken for nearly eight standard years, and hearing it now I felt sad and foolish. My birthright; my people, my language. Eight years away, eight years in the wilderness. My great adventure, my renunciation of what seemed to me sterile and lifeless to plunge into a more vital society, my grand gesture ... well, now it seemed like an empty gesture, now it looked like a stupid, petulant thing to have done.

I drank some more of the sharp-tasting spirit. The gun gibbered on, talking about beam-spread diameters, gyroscopic weave patterns, gravity-contour mode, line-of-sight mode, curve shots, spatter and pierce settings ... I thought about glanding something soothing and cool, but I didn't; I had vowed not to use those cunningly altered glands eight years ago, and I'd broken that vow only twice, both times when I was in severe pain. Had I been courageous I'd have had the whole damn lot taken out, returned to their human-normal state, our original animal inheritance ... but I am not courageous. I dread pain, and cannot face it naked, as these people do. I admire them, fear them, still cannot understand them. Not even Maust. In fact, least of all Maust. Perhaps you cannot ever love what you completely understand.

Eight years in exile, lost to the Culture, never hearing that silky, subtle, complexly simple language, and now when I do hear Marain, it's from a gun, telling me how to fire it so I can kill ... what? Hundreds of people? Maybe thousands; it will depend on where the ship falls, whether it explodes (could primitive starships explode? I had no idea; that was never my field). I took another drink, shook my head. I couldn't do it.

I am Wrobik Sennkil, Vreccile citizen number ... (I always forget; it's on my papers), male, prime race, aged thirty; part-time freelance journalist (between jobs at the moment), and full-time gambler (I tend to lose but I enjoy myself, or at least I did until last night). But I am, also, still Bahlln-Eucharsa Wrobich Vress Schennil dam Flaysse, citizen of the Culture, born female, species mix too complicated to remember, aged sixty-eight, standard, and one-time member of the Contact section.

And a renegade; I chose to exercise the freedom the Culture is so proud of bestowing upon its inhabitants by leaving it altogether. It let me go, even helped me, reluctant though I was (but could I have forged my own papers, made all the arrangements by myself? No, but at least, after my education into the ways of the Vreccile Economic Community, and after the module rose, dark and silent, back into the night sky and the waiting ship, I have turned only twice to the Culture's legacy of altered biology, and not once to its artefacts. Until now; the gun rambles on.) I abandoned a paradise I considered dull for a cruel and greedy system bubbling with life and incident; a place I thought I might find ... what? I don't know. I didn't know when I left and I don't know yet, though at least here I found Maust, and when I am with him my searching no longer seems so lonely.

Until last night that search still seemed worthwhile. Now utopia sends a tiny package of destruction, a casual, accidental message.

Where *did* Kaddus and Cruizell get the thing? The Culture guards its weaponry jealously, even embarrassedly. You can't buy Culture weapons, at least not from the Culture. I suppose things go missing though; there is so much of everything in the Culture that objects must be mislaid occasionally. I took another drink, listening to the gun, and watching that watery, rainy-season sky over the rooftops, towers, aerials, dishes and domes of the Great City. Maybe guns slip out of the Culture's manicured grasp more often than other products do; they betoken danger, they signify threat, and they will only be needed where there must be a fair chance of losing them, so they must disappear now and again, be taken as prizes.

That, of course, is why they're built with inhibiting circuits which only let the weapons work for Culture people (sensible, non-violent, non-acquisitive Culture people, who *of course* would only use a gun in self-defence, for example, if threatened by some comparative barbarian ... oh the self-satisfied Culture: its imperialism of smugness). And even this gun is antique; not obsolescent (for that is not a concept the Culture really approves of – it builds to last), but outdated; hardly more intelligent than a household pet, whereas modern Culture weaponry is sentient.

The Culture probably doesn't even make handguns any more. I've seen what it calls Personal Armed Escort Drones, and if, somehow, one of those fell into the hands of people like Kaddus and Cruizell, it would immediately signal for help, use its motive power to try and escape, shoot to injure or even kill anybody trying to use or trap it, attempt to bargain its way out, and destruct if it thought it was going to be taken apart or otherwise interfered with.

I drank some more jahl. I looked at the time again; Maust was late. The club always closed promptly, because of the police. They weren't allowed to talk to the customers after work: he always came straight back ... I felt the start of fear, but pushed it away. Of course he'd be all right. I had other things to think about. I had to think this thing through. More jahl.

No, I couldn't do it. I left the Culture because it bored me, but also because the evangelical, interventionist morality of Contact sometimes meant doing just the sort of thing we were supposed to prevent others doing; starting wars, assassinating ... all of it, all the bad things ... I was never involved with Special Circumstances directly, but I knew what went on (Special Circumstances; Dirty Tricks, in other words. The Culture's tellingly unique euphemism.) I refused to live with such hypocrisy and chose instead this honestly selfish and avaricious society, which doesn't pretend to be good, just ambitious.

But I have lived here as I lived there, trying not to hurt others, trying just to be myself; and I cannot be myself by destroying a ship full of people, even if they are some of the rulers of this cruel and callous society. I can't use the gun; I can't let Kaddus and Cruizell find me. And I will not go back, head bowed, to the Culture.

I finished the glass of jahl.

I had to get out. There were other cities, other planets, besides Vreccis; I just had to run; run and hide. Would Maust come with me though? I looked at the time again; he was half an hour late. Not like him. Why was he late? I went to the window, looking down to the street, searching for him.

A police APC rumbled through the traffic. Just a routine cruise; siren off, guns stowed. It was heading for the Outworlders' Quarter, where the police had been making shows of strength recently. No sign of Maust's svelte shape swinging through the crowds.

Always the worry. That he might be run over, that the police might arrest him at the club (indecency, corrupting public morals, and homosexuality; that great crime, even worse than not making your pay-off!), and, of course, the worry that he might meet somebody else.

Maust. Come home safely, come home to me.

I remember feeling cheated when I discovered, towards the end of my regendering, that I still felt drawn to men. That was long ago, when I was happy in the Culture, and like many people I had wondered what it would be like to love those of my own original sex; it seemed terribly unfair that my desires did not alter with my physiology. It took Maust to make me feel I had not been cheated. Maust made everything better. Maust was my breath of life.

Anyway, I would not be a woman in this society.

I decided I needed a refill. I walked past the table.

'... will not affect the line-stability of the weapon, though recoil will be increased on power-priority, or power decreased –'

'Shut up!' I shouted at the gun, and made a clumsy attempt to hit its Off button; my hand hit the pistol's stubby barrel. The gun skidded across the table and fell to the floor.

'Warning!' the gun shouted. 'There are no user-serviceable parts inside! Irreversible deactivation will result if any attempt is made to dismantle or –'

'Quiet, you little bastard,' I said (and it did go quiet). I picked it up and put it in the pocket of a jacket hanging over a chair. Damn the Culture; damn all guns. I went to get more drink, a heaviness inside me as I looked at the time again. Come home, please come home ... and then come away, come away with me ...

I fell asleep in front of the screen, a knot of dull panic in my belly competing with the spinning sensation in my head as I watched the news and worried about Maust, trying not to think of too many things. The news was full of executed terrorists and famous victories in small, distant wars against aliens, outworlders, subhumans. The last report I remember was about a riot in a city on another planet; there was no mention of civilian deaths, but I remember a shot of a broad street littered with crumpled shoes. The item closed with an injured policeman being interviewed in hospital.

I had my recurring nightmare, reliving the demonstration I was caught up in three years ago; looking, horrified, at a wall of drifting, sun-struck stun gas and seeing a line of police mounts come charging out of it, somehow more appalling than armoured cars or even tanks, not because of the visored riders with their long shock-batons, but because the tall animals were also armoured and gas-masked; monsters from a ready-made, mass-produced dream; terrorizing.

Maust found me there hours later, when he got back. The club had been raided and he hadn't been allowed to contact me. He held me as I cried, shushing me back to sleep.

'Wrobik, I can't. Risåret's putting on a new show next season and he's looking for new faces; it'll be big-time, straight stuff. A High City deal. I can't leave now; I've got my foot in the door. Please understand.' He reached over the table to take my hand. I pulled it away.

'I can't do what they're asking me to do. I can't stay. So I have to go; there's nothing else I can do.' My voice was dull. Maust started to clear away the plates and containers, shaking his long, graceful head. I hadn't eaten much; partly hangover, partly nerves. It was a muggy, enervating mid-morning; the tenement's conditioning plant had broken down again.

'Is what they're asking really so terrible?' Maust pulled his robe tighter, balancing plates expertly. I watched his slim back as he moved to the kitchen. 'I mean, you won't even tell me. Don't you trust me?' His voice echoed.

What could I say? That I didn't know if I did trust him? That I loved him but: only he had known I was an outworlder. That had been my secret, and I'd told only him. So how did Kaddus and Cruizell know? How did Bright Path know? My sinuous, erotic, faithless dancer. Did you think because I always remained silent that I didn't know of all the times you deceived me?

'Maust, please; it's better that you don't know.'

'Oh.' Maust laughed distantly; that aching, beautiful sound, tearing at me. 'How terribly dramatic. You're protecting me. How awfully gallant.'

'Maust, this is serious. These people want me to do something I just can't do. If I don't do it they'll ... they'll at least hurt me, badly. I don't know what they'll do. They ... they might even try to hurt me through you. That was why I was so worried when you were late; I thought maybe they'd taken you.'

'My dear, poor Wrobbie,' Maust said, looking out from the kitchen, 'it has been a long day; I think I pulled a muscle during my last number, we may not get paid after the raid – Stelmer's sure to use that as an excuse even if the filth didn't swipe the takings – and my ass is still sore from having one of those queer-bashing pigs poking his finger around inside me. Not as romantic as your dealings with gangsters and baddies, but important to me. I've enough to worry about. You're overreacting. Take a pill or something; go back to sleep; it'll look better later.' He winked at me, disappeared. I listened to him moving about in the kitchen. A police siren moaned overhead. Music filtered through from the apartment below.

I went to the door of the kitchen. Maust was drying his hands. 'They want me to shoot down the starship bringing the Admiral of the Fleet back on Ninthday,' I told him. Maust looked blank for a second, then sniggered. He came up to me, held me by the shoulders.

'Really? And then what? Climb the outside of the Lev and fly to the sun on your magic bicycle?' He smiled tolerantly, amused. I put my hands on his and removed them slowly from my shoulders.

'No. I just have to shoot down the ship, that's all. I have ... they gave me a gun that can do it.' I took the gun from the jacket. He frowned, shaking his head, looked puzzled for a second, then laughed again.

'With that, my love? I doubt you could stop a motorized pogo-stick with that little –'

'Maust, please; believe me. This can do it. My people made it and the ship ... the state has no defence against something like this.'

Maust snorted, then took the gun from me. Its lights flicked off. 'How do you switch it on?' He turned it over in his hand.

'By touching it; but only I can do it. It reads the genetic make-up of my skin, knows I am Culture. Don't look at me like that; it's true. Look.' I showed him. I had the gun recite the first part of its monologue and switched the tiny screen to holo. Maust inspected the gun while I held it.

'You know,' he said after a while, 'this might be rather valuable.'

'No, it's worthless to anyone else. It'll only work for me, and you can't get round its fidelities; it'll deactivate.'

'How ... faithful,' Maust said, sitting down and looking steadily at me. 'How neatly everything must be arranged in your "Culture". I didn't really believe you when you told me that tale, did you know that, my love? I thought you were just trying to impress me. Now I think I believe you.'

I crouched down in front of him, put the gun on the table and my hands on his lap. 'Then believe me that I can't do what they're asking, and that I am in danger; perhaps we both are. We have to leave. Now. Today or tomorrow. Before they think of another way to make me do this.'

Maust smiled, ruffled my hair. 'So fearful, eh? So desperately anxious.' He bent, kissed my forehead. 'Wrobbie, Wrobbie; I can't come with you. Go if you feel you must, but I can't come with you. Don't you know what this chance means to me? All my life I've wanted this; I may not get another opportunity. I have to stay, whatever. You go; go for as long as you must and don't tell me where you've gone. That way they can't use me, can they? Get in touch through a friend, once the dust has settled. Then we'll see. Perhaps you can come back; perhaps I'll have missed my big chance anyway and I'll come to join you. It'll be all right. We'll work something out.'

I let my head fall to his lap, wanting to cry. 'I can't leave you.'

He hugged me, rocking me. 'Oh, you'll probably find you're glad of the change. You'll be a hit wherever you go, my beauty; I'll probably have to kill some knife-fighter to win you back.'

'Please, please come with me,' I sobbed into his gown.

'I can't, my love, I just can't. I'll come to wave you goodbye, but I can't come with you.'

He held me while I cried; the gun lay silent and dull on the table at his side, surrounded by the debris of our meal.

I was leaving. Fire escape from the flat just before dawn, over two walls clutching my travelling bag, a taxi from General Thetropsis Avenue to Intercontinental Station ... then I'd catch a Railtube train to Bryme and take the Lev there; hoping for a standby on almost anything heading Out, either trans or inter. Maust had lent me some of his savings, and I still had a little high-rate credit left; I could make it. I left my terminal in the apartment. It would have been useful, but the rumours are true; the police can trace them, and I wouldn't put it past Kaddus and Cruizell to have a tame cop in the relevant department.

The station was crowded. I felt fairly safe in the high, echoing halls, surrounded by people and business. Maust was coming from the club to see me off; he'd promised to make sure he wasn't followed. I had just enough time to leave the gun at Left Luggage. I'd post the key to Kaddus, try to leave him a little less murderous.

There was a long queue at Left Luggage; I stood, exasperated, behind some naval cadets. They told me the delay was caused by the porters searching all bags and cases for bombs; a new security measure. I left the queue to go and meet Maust; I'd have to get rid of the gun somewhere else. Post the damn thing, or even just drop it in a waste bin.

I waited in the bar, sipping at something innocuous. I kept looking at my wrist, then feeling foolish. The terminal was back at the apartment; use a public phone, look for a clock. Maust was late.

There was a screen in the bar, showing a news bulletin. I shook off the absurd feeling that somehow I was already a wanted man, face liable to appear on the news broadcast, and watched today's lies to take my mind off the time.

They mentioned the return of the Admiral of the Fleet, due in two days. I looked at the screen, smiling nervously. *Yeah, and you'll never know how close the bastard came to getting blown out of the skies.* For a moment or two I felt important, almost heroic.

Then the bombshell; just a mention – an aside, tacked on, the sort of thing they'd have cut had the programme been a few seconds over – that the Admiral would be bringing a guest with him; an ambassador from the Culture. I choked on my drink.

Was *that* who I'd really have been aiming at if I'd gone ahead?

What was the Culture doing anyway? An ambassador? The Culture knew everything about the Vreccile Economic Community, and was watching, analyzing; content to leave well enough alone for now. The Vreccile people had little idea how advanced or widely spread the Culture was, though the court and Navy had a fairly good idea. Enough to make them slightly (though had they known it, still not remotely sufficiently) paranoid. What was an ambassador for?

And who was really behind the attempt on the ship? Bright Path would be indifferent to the fate of a single outworlder compared to the propaganda coup of pulling down a starship, but what if the gun hadn't come from them, but from a grouping in the court itself, or from the Navy? The VEC had problems; social problems, political problems. Maybe the President and his cronies were thinking about asking the Culture for aid. The price might involve the sort of changes some of the more corrupt officials would find terminally threatening to their luxurious lifestyles.

Shit, I didn't know; maybe the whole attempt to take out the ship was some loony in Security or the Navy trying to settle an old score, or just skip the next few rungs on the promotion ladder. I was still thinking about this when they paged me.

I sat still. The station PA called for me, three times. A phonecall. I told myself it was just Maust, calling to say he had been delayed; he knew I was leaving the terminal at the apartment so he couldn't call me direct. But would he announce my name all over a crowded station when he knew I was trying to leave quietly and unseen? Did he still take it all so lightly? I didn't want to answer that call. I didn't even want to think about it.

My train was leaving in ten minutes; I picked up my bag. The PA asked for me again, this time mentioning Maust's name. So I had no choice.

I went to Information. It was a viewcall.

'Wrobik,' Kaddus sighed, shaking his head. He was in some office; anonymous, bland. Maust was standing, pale and frightened, just behind Kaddus' seat. Cruizell stood right behind Maust, grinning over his slim shoulder. Cruizell moved slightly, and Maust flinched. I saw him bite his lip. 'Wrobik,' Kaddus said again. 'Were you going to leave so soon? I thought we had a date, yes?'

'Yes,' I said quietly, looking at Maust's eyes. 'Silly of me. I'll ... stick around for ... a couple of days. Maust, I –' The screen went grey.

I turned round slowly in the booth and looked at my bag, where the gun was. I picked the bag up. I hadn't realized how heavy it was.

I stood in the park, surrounded by dripping trees and worn rocks. Paths carved into the tired top-soil led in various directions. The earth smelled warm and damp. I looked down from the top of the gently sloped escarpment to where pleasure boats sailed in the dusk, lights reflecting on the still waters of the boating lake. The duskward quarter of the city was a hazy platform of light in the distance. I heard birds calling from the trees around me.

The aircraft lights of the Lev rose like a rope of flashing red beads into the blue evening sky; the port at the Lev's summit shone, still uneclipsed, in sunlight a hundred kilometres overhead. Lasers, ordinary searchlights and chemical fireworks began to make the sky bright above the Parliament buildings and the Great Square of the Inner City; a display to greet the returning, victorious Admiral, and maybe the ambassador from the Culture, too. I couldn't see the ship yet.

I sat down on a tree stump, drawing my coat about me. The gun was in my hand; on, ready, ranged, set. I had tried to be thorough and professional, as though I knew what I was doing; I'd even left a hired motorbike in some bushes on the far side of the escarpment, down near the busy parkway. I might actually get away with this. So I told myself, anyway. I looked at the gun.

I considered using it to try and rescue Maust, or maybe using it to kill myself; I'd even considered taking it to the police (another, slower form of suicide). I'd also considered calling Kaddus and telling him I'd lost it, it wasn't working, I couldn't kill a fellow Culture citizen ... anything. But in the end; nothing.

If I wanted Maust back I had to do what I'd agreed to do.

Something glinted in the skies above the city; a pattern of falling, golden lights. The central light was brighter and larger than the others.

I had thought I could feel no more, but there was a sharp taste in my mouth, and my hands were shaking. Perhaps I would go berserk, once the ship was down, and attack the Lev too; bring the whole thing smashing down (or would part of it go spinning off into space? Maybe I ought to do it just to see.) I could bombard half the city from here (hell, don't forget the curve shots; I could bombard the *whole* damn city from here); I could bring down the escort vessels and attacking planes and police cruisers; I could give the Vreccile the biggest shock they've ever had, before they got me ...

The ships were over the city. Out of the sunlight, their laser-proof mirror hulls were duller now. They were still falling; maybe five kilometres up. I checked the gun again.

Maybe it wouldn't work, I thought.

Lasers shone in the dust and grime above the city, producing tight spots on high and wispy clouds. Searchlight beams faded and spread in the same haze, while fireworks burst and slowly fell, twinkling and sparkling. The sleek ships dropped majestically to meet the welcoming lights. I looked about the tree-lined ridge; alone. A warm breeze brought the grumbling sound of the parkway traffic to me.

I raised the gun and sighted. The formation of ships appeared on the holo display, the scene noon-bright. I adjusted the magnification, fingered a command stud; the gun locked on to the flagship, became rock-steady in my hand. A flashing white point in the display marked the centre of the vessel.

I looked round again, my heart hammering, my hand held by the field-anchored gun. Still nobody came to stop me. My eyes stung. The ships hung a few hundred metres above the state buildings of the Inner City. The outer vessels remained there; the centre craft, the flagship, stately and massive, a mirror held up to the glittering city, descended towards the Great Square. The gun dipped in my hand, tracking it.

Maybe the Culture ambassador wasn't aboard the damn ship anyway. This whole thing might be a Special Circumstances set-up; perhaps the Culture was ready to interfere now and it amused the planning Minds to have me, a heretic, push things over the edge. The Culture ambassador might have been a ruse, just in case I started to suspect ... I didn't know. I didn't know anything. I was floating on a sea of possibilities, but parched of choices.

I squeezed the trigger.

The gun leapt backwards, light flared all around me. A blinding line of brilliance flicked, seemingly instantaneously, from me to the starship ten kilometres away. There was a sharp detonation of sound somewhere inside my head. I was thrown off the tree stump.

When I sat up again the ship had fallen. The Great Square blazed with flames and smoke and strange, bristling tongues of some terrible lightning; the remaining lasers and fireworks were made dull. I stood, shaking, ears ringing, and stared at what I'd done. Late-reacting sprinterceptiles from the escorts criss-crossed the air above the wreck and slammed into the ground, automatics fooled by the sheer velocity of the plasma bolt. Their warheads burst brightly among the boulevards and buildings of the Inner City, a bruise upon a bruise.

The noise of the first explosion smacked and rumbled over the park.

The police and the escort ships themselves were starting to react. I saw the lights of police cruisers rise strobing from the Inner City; the escort craft began to turn slowly above the fierce, flickering radiations of the wreck.

I pocketed the gun and ran down the damp path towards the bike, away from the escarpment's lip. Behind my eyes, burnt there, I could still see the line of light that had briefly joined me to the starship; bright path indeed, I thought, and nearly laughed. A bright path in the soft darkness of the mind.

I raced down to join all the other poor folk on the run.

ONLINE: **ONE/8** *Subject*: William Bailey, murderer

Murder Will In

Frank Herbert

INFO: One day, the computer will become god-like and make crime and murder things of the past. It will even be able to turn killers into funlovers. At least *that* is the theory of some computer scientists. But here is a little warning that even then we may not be able to legislate for *every* sort of human being.

Frank Herbert is the author of *Dune* (1965) and its various sequels which describe life on the desert planet Arrakis, where the inhabitants conserve water with fanatical energy. Together the novels have exerted a huge influence on contemporary sf. Frank, who was born in Tacoma, Washington, worked as a professional photographer, TV cameraman, oyster diver, lay analyst and West Coast newspaperman before launching out on a career as an sf writer with *Dragon in the Sea* (1964), a thriller about a submarine of the future. It was the success of *Dune*, however, and the spectacular movie adaptation, which brought his work to international attention. Another of his highly regarded novels is *Destination: Void* (1966), in which he explored the idea that computers might ultimately become omnipotent – a theme he returns to again in 'Murder Will In', written for the *Magazine of Fantasy and Science Fiction* in 1970.

As the body died, the Tegas/Bacit awoke. Unconsciousness had lasted its usual flickering instant for the Tegas element. He came out of it with his Bacit negative identity chanting: '... not William Bailey – I'm not William Bailey – I'm not William Bailey ...'

It was a painful, monotonous refrain – schismatic, important. The Tegas had to separate its identity from this fading flesh. Behind the chant lay a sense of many voices clamoring.

Awareness began to divide, a splitting seam that separated him from the compressed contact which controlled the host. There came a sensation of tearing fabric and he rode free, still immersed in the dying neural system because he had no other place to go, but capable of the identity leap.

Bacit and Tegas now functioning together, sticking him to each instant. He searched his surroundings: twenty meters ... twenty meters ...

Flickering, pale emotions registered on his awareness. Another attendant. The man passed out of range. Cold-cold-cold.

Nothing else.

What a rare joke this was, he thought. What a mischievous thing for fate to do. A Tegas to be caught like this! Mischievous. Mischievous. It wasn't fair. Hadn't he always treated the captive flesh with gentle care? Hadn't he made fun-lovers out of killers? Fate's mischief was cruel, not kindly in the manner of the Tegas.

The Bacit negative identity projected terror, accusation, embarrassment. He had lived too long in the William Bailey flesh. Too long. He had lived down where men were, where things were made – in the thick of being. He'd loved the flesh too much. He should've stopped occasionally and looked around him. The great Tegas curiosity which masqueraded as diffidence to hide itself had failed to protect him.

Failed ... failed ...

Within the dying neural system, frantic messages began darting back and forth. His mind was a torrent, a flare of being. Thoughts flew off like sparks from a grinding wheel.

'It's decided,' the Tegas transmitted, seeking to quiet his negative self. The communicative contact returned a sharp feeling of shame and loss.

The Bacit shifted from terror to fifth-order displeasure, which was almost as bad as the terror. All the lost experiences. Lost ... lost ... lost ...

'I had no idea the Euthanasia Center would be that simple and swift,' the Tegas transmitted. 'The incident is past changing. What can we do?'

He thought of the one vid-call he'd permitted himself, to check on the center's hours and routine. A gray-haired, polished contact-with-the-public type had appeared on the screen.

'We're fast, clean, neat, efficient, sanitary, and reverent,' the man had said.

'Fast?'

'Who would want a slow death?'

The Tegas wished in this instant for nothing more than a slow death. If only he'd checked further. He'd expected this place to be seething with emotions. But it was emotionally dead – silent as a tomb. The joke-thought fell on inner silence.

The Bacit transfixed their composite self with a projection of urgent measurement – the twenty meters limit across which the Tegas could launch them into a new host.

But there'd been no way of knowing this place was an emotional vacuum until the Tegas element had entered here, probed the place. And these chambers where he now found himself were much farther from the street than twenty meters.

Momentarily, the Tegas was submerged in accusatory terror. *This death isn't like murder at all!*

Yet, he'd thought it would be *like* murder. And it was murder that'd been the saving device of the Tegas/Bacit for centuries. A murderer could be depended upon for total emotional involvement. A murderer could be lured close ... close ... close, much closer than twenty meters. It'd been so easy to goad the human creatures into that violent act, to set up the ideal circumstances for the identity leap. The Tegas absolutely required profound emotions in a prospective host. One couldn't focus on the neural totality without it. Bits of the creature's awareness center tended to escape. That could be fatal – as fatal as the trap in which he now found himself.

Murder.

The swift outflow of life from the discarded host, the emotional concentration of the new host – and before he knew it, the murderer was captive of the Tegas, captive in his own body. The captive awareness cried out silently, darting inward with ever tightening frenzy until it was swallowed.

And the Tegas could get on about its business of enjoying life.

This world had changed, though, in the past hundred years of the William Bailey period. Murder had been virtually eliminated by the new predictive techniques and computers of the Data Center. The android law-niks were everywhere, anticipating violence, preventing it. This was an elliptical development of society and the Tegas realized he should've taken it into account long ago. But life tended to be so pleasant when it held the illusion of never ending. For the Tegas, migrating across the universe with its hosts, moving as a predator in the dark of life, the illusion could be a fact.

Unless it ended here.

It didn't help matters that decisions had been forced upon him. Despite a fairly youthful appearance, the host flesh of William Bailey had been failing. The Tegas could keep its host going far beyond the normal span, but when the creature began to fail, collapse could be massive and abrupt.

I should've tried to attack someone in circumstances where I'd have been killed, he thought. But he'd seen the flaw there. The emotionless law-niks would have been on him almost instantly. Death might've escaped him. He could've been trapped in a crippled, dying host surrounded by android blankness or, even worse, surrounded by humans rendered almost emotionless by that damnable 'Middle Way' and 'Eight-fold Karma'.

And the hounds were on his trail. He knew they were. He'd seen plenty of evidence, sensed the snoopers. He'd lived too long as William Bailey. The ones who thrived on suspicion had become suspicious. And they couldn't be allowed to examine a Tegas host too closely. He knew what'd put them on his trail: that diabolical 'total profile of motive'. The Tegas in William Bailey was technically a murderer thousands of times over. Not that he went on killing and killing; once in a human lifetime was quite enough. Murder could take the fun out of life.

Thoughts were useless now, he realized. He had, after all, been trapped. Thinking about it led only to Bacit accusations. And while he jumped from thought to thought, the William Bailey body moved nearer and nearer to dissolution. The body now held only the faintest contact with life, and that only because of desperate Tegas efforts. A human medic would've declared Bailey dead. Breathing had stopped. Abruptly, the heart fibrillated, ceased function.

Less than five minutes remained for the Tegas. He had to find a new host in five minutes with this one.

'Murder-murder-murder,' the Bacit intruded. 'You said euthanasia would be murder.'

The Tegas felt William Bailey-shame. He cursed inwardly. The Bacit, normally such a useful function for a Tegas (driving away intellectual loneliness, providing companionship and caution) had become a distracting liability. The intrusion of terrifying urgency stopped thought.

Why couldn't the Bacit be silent and let him think?

Momentarily, the Tegas realized he'd never before considered the premises of his own actions.

What was the Bacit?

He'd never hungered after his own kind, for he had the Bacit. But what, after all, was the Bacit? Why, for example, would it let him captivate only males? Female thinking might be a help in this emergency. Why couldn't he mix the sexes?

The Bacit used the inner shout: 'Now we have time for philosophy?'

It was too much.

'Silence!' the Tegas commanded.

An immediate sense of loneliness rocked him. He defied it, probed his surroundings. Any host would do in this situation – even a lower animal, although he hadn't risked one of those in aeons. Surely there must be some emotional upset in this terrible place ... something ... anything ...

He remembered a long-ago incident when he'd allowed himself to be slain by a type who'd turned out to be completely emotionless. He'd barely managed to shift in time to an eye-witness to the crime. The moment had been like this one in its sudden emergency, but who was eye-witness to this killing? Where was an alternative host?

He searched fruitlessly.

Synapses began snapping in the William Bailey neural system. The Tegas withdrew to the longest-lived centers, probed with increasing frenzy.

A seething emotional mass lifted itself on his awareness, horizon. Fear, self-pity, revenge, anger: a lovely prospect, like a rescue steamer bearing down on a drowning mariner.

'I'm not William Bailey,' he reminded himself and launched outwards, homing on that boiling tangle of paradox, that emotional beacon ...

There came the usual bouncing shock as he grabbed for the new host's identity centers. He poured out through a sensorium, discovered his own movements, felt something cold against a wrist. It was not yet completely his wrist, but the eyes were sufficiently under control for him to force them towards the source of sensation.

A flat, gray metallic object swam into focus. It was pressed against *his* wrist. Simultaneously, there occurred a swarming sense of awareness within the host. It was a sighing-out – not submission, but negative exaltation. The Tegas felt an old heart begin to falter, looked at an attendant: unfamiliar face – owlish features around a sharp nose.

But no emotional intensity, no central hook of being to be grabbed and captivated.

The room was a twin to the one in which he'd been captured by this system. The ceiling's time read-out said only eight minutes had passed since that other wrist had been touched by death.

'If you'll be so kind as to go through the door behind you,' the owl-faced attendant said. 'I do hope you can make it. Had to drag three of you in there already this shift; I'm rather weary. Let's get moving, eh?'

Weary? Yes – the attendant radiated only emotional weariness. It was nothing a Tegas could grasp.

The new host responded to the idea of urgency, pushed up out of a chair, shambled towards an oval door. The attendant hurried him along with an arm across the old shoulders.

The Tegas moved within the host, consolidated neural capacity, swept in an unresisting awareness. It wasn't an awareness he'd have taken out of choice – defeated, submissive. There was something strange about it. The Tegas detected a foreign object pressed against the host's spine. A capsule of some kind – neural transmitter/receiver. It radiated an emotional-damper effect, commands of obedience.

The Tegas blocked it off swiftly, terrified by the implications of such an instrument.

He had the host's identity now: James Daggett; that was the name. Age seventy-one. The body was a poor, used-up relic, weaker, more debilitated than William Bailey had been at 236. The host's birdlike awareness, giving itself up to the Tegas as it gave up to death, radiated oddly mystical thoughts, confusions, assumptions, filterings.

The Tegas was an angel 'come to escort me'.

Still trailing wisps of William Bailey, the Tegas avoided too close a linkage with this new host. The name and self-recognition centers were enough.

He realized with a twisted sense of defeat that the old body was being strapped on to a hard surface. The ceiling loomed over him a featureless gray. Dulled nostrils sniffed at an antiseptic breeze.

'Sleep well, paisano,' the attendant said.

Not again! the Tegas thought.

His Bacit half reasserted itself: 'We can jump from body to body – dying a little each time. What fun!'

The Tegas transmitted a remote obscenity from another world and another aeon, describing what the Bacit half could do with its bitterness.

Vacuity replaced the intrusion.

Defeat ... defeat ...

Part of this doomed mood, he realized, came out of the James Daggett personality. The Tegas took the moment to probe that host's memories, found the time when the transmitter had been attached to his spine.

Defeat-obedience-defeat ...

It stemmed from that surgical instant.

He restored the blocks, quested outwards for a new host. Questing, he searched his Tegas memory. There must be a clue somewhere, a hint, a thought – some way of escape. He missed the Bacit contribution, parts of his memory felt cut off. The neural linkage with the dying James Daggett clung like dirty mud to his thoughts.

Ancient, dying James Daggett remained filled with mystical confusions until he was swallowed by the Tegas. It was a poor neural connection. The host was supposed to resist. That strengthened the Tegas grip. Instead, the Tegas ran into softly dying walls of other-memory. Linkages slipped. He felt his awareness range contracting.

Something swam into the questing field – anger, outrage of the kind frequently directed against stupidities. The Tegas waited, wondering if this could be another *client* of the center.

Now, trailing the angry one came another identity. Fear dominated this one. The Tegas went into a mental crouch, focused its awareness hungrily. An object of anger, a fearful one – there was one a Tegas could grab.

Voices came to him from the hallway outside the alcove – rasping, attacking and (delayed) fearful.

James Daggett's old and misused ears cut off overtones, reduced volume. There wasn't time to strengthen the host's hearing circuits, but the Tegas grasped the sense of the argument.

'… told to notify … immediately if … Bailey! William Bailey! … saw the … your desk …'

And the fearful one: '…. busy … you've no idea how … and understaffed and … teen an hour … only … this shift …'

The voices receded, but the emotional auras remained within Tegas range.

'Dead!' It was the angry one, a voice-blast accompanied by a neural overload that rolled across the Tegas like a giant wave.

At the instant of rage, the fearful one hit a momentary fear peak: abject retreat.

The Tegas pounced, quitting James Daggett in the blink-out as life went under. It was like stepping off a sinking boat into a storm-racked cockleshell. He was momentarily lost in the tracery of material spacetime which was the chosen host. Abruptly, he realized the fearful one had husbanded a reserve of supercilious hate, an ego corner fortified by resentments against authority accumulated over many years. The bouncing shock of the contact was accompanied by an escape of the host's awareness into the fortified corner.

The Tegas knew then he was in for a fight such as he'd never before experienced. The realization was accompanied by a blurred glimpse through host-eyes of a darkly suspicious face staring at him across a strapped-down body. The death-locked features of the body shook him – William Bailey! He almost lost the battle right there.

The host took control of the cheeks, contorted them. The eyes behaved independently: one looking up, the other down. He experienced direct perception, seeing with the fingertips (pale glowing), hearing with the lips (an itch of sound). Skin trembled and flushed. He staggered, heard a voice shout: 'Who're you? What you doing to me?'

It was the host's voice, and the Tegas, snatching at the vocal centers, could only burr the edges of sound, not blank out intelligibility. He glimpsed the dark face across from him in an eye-swirling flash. The other had recoiled, staring.

It was one of the suspicious ones, the hated ones, the ones-who-rule. No time to worry about that now. The Tegas was fighting for survival. He summoned every trick he'd ever learned – cajolery, mystical subterfuges, a flailing of religious illusion, love, hate, word play. Men were an instrument of language and could be snared by it. He went in snake-striking dashes along the neural channels.

The name! He had to get the name!

'Carmy ... Carmichael!'

He had half the name then, a toehold on survival. Silently, roaring inward along synaptic channels, he screamed the name –

'I'm Carmichael! I'm Carmichael!'

'No!'

'Yes! I'm Carmichael!'

'You're not! You're not!'

'I'm Carmichael!'

The host was bludgeoned into puzzlement: 'Who're you? You can't be me. I'm ... Joe – Joe Carmichael!'

The Tegas exulted, snapping up the whole name: 'I'm Joe Carmichael!'

The host's awareness spiralled inward, darting, frenzied. Eyes rolled. Legs trembled. Arms moved with a disjointed flapping. Teeth gnashed. Tears rolled down the cheeks.

The Tegas smashed at him now: 'I'm Joe Carmichael!'

'No ... no ... no ...' It was a fading inner scream, winking out ... back ... out ...

Silence.

'I'm Joe Carmichael,' the Tegas thought.

It was a Joe Carmichael thought faintly touched by Tegas inflections and Bacit's reproving: 'That was too close.'

The Tegas realized he lay flat on his back on the floor. He looked up into dark features identified by host-memories: 'Chadrick Vicentelli, Commissioner of Crime Prevention.'

'Mr Carmichael,' Vicentelli said. 'I've summoned help. Rest quietly. Don't try to move just yet.'

What a harsh, unmoving face, the Tegas thought. Vicentelli's was a Noh mask face. And the voice: wary, cold, suspicious. This violent incident wasn't on any computer's predictives ... Or was it? No matter – a suspicious man had seen too much. Something had to be done – immediately. Feet already could be heard pounding along the corridor.

'Don't know what's wrong with me,' the Tegas said, managing the Carmichael voice with memory help from the Bailey period. 'Dizzy ... whole world seemed to go red ...'

'You look alert enough now,' Vicentelli said.

There was no *give* in that voice, no love. Violence there, suspicious hate contained in sharp edges.

'You look alert enough now.'

A Tegas shudder went through the Carmichael body. He studied the probing, suspicious eyes. This was the breed Tegas avoided. Rulers possessed terrible resources for the inner battle. That was one of the reasons they ruled. Tegas had been swallowed by rulers – dissolved, lost. Mistakes had been made in the dim beginnings before Tegas learned to avoid ones such as this. Even on this world, the Tegas recalled early fights, near things that had resulted in rumors and customs, myths, racial fears. All primitives knew the code: *'Never reveal your true name!'*

And here was a ruler who had seen too much in times when that carried supreme danger. Suspicion was aroused. A sharp intelligence weighed data it should never have received.

Two red-coated android law-niks, as alike in their bland-featured intensity as obedient dogs, swept through the alcove hangings, came to a stop waiting for Vicentelli's orders. It was unnerving: even with androids, the ones-who-submitted never hesitated in looking first to a ruler for their orders.

The Tegas thought of the control capsule that had been on James Daggett's spine. A new fear trembled through him. The host's mouth was dry with a purely Carmichael emotion.

'This is Joseph Carmichael,' Vicentelli said, pointing. 'I want him taken to IC for a complete examination and motivational profile. I'll meet you there. Notify the appropriate cadres.'

The law-niks helped the Tegas to his new feet.

IC – Investigation Central, he thought.

'Why're you taking me to IC?' he demanded. 'I should go to a hospital for –'

'We've medical facilities,' Vicentelli said. He made it sound ominous.

Medical facilities for what?

'But why –'

'Be quiet and obey,' Vicentelli said. He glanced at William Bailey's body, back to Carmichael. It was a look full of weighted suspicions, half knowledge, educated assumptions.

The Tegas glanced at William Bailey's body, was caught by an inward-memory touch that wrenched at his new awareness. It had been a superior host, flesh deserving of love. The nostalgia passed. He looked back at Vicentelli, formed a vacant stare of confusion. It was not a completely feigned reaction. The Carmichael takeover had occurred in the presence of the suspected William Bailey – no matter that William Bailey was a corpse; that merely fed the suspicions. Vicentelli, assuming an unknown presence in William Bailey, would think it had leaped from the corpse to Carmichael.

'We're interested in you,' Vicentelli said. 'Very interested. Much more interested than we were before your recent ... ahhh, seizure.' He nodded to the androids.

Seizure! the Tegas thought.

Firm, insistent hands propelled him through the alcove curtains into the hallway, down the hall, through the antiseptic white of the employees' dressing room and out of the back door.

The day he'd left such a short time before as William Bailey appeared oddly transformed to the Carmichael eyes. There was a slight change in the height of the eyes, of course – a matter of perhaps three centimeters taller for Carmichael. He had to break his visual reactions out of perspective habits formed by more than two centuries at Bailey's height. But the change was more than that. He felt that he was seeing the day through many eyes – many more than the host's two.

The sensation of multi-ocular vision confused him, but he hadn't time to examine it before the law-niks pushed him into the one-way glass cage of an aircar. The door hissed closed, thumping on its seals, and he was alone, peering out through the blue-gray filtering of the windows. He leaned back on padded plastic.

The aircar leaped upward out of the plastrete canyon, sped across the great tableland roof of the Euthanasia Center toward the distant man-made peaks of IC. The central complex of government was an area the Tegas always had avoided. He wished nothing more now than to continue avoiding it.

A feeling came over him that his universe had shattered. He was trapped here – not just trapped in the aircar flitting towards the plastrete citadel of IC, but trapped in the ecosystem of the planet. It was a sensation he'd never before experienced – not even on that aeons-distant day when he'd landed here in a conditioned host at the end of a trip which had taxed the limits of the host's viability. It was the way of the Tegas, though, to reach out for new planets, new hosts. It had become second nature to choose the right kind of planet, the right kind of developing life forms. The right kind always developed star travel, releasing the Tegas for a new journey, new explorations, new experiences. That way, boredom never intervened. The creatures of this planet were headed towards the stellar leap, too – given time.

But the Tegas, experiencing a new fear for him, realized he might not be around to take advantage of that stellar leap. It was a realization that left him feeling exhausted, time-scalded, injured in his responses like a mistreated instrument.

Where did I go wrong? he wondered. *Was it in the original choice of the planet?*

His Bacit half, usually so explicit in reaction to inner searching, spread across their mutual awareness a projected sense of the fuzzy unknowns ahead.

This angered the Tegas. The future always was unknown. He began exploring his host-self, assessing what he could use in the coming showdown. It was a good host – healthy, strong, its musculature and neural system capable of excellent Tegas reinforcement and intensification. It was a host that could give good service, perhaps even longer than William Bailey. The Tegas began doing what he could in the time available, removing inhibitory blocks for quicker and smoother neural responses, setting up a heart and vascular system buffer. He took a certain pride in the work; he'd never misused a host as long as it remained viable.

The natural Tegas resilience, the thing that kept him going, kept him alive and interested – the endless curiosity – reasserted itself. Whatever was about to happen, it would be new. He seated himself firmly in the host, harnessed the Carmichael memory system to his Tegas responses, and readied himself to meet the immediate future.

A thought crept into his mind:

In the delicate immensity that was his own past there lay nonhuman experiences. How subtle was this 'Total Profile of Personality'? Could it detect the nonhuman? Could it cast a template which would compare too closely with William Bailey ... or any of the others they might have on their Data Center lists?

He sensed the dance of the intellects within him, pounding out their patterns on the floor of his awareness. In a way, he knew he was all the captive stalks bound up like a sheaf of grain.

The city-scape passing beneath the aircar became something sensed rather than seen. Tiny frenzies of fear began to dart about in him. What tools of psychometry would his interrogators use? How discreet? How subtle? Beneath their probes, he must be nothing other than Joe

Carmichael. Yet ... he was far more. He felt the current of *now* sweeping his existence toward peril.

Danger-danger-danger. He could see it intellectually as Tegas. He responded to it as Joe Carmichael.

Sweat drenched his body.

The aircar began to descend. He stared at the backs of the androids' heads visible through the glass of the control cab. They were two emotionless blobs; no help there. The car left the daylight, rocked once in a recognition-field, slid down a tube filled with cold aluminium light into the yellow glowing of a gigantic plastrete parking enclosure – tawny walls and ceiling, a sense of cavernous distance humming with activity.

It made the Tegas think of a hive society he'd once experienced; not one of his better memories. He shuddered.

The aircar found its parking niche, stopped. Presently, the doors hissed open. The androids flanked the opening. One gestured for him to emerge.

The Tegas swallowed in a dry Carmichael throat, climbed out, stared around at the impersonal comings and goings of androids. Neither by eye or emotional aura could he detect a human in the region around him. Intense loneliness came over him.

Still without speaking, the androids took his arms, propelled him across an open space into the half-cup of a ring lift. The field grabbed them, shot them upward past blurred walls and flickers of openings. The lift angled abruptly, holding them softly with their faces tipped downward at something near forty-five degrees. The androids remained locked beside him like two fish swimming in the air. The lift grip returned to vertical, shot them upward into the center of an amphitheater room.

The lift hole became floor beneath his feet.

The Tegas stared up and around at a reaching space, immense blue skylight, people-people-people, tiers of them peering down at him, tiers of them all around.

He probed for emotions, met the terrifying aura of the place, an icy neural stare, a psychic *chutzpah*. The watchers – rulers all, their minds disconnected from any religion except the *self*, no nervous coughs, no impatient stirrings.

They were an iceberg of silent waiting.

He had never imagined such a place even in a nightmare. But he knew this place, recognized it immediately. If a Tegas must end, he thought, then it must be in some such place as this. All the lost experiences that might come to an end here began wailing through him.

Someone emerged from an opening on his left, strode toward him across the floor of the amphitheater: Vicentelli.

The Tegas stared at the approaching man, noted the eyes favored by deep shadows: dense black eyes cut into a face where lay a verseless record – hard glyphs of cheeks, stone-cut mouth. Everything was labor in that face: work-work-work. It held no notion of fun. It was a contrivance for asserting violence, both spectator and participant. It rode the flesh, cherishing no soft thing at all.

A vat of liquid as blue as glowing steel arose from the floor beside the Tegas. Android hands gripped him tightly as he jerked with surprise.

Vicentelli stopped in front of him, glanced once at the surrounding banks of faces, back to his victim.

'Perhaps you're ready to save us the trouble of an interrogation in depth,' he said.

The Tegas felt his body tremble, shook his head.

Vicentelli nodded.

With impersonal swiftness, the androids stripped the clothing from the Tegas' host, lifted him into the vat. The liquid felt warm and tingling. A harness was adjusted to hold his arms and keep his face just above the surface. An inverted dome came down to rest just above his head. The day became a blue stick of light and he wondered inanely what time it was. It'd been early when he'd entered the Euthanasia Center, now, it was very late. Yet, he knew the day had hardly advanced past mid-morning.

Again, he probed the emotional aura, recoiled from it.

What if they kill me coldly? he wondered.

Where he could single out individuals, he was reminded of the play of lightning on a far horizon. The emotional beacons were thin, yet filled with potency.

A room full of rulers. The Tegas could imagine no more hideous place.

Something moved across his stick of light: Vicentelli.

'Who are you?' Vicentelli asked.

I'm Joe Carmichael, he thought. *I must be only Joe Carmichael.*

But Carmichael's emotions threatened to overwhelm him. Outrage and submissive terror flickered through the neural exchanges. The host body twitched. Its legs made faint running motions.

Vicentelli turned away, spoke to the surrounding watchers:

'The problem with Joseph Carmichael is this violent incident which you're now seeing on your recorders. Let me impress upon you that this incident was not predicted. It was outside our scope. We must assume, therefore, that it was not a product of Joseph Carmichael. During this examination, each of you will study the exposed profile. I want each of you to record your reactions and suggestions. Somewhere here there will be a clue to the unknowns we observed in William Bailey and before that in Almiro Hsing. Be alert, observant.'

God of Eternity! the Tegas thought. *They've traced me from Hsing to Bailey!*

This change in human society went back farther than he'd suspected. How far back?

'You will note, please,' Vicentelli said, 'that Bailey was in the immediate vicinity when Hsing fell from the Peace Tower at Canton and died. Pay particular attention to the material which points to a previous association between Hsing and Bailey. There is a possibility Bailey was at that particular place on Hsing's invitation. This could be important.'

The Tegas tried to withdraw his being, to encyst his emotions. The ruling humans had gone down a developmental side path he'd never expected. They had left him somewhere.

He knew why: Tegas-like, he had immersed himself in the concealing presence of the mob, retreated into daily drudgery, lived like the living. Yet, he had never loved the flesh more than in this moment when he knew he could lose it for ever. He loved the flesh the way a man might love a house. This intricate structure was a house that breathed and felt.

Abruptly, he underwent a sense of union with the flesh more intimate than anything of his previous experience. He knew for certain in this instant how a man would feel here. Time had never been an enemy of the Tegas. But Time was man's enemy. He was a man now and he prepared his flesh for maximum reactions, for high-energy discharge.

Control: that was what this society was up to – super control.

Vicentelli's face returned to the stick of light.

'For the sake of convenience,' he said, 'I'll continue to call you Carmichael.'

The statement told him baldly that he was in a corner and Vicentelli knew it. If the Tegas had any doubts, Vicentelli now removed them.

'Don't try to kill yourself,' Vicentelli said. 'The mechanism in which you now find yourself can sustain your life even when you least wish that life to continue.'

Abruptly, the Tegas realized his Carmichael self should be panic-stricken. There could be no Tegas watchfulness or remoteness here.

He was panic-stricken.

The host body thrashed in the liquid, surged against the bonds. The liquid was heavy – oily, but not oily. It held him as an elastic suit might, dampening his movements, always returning him to the quiescent, fishlike floating.

'Now,' Vicentelli said.

There was a loud click.

Light dazzled the Carmichael eyes. Color rhythms appeared within the light. The rhythms held an epileptic beat. They jangled his mind, shook the Tegas awareness like something loosed in a violent cage.

Out of the voice which his universe had become there appeared questions. He knew they were spoken questions, but he saw them: word shapes tumbling in a torrent.

'Who are you?'

'What are you?'

'We see you for what you are. Why don't you admit what you are? We know you.'

The aura of the surrounding watchers drummed at him with accusing vibrations: 'We know you – know you – know you – know you ...'

The Tegas felt the words rocking him, subduing him.

No Tegas can be hypnotized, he told himself. But he could feel his being coming out in shreds. Something was separating. Carmichael! The Tegas was losing his grip on the host! But the flesh was being reduced to a mesmerized idiot. The sense of separation intensified.

Abruptly, there was an inner sensation of stirring, awakening. He felt the host ego awakening, was powerless to counter it.

Thoughts crept along the dancing, shimmering neural paths –

'Who ... what are ... where do ...'

The Tegas punched frantically at the questings: 'I'm Joe Carmichael ... I'm Joe Carmichael ... I'm Joe Carmichael ...'

He found vocal control, mouthed the words in dumb rhythm, making this the one answer to all questions. Slowly, the host fell silent, smothered in a Tegas envelope.

The blundering, bludgeoning interrogation continued.

Shake-rattle-question.

He felt himself losing all sense of distinction between Tegas and Carmichael. The Bacit half, whipped and terrorized by the unexpected sophistication of this attack, strewed itself in tangles through the identity net.

Voices of old hosts came alive in his mind: '... you can't ... mustn't ... I'm Joe Carmichael ... stop them ... why can't we ...'

'You're murdering me!' he screamed.

The ranked watchers in the amphitheater united in an aura of pouncing glee.

'They're monsters!' Carmichael thought.

It was a pure Carmichael thought, unmodified by Tegas awareness, an unfettered human expression surging upwards from within.

'You hear me, Tegas?' Carmichael demanded. 'They're monsters!'

The Tegas crouched in the flesh not knowing how to counter this. Never before had he experienced direct communication from a host after that final entrapment. He tried to locate the source of communication, failed.

'Look at 'em staring down at us like a pack of ghouls!' Carmichael thought.

The Tegas knew he should react, but before he could bring himself to it, the interrogation assumed a new intensity: shake-rattle-question.

'Where do you come from? Where do you come from? Where do you come from?'

The question tore at him with letters tall as giant buildings – faceless eyes, thundering voices, shimmering words.

Carmichael anger surged across the Tegas.

Still, the watchers radiated their chill amusement.

'Let's die and take one of 'em!' Carmichael insisted.

'Who speaks?' the Bacit demanded. 'How did you get away? Where are you?'

'God! How cold they are.' That had been a Bailey thought.

'Where do you come from?' the Bacit demanded, seeking the host awareness. 'You are here, but we cannot find you.'

'I come from Zimbue,' Carmichael projected.

'You cannot come from Zimbue,' the Tegas countered. 'I come from Zimbue.'

'But Zimbue is nowhere,' the Bacit insisted.

And all the while – shake-rattle-question – Vicentelli's interrogation continued to jam circuits.

The Tegas felt he was being bombarded from all sides and from within. How could Carmichael talk of Zimbue?

'Then whence comest thou?' Carmichael asked.

How could Carmichael know of this matter? the Tegas asked himself. Whence had all Tegas come? The answer was a rote memory at the bottom of all his experiences: at the instant time began, the Tegas intruded upon the blackness where no star – not even a primal dust fleck – had tracked the dimensions with its being. They had been where senses had not been. How could Carmichael's ego still exist and know to ask of such things?

'And why shouldn't I ask?' Carmichael insisted. 'It's what Vicentelli asks.'

But where had the trapped ego of the host flesh hidden? Whence took it an existence to speak now?

The Bacit half had experienced enough. 'Say him down!' the Bacit commanded. 'Say him down! We are Joe Carmichael! You are Joe Carmichael! I am Joe Carmichael!'

'Don't panic,' Carmichael soothed. 'You are Tegas/Bacit, one being. I am Joe Carmichael.'

And from the outer world, Vicentelli roared: 'Who are you? I command you to tell me who you are! You must obey me! Are you William Bailey?'

Silence – inward and outward.

In the silence, the Tegas probed the abused flesh, understood part of the nature behind Vicentelli's attack. The liquid in which the host lay immersed: it was an anesthetic. The flesh was being robbed of sensation until only inner nerve tangles remained. Even more – the anesthetized flesh had been invaded by a control device. A throbbing capsule lay against the Carmichael spine – signalling, commanding, interfering.

'The capsule has been attached,' Vicentelli said. 'I will take him now to the lower chamber where the interrogation can proceed along normal channels. He's completely under our control now.'

In the trapped flesh, the Bacit half searched out neural connections of the control capsule, tried to block them, succeeded only partly. Anesthetized flesh resisted Bacit probes. The Tegas, poised like a frightened spider in the host awareness, studied the softly throbbing neural currents for a solution. Should he attack, resume complete control? What could he attack? Vicentelli's interrogation had tangled identities in the host in a way that might never be unravelled.

The control capsule pulsed.

Carmichael's flesh obeyed a new command. Restraining bands slid aside. The Tegas stood up in the tank on unfeeling feet. Where his chest was exposed, sensation began to return. The inverted hemisphere was lifted from his head.

'You see,' Vicentelli said, addressing the watchers above them. 'He obeys perfectly.'

Inwardly, Carmichael asked: 'Tegas, can you reach out and see how they feel about all this? There might be a clue in their emotions.'

'Do it!' the Bacit commanded.

The Tegas probed surrounding space, felt boredom, undertones of suspicion, a cat-licking sense of power. Yes, the mouse lay trapped between claws. The mouse could not escape.

Android hands helped the Tegas out of the tank, stood him on the floor, steadied him.

'Perfect control,' Vicentelli said.

As the control capsule commanded, the Carmichael eyes stared straight ahead with a blank emptiness.

The Tegas sent a questing probe along the nearest channels, met Bacit, Carmichael, uncounted bits of others.

'How can you be here, Joe Carmichael?' he asked.

The host flesh responded to a capsule command, walked straight ahead across the floor of the amphitheater.

'Why aren't you fleeing or fighting me?' the Tegas insisted.

'No need,' Carmichael responded. 'We're all mixed up together, as you can see.'

'Why aren't you afraid?'

'I was ... am ... hope not to be.'

'How do you know about the Tegas?'

'How not? We're each other.'

The Tegas experienced a shock-blink of awareness at this, felt an uneasy Bacit-projection. Nothing in all Tegas experience recalled such an inner encounter. The host fought and lost or the Tegas ended there. And the lost host went ... where? A fearful questing came from the Bacit, a sense of broken continuity.

That damnable interrogation!

The host flesh, responding to the capsule's commands, had walked through a doorway into a blue hallway. As sensation returned, Tegas/Carmichael/Bacit grew aware of Vicentelli following ... and other footsteps – android law-niks.

'What do you want, Joe Carmichael?' the Tegas demanded.

'I want to share.'

'Why?'

'You're ... more than I was. You can give me ... longer life. You're curious ... interesting. Half the creeps we got at the E-Center were worn down by boredom, and I was almost at that stage myself. Now ... living is interesting once more.'

'How can we live together – in here?'

'We're doing it.'

'But I'm Tegas! I must rule in here!'

'So rule.'

And the Tegas realized he had been restored to almost complete contact with the host's neural system. Still, the intrusive Carmichael ego remained. And the Bacit was doing nothing about this situation, appeared to have withdrawn to wherever the Bacit went. Carmichael remained – a slithering, mercuric thing: right there! No! Over here! No ... no ... not there, not here. Still, he remained.

'The host must submit without reservation,' the Tegas commanded.

'I submit,' Carmichael agreed.

'Then where are you?'

'We're all in here together. You're in command of the flesh, aren't you?'

The Tegas had to admit he was in command.

'What do you want, Joe Carmichael?' he insisted.

'I've told you.'

'You haven't.'

'I want to ... watch ... to share.'

'Why should I let you do that?'

Vicentelli and his control capsule had brought the host flesh now to a drop chute. The chute's field gripped the Carmichael flesh, sent it whispering downward ... downward ... downward.

'Maybe you have no choice in whether I stay and watch,' Joe Carmichael responded.

'I took you once,' the Tegas countered. 'I can take you again.'

'What happens when they resume the interrogation?' Carmichael asked.

'What do you mean?'

'He means,' the Bacit intruded, 'that the true Joe Carmichael can respond with absolute verisimilitude to their search for a profile comparison.'

The drop chute disgorged him into a long icy-white laboratory space. Through the fixated eyes came a sensation of metal shapes, of instruments, of glitterings and flashings, of movement.

The Tegas stood in capsule-induced paralysis. It was a condition any Tegas could override, but he dared not. No human could surmount this neural assault. The merest movement of a finger now amounted to exposure.

In the shared arena of their awareness, Carmichael said: 'Okay, let me have the con for a while. Watch. Don't intrude at all.'

The Tegas hesitated.

'Do it!' the Bacit commanded.

The Tegas withdrew. He found himself in emptiness, a nowhere of the mind, an unseen place, constrained vacuity ... nothing ... never ... an unspoken, unspeaking pill of absence ... uncontained. This was a place where senses had not been, could not be. He feared it, but felt protected by it – hidden.

A sense of friendship and reassurance came to him from Carmichael. The Tegas felt a hopeless sense of gratitude for the first other-creature friendship he'd ever experienced. But why should Carmichael-ego be friendly? Doubt worried at him, nipped and nibbled. Why?

No answer came, unless an unmeasured simplicity radiating from the Bacit could be interpreted as answer. The Tegas found he had an economy of reservations about his position. This astonished him. He recognized he was making something new with all the dangers inherent in newness. It wasn't logical, but he knew thought might be the least careless when it was the least logical.

Time is the enemy of the flesh, he reminded himself. *Time is not my enemy.*

Reflections of meaning, actions, and intentions began coming to him from the outer-being-place where Carmichael sat. Vicentelli had returned to the attack with induced colors, shapes, flarings and dazzles. Words leaped across a Tegas mind-sky: 'Who are you? Answer! I know you're there! Answer! Who are you?'

Joe Carmichael mumbled half-stupefied protests: 'Why're you torturing me? What're y'doing?'

Shake-rattle-question: 'STOP HIDING FROM ME!'

Carmichael's response wiggled outwards: 'Wha' y'doing?'

Silence enveloped the flesh.

The Tegas began receiving muted filterings of a debate: 'I tell you, his profile matches the Carmichael identity with exactness.' ... 'Saw him change.' ... '... perhaps chemical poisoning ... Euthanasia Center ... consistent with ingestion of picrotoxin ... coincidence ...'

Creeping out into the necessary neural channels, the Tegas probed his surroundings for the emotional aura, found only Vicentelli and two androids. The androids were frigid, emotionless shells. Vicentelli was a blazing core of frustrated anger.

Voices rained from a communications screen in the lab ceiling: 'Have an end to it!' 'Eliminate him and have done with it!' 'This is a waste of time!' 'You're mistaken, Vic!' 'Stop wasting our time!'

They were commanding death for the Carmichael flesh, the Tegas realized. He thought of an arena, its rim dripping with thumbs: death. Those had been the days – short-lived hosts and easy transfers. But now: would he dare tackle Vicentelli? It was almost certain failure, and the Tegas knew it. The hard shell of a ruler's ego could resist any assault.

A sharp 'snap!' echoed in the lab. The communications screen went blank.

What now? the Tegas wondered.

'If Bailey's death didn't eliminate it,' Vicentelli muttered, 'why should the death of Carmichael be any different? What can stop it? The thing survived Hsing, and lord knows how many before that.'

The Tegas felt his Bacit half flexing unseen membranes.

'If I'm right,' Vicentelli muttered, 'the thing lives on for ever in host bodies. It lives – enjoys ... What if life were not ... enjoyable?'

'The death of this human has been commanded,' one of the androids said. 'Do you wish us to leave?'

'Leave ... yes,' Vicentelli said.

The frigid android radiations receded, were gone.

The other rulers who'd been watching through the screen were convinced Vicentelli was wrong, the Tegas realized. But they'd commanded death for Carmichael. The androids had been sent away, of course: they could have no part in a human death.

The Tegas felt Carmichael cringing, demanding: 'What'll we do?'

The Bacit tested a muscle in the host's left arm, a muscle the Tegas host had never before consciously sensed. Flesh rippled, relaxed.

'Exposure means final dissolution,' the Tegas warned. It was his most basic inhibition. 'We must remain cryptic in color and behaviour, impossible to separate from any background.'

'We're already exposed!' It was a pure Joe Carmichael thought. 'What'll we do?'

A sensation of flowing wetness radiated from the control capsule on the host's spine.

'All right,' Vicentelli said. 'They don't believe me. But we're alone now.' He stared into Carmichael eyes. 'And I can try whatever I want. What if your life isn't enjoyable, eh?'

The sensation of wetness reached the brain.

Immediate blackness!

The Tegas recoiled upward, fighting past the neural shock, regaining some awareness. Carmichael's neurosystem quivered and rolled, filtered out some sounds, let others through with a booming roar. The Tegas felt outraged by scraping tactility – harsh movements, rollings.

Vicentelli was doing something at a glittering console directly in front of him.

The rolling sensation went on and on and on – swaying, dipping, gliding ... and pain.

Tegas, measuring out his attention, felt the shuttlecock entanglements of his being with that of Carmichael. Blank spots were Carmichael ... fuzzy grayness ... and tightly stretched threads that linked bulbs of ego-reserve. There! There! And there! Pieces of Carmichael, all quiescent.

The Bacit nudged his awareness, an inner touch like the prickling of cactus spines. Whisper-thoughts came: 'Got to get out of here. Trapped. Got to get out of here. Trapped-trapped.'

He was forming verbal concepts in thousands of languages simultaneously.

What was Vicentelli doing?

The Tegas felt a pulse from the control capsule. A leg twitched. He snapped a reflex block on to that neural region to resume control. One eye opened, rolled. The Tegas fought for control of the visual centers, saw a multi-faceted creation of wires and crystals directly above him, blurs of green movement. All focused on the control capsule. The host's flesh felt as though it had been encased in a tight skin.

Vicentelli swam into his range of vision.

'Now, let us see how long you can hide,' Vicentelli said. 'We call this the torture skin.' He moved something on the control console.

Tegas felt alertness return. He moved a left foot. Pain slashed at knee and ankle.

He gasped. Pain raked his back and chest.

'Very good,' Vicentelli said. 'It's the movements you make, do you understand? Remain unmoving, no pain. Move – pain.'

Tegas permitted his host to take a deep, quivering breath. Knives played with his chest and spine.

'To breathe, to flex a wrist, to walk – all equal pain,' Vicentelli said. 'The beauty of it is there's no bodily harm. But you'll pray for something simple as injury unless you give up.'

'You're an animal!' the Tegas managed. Agony licked along his jaw and lips, flayed his temples.

'Give up,' Vicentelli said.

'Animal,' the Tegas whispered. He felt his Bacit half throwing pain blocks into the neural system, tried a shallow breath. Faint irritation rewarded the movement, but he simulated a pain reaction – closed his eyes. Fire crept along his brows. A swift block eased the pain.

'Why prolong it?' Vicentelli asked. 'What are you?'

'You're insane,' Tegas whispered. He waited, feeling the pain blocks click into place.

Darting lights glittered in Vicentelli's eyes. 'Do you really feel the pain?' he asked. He moved a handle on the console.

The host was hurled to the floor by a flashing command from the control capsule.

Under Bacit guidance, he writhed with the proper pain reactions, allowed them to subside slowly.

'You feel it,' Vicentelli said. 'Good.' He reached down, jerked his victim upright, steadied him.

The Bacit had almost all the pain under control, signalling proper concealment reactions. The host flesh grimaced, resisted movement, stood awkwardly.

'I have all the time I need,' Vicentelli said. 'You cannot outlast me. Surrender. Perhaps I may even find a use for you. I know you're there, whatever you are. You must realize this by now. You can speak candidly with me. Confess. Explain yourself. What are you? What use can I make of you?'

Moving his lips stiffly as though against great pain, Tegas said: 'If I were what you suggest, what would I fear from such as you?'

'Very good!' Vicentelli crowed. 'We progress. What should you fear from me? Hah! And what should I fear from you?'

'Madman,' Tegas whispered.

'Ahh, now,' Vicentelli said. 'Hear if this is mad: my profile on you says I should fear you only if you die. Therefore, I will not kill you. You may wish to die, but I will not permit you to die. I can keep the body alive indefinitely. It will not be an enjoyable life, but it will be life. I can make you breathe. I can make your heart work. Do you wish a full demonstration?'

The inner whispers resumed and the Tegas fought against them. 'We can't escape. Trapped.'

The Bacit radiated hesitant uncertainty.

A Bailey thought: 'It's a nightmare! That's what!'

Tegas stood in wonder: a Bailey thought!

Bacit admonitions intruded: 'Be still. We must work together, Serenity ... serenity ... serenity ...'

The Tegas felt himself drifting off on waves of tranquility, was shocked by a Bacit thought-scream: 'NOT YOU!'

Vicentelli moved one of his console controls.

Tegas let out a muffled scream as both his arms jerked upward.

Another Vicentelli adjustment and Tegas bent double, whipped upright.

Bacit-prompted whimpering sounds escaped his lips.

'What are you?' Vicentelli asked in his softest voice.

Tegas sensed the frantic inner probings as the Bacit searched out the neural linkages, blocked them. Perspiration bathed the host flesh.

'Very well,' Vicentelli said. 'Let us go for a long hike.'

The host's legs began pumping up and down in a stationary march. Tegas stared straight ahead, pop-eyed with simulation of agony.

'This will end when you answer my questions,' Vicentelli said. 'What are you? Hup-two-three-four. Who are you? Hup-two-three-four ...'

The host flesh jerked with obedience to the commands.

Tegas again felt the thousands of old languages taking place within him – a babble. With an odd detachment, he realized he must be a museum of beings and remembered energies.

'Ask yourself how long you can stand this,' Vicentelli said.

'I'm Joe Carmichael,' he gasped.

Vicentelli stepped close, studied the evidences of agony. 'Hup-two-three-four ...'

Still, the babble persisted. He was a flow of energy, Tegas realized. Energy ... energy ... energy. Energy was the only *solid* in the universe. He was wisdom seated in a bed of languages. But wisdom chastised the wise and spat upon those who came to pay homage. Wisdom was for copyists and clerks.

Power, then, he thought.

But power, when exercised, fragmented.

How simple to attack Vicentelli now, Tegas thought. *We're alone. No one is watching. I could strike him down in an instant.*

The habits of all that aeons-long history inhibited action. Inevitably, he had picked up some of the desires, hopes and fears – especially the fears – of his uncounted hosts. Their symbols sucked at him now.

A pure Bailey thought: 'We can't keep this up for ever.'

The Tegas felt Bailey's sharings, the Carmichael's, the mysterious coupling of selves, the never-before engagement with the captive.

'One clean punch,' Carmichael insisted.

'Hup-two-three-four,' Vicentelli said, peering closely at his victim.

Abruptly, the Tegas felt himself looking inward from the far end of his being. He saw all his habits of thought contained in the shapes of every action he'd ever contemplated. The thoughts took form to control flesh, a blaze of energy, a *solid*. In that flaring instant, he became pure performance. All the violent killers the Tegas had overwhelmed rose up in him, struck outward, and he *was* the experience – overpoweringly single with it, not limited by any description ... without symbols.

Vicentelli lay unconscious on the floor.

Tegas stared at his own right hand. The thing had taken on a life of its own. Its movement had been unique to the moment, a flashing jab with fingers extended, a crushing impact against a nerve bundle in Vicentelli's neck.

Have I killed him? he wondered.

Vicentelli stirred, groaned.

So there'd been Tegas inhibitions on the blow, an exquisite control that could overpower but not kill, the Tegas thought.

Tegas moved to Vicentelli's head, stooped to examine him. Moving, he felt the torture skin relax, glanced up at the green-gloving construction, realized the thing's field was limited.

Again, Vicentelli groaned.

Tegas pressed the nerve bundle in the man's neck. Vicentelli subsided, went limp.

Pure Tegas thoughts rose up in the Carmichael neural system. He realized he'd been living for more than a century immersed in a culture which had regressed. They had invented a new thing – almost absolute control – but it held an old pattern. The Egyptians had tried it, and many before them, and a few since. The Tegas thought of the phenomenon as the man-machine. Pain controlled it – and food ... pleasure, ritual.

The control capsule irritated his senses. He felt the aborted action message, a faint echo, Bacit-repressed: 'Hup-two-three-four ...' With the action message went the emotional inhibitions deadly to Tegas survival.

The Tegas felt sensually subdued. He thought of a world where no concentrated emotions remained, no beacons upon which he could home his short-burst transfer of identity.

The Carmichael flesh shuddered to a Tegas response. The Bacit stirred, transmitting sensations of urgency.

Yes, there was urgency. Androids might return. Vicentelli's fellow rulers might take it upon themselves to check the activity of this room.

He reached around to his back, felt the control capsule: a flat, tapered package ... cold, faintly pulsing. He tried to insert a finger beneath it, felt the flesh rebel. Ahhh, the linkage was mortal. The diabolic thing joined the spine. He explored the connections internally, realized the thing could be removed, given time and the proper facilities.

But he had not the time.

Vicentelli's lips made feeble writhings – a baby's mouth searching for the nipple.

Tegas concentrated on Vicentelli. A ruler. Tegas rightly avoided such as this. Vicentelli's kind knew how to resist the mind-swarm. They had ego power.

Perhaps the Vicentellis had provided the key to their own destruction, though. Whatever happened, the Tegas knew he could never return into the human mass. The new man-machine provided no hiding place. In this day of new things, another new thing had to be tried.

Tegas reached for the control capsule on his back, inserted three fingers beneath it. With the Bacit blocking off the pain, he wrenched the capsule free.

All sensation left his lower limbs. He collapsed across Vicentelli, brought the capsule around to study it. The removal had dealt a mortal blow to the Carmichael host, but there were no protests in their shared awareness, only a deep curiosity about the capsule.

Simple, deadly thing – operation obvious. Barbed needles protruded along its inner surface. He cleaned shreds of flesh from them, working fast. The host was dying rapidly, blood pumping on to the floor – and spinal fluid. He levered himself on to one elbow, rolled Vicentelli on to one side, pulled away the man's jacket and shirt. A bit of fleshly geography, a ridge of spine lay exposed.

Tegas knew this landscape from the inward examination of the capsule. He gauged the position required, slapped the capsule home.

Vicentelli screamed.

He jerked away, scrabbled across the floor, leaped upright.

'Hup-two-three-four ...'

His legs jerked up and down in terrible rhythm. Sounds of agony escaped his lips. His eyes rolled.

The Carmichael body slumped to the floor, and Tegas waited for the host to die. Too bad about this host – a promising one – but he was committed now. No turning back.

Death came as always, a wink-out, and after the flicker of blankness, he centered on the emotional scream which was Vicentelli. The Tegas divided from dead flesh, bore away with that always-new sensation of supreme discovery – a particular thing, relevant to nothing else in the universe except himself.

He was pain.

But it was pain he had known, analyzed, understood and could isolate. The pain contained all there was of Vicentelli's identity. Encapsulated that way, it could be absorbed piecemeal, shredded off at will. And the new host's flesh was grateful. With the Tegas came surcease from pain.

Slowly, the marching subsided.

The Tegas blocked off control circuits, adjusted Vicentelli's tunic to conceal the capsule on his back, paused to contemplate how easy this capture had been. It required a dangerous change of pattern, yes: a Tegas must dominate, risk notice – not blend with his surroundings.

With an abrupt sense of panic, William Bailey came alive in his awareness. 'We made it!'

In that instant, the Tegas was hanging by the hook of his being, momentarily lost in the host he'd just captured. The intermittency of mingled egos terrified and enthralled. As he had inhabited others, now he was inhabited.

Even the new host – silent, captivated – became part of a changed universe, one that threatened in a different way: all maw. He realized he'd lost contact with the intellectual centers. His path touched only nerve ends. He had no home for his breath, couldn't find the flesh to wear it.

Bacit signals darted around him: a frantic, searching clamor. The flesh – the flesh – the flesh ...

He'd worn the flesh too gently, he realized. He'd been lulled by its natural laws and his own. He'd put aside all reaching questions about the organism, had peered out of the flesh unconcerned, leaving all worries to the Bacit.

One axiom had soothed him: *The Bacit knows.*

But the Bacit was loosed around him and he no longer held the flesh. The flesh held him, a grip so close it threatened to choke him.

The flesh cannot choke me, he thought. *It cannot. I love the flesh.*

Love – there was a toehold, a germ of contact. The flesh remembered how he had eased its agony. Memories of other flesh intruded. Tendrils of association accumulated. He thought of all the flesh he'd loved on this world: the creatures with their big eyes, their ears flat against their heads, smooth caps of hair, beautiful mouths and cheeks. The Tegas always noticed mouths. The mouth betrayed an infinite variety of things about the flesh around it.

A Vicentelli self-image came into his awareness, swimming like a ghost in a mirror. The Tegas thought about the verseless record, the stone-cut mouth. No notion of fun – that was the thing about Vicentelli's mouth.

He'll have to learn fun now, the Tegas thought.

He felt the feet then, hard against the floor, and the Bacit was with him. But the Bacit had a voice that touched the auditory centers from within. It was the voice of William Bailey and countless others.

'Remove the signs of struggle before the androids return,' the voice said.

He obeyed, looked down at the empty flesh which had been Joe Carmichael. But Joe Carmichael was with him in this flesh, Vicentelli's flesh, which still twitched faintly to the broadcast commands transmitted through the capsule on his spine.

'Have to remove the capsule as soon as possible,' the Bacit voice reminded. 'You know the way to do it.'

The Tegas marveled at the Vicentelli overtones suddenly noticeable in the voice. Abruptly, he glimpsed the dark side of his being through Vicentelli, and he saw an aspect of the Bacit he'd never suspected. He realized he was a net of beings who enjoyed their captivity, were strong in their captivity, would not exchange it for any other existence.

They *were* Tegas in a real sense, moving him by habits of thought, shaping actions out of uncounted mediations. The Bacit half had accumulated more than forty centuries of mediations on this one world. And there were uncounted worlds before this one.

Language and thought.

Language was the instrument of the sentient being – yet, the being was the instrument of language as Tegas was the instrument of the Bacit. He searched for significant content in this new awareness, was chided by the Bacit's sneer. To search for content was to search for limits where there were no limits. Content was logic and classification. It was a word sieve through which to judge experience. It was nothing in itself, could never satisfy.

Experience, that was the thing. Action. The infinite reenactment of life accompanied by its endless procession of images.

There are things to be done, the Tegas thought.

The control capsule pulsed on his spine.

The capsule, yes – and many more things.

They have bugged the soul, he thought. *They've mechanized the soul and are for ever damned. Well, I must join them for a while.*

He passed a hand through a call beam, summoned the androids to clear away the discarded host that had been Carmichael.

A door opened at the far end of the lab. Three androids entered, marching in line towards him. They were suddenly an amusing six-armed figure, their arms moving that way in obedient cadence.

The Vicentelli mouth formed an unfamiliar smile.

Briefly he set the androids to the task of cleaning up the mess in the lab. Then, the Tegas began the quiet exploration of his new host, a task he found remarkably easy with his new understanding. The host cooperated. He explored Vicentelli slowly – strong, lovely, healthy flesh – explored as one might explore a strange land, swimming across coasts of awareness that loomed and receded.

A host had behavior that must be learned. It was not well to dramatize the Tegas difference. There would be changes, of course – but slow ones; nothing dramatic in its immediacy.

While he explored he thought of the mischief he could do in this new role. There were so many ways to disrupt the man-machine, to revive individualism, to have fun. Lovely mischief.

Intermittently, he wondered what had become of the Bailey ego and the Joe Carmichael ego. Only the Bacit remained in the host with him, and the Bacit transmitted a sensation of laughter.

TWO
ROBOT CRIME

INTERFACE:/
A human being may shoot a robot which has come out of a General Electrics factory, and to his surprise see it weep and bleed. And the dying robot may shoot back and, to its surprise, see a wisp of grey smoke arise from the electric pump that it supposed was the human's beating heart. It would be rather a great moment of truth for both of them.

Philip K. Dick
The Android and the Human (1973)

ONLINE: **TWO/1** Subject: The Rackets Game

The Undercity

Dean Koontz

INFO: In the Undercity, robots run most things and there's not a lot of the old-time crime that is still illegal. But a man can always find a racket of some kind or another in which to make a quick buck. In this particular scam, cybernetics meets hard-boiled fiction.

Dean Koontz is one of the few authors whose worldwide sales come near to matching those of Stephen King. Despite his fame as a horror novelist – although his books are much more diverse than that – Dean actually started out writing science fiction. Several of his stories featured robots and cyborgs as central characters, including 'Killerbot' and 'A Third Hand', plus his novels *Anti-Man* (1970) and *A Werewolf Among Us* (1973). Born in Bedford, Pennsylvania, Dean began to write while he was struggling to make a living as a teacher, and published a number of sf and suspense paperbacks under various pen-names. (One of his early novels, *Invasion* by 'Aaron Wolfe', was for a time rumoured to have been written by Stephen King.) Dean is an admirer of the hard-boiled school of crime fiction and rates Dick Francis as one of the best contemporary writers in this tradition. Criminal killers have featured in some of his most recent books – notably *Mr Murder*, published in 1993, which many fans rate as his best work. 'The Undercity' was originally published in *Future City* in 1973.

Well, kid, it was a busy day. You might even say it was a harrowing day, and you might be tempted to think that it was somehow out of the ordinary. But you must understand, straight off, that it was perfectly normal as business days go, no better and no worse than ten thousand days before it. And if I live so long, it won't be appreciably different from any of ten thousand days to follow. Remember that. If you want to enter the family business, kid, you have to be able to cope with long strings of days like this one, calendars full of them.

Once, when the cities weren't a tenth as large as they are now, when a man might travel and might have business contacts throughout the world, we were called The Underworld, and we were envied and feared. We are still envied and feared, but now we're called The Undercity, because that is the world to us, and more than we can rightly handle anyway. I, for one, would be happy to roll things back, to break down these hundred-story megalopolises and live in a time where we could call ourselves a part of The Underworld, because things were a hell of a lot easier then for our type. Just consider ...

Nearly all forms of gambling were illegal back then. An enterprising young man could step in, buck the law, and clean up a tidy sum with a minimal financial outlay and with almost no personal risk at all. Cops and judges were on the take, clandestine casinos, street games and storefront betting shops thrived. No longer. They legalized it, and they gave us bank clerks for casino managers, CPAs instead of bouncers. They made gambling respectable – and boring.

Drugs were illegal then, too. Grass, hash, skag, coke, speed ... God, an enterprising young kid like yourself could make a fortune in a year. But now grass and hash are traded on the open market, and all the harder drugs are available to all the loonies who will sign a health waiver and buy them from the government. Where's the thrill now? Gone. And where's the profit? Gone, too.

Sex. Oh, kid, the money to be made on sex, back then. It was *all* illegal: prostitution, dirty movies, picture postcards, erotic dancing, adultery, you name it! Now the government licenses the brothels, both male and female, and the wife or husband without a lover on the side is considered a throwback. Is this any way to make a buck?

Hell, kid, even murder was illegal in those days, and a man could buy the big trip for wiping someone off the slate. As you know, some folks never can seem to learn the niceties of civilized life – their manners are atrocious, their business methods downright devious, their insults unnecessarily public and demanding – and these people need to be eliminated from the social sphere. Now we have the code duello, through which a man can settle his grudges and satisfy his honor, all legally. The once-lucrative career as a hired assassin has gone the way of the five-dollar streetwalker.

Now, kid, you have got to hustle all day, every day, if you want to survive in this business. You've got to be resourceful, clever and forward-thinking if you expect to meet the competition. Let me tell you how the day went, because it was a day like all days ...

I bolted down a breakfast of protein paste and cafa, then met Lew Boldoni on the fifth subbasement level in Wing-L, where only the repair robots go. Boldoni was waiting on the robotwalk beside the beltway, carrying his tool satchel, watching the cartons of perishables move past him.

'On time,' he said.

I said, 'As usual.' Time is money; cliché but true.

We removed the access plate to the beltway workings, went down under the robotwalk. In less than five minutes, we were directly beneath the big belt, barely able to shout above the roar, buffeted by the wind of its continuous passage. Together, we opened one of the hydraulic lines and let the lubricant spew out over the traffic computer terminal, where it was sure to seep through and do some damage. Before a fire could start, we were out of there, up on the sidewalk again, putting the access plate back where it belonged. That done, just as the alarms were beginning to clang, we went in different directions.

We both had other business.

This bit of sabotage wouldn't pay off until much later in the day.

At 9:30 in the morning, right on time, I met a young couple – Gene and Miriam Potemkin – in a public hydroponics park on the eighty-third level, in that neighborhood they call Chelsea. She was twenty-one and a looker, bright and curious and unhappy. He was a year older than she was, but that was the only real difference between them. They sat on a bench by an artificial waterfall, both of them leaning forward as I approached, both with their hands folded in their laps, more like sister and brother than like wife and husband.

'Did you bring it?' he asked.

I removed a sealed envelope from my pocket, popped the seal and let them see the map inside, though I was careful not to let them handle it just then. I said, 'And you?'

She lifted a small plastic satchel from the ground beside her and took another sealed envelope from it, reluctantly handed it over.

I opened it, counted the money, nodded, tucked the envelope into my pocket and gave them the map.

'Wait a minute, here!' Mr Potemkin said. 'According to this damn map, we'll be going out through the sewer! You know that's not possible. Sewage is pumped at pressure, and there's no way to survive in the system.'

'True enough,' I said. 'But if you'll look closely at the map, you'll see that the sewage line is encased inside a larger pipe, from which repairs can be made to the system. This larger pipe is everywhere twenty feet in diameter, sometimes as much as thirty, and is always enough larger than the sewage pipe itself to give you adequate crawl space.'

'I don't know,' he said. 'It doesn't look easy ...'

'No way out of the city is easy, for God's sake!' I told him. 'Look, Potemkin, the city fathers say that the open land, beyond the cities, is unlivable. It's full of poisoned air, poisoned water, plague, and hostile plant and animal life. That's why the air freight exits are the only ones that are maintained, and that's why they're so carefully supervised. City law forbids anyone to leave the city for fear they'll return bearing one of the plagues from Outside. Now, considering all of this, could you reasonably expect me to provide you with an *easy* way out?'

'I suppose not.'

'And that's damn straight.'

Ms Potemkin said, 'It's really not like that Outside, is it? The stories of plagues, poisoned air and water, monsters – all of that's just so much bunk.'

'I wouldn't know,' I said.

'But you must know!'

'Oh?'

'You've shown us the way out,' she said. 'You must have seen what's beyond the city.'

'I'm afraid not,' I said. 'I employ engineers, specialists, who work from diagrams and blueprints. None of my people would consider leaving the city; we've got too much going for us here.'

'But,' she insisted, 'by sending us, you're showing your distrust of the old stories about the Outside.'

'Not at all,' I explained. 'Once you've gone, my men will seal off this escape route so you can't come back that way, just in case you might bring a plague with you.'

'And you won't sell it again?'

'No. We'll find other ways out. There are millions of them.'

They looked at each other, unsure of themselves now.

I said, 'Look, you haven't committed the map to memory. If you want, I can take it back and return half your money.'

'No,' he said.

She said, 'We've made up our minds. We need open land, something more than layer on layer of enclosed streets and corridors.'

'Suit yourself,' I said. 'And good luck.'

I shook their hands and got the hell out of there; things to do, things to do ...

Moving like a maintenance robot on an emergency call, I dropped down to the subbasements again, to the garbage monitoring decks, where I met with the day-shift manager, K. O. Wilson. We shook hands at precisely 10:20, five minutes behind schedule, and we went into the retrieval chamber, where he had the first two hours of discoveries laid out in neat, clean order.

Kid, I don't think I've ever talked about this angle of the family business before, because I'm not that proud of it. It's the cheapest form of scavenging, no matter how lucrative it is. And it *is* lucrative. You see, the main pipes of the garbage shuttle system are monitored electronically and filtered to remove any articles of value that might otherwise be funneled into the main sewage lines and pumped out of the city. I've got K. O. Wilson, of the first shift, and Marty Linnert, of the second shift, on my payroll. They see to it that I have time to look over the day's findings before they're catalogued and sent up to the city's lost-and-found bureau. Before you think too badly of your old man, consider that 20 per cent of the family's gross comes from the garbage operation.

'Six valuable rings, a dozen good watches, what appears to be one folder of a top-quality coin collection, a diamond tiara, and a mess of other junk,' Wilson told me, pointing to the good items, which he had set aside for me.

I ignored the watches, took two of the rings, the tiara and the damp folder full of old coins. 'Nothing else?'

'A corpse,' he said. 'That'll interest the cops. I put it on ice until you could get in and check over your stuff first.'

'A murder?' I asked.

'Yeah.'

Kid, the code duello hasn't solved everything. There are still those who are afraid to fight, who prefer to sneak about and repay their enemies illegally. And there are also those who aren't satisfied with taking economic and emotional revenge from those not eligible for the duels; they insist on blood, and they have it. Eventually, the law has them. We're not involved with people of this sort, but you should know the kind of scum that the city still supports.

I told Wilson, 'I'll send a man around after noon to see what else you've got by then.'

Ten minutes later, at 10:53, I walked into the offices of Boldoni and Gia Cybernetic Repairs, on the ninety-second floor, Wing-B, where I acted very shocked about the breakdown in the beltway system.

'City Engineer Willis left an urgent message for you,' my secretary said. She handed it to me and said, 'It's a beltway carrying perishables in the fifth subbasement.'

'Is Mr Boldoni there?' I asked.

'He accompanied the first repair team,' she said.

'Call down and tell Willis I'm on my way.'

I used the express drop and almost lost my protein paste and cafa – any inconvenience for a good customer, and the city is the best customer that Boldoni and Gia Cybernetic Repairs has on its list.

Willis was waiting for me by the beltway. He's a small man with very black hair and very dark eyes and a way of moving that makes you think of a maintenance robot with a short between his shoulder blades. He scuttled toward me and said, 'What a mess!'

'Tell me,' I said.

'The main hydraulic line broke over the traffic computer terminal and a fire started in the works.'

'That doesn't sound so bad,' I said.

He wiped his small face with one large hand and said, 'It wouldn't have been if it had stopped there. We've got the fire out already. The only trouble is that the lubricant has run back the lines into the main traffic computer and the damn thing won't shut down. I've got perishables moving up out of the subterranean coolers, and no way to move them or stop them. They're piling up on me fast, Mr Gia. I have to have this beltway moving inside the hour or the losses are going to be staggering.'

'We'll do the job,' I assured him.

'I went out on the limb, calling you before you could deliver a quick computerized estimate. But I knew you people were the fastest, and I needed someone who could be here immediately.'

'Don't you worry about it,' I told him. 'Whatever the B & G Computer estimates we'll shave by ten per cent to keep your bosses happy.'

Willis was ecstatic, thanking me again and again. He didn't understand that the Boldoni and Gia house computer always estimated an additional and quite illegal 15 per cent surprofit, more than negating the 10 per cent discount I'd given him.

While he was still thanking me, Lew Boldoni came up from the access tunnel, smeared with lubricant, looking harried and nervous and exhausted. Lew is an excellent actor, and that is another qualification for success in this business.

'How is it down there?' I asked.

'Bad,' Boldoni said.

Willis groaned.

Boldoni said, 'But we're winning it.'

'How long?' I asked.

'We'll have the beltway moving in an hour, with a jury-rigged system, and then we can take our time with the permanent repairs.'

Willis groaned again, differently this time: in happiness.

I said, 'Mr Boldoni has everything in control, Mr Willis. I'm sure that you'll be in business as usual shortly. Now, if you'll excuse me, I've got some other urgent business to attend to.'

I went up in the express elevator, which was worse than coming down, since my stomach seemed to reach the fifty-ninth floor seconds before the rest of me.

I boarded a horizontal beltway and rode twelve miles east, the last six down Y-Wing. At 11:40, ten minutes behind schedule, I entered an office in the Chesterfield District where a nonexistent Mr Lincoln Pliney supposedly did business. There, I locked the outer door, apologized for my tardiness to the two people waiting in the reception area, then led them into Lincoln Pliney's private office. I locked that door too, went to the desk, checked out my bug-detecting equipment, made sure the room hadn't been tapped, then sat down behind my desk, offered the customers a drink, poured, sat back and introduced myself under a false name.

My visitors were Arthur Coleman, a rather successful industrialist with offices on the hundredth level, and Eileen Romaine, a lovely girl, fifteen years Coleman's junior. We had all come together in order to negotiate a marriage between Coleman and Romaine, an illegal marriage.

'Tell me, Mr Coleman,' I said, 'just why you wish to risk the fines and prison sentences involved with this violation of the Equal Rights Act?'

He squirmed a bit and said, 'Do you have to put it that way?'

I said, 'I believe a customer must know the consequences before he can be fairly expected to enter a deal like this.'

'Okay,' he said. 'Well, I've been married four times under the standard city contract, and all four marriages have terminated in divorce at my instigation. I'm a very unhappy man, sir. I've got this ... well, perversion that dominates the course of my private life. I need a wife who ... who is not my equal, who is subservient, who plays a dated role as nothing more than my bedmate and my housekeeper. I want to dominate any marital situation that I enter.'

I said, 'Conscious male chauvinism is a punishable crime.'

'As I'm aware.'

'Have you seen a robopsych?' I asked. 'Perhaps one of those could cure you of your malady.'

'I'm sure it could,' he said. 'But you see, I don't really want to be cured. I *like* myself the way I am. I *like* the idea of a woman waiting on me and making her own life conditioned to mine.'

'And you?' I asked Eileen.

She nodded, an odd light in her eyes, and she said, 'I don't like the responsibility of the standard marriage. I want a man who will put me in my place, a man I can look up to, admire, depend on.'

I tell you, kids, these antiquated lusts of theirs were distasteful to me. However, I believe in rebels, both good and bad, being a rebel myself, and I was ready to help them. Both had come to me by word-of-mouth referral within the past month. I'd researched the lives of both, built up two thick dossiers, matched them, and called them here for their first and final meeting under my auspices.

'You have both paid me a finder's fee,' I told them. 'Now, you will have sixty days to get to know each other. At the end of that time, you will either fail to contact me about a finalization of the contract, in which case I'll know you've found each other unsuitable, or you'll come back here and set up an appointment with my robosec. If you find you like each other, it will be a simple matter to arrange an illegal marriage, without the standard city contract.'

Coleman wasn't satisfied with that. He said, 'Just how will you pull this off, Mr Pliney?'

'The first step, of course, is to have Eileen certified dead and disposed of. My people will falsify a death report and have it run through the city records. This may sound like an incredible feat to you; it is nevertheless possible. Once Eileen Romaine has ceased to exist, we will create a false persona in the name of Eileen Coleman. She will be identified as your sister; an entire series of life records will be planted in the computers to solidify her false identity. She can, naturally, then come to live with you, without the city records people realizing that there is anything sexual in your cohabitation.'

'If you can do it,' Coleman said, 'you're a genius.'

'No, just clever,' I said. 'And I will do it. In fact, on any date you pick, I'll have a man at your apartment to officiate at a clandestine wedding using the ancient, male chauvinist rituals.'

'There will be no psycheprobes, as there are in other marriages?' she asked.

'Of course not,' I said. 'The city will have no reason to psycheprobe you under the Equal Rights Act because you won't, so far as the city is concerned, be married at all.'

At that point, she burst into tears and said, 'Mr Pliney, you are the first person, outside of Arthur here, who's ever understood me.'

I set her straight on that, kid, believe me. I said, 'Lady, I don't understand you at all, but I sympathize with rebels. You're chucking out total equality and everything a normal human being should desire in return for a lifestyle that has long been shown to be inadequate. You're risking prison and fines for knowingly circumventing the Equal Rights Act. It's all crazy, but you've a right to be nuts.'

'But if you don't understand us, not at all, why are you risking –'

'For the profit, Eileen,' I said. 'If this is pulled off, Mr Coleman will owe me a tidy sum.' I stood up. 'Now, I must see you out. I've many, many things to do yet today.'

When I was finally rid of the happy couple, I boarded an entertainment beltway into a restaurant district in Wing-P, and there I had my lunch: a fillet of reconstituted sea bass, a baked potato, strawberries from a hydroponic garden immersed in simulated cream. It was a rich lunch, but one that was easily digested.

A warning, kid: stay away from greasy foods for lunch. In this business, your stomach can be the end of you; it curdles grease and plagues you with murderous heartburn.

By 1:30, I was back on the street. I phoned in to the offices of Boldoni and Gia and learned that the beltway on the fifth subbasement level was rolling again, though Boldoni now estimated permanent repairs as a two- or three-day job. It seemed that one of the B & G workmen had found a second potential break in the hydraulic line just before it was ready to go. He'll get a bonus for that, however he managed it.

At 1:45, I stopped around to see K. O. Wilson again, down at the garbage monitoring decks, picked up the best part of a set of pure silver dinnerware, an antique oil lantern, and a somewhat soiled set of twentieth-century pornographic photographs, which, while no longer titillating to the modern man, are well worth a thousand duo-creds as prime, comic nostalgia. Kid, the strangest damn stuff shows up in the garbage, sometimes so strange you won't believe it. Just remember that there are thirty million people in this damn hive, and that among them they own and accidentally throw out about anything a man could hope to find.

I delivered the dinnerware, lantern and pornography to Petrone, the family fence, and then got my ass on the move. I was twenty minutes behind the day's schedule.

At 2:15, I met a man named Talmadge at a sleazy little drug bar in one of the less pleasant entertainment districts on the forty-sixth level. He was sitting at a table in a dark corner, clasping his water pipe in both hands and staring down at the mouthpiece that appeared to have fallen from his lips to the tabletop.

'Sorry I'm late,' I said.

He looked up, dreamy-eyed, smiled at me more than he had to, and said, 'That's all right. I'm feeling fine, just fine.'

'Good for you,' I said. 'But are you feeling too fine to go through with this?'

'No, no!' he said. 'I've waited much too long already, months and months – even years!'

'Come on, then,' I said.

I took him out of the drug bar and helped him board a public beltway that took us quickly away from the entertainment zone and deep into a residential area on the same level.

Leaning close to me, in a stage whisper, as if he enjoyed the role of a conspirator, Talmadge said, 'Tell me again how big the apartment is.'

I looked around, saw that no one was close to us, and, knowing that he would just grow louder and more boisterous if I refused to speak of it, I said, 'Three times as large as regulations permit a single man like you. It has nine rooms and two baths.'

'And I don't have to share the baths?'

'Of course not.'

He was ecstatic.

Now, kid, this is the racket you'll be starting out in to get some experience in the business, and you should pay especially close attention. Even when your mother was alive, we had a bigger apartment than city regulations permit; now, with your mother gone, it's *much* bigger than allowed. How was this achieved, this lavish suite? Simple. We bought up the small apartments all around this, knocked out walls, refitted and redecorated. Then, through a falsification of land records in the city real estate office, we made it look as if the outsize apartment had always been here, was a fluke in the original designs. Now, although living space is at a premium, and though the city tries to force everyone into relatively similar accommodations, the government repair robots are far too busy to have the time to section up the large apartment, throw up new walls and so forth. Instead, because this sort of thing happens so seldom, the city allows the oversize apartment to exist and merely doubles or triples the tax assessment on whoever lives there. In a city of fifteen million apartments, you can pull a hustle like this at least twice a month, without drawing undue official concern, and you can clean up a very tidy sum from rich folks who need more than the legal living space.

At 2:38, Mr Talmadge and I arrived at the entrance to his new home, keyed it and went inside. I took him on a grand tour of the place, waited while he checked the Tri-D fakeview in all the rooms, tested the beds, flushed the toilets in both johns, and finally paid me the money yet outstanding on our contract. In return, I gave him his ownership papers, copies of the falsified real estate claims, and his first tax assessment.

At 3:00, half an hour behind schedule, I got out of there.

On my way up to the offices of Boldoni and Gia, in the standard elevator, I had time to catch a news flash on the comscreen, and it was such bad news that it shattered the hell out of my schedule. You heard about it. Ms and Mr Potemkin, my first clients of the day, were apprehended in their attempt to sneak out of the city through the sewage service pipes. They accidentally ran into a crew of maintenance robots who gave pursuit. They'd only just then been brought to city police headquarters, but they wouldn't need long to fold up under a stiff interrogation.

I canceled my original destination on the elevator board, punched out the twenty-sixth level and dropped down in agonizingly slow motion, wishing to hell I'd used the express drop.

At 3:11, I rode by the offices of Cargill Marriage Counseling, which was the front I used for selling routes out of the city to people like the Potemkins. The place didn't seem to be under surveillance, so I came back on another beltway, opened up, went inside and set to work. I opened the safe, took out what creds I had bundled there, stuffed half a dozen different maps in my pockets, looked around to be sure I'd not left anything of value behind, then set fire to the place and beat it out of there. I had always used the name Cargill in that racket, and I'd always worn transparent plastic fingertip shields to keep from leaving prints; however, one can never be too careful, kid.

At 3:47, I rode back upstairs to the offices of Boldoni and Gia, checked on the beltway repair job with Lew, who had returned to the office. It was going well; the profit would keep Boldoni and Gia in the black; we're always in the black; we see to that.

I sent a man down to see K. O. Wilson before shifts changed, then dialed the number for Mr Lincoln Pliney (who is me, you recall), on the fifty-ninth floor in the Chesterfield District. The robosec answered on a cut-in, and I asked for messages.

In a metallic voice, the robosec said, 'Mr Arthur Coleman just stopped in and asked for an appointment, sir.'

'Coleman? I just talked to him this morning.'

'Yes, sir. But he left a number for you.'

I took the number, hung up, dialed Coleman and said hello and identified myself to him.

He said, 'Eileen and I want to go through with the deal.'

'You've just met each other,' I said.

'I know, but I think we're perfect for each other.'

I said, 'What does Eileen think?'

'The same as I do, of course.'

'In one afternoon, you can't learn enough about each other –'

Coleman said, 'It's true love.'

I said, 'Well, it's obviously true *something*.'

'We'd like to finalize things tonight.'

'Impossible.'

'Then we'll go somewhere else.'

'To whom?'

'We'll find someone,' he said.

I said, 'You'll find some incompetent criminal hack who'll botch the falsification of Eileen's death certificate, and in the end you'll have to tell the police about me.'

He didn't respond.

'Oh, hell!' I snapped. 'Meet me in my Chesterfield District office in half an hour, with Eileen.'

I hung up.

I'd intended to see a man who wanted to purchase a falsified Neutral Status Pass to keep him safe from duel challenges. See, kid, there are a lot of people who are healthy enough to have to go armed but who want to avoid having to accept challenges. The government has no sympathy with them and forces them to comply with the system. I'm always ready, however, to give them a paper disability to keep them whole and sane. I sympathize with rebels, like I said. And there's a profit in it, too. Anyway, I had to call the guy who wanted the Neutral Status Pass and postpone our appointment until tomorrow.

Then I ran off to tie the nuptial knots for Coleman and his lady.

You see, now, why I was late getting home. Scare you? I didn't think it would. Tomorrow, you can come along with me, watch me work, pick up some tips about the business. You're fifteen, plenty old enough to learn. I tell you, kid, you're going to be a natural for this business. I wish your mother could have lived to see what kind of daughter she brought into this world.

Well, kid, you better turn in. It's going to be a busy day.

ONLINE: **TWO/2** *Subject:* Killer Robot

Imposter

Philip K. Dick

INFO: A killer robot that looks just like a man is on the loose. It has been programmed to destruct causing the maximum mayhem unless caught. But when an arrest *does* take place, it proves to be only the prelude to an even stranger dilemma.

Philip K. Dick has been described as one of the half dozen most important authors in 20th century American sf and his reputation continues to grow with screen adaptations of his work following the brilliant Ridley Scott production, *Blade Runner*, in 1982. This landmark movie with its remarkable special effects was based on his novel, *Do Androids Dream of Electric Sheep?* (1968), about the hunt for Martian androids which have been illegally imported to Earth.

Philip was born in California – which appears, thinly disguised, in much of his work – and worked as a radio dj while developing his remarkable talent as a writer of speculative and idiosyncratic fiction. Androids, robots, cyborgs and a variety of other mechanical simulacra have appeared as important figures in his work: especially the novels *Dr Futurity* (1953), *We Can Build You* (1962), *Warning: We Are Your Police* (1967), *Ubik* (1969) and short stories including 'Imposter', 'A. Lincoln, Simulacrum' and – notoriously – 'We Can Remember It for You Wholesale' (1965), filmed in 1990 as *Total Recall*, with Arnold Schwarzenegger playing Doug Quail, the construction worker pursued by a merciless android killer named Michael Ironsides. 'Imposter', which appeared in *Astounding*, June 1953, has also recently been optioned for a movie by Miramax Films.

'One of these days I'm going to take time off,' Spence Olham said at first-meal. He looked around at his wife. 'I think I've earned a rest. Ten years is a long time.'

'And the Project?'

'The war will be won without me. This ball of clay of ours isn't really in much danger.' Olham sat down at the table and lit a cigarette. 'The newsmachines alter dispatches to make it appear the Outspacers are right on top of us. You know what I'd like to do on my vacation? I'd like to take a camping trip to those mountains outside of town, where we went that time. Remember? I got poison oak and you almost stepped on a gopher snake.'

'Sutton Wood?' Mary began to clear away the food dishes. 'The Wood was burned a few weeks ago. I thought you knew. Some kind of flash fire.'

Olham sagged. 'Didn't they even try to find the cause?' His lips twisted. 'No one cares anymore. All they can think of is the war.' He clamped his jaws together, the whole picture coming up in his mind, the Outspacers, the war, the needle-ships.

'How can we think about anything else?'

Olham nodded. She was right, of course. The dark little ships out of Alpha Centauri had bypassed the Earth cruisers easily, leaving them like helpless turtles. It had been one-way fights, all the way back to Terra.

All the way, until the protec-bubble was demonstrated by Westinghouse Labs. Thrown around the major Earth cities and finally the planet itself, the bubble was the first real defense, the first legitimate answer to the Outspacers – as the newsmachines labeled them.

But to win the war, that was another thing. Every lab, every project was working night and day, endlessly, to find something more: a weapon for positive combat. His own project, for example. All day long, year after year.

Olham stood up, putting out his cigarette. 'Like the Sword of Damocles. Always hanging over us. I'm getting tired. All I want to do is take a long rest. But I guess everybody feels that way.'

He got his jacket from the closet and went out on the front porch. The shoot would be along any moment, the fast little bug that would carry him to the Project.

'I hope Nelson isn't late.' He looked at his watch. 'It's almost seven.'

'Here the bug comes,' Mary said, gazing between the rows of houses.

The sun glittered behind the roofs, reflecting against the heavy lead plates. The settlement was quiet; only a few people were stirring. 'I'll see you later. Try not to work beyond your shift, Spence.'

Olham opened the car door and slid inside, leaning back against the seat with a sigh. There was an older man with Nelson.

'Well?' Olham said, as the bug shot ahead. 'Heard any interesting news?'

'The usual,' Nelson said. 'A few Outspace ships hit, another asteroid abandoned for strategic reasons.'

'It'll be good when we get the Project into final stage. Maybe it's just the propaganda from the newsmachines, but in the last month I've gotten weary of all this. Everything seems so grim and serious, no color to life.'

'Do you think the war is in vain?' the older man said suddenly. 'You are an integral part of it, yourself.'

'This is Major Peters,' Nelson said. Olham and Peters shook hands. Olham studied the older man.

'What brings you along so early?' he said. 'I don't remember seeing you at the Project before.'

'No, I'm not with the Project,' Peters said, 'but I know something about what you're doing. My own work is altogether different.'

A look passed between him and Nelson. Olham noticed it and he frowned. The bug was gaining speed, flashing across the barren, lifeless ground toward the distant rim of the Project building.

'What is your business?' Olham said. 'Or aren't you permitted to talk about it?'

'I'm with the government,' Peters said. 'With FSA, the security organ.'

'Oh?' Olham raised an eyebrow. 'Is there any enemy infiltration in this region?'

'As a matter of fact I'm here to see you, Mr Olham.'

Olham was puzzled. He considered Peters' words, but he could make nothing of them. 'To see me? Why?'

'I'm here to arrest you as an Outspace spy. That's why I'm up so early this morning. *Grab him, Nelson –*'

The gun drove into Olham's ribs. Nelson's hands were shaking, trembling with released emotion, his face pale. He took a deep breath and let it out again.

'Shall we kill him now?' he whispered to Peters. 'I think we should kill him now. We can't wait.'

Olham stared into his friend's face. He opened his mouth to speak, but no words came. Both men were staring at him steadily, rigid and grim with fright. Olham felt dizzy. His head ached and spun.

'I don't understand,' he murmured.

At that moment the shoot car left the ground and rushed up, heading into space. Below them the Project fell away, smaller and smaller, disappearing. Olham shut his mouth.

'We can wait a little,' Peters said. 'I want to ask him some questions first.'

Olham gazed dully ahead as the bug rushed through space.

'The arrest was made all right,' Peters said into the vidscreen. On the screen the features of the security chief showed. 'It should be a load off everyone's mind.'

'Any complications?'

'None. He entered the bug without suspicion. He didn't seem to think my presence was too unusual.'

'Where are you now?'

'On our way out, just inside the protec-bubble. We're moving at a maximum speed. You can assume that the critical period is past. I'm glad the takeoff jets in this craft were in good working order. If there had been any failure at that point —'

'Let me see him,' the security chief said. He gazed directly at Olham where he sat, his hands in his lap, staring ahead.

'So that's the man.' He looked at Olham for a time. Olham said nothing. At last the chief nodded to Peters. 'All right. That's enough.' A faint trace of disgust wrinkled his features. 'I've seen all I want. You've done something that will be remembered for a long time. They're preparing some sort of citation for both of you.'

'That's not necessary,' Peters said.

'How much danger is there now? Is there still much chance that —'

'There is some chance, but not too much. According to my understanding it requires a verbal key phrase. In any case we'll have to take the risk.'

'I'll have the Moon base notified you're coming.'

'No.' Peters shook his head. 'I'll land the ship outside, beyond the base. I don't want it in jeopardy.'

'Just as you like.' The chief's eyes flickered as he glanced again at Olham. Then his image faded. The screen blanked.

Olham shifted his gaze to the window. The ship was already through the protec-bubble, rushing with greater and greater speed all the time. Peters was in a hurry; below him, rumbling under the floor, the jets were wide-open. They were afraid, hurrying frantically, because of him.

Next to him on the seat, Nelson shifted uneasily. 'I think we should do it now,' he said. 'I'd give anything if we could get it over with.'

'Take it easy,' Peters said. 'I want you to guide the ship for a while so I can talk to him.'

He slid over beside Olham, looking into his face. Presently he reached out and touched him gingerly, on the arm and then on the cheek.

Olham said nothing. *If I could let Mary know*, he thought again. *If I could find some way of letting her know*. He looked around the ship. How? The vidscreen? Nelson was sitting by the board, holding the gun. There was nothing he could do. He was caught, trapped.

But why?

'Listen,' Peters said, 'I want to ask you some questions. You know where we're going. We're moving Moonward. In an hour we'll land on the far side, on the desolate side. After we land you'll be turned over immediately to a team of men waiting there. Your body will be destroyed at once. Do you understand that?' He looked at his watch. 'Within two hours your parts will be strewn over the landscape. There won't be anything left of you.'

Olham struggled out of his lethargy. 'Can't you tell me –'

'Certainly, I'll tell you.' Peters nodded. 'Two days ago we received a report that an Outspace ship had penetrated the protec-bubble. The ship let off a spy in the form of a humanoid robot. The robot was to destroy a particular human being and take his place.'

Peters looked calmly at Olham.

'Inside the robot was a U-Bomb. Our agent did not know how the bomb was to be detonated, but he conjectured that it might be by a particular spoken phrase, a certain group of words. The robot would live the life of the person he killed, entering into his usual activities, his job, his social life. He had been constructed to resemble that person. No one would know the difference.'

Olham's face went sickly chalk.

'The person whom the robot was to impersonate was Spence Olham, a high-ranking official at one of the research Projects. Because this particular Project was approaching crucial stage, the presence of an animate bomb, moving toward the center of the Project –'

Olham stared down at his hands. *'But I'm Olham!'*

'Once the robot had located and killed Olham it was a simple matter to take over his life. The robot was released from the ship eight days ago. The substitution was probably accomplished over the last weekend, when Olham went for a short walk in the hills.'

'But I'm Olham.' He turned to Nelson, sitting at the controls. 'Don't you recognize me? You've known me for twenty years. Don't you remember how we went to college together?' He stood up. 'You and I were at the University. We had the same room.' He went toward Nelson.

'Stay away from me!' Nelson snarled.

'Listen. Remember our second year? Remember that girl? What was her name –' He rubbed his forehead. 'The one with the dark hair. The one we met over at Ted's place.'

'Stop!' Nelson waved the gun frantically. 'I don't want to hear any more. You killed him! You ... machine.'

Olham looked at Nelson. 'You're wrong. I don't know what happened, but the robot never reached me. Something must have gone wrong. Maybe the ship crashed.' He turned to Peters. 'I'm Olham. I know it. No transfer was made. I'm the same as I've always been.'

He touched himself, running his hands over his body. 'There must be some way to prove it. Take me back to Earth. An X-ray examination, a neurological study, anything like that will show you. Or maybe we can find the crashed ship.'

Neither Peters nor Nelson spoke.

'I am Olham,' he said again. 'I know I am. But I can't prove it.'

'The robot,' Peters said, 'would be unaware that he was not the real Spence Olham. He would become Olham in mind as well as body. He was given an artificial memory system, false recall. He would look like him, have his memories, his thoughts and interests, perform his job.

'But there would be one difference. Inside the robot is a U-Bomb, ready to explode at the trigger phrase.' Peters moved a little away. 'That's the one difference. That's why we're taking you to the Moon. They'll disassemble you and remove the bomb. Maybe it will explode, but it won't matter, not there.'

Olham sat down slowly.

'We'll be there soon,' Nelson said.

He lay back, thinking frantically, as the ship dropped slowly down. Under them was the pitted surface of the Moon, the endless expanse of ruin. What could he do? What would save him?

'Get ready,' Peters said.

In a few minutes he would be dead. Down below he could see a tiny dot, a building of some kind. There were men in the building, the demolition team, waiting to tear him to bits. They would rip him open, pull off his arms and legs, break him apart. When they found no bomb they would be surprised; they would know, but it would be too late.

Olham looked around the small cabin. Nelson was still holding the gun. There was no chance there. If he could get to a doctor, have an examination made – that was the only way. Mary could help him. He thought frantically, his mind racing. Only a few minutes, just a little time left. If he could contact her, get word to her some way.

'Easy,' Peters said. The ship came down slowly, bumping on the rough ground. There was silence.

'Listen,' Olham said thickly. 'I can prove I'm Spence Olham. Get a doctor. Bring him here –'

'There's the squad,' Nelson pointed. 'They're coming.' He glanced nervously at Olham. 'I hope nothing happens.'

'We'll be gone before they start work,' Peters said. 'We'll be out of here in a moment.' He put on his pressure suit. When he had finished he took the gun from Nelson. 'I'll watch him for a moment.'

Nelson put on his pressure suit, hurrying awkwardly. 'How about him?' He indicated Olham. 'Will he need one?'

'No.' Peters shook his head. 'Robots probably don't require oxygen.'

The group of men were almost to the ship. They halted, waiting. Peters signaled to them.

'Come on!' He waved his hand and the men approached warily; stiff, grotesque figures in their inflated suits.

'If you open the door,' Olham said, 'it means my death. It will be murder.'

'Open the door,' Nelson said. He reached for the handle.

Olham watched him. He saw the man's hand tighten around the metal rod. In a moment the door would swing back, the air in the ship would rush out. He would die, and presently they would realize their mistake. Perhaps at some other time, when there was no war, men might not act this way, hurrying an individual to his death because they were afraid. Everyone was frightened, everyone was willing to sacrifice the individual because of the group fear.

He was being killed because they could not wait to be sure of his guilt. There was not enough time.

He looked at Nelson. Nelson had been his friend for years. They had gone to school together. He had been best man at his wedding. Now Nelson was going to kill him. But Nelson was not wicked; it was not his fault. It was the times. Perhaps it had been the same way during the plagues. When men had shown a spot they probably had been killed, too, without a moment's hesitation, without proof, on suspicion alone. In times of danger there was no other way.

He did not blame them. But he had to live. His life was too precious to be sacrificed. Olham thought quickly. What could he do? Was there anything? He looked around.

'Here goes,' Nelson said.

'You're right,' Olham said. The sound of his own voice surprised him. It was the strength of desperation. 'I have no need of air. Open the door.'

They paused, looking at him in curious alarm.

'Go ahead. Open it. It makes no difference.' Olham's hand disappeared inside his jacket. 'I wonder how far you two can run?'

'Run?'

'You have fifteen seconds to live.' Inside his jacket his fingers twisted, his arm suddenly rigid. He relaxed, smiling a little. 'You were wrong about the trigger phrase. In that respect you were mistaken. Fourteen seconds, now.'

Two shocked faces stared at him from the pressure suits. Then they were struggling, running, tearing the door open. The air shrieked out, spilling into the void. Peters and Nelson bolted out of the ship. Olham came after them. He grasped the door and dragged it shut. The automatic pressure system chugged furiously, restoring the air. Olham let his breath out with a shudder.

One more second –

Beyond the window the two men had joined the group. The group scattered, running in all directions. One by one they threw themselves down, prone on the ground. Olham seated himself at the control board, He moved the dials into place. As the ship rose up into the air the men below scrambled to their feet and stared up, their mouths open.

'Sorry,' Olham murmured, 'but I've got to get back to Earth.'

He headed the ship back the way it had come.

It was night. All around the ship crickets chirped, disturbing the chill darkness. Olham bent over the vidscreen. Gradually the image formed; the call had gone through without trouble. He breathed a sigh of relief.

'Mary,' he said. The woman stared at him. She gasped.

'Spence! Where are you? What's happened?'

'I can't tell you. Listen, I have to talk fast. They may break this call off any minute. Go to the Project grounds and get Dr Chamberlain. If he isn't there, get any doctor. Bring him to the house and have him stay there. Have him bring equipment, X-ray, fluoroscope, everything.'

'But –'

'Do as I say. Hurry. Have him get it ready in an hour.' Olham leaned toward the screen. 'Is everything all right? Are you alone?'

'Alone?'

'Is anyone with you? Has … has Nelson or anyone contacted you?'

'No. Spence, I don't understand.'

'All right. I'll see you at the house in an hour. And don't tell anyone anything. Get Chamberlain there on any pretext. Say you're very ill.'

He broke the connection and looked at his watch. A moment later he left the ship, stepping down into the darkness. He had a half mile to go.

He began to walk.

One light showed in the window, the study light. He watched it, kneeling against the fence. There was no sound, no movement of any kind. He held his watch up and read it by starlight. Almost an hour had passed.

Along the street a shoot bug came. It went on.

Olham looked toward the house. The doctor should have already come. He should be inside, waiting with Mary. A thought struck him. Had she been able to leave the house? Perhaps they had intercepted her. Maybe he was moving into a trap.

But what else could he do?

With a doctor's records, photographs and reports, there was a chance, a chance of proof. If he could be examined, if he could remain alive long enough for them to study him —

He could prove it that way. It was probably the only way. His one hope lay inside the house. Dr Chamberlain was a respected man. He was the staff doctor for the Project. He would know, his word on the matter would have meaning. He could overcome their hysteria, their madness, with facts.

Madness — that was what it was. If only they would wait, act slowly, take their time. But they could not wait. He had to die, die at once, without proof, without any kind of trial or examination. The simplest test would tell, but they had no time for the simplest test. They could think only of the danger. Danger, and nothing more.

He stood up and moved toward the house. He came up on the porch. At the door he paused, listening. Still no sound. The house was absolutely still.

Too still.

Olham stood on the porch, unmoving. They were trying to be silent inside. Why? It was a small house; only a few feet away, beyond the door, Mary and Dr Chamberlain should be standing. Yet he could hear nothing, no sound of voices, nothing at all. He looked at the door. It was a door he had opened and closed a thousand times, every morning and every night.

He put his hand on the knob. Then, all at once, he reached out and touched the bell instead. The bell pealed, off some place in the back of the house. Olham smiled. He could hear movement.

Mary opened the door. As soon as he saw her face he knew.

He ran, throwing himself into the bushes. A security officer shoved Mary out of the way, firing past her. The bushes burst apart. Olham wriggled around the side of the house. He leaped up and ran, racing frantically into the darkness. A searchlight snapped on, a beam of light circling past him.

He crossed the road and squeezed over a fence. He jumped down and made his way across a backyard. Behind him men were coming, security officers, shouting to each other as they came. Olham gasped for breath, his chest rising and falling.

Her face — he had known at once. The set lips, the terrified, wretched eyes. Suppose he had gone ahead, pushed open the door and entered! They had tapped the call and come at once, as soon as he had broken off. Probably she believed their account. No doubt she thought he was the robot, too.

Olham ran on and on. He was losing the officers, dropping them behind. Apparently they were not much good at running. He climbed a hill and made his way down the other side. In a moment he would be back at the ship. But where to, this time? He slowed down, stopping. He could see the ship already, outlined against the sky, where he had parked it. The settlement was behind him; he was on the outskirts of the wilderness between the inhabited places, where the forests and desolation began. He crossed a barren field and entered the trees.

As he came toward it, the door of the ship opened.

Peters stepped out, framed against the light. In his arms was a heavy Boris gun. Olham stopped, rigid. Peters stared around him, into the darkness. 'I know you're there, some place,' he said. 'Come on up here, Olham. There are security men all around you.'

Olham did not move.

'Listen to me. We will catch you very shortly. Apparently you still do not believe you're the robot. Your call to the woman indicates that you are still under the illusion created by your artificial memories.

'But you *are* the robot. You are the robot, and inside you is the bomb. Any moment the trigger phrase may be spoken, by you, by someone else, by anyone. When that happens the bomb will destroy everything for miles around. The Project, the woman, all of us will be killed. Do you understand?'

Olham said nothing. He was listening. Men were moving toward him, slipping through the woods.

'If you don't come out, we'll catch you. It will only be a matter of time. We no longer plan to remove you to the Moon base. You will be destroyed on sight, and we will have to take the chance that the bomb will detonate. I have ordered every available security officer into the area. The whole county is being searched, inch by inch. There is no place you can go. Around this wood is a cordon of armed men. You have about six hours left before the last inch is covered.'

Olham moved away. Peters went on speaking; he had not seen him at all. It was too dark to see anyone. But Peters was right. There was no place he could go. He was beyond the settlement, on the outskirts where the woods began. He could hide for a time, but eventually they would catch him.

Only a matter of time.

Olham walked quietly through the wood. Mile by mile, each part of the county was being measured off, laid bare, searched, studied, examined. The cordon was coming all the time, squeezing him into a smaller and smaller space.

What was there left? He had lost the ship, the one hope of escape. They were at his home; his wife was with them, believing, no doubt, that the real Olham had been killed. He clenched his fists. Some place there was a wrecked Outspace needle-ship, and in it the remains of the robot. Somewhere nearby the ship had crashed and broken up.

And the robot lay inside, destroyed.

A faint hope stirred him. What if he could find the remains? If he could show them the wreckage, the remains of the ship, the robot –

But where? Where would he find it?

He walked on, lost in thought. Some place, not too far off, probably. The ship would have landed close to the Project; the robot would have expected to go the rest of the way on foot. He went up the side of the hill and looked around. Crashed and burned. Was there some clue, some hint? Had he read anything, heard anything? Some place close by, within walking distance. Some wild place, a remote spot where there would be no people.

Suddenly Olham smiled. Crashed and burned –

Sutton Wood.

He increased his pace.

It was morning. Sunlight filtered down through the broken trees, on to the man crouching at the edge of the clearing. Olham glanced up from time to time, listening. They were not far off, only a few minutes away. He smiled.

Down below him, strewn across the clearing and into the charred stumps that had been Sutton Wood, lay a tangled mass of wreckage. In the sunlight it glittered a little, gleaming darkly. He had not had too much trouble finding it. Sutton Wood was a place he knew well; he had climbed around it many times in his life, when he was younger. He had known where he would find the remains. There was one peak that jutted up suddenly, without a warning.

A descending ship, unfamiliar with the Wood, had little chance of missing it. And now he squatted, looking down at the ship, or what remained of it.

Olham stood up. He could hear them, only a little distance away, coming together, talking in low tones. He tensed himself. Everything depended on who first saw him. If it was Nelson, he had no chance. Nelson would fire at once. He would be dead before they saw the ship. But if he had time to call out, hold them off for a moment – that was all he needed. Once they saw the ship he would be safe.

But if they fired first –

A charred branch cracked. A figure appeared, coming forward uncertainly. Olham took a deep breath. Only a few seconds remained, perhaps the last seconds of his life. He raised his arms, peering intently.

It was Peters.

'Peters!' Olham waved his arms. Peters lifted his gun, aiming. 'Don't fire!' His voice shook. 'Wait a minute. Look past me, across the clearing.'

'I've found him,' Peters shouted. Security men came pouring out of the burned woods around him.

'Don't shoot. Look past me. The ship, the needle-ship. The Outspace ship. Look!'

Peters hesitated. The gun wavered.

'It's down there,' Olham said rapidly. 'I knew I'd find it here. The burned wood. Now you believe me. You'll find the remains of the robot in the ship. Look, will you?'

'There is something down there,' one of the men said nervously.

'Shoot him!' a voice said. It was Nelson.

'Wait.' Peters turned sharply. 'I'm in charge. Don't anyone fire. Maybe he's telling the truth.'

'Shoot him,' Nelson said. 'He killed Olham. Any minute he may kill us all. If the bomb goes off –'

'Shut up.' Peters advanced toward the slope. He stared down. 'Look at that.' He waved two men up to him. 'Go down there and see what that is.'

The men raced down the slope, across the clearing. They bent down, poking in the ruins of the ship.

'Well?' Peters called.

Olham held his breath. He smiled a little. It must be there; he had not had time to look, himself, but it had to be there. Suddenly doubt assailed him. Suppose the robot had lived long enough to wander away? Suppose his body had been completely destroyed, burned to ashes by the fire?

He licked his lips. Perspiration came out on his forehead. Nelson was staring at him, his face still livid. His chest rose and fell.

'Kill him,' Nelson said. 'Before he kills us.'

The two men stood up.

'What have you found?' Peters said. He held the gun steady. 'Is there anything there?'

'Looks like something. It's a needle-ship, all right. There's something beside it.'

'I'll look.' Peters strode past Olham. Olham watched him go down the hill and up to the men. The others were following after him, peering to see.

'It's a body of some sort,' Peters said. 'Look at it!'

Olham came along with them. They stood around in a circle, staring down.

On the ground, bent and twisted in a strange shape, was a grotesque form. It looked human, perhaps; except that it was bent so strangely, the arms and legs flung off in all directions. The mouth was open; the eyes stared glassily.

'Like a machine that's run down,' Peters murmured. Olham smiled feebly. 'Well?' he said.

Peters looked at him. 'I can't believe it. You were telling the truth all the time.'

'The robot never reached me,' Olham said. He took out a cigarette and lit it. 'It was destroyed when the ship crashed. You were all too busy with the war to wonder why an out-of-the-way wood would suddenly catch fire and burn. Now you know.'

He stood smoking, watching the men. They were dragging the grotesque remains from the ship. The body was stiff, the arms and legs rigid.

'You'll find the bomb now,' Olham said. The men laid the body on the ground. Peters bent down.

'I think I see the corner of it.' He reached out, touching the body.

The chest of the corpse had been laid open. Within the gaping tear something glinted, something metal. The men stared at the metal without speaking.

'That would have destroyed us all, if it had lived,' Peters said. 'That metal box there.'

There was silence.

'I think we owe you something,' Peters said to Olham. 'This must have been a nightmare to you. If you hadn't escaped, we would have –' He broke off.

Olham put out his cigarette. 'I knew, of course, that the robot had never reached me. But I had no way of proving it. Sometimes it isn't possible to prove a thing right away. That was the whole trouble. There wasn't any way I could demonstrate that I was myself.'

'How about a vacation?' Peters said. 'I think we might work out a month's vacation for you. You could take it easy, relax.'

'I think right now I want to go home,' Olham said.

'All right, then,' Peters said. 'Whatever you say.'

Nelson had squatted down on the ground, beside the corpse. He reached out toward the glint of metal visible within the chest.

'Don't touch it,' Olham said. 'It might still go off. We better let the demolition squad take care of it later on.'

Nelson said nothing. Suddenly he grabbed hold of the metal, reaching his hand inside the chest. He pulled.

'What are you doing?' Olham cried.

Nelson stood up. He was holding on to the metal object. His face was blank with terror. It was a metal knife, an Outspace needle-knife, covered with blood.

'This killed him,' Nelson whispered. 'My friend was killed with this.' He looked at Olham. 'You killed him with this and left him beside the ship.'

Olham was trembling. His teeth chattered. He looked from the knife to the body. 'This can't be Olham,' he said. His mind spun, everything was whirling. 'Was I wrong?'

He gaped.

'But if that's Olham, then I must be –'

He did not complete the sentence, only the first phrase. The blast was visible all the way to Alpha Centauri.

ONLINE: TWO/3 Subject: Homicidal android

Fondly Fahrenheit

Alfred Bester

INFO: Androids are man's best friends – they're programmed to be. Most of the time they act as all-purpose helpers to their less capable flesh and blood masters. But when a murder is involved and the narrator of a story switches unnervingly between referring to his organic friend as 'him' and 'me', there are clearly sinister implications ...

Alfred Bester was a writer ahead of his time, his hard-edged, innovative storytelling marking him down as a forerunner of the cyberpunk generation. Despite a comparatively small *oeuvre*, he produced several landmark novels and was probably not given the recognition or awards he deserved. Born in New York, Bester studied psychology at the University of Pennsylvania, and began his working life in the comic book industry scripting for several of the crime-fighting superheroes including *Superman*, *Batman* and *The Green Lantern*. It was while he was writing for television – in particular the weekly series *Tom Corbett, Space Cadet* – that he began to produce the short stories and later the novels on which his reputation rests. Foremost among these are *The Demolished Man* (1953) about a successful murder in a society where such things are unknown because telepathic detectives normally sense the intention before the crime is committed; *Tiger! Tiger!* (1956) featuring a man's quest for revenge in a corrupt 25th century future; and *Golem 100* (1980) which deals with a future New York where vice, corruption and death are commonplace. 'Fondly Fahrenheit' was originally published in *Fantasy and Science Fiction* magazine in 1954 and earned Alfred Bester one of his few awards from the *Science Fiction Hall of Fame*.

He doesn't know which of us I am these days, but they know one truth. You must own nothing but yourself. You must make your own life, live your own life and die your own death ... or else you will die another's.

The rice fields on Paragon III stretch for hundreds of miles like checkerboard tundras, a blue and brown mosaic under a burning sky of orange. In the evening, clouds whip like smoke, and the paddies rustle and murmur.

A long line of men marched across the paddies the evening we escaped from Paragon III. They were silent, armed, intent; a long rank of silhouetted statues looming against the smoking sky. Each man carried a gun. Each man wore a walkie-talkie belt pack, the speaker button in his ear, the microphone bug clipped to his throat, the glowing view-screen strapped to his wrist like a green-eyed watch. The multitude of screens showed nothing but a multitude of individual paths through the paddies. The annunciators uttered no sound but the rustle and splash of steps. The men spoke infrequently, in heavy grunts, all speaking to all.

'Nothing here.'
'Where's here?'
'Jenson's fields.'
'You're drifting too far west.'
'Close in the line there.'
'Anybody covered the Grimson paddy?'
'Yeah. Nothing.'
'She couldn't have walked this far.'
'Could have been carried.'
'Think she's alive?'
'Why should she be dead?'

The slow refrain swept up and down the long line of beaters advancing toward the smoky sunset. The line of beaters wavered like a writhing snake, but never ceased its remorseless advance. One hundred men spaced fifty feet apart. Five thousand feet of ominous search. One mile of angry determination stretching from east to west across a compass of heat. Evening fell. Each man lit his search lamp. The writhing snake was transformed into a necklace of wavering diamonds.

'Clear here. Nothing.'
'Nothing here.'
'Nothing.'

'What about the Allen paddies?'
'Covering them now.'
'Think we missed her?'
'Maybe.'
'We'll beat back and check.'
'This'll be an all-night job.'
'Allen paddies clear.'
'God damn! We've got to find her!'
'We'll find her.'
'Here she is. Sector seven. Tune in.'

The line stopped. The diamonds froze in the heat. There was silence. Each man gazed into the glowing green screen on his wrist, tuning to sector seven. All tuned to one. All showed a small nude figure awash in the muddy water of a paddy. Alongside the figure an owner's stake of bronze read: VANDALEUR. The ends of the line converged toward the Vandaleur field. The necklace turned into a cluster of stars. One hundred men gathered around a small nude body, a child dead in a rice paddy. There was no water in her mouth. There were fingermarks on her throat. Her innocent face was battered. Her body was torn. Clotted blood on her skin was crusted and hard.

'Dead three–four hours at least.'
'Her mouth is dry.'
'She wasn't drowned. Beaten to death.'

In the dark evening heat the men swore softly. They picked up the body. One stopped the others and pointed to the child's fingernails. She had fought her murderer. Under the nails were particles of flesh and bright drops of scarlet blood, still liquid, still uncoagulated.

'That blood ought to be clotted too.'
'Funny.'
'Not so funny. What kind of blood don't clot?'
'Android.'
'Looks like she was killed by one.'
'Vandaleur owns an android.'
'She couldn't be killed by an android.'
'That's android blood under her nails.'
'The police better check.'
'The police'll prove I'm right.'
'But androids can't kill.'
'That's android blood, ain't it?'
'Androids can't kill. They're made that way.'
'Looks like one android was made wrong.'
'Jesus!'

And the thermometer that day registered 92.9° gloriously Fahrenheit.

So there we were aboard the *Paragon Queen* enroute for Megaster V, James Vandaleur and his android. James Vandaleur counted his money and wept. In the second-class cabin with him was his android, a magnificent synthetic creature with classic features and wide blue eyes. Raised on its forehead in a cameo of flesh were the letters MA, indicating that this was one of the rare multiple aptitude androids, worth $57,000 on the current exchange. There we were, weeping and counting and calmly watching.

'Twelve, fourteen, sixteen. Sixteen hundred dollars,' Vandaleur wept. 'That's all. Sixteen hundred dollars. My house was worth ten thousand. The land was worth five. There was furniture, cars, my paintings, etchings, my plane, my – And nothing to show for everything but sixteen hundred dollars. Christ!'

I leaped up from the table and turned on the android. I pulled a strap from one of the leather bags and beat the android. It didn't move.

'I must remind you,' the android said, 'that I am worth fifty-seven thousand dollars on the current exchange. I must warn you that you are endangering valuable property.'

'You damned crazy machine,' Vandaleur shouted.

'I am not a machine,' the android answered. 'The robot is a machine. The android is a chemical creation of synthetic tissue.'

'What got into you?' Vandaleur cried. 'Why did you do it? Damn you!' He beat the android savagely.

'I must remind you that I cannot be punished,' I said. 'The pleasure-pain syndrome is not incorporated in the android synthesis.'

'Then why did you kill her?' Vandaleur shouted. 'If it wasn't for kicks, why did you –'

'I must remind you,' the android said, 'that the second-class cabins in these ships are not soundproofed.'

Vandaleur dropped the strap and stood panting, staring at the creature he owned.

'Why did you do it? Why did you kill her?' I asked.

'I don't know,' I answered.

'First it was malicious mischief. Small things. Petty destruction. I should have known there was something wrong with you then. Androids can't destroy. They can't harm. They –'

'There is no pleasure-pain syndrome incorporated in the android synthesis.'

'Then it got to arson. Then serious destruction. Then assault ... that engineer on Rigel. Each time worse. Each time we had to get out faster. Now it's murder. Christ! What's the matter with you? What's happened?'

'There are no self-check relays incorporated in the android brain.'

'Each time we had to get out, it was a step downhill. Look at me. In a second-class cabin. Me. James Paleologue Vandaleur. There was a time when my father was the wealthiest – Now, sixteen hundred dollars in the world. That's all I've got. And you. Christ damn you!'

Vandaleur raised the strap to beat the android again, then dropped it and collapsed on a berth, sobbing. At last he pulled himself together.

'Instructions,' he said.

The multiple aptitude android responded at once. It arose and awaited orders.

'My name is now Valentine. James Valentine. I stopped off on Paragon III for only one day to transfer to this ship for Megaster V. My occupation: Agent for one privately owned MA android which is for hire. Purpose of visit: To settle on Megaster V. Fix the papers.'

The android removed Vandaleur's passport and papers from a bag, got pen and ink and sat down at the table. With an accurate, flawless hand – an accomplished hand that could draw, write, paint, carve, engrave, etch, photograph, design, create and build – it meticulously forged new credentials for Vandaleur. Its owner watched me miserably.

'Create and build,' I muttered. 'And now destroy. Oh, God! What am I going to do? Christ! If I could only get rid of you. If I didn't have to live off you. God! If only I'd inherited some guts instead of you.'

Dallas Brady was Megaster's leading jewelry designer. She was short, stocky, amoral and a nymphomaniac. She hired Vandaleur's multiple aptitude android and put me to work in her shop. She seduced Vandaleur. In her bed one night, she asked abruptly: 'Your name's Vandaleur, isn't it?'

'Yes,' I murmured. Then: 'No! No! It's Valentine. James Valentine.'

'What happened on Paragon?' Dallas Brady asked. 'I thought androids couldn't kill or destroy property. Prime Directives and Inhibitions set up for them when they're synthesized. Every company guarantees they can't.'

'Valentine!' Vandaleur insisted.

'Oh, come off it,' Dallas Brady said. 'I've known for a week. I haven't hollered copper, have I?'

'The name is Valentine.'

'You want to prove it? You want I should call the cops?' Dallas reached out and picked up the phone.

'For God's sake, Dallas!' Vandaleur leaped up and struggled to take the phone from her. She fended him off, laughing at him, until he collapsed and wept in shame and helplessness.

'How did you find out?' he asked at last.

'The papers are full of it. And Valentine was a little too close to Vandaleur. That wasn't smart, was it?'

'I guess not. I'm not very smart.'

'Your android's got quite a record, hasn't it? Assault. Arson. Destruction. What happened on Paragon?'

'It kidnapped a child. Took her out into the rice fields and murdered her.'

'Raped her?'

'I don't know.'

'They're going to catch up with you.'

'Don't I know it? Christ! We've been running for two years now. Seven planets in two years. I must have abandoned fifty thousand dollars' worth of property in two years.'

'You better find out what's wrong with it.'

'How can I? Can I walk into a repair clinic and ask for an overhaul? What am I going to say? "My android's just turned killer. Fix it." They'd call the police right off.' I began to shake. 'They'd have that android dismantled inside one day. I'd probably be booked as accessory to murder.'

'Why didn't you have it repaired before it got to murder?'

'I couldn't take the chance,' Vandaleur explained angrily. 'If they started fooling around with lobotomies and body chemistry and endocrine surgery, they might have destroyed its aptitudes. What would I have left to hire out? How would I live?'

'You could work yourself. People do.'

'Work at what? You know I'm good for nothing. How could I compete with specialist androids and robots? Who can, unless he's got a terrific talent for a particular job?'

'Yeah. That's true.'

'I lived off my old man all my life. Damn him! He had to go bust just before he died. Left me the android and that's all. The only way I can get along is living off what it earns.'

'You better sell it before the cops catch up with you. You can live off fifty grand. Invest it.'

'At 3 per cent? Fifteen hundred a year? When the android returns 15 per cent on its value? Eight thousand a year. That's what it earns. No, Dallas. I've got to go along with it.'

'What are you going to do about its violence kick?'

'I can't do anything ... except watch it and pray. What are you going to do about it?'

'Nothing. It's none of my business. Only one thing ... I ought to get something for keeping my mouth shut.'

'What?'

'The android works for me for free. Let somebody else pay you, but I get it for free.'

The multiple aptitude android worked. Vandaleur collected its fees. His expenses were taken care of. His savings began to mount. As the warm spring of Megaster V turned to hot summer, I began investigating farms and properties. It would be possible, within a year or two, for us to settle down permanently, provided Dallas Brady's demands did not become rapacious.

On the first hot day of summer, the android began singing in Dallas Brady's workshop. It hovered over the electric furnace which, along with the weather, was broiling the shop, and sang an ancient tune that had been popular half a century before.

Oh, it's no feat to beat the heat.
All reet! All reet!
So jeet your seat
Be fleet be fleet
Cool and discreet
Honey ...

It sang in a strange, halting voice, and its accomplished fingers were clasped behind its back, writhing in a strange rumba all their own. Dallas Brady was surprised.

'You happy or something?' she asked.

'I must remind you that the pleasure-pain syndrome is not incorporated in the android synthesis,' I answered. 'All reet! All reet! Be fleet be fleet, cool and discreet, honey ...'

Its fingers stopped their writhing and picked up a heavy pair of iron tongs. The android poked them into the glowing heart of the furnace, leaning far forward to peer into the lovely heat.

'Be careful, you damned fool!' Dallas Brady exclaimed. 'You want to fall in?'

'I must remind you that I am worth fifty-seven thousand dollars on the current exchange,' I said. 'It is forbidden to endanger valuable property. All reet! All reet! Honey ...'

It withdrew a crucible of glowing gold from the electric furnace, turned, capered hideously, sang crazily, and splashed a sluggish gobbet of molten gold over Dallas Brady's head. She screamed and collapsed, her hair and clothes flaming, her skin crackling. The android poured again while it capered and sang.

'Be fleet be fleet, cool and discreet, honey ...' It sang and slowly poured and poured the molten gold. Then I left the workshop and rejoined James

Vandaleur in his hotel suite. The android's charred clothes and squirming fingers warned its owner that something was very much wrong.

Vandaleur rushed to Dallas Brady's workshop, stared once, vomited and fled. I had enough time to pack one bag and raise nine hundred dollars on portable assets. He took a third-class cabin on the *Megaster Queen* which left that morning for Lyra Alpha. He took me with him. He wept and counted his money and I beat the android again.

And the thermometer in Dallas Brady's workshop registered 98.1° beautifully Fahrenheit.

On Lyra Alpha we holed up in a small hotel near the university. There, Vandaleur carefully bruised my forehead until the letters MA were obliterated by the swelling and the discoloration. The letters would reappear again, but not for several months, and in the meantime Vandaleur hoped the hue and cry for an MA android would be forgotten. The android was hired out as a common laborer in the university power plant. Vandaleur, as James Venice, ĕked out life on the android's small earnings.

I wasn't too unhappy. Most of the other residents in the hotel were university students, equally hard up, but delightfully young and enthusiastic. There was one charming girl with sharp eyes and a quick mind. Her name was Wanda, and she and her beau, Jed Stark, took a tremendous interest in the killing android which was being mentioned in every paper in the galaxy.

'We've been studying the case,' she and Jed said at one of the casual student parties which happened to be held this night in Vandaleur's room. 'We think we know what's causing it. We're going to do a paper.' They were in a high state of excitement.

'Causing what?' somebody wanted to know.

'The android rampage.'

'Obviously out of adjustment, isn't it? Body chemistry gone haywire. Maybe a kind of synthetic cancer, yes?'

'No.' Wanda gave Jed a look of suppressed triumph.

'Well, what is it?'

'Something specific.'

'What?'

'That would be telling.'

'Oh, come on.'

'Nothing doing.'

'Won't you tell us?' I asked intently. 'I ... We're very much interested in what could go wrong with an android.'

'No, Mr Venice,' Wanda said. 'It's a unique idea and we've got to protect it. One thesis like this and we'll be set up for life. We can't take the chance of somebody stealing it.'

'Can't you give us a hint?'

'No. Not a hint. Don't say a word, Jed. But I'll tell you this much, Mr Venice. I'd hate to be the man who owns that android.'

'You mean the police?' I asked.

'I mean projection, Mr Venice. Projection! That's the danger ... and I won't say any more. I've said too much as it is.'

I heard steps outside, and a hoarse voice singing softly: 'Be fleet be fleet, cool and discreet, honey ...' My android entered the room, home from its tour of duty at the university power plant. It was not introduced. I motioned to it and I immediately responded to the command and went to the beer keg and took over Vandaleur's job of serving the guests. Its accomplished fingers writhed in a private rumba of their own. Gradually they stopped their squirming, and the strange humming ended.

Androids were not unusual at the university. The wealthier students owned them along with cars and planes. Vandaleur's android provoked no comment, but young Wanda was sharp-eyed and quick-witted. She noted my bruised forehead and she was intent on the history-making thesis she and Jed Stark were going to write. After the party broke up, she consulted with Jed walking upstairs to her room.

'Jed, why'd that android have a bruised forehead?'

'Probably hurt itself, Wanda. It's working in the power plant. They fling a lot of heavy stuff around.'

'That all?'

'What else?'

'It could be a convenient bruise.'

'Convenient for what?'

'Hiding what's stamped on its forehead.'

'No point to that, Wanda. You don't have to see marks on a forehead to recognize an android. You don't have to see a trademark on a car to know it's a car.'

'I don't mean it's trying to pass as a human. I mean it's trying to pass as a lower grade android.'

'Why?'

'Suppose it had MA on its forehead.'

'Multiple aptitude? Then why in hell would Venice waste it stoking furnaces if it could earn more – Oh. Oh! You mean it's –?'

Wanda nodded.

'Jesus!' Stark pursed his lips. 'What do we do? Call the police?'

'No. We don't know if it's an MA for a fact. If it turns out to be an MA and the killing android, our paper comes first anyway. This is our big chance, Jed. If it's *that* android we can run a series of controlled tests and –'

'How do we find out for sure?'

'Easy. Infrared film. That'll show what's under the bruise. Borrow a camera. Buy some film. We'll sneak down to the power plant tomorrow afternoon and take some pictures. Then we'll know.'

They stole down into the university power plant the following afternoon. It was a vast cellar, deep under the earth. It was dark, shadowy, luminous with burning light from the furnace doors. Above the roar of the fires they could hear a strange voice shouting and chanting in the echoing vault: 'All reet! All reet! So jeet your seat. Be fleet be fleet, cool and discreet, honey....' And they could see a capering figure dancing a lunatic rumba in time to the music it shouted. The legs twisted. The arms waved. The fingers writhed.

Jed Stark raised the camera and began shooting his spool of infrared film, aiming the camera sights at that bobbing head. Then Wanda shrieked, for I saw them and came charging down on them, brandishing a polished steel shovel. It smashed the camera. It felled the girl and then the boy. Jed fought me for a desperate hissing moment before he was bludgeoned into helplessness. Then the android dragged them to the furnace and fed them to the flames, slowly, hideously. It capered and sang. Then it returned to my hotel.

The thermometer in the power plant registered 100.9° murderously Fahrenheit. All reet! All reet!

We bought steerage on the *Lyra Queen* and Vandaleur and the android did odd jobs for their meals. During the night watches, Vandaleur would sit alone in the steerage head with a cardboard portfolio on his lap, puzzling over its contents. That portfolio was all he had managed to bring with him from Lyra Alpha. He had stolen it from Wanda's room. It was labeled ANDROID. It contained the secret of my sickness.

And it contained nothing but newspapers. Scores of newspapers from all over the galaxy, printed, microfilmed, engraved, etched, offset, photostated ... Rigel *Star-Banner* ... Paragon *Picayune* ... Megaster *Times-Leader* ... Lalande *Herald* ... Lacaille *Journal* ... Indi *Intelligencer* ... Eridani *Telegram-News*. All reet! All reet!

Nothing but newspapers. Each paper contained an account of one crime in the android's ghastly career. Each paper also contained news, domestic and foreign, sports, society, weather, shipping news, stock exchange quotations, human interest stories, features, contests, puzzles. Somewhere in that mass of uncollated facts was the secret Wanda and Jed Start had discovered. Vandaleur pored over the papers helplessly. It was beyond him. So jeet your seat!

'I'll sell you,' I told the android. 'Damn you. When we land on Terra, I'll sell you. I'll settle for 3 per cent on whatever you're worth.'

'I am worth fifty-seven thousand dollars on the current exchange,' I told him.

'If I can't sell you, I'll turn you in to the police,' I said.

'I am valuable property,' I answered. 'It is forbidden to endanger valuable property. You won't have me destroyed.'

'Christ damn you!' Vandaleur cried. 'What? Are you arrogant? Do you know you can trust me to protect you? Is that the secret?'

The multiple aptitude android regarded him with calm accomplished eyes. 'Sometimes,' it said, 'it is a good thing to be property.'

It was three below zero when the *Lyra Queen* dropped at Croydon Field. A mixture of ice and snow swept across the field, fizzing and exploding into steam under the *Queen*'s tail jets. The passengers trotted numbly across the blackened concrete to customs inspection, and thence to the airport bus that was to take them to London. Vandaleur and the android were broke. They walked.

By midnight they reached Piccadilly Circus. The December ice storm had not slackened and the statue of Eros was encrusted with ice. They turned right, walked down to Trafalgar Square and then along the Strand toward Soho, shaking with cold and wet. Just above Fleet Street, Vandaleur saw a solitary figure coming from the direction of St Paul's. He drew the android into an alley.

'We've got to have money,' he whispered. He pointed at the approaching figure. 'He has money. Take it from him.'

'The order cannot be obeyed,' the android said.

'Take it from him,' Vandaleur repeated. 'By force. Do you understand? We're desperate.'

'It is contrary to my prime directive,' I said. 'I cannot endanger life or property. The order cannot be obeyed.'

'For God's sake!' Vandaleur burst out. 'You've attacked, destroyed, murdered. Don't gibber about prime directives. You haven't any left. Get his money. Kill him if you have to. I tell you, we're desperate!'

'It is contrary to my prime directive,' the android repeated. 'The order cannot be obeyed.'

I thrust the android back and leaped out at the stranger. He was tall, austere, competent. He had an air of hope curdled by cynicism. He carried a cane. I saw he was blind.

'Yes?' he said. 'I hear you near me. What is it?'

'Sir ...' Vandaleur hesitated. 'I'm desperate.'

'We are all desperate,' the stranger replied. 'Quietly desperate.'

'Sir ... I've got to have some money.'

'Are you begging or stealing?' The sightless eyes passed over Vandaleur and the android.

'I'm prepared for either.'

'Ah. So are we all. It is the history of our race.' The stranger motioned over his shoulder. 'I have been begging at St Paul's, my friend. What I desire cannot be stolen. What is it you desire that you are lucky enough to be able to steal?'

'Money,' Vandaleur said.

'Money for what? Come, my friend, let us exchange confidences. I will tell you why I beg, if you will tell me why you steal. My name is Blenheim.'

'My name is ... Vole.'

'I was not begging for sight at St Paul's, Mr Vole. I was begging for a number.'

'A number.'

'Ah yes. Numbers rational, numbers irrational. Numbers imaginary. Positive integers. Negative integers. Fractions, positive and negative. Eh? You have never heard of Blenheim's immortal treatise on Twenty Zeros, or The Differences in Absence of Quantity?' Blenheim smiled bitterly. 'I am the wizard of the Theory of Number, Mr Vole, and I have exhausted the charm of number for myself. After fifty years of wizardry, senility approaches and the appetite vanishes. I have been praying in St Paul's for inspiration. Dear God, I prayed, if You exist, send me a number.'

Vandaleur slowly lifted the cardboard portfolio and touched Blenheim's hand with it. 'In here,' he said, 'is a number. A hidden number. A secret number. The number of a crime. Shall we exchange, Mr Blenheim? Shelter for a number?'

'Neither begging nor stealing, eh?' Blenheim said. 'But a bargain. So all life reduces itself to the banal.' The sightless eyes again passed over Vandaleur and the android. 'Perhaps the All-Mighty is not God but a merchant. Come home with me.'

On the top floor of Blenheim's house we shared a room – two beds, two closets, two washstands, one bathroom. Vandaleur bruised my forehead again and sent me out to find work, and while the android worked, I consulted with Blenheim and read him the papers from the portfolio, one by one. All reet! All reet!

Vandaleur told him so much and no more. He was a student, I said, attempting a thesis on the murdering android. In these papers which he had collected were the facts that would explain the crimes of which Blenheim had heard nothing. There must be a correlation, a number, a statistic, something which would account for my derangement, I explained, and Blenheim was piqued by the mystery, the detective story, the human interest of number.

We examined the papers. As I read them aloud, he listed them and their contents in his blind, meticulous writing. And then I read his notes to him. He listed the papers by type, by type face, by fact, by fancy, by article, spelling, words, theme, advertising, pictures, subject, politics, prejudices. He analyzed. He studied. He meditated. And we lived together in that top floor, always a little cold, always a little terrified, always a little closer ... brought together by our fear of it, our hatred between us. Like a wedge driven into a living tree and splitting the trunk, only to be forever incorporated into the scar tissue, we grew together. Vandaleur and the android. Be fleet be fleet!

And one afternoon Blenheim called Vandaleur into his study and displayed his notes. 'I think I've found it,' he said, 'but I can't understand it.'

Vandaleur's heart leaped.

'Here are the correlations,' Blenheim continued. 'In fifty papers there are accounts of the criminal android. What is there, outside the depredations, that is also in fifty papers?'

'I don't know, Mr Blenheim.'

'It was a rhetorical question. Here is the answer. The weather.'

'What?'

'The weather.' Blenheim nodded. 'Each crime was committed on a day when the temperature was above 90 degrees Fahrenheit.'

'But that's impossible,' Vandaleur exclaimed. 'It was cool on Lyra Alpha.'

'We have no record of any crime committed on Lyra Alpha. There is no paper.'

'No. That's right. I –' Vandaleur was confused. Suddenly he exclaimed. 'No. You're right. The furnace room. It was hot there. Hot! Of course. My God, yes! That's the answer. Dallas Brady's electric furnace ... The rice deltas on Paragon. So jeet your seat. Yes. But why? Why? My God, why?'

I came into the house at that moment, and passing the study, saw Vandaleur and Blenheim. I entered, awaiting commands, my multiple aptitudes devoted to service.

'That's the android, eh?' Blenheim said after a long moment.

'Yes,' Vandaleur answered, still confused by the discovery. 'And that explains why it refused to attack you that night on the Strand. It wasn't hot enough to break the prime directive. Only in the heat ... The heat, all reet!' He looked at the android. A lunatic command passed from man to android. I refused. It is forbidden to endanger life. Vandaleur gestured furiously, then seized Blenheim's shoulders and yanked him back out of his desk chair to the floor. Blenheim shouted once. Vandaleur leaped on him like a tiger, pinning him to the floor and sealing his mouth with one hand.

'Find a weapon,' he called to the android.

'It is forbidden to endanger life.'

'This is a fight for self-preservation. Bring me a weapon!' He held the squirming mathematician with all his weight. I went at once to a cupboard where I knew a revolver was kept. I checked it. It was loaded with five cartridges. I handed it to Vandaleur. I took it, rammed the barrel against Blenheim's head and pulled the trigger. He shuddered once.

We had three hours before the cook returned from her day off. We looted the house. We took Blenheim's money and jewels. We packed a bag with clothes. We took Blenheim's notes, destroyed the newspapers; and we left, carefully locking the door behind us. In Blenheim's study we left a pile of crumpled papers under a half inch of burning candle. And we soaked the rug around it with kerosene. No, I did all that. The android refused. I am forbidden to endanger life or property.

All reet!

They took the tube to Leicester Square, changed trains and rode to the British Museum. There they got off and went to a small Georgian house just off Russell Square. A shingle in the window read: NAN WEBB, PSYCHO-METRIC CONSULTANT. Vandaleur had made a note of the address some weeks earlier. They went into the house. The android waited in the foyer with the bag. Vandaleur entered Nan Webb's office.

She was a tall woman with gray shingled hair, very fine English complexion and very bad English legs. Her features were blunt, her expression acute. She nodded to Vandaleur, finished a letter, sealed it and looked up.

'My name,' I said, 'is Vanderbilt. James Vanderbilt.'

'Quite.'

'I'm an exchange student at London University.'

'Quite.'

'I've been researching on the killing android, and I think I've discovered something very interesting. I'd like your advice on it. What is your fee?'

'What is your college at the university?'

'Why?'

'There is a discount for students.'

'Merton College.'

'That will be two pounds, please.'

Vandaleur placed two pounds on the desk and added to the fee Blenheim's notes. 'There is a correlation,' he said, 'between the crimes of the android and the weather. You will note that each crime was committed when the temperature rose above 90 degrees Fahrenheit. Is there a psychometric answer for this?'

Nan Webb nodded, studied the notes for a moment, put down the sheets of paper and said: 'Synesthesia, obviously.'

'What?'

'Synesthesia,' she repeated. 'When a sensation, Mr Vanderbilt, is interpreted immediately in terms of a sensation from a different sense organ from the one stimulated, it is called synesthesia. For example: a sound stimulus gives rise to a simultaneous sensation of definite color. Or color gives rise to a sensation of taste. Or a light stimulus gives rise to a sensation of sound. There can be confusion or short circuiting of any sensation of taste, smell, pain, pressure, temperature and so on. D'you understand?'

'I think so.'

'Your research has uncovered the fact that the android most probably reacts to temperature stimulus above the 90-degree level synesthetically. Most probably there is an endocrine response. Probably a temperature linkage with the android adrenal surrogate. High temperature brings about a response of fear, anger, excitement and violent physical activity ... all within the province of the adrenal gland.'

'Yes. I see. Then if the android were to be kept in cold climates ...'

'There would be neither stimulus nor response. There would be no crimes. Quite.'

'I see. What is projection?'

'It is the danger of believing what is implied. If you live with a psychotic who projects his sickness upon you, there is a danger of falling into his psychotic pattern and becoming virtually psychotic yourself. As, no doubt, is happening to you, Mr Vandaleur.'

Vandaleur leaped to his feet.

'You are an ass,' Nan Webb went on crisply. She waved the sheets of notes. 'This is no exchange student's writing. It's the unique cursive of the famous Blenheim. Every scholar in England knows this blind writing. There is no Merton College at London University. That was a miserable guess. Merton is one of the Oxford colleges. And you, Mr Vandaleur, are so obviously infected by association with your deranged android ... by projection, if you will ... that I hesitate between calling the Metropolitan Police and the Hospital for the Criminally Insane.'

I took the gun and shot her.

'Antares II, Alpha Aurigae, Acrux IV, Pollux IX, Rigel Centaurus,' Vandaleur said. 'They're all cold. Cold as a witch's kiss. Mean temperatures of 40 degrees Fahrenheit. Never get hotter than 70. We're in business again. Watch that curve.'

The multiple aptitude android swung the wheel with its accomplished hands. The car took the curve sweetly and sped on through the northern marshes, the reeds stretching for miles, brown and dry, under the cold English sky. The sun was sinking swiftly. Overhead, a lone flight of bustards flapped clumsily eastward. High above the flight, a lone helicopter drifted toward home and warmth.

'No more warmth for us,' I said. 'No more heat. We're safe when we're cold. We'll hole up in Scotland, make a little money, get across to Norway, build a bankroll and then ship out. We'll settle on Pollux. We're safe. We've licked it. We can live again.'

There was a startling *bleep* from overhead, and then a ragged roar: 'ATTENTION JAMES VANDALEUR AND ANDROID. ATTENTION JAMES VANDALEUR AND ANDROID!'

Vandaleur started and looked up. The lone helicopter was floating above them. From its belly came amplified commands: 'YOU ARE SURROUNDED. THE ROAD IS BLOCKED. YOU ARE TO STOP YOUR CAR AT ONCE AND SUBMIT TO ARREST. STOP AT ONCE!'

I looked at Vandaleur for orders.

'Keep driving,' Vandaleur snapped.

The helicopter dropped lower. 'ATTENTION ANDROID. YOU ARE IN CONTROL OF THE VEHICLE. YOU ARE TO STOP AT ONCE. THIS IS A STATE DIRECTIVE SUPERSEDING ALL PRIVATE COMMANDS.'

'What the hell are you doing?' I shouted.

'A state directive supersedes all private commands,' the android answered. 'I must point out to you that —'

'Get the hell away from the wheel,' Vandaleur ordered. I clubbed the android, yanked him sideways and squirmed over him to the wheel. The car veered off the road in that moment and went churning through the frozen mud and dry reeds. Vandaleur regained control and continued westward through the marshes toward a parallel highway five miles distant.

'We'll beat their God damned block,' he grunted.

The car pounded and surged. The helicopter dropped even lower. A searchlight blazed from the belly of the plane.

'ATTENTION JAMES VANDALEUR AND ANDROID. SUBMIT TO ARREST. THIS IS A STATE DIRECTIVE SUPERSEDING ALL PRIVATE COMMANDS.'

'He can't submit,' Vandaleur shouted wildly. 'There's no one to submit to. He can't and I won't.'

'Christ!' I muttered. 'We'll beat them yet. We'll beat the block. We'll beat the heat. We'll —'

'I must point out to you,' I said, 'that I am required by my prime directive to obey state directives which supersede all private commands. I must submit to arrest.'

'Who says it's a state directive?' Vandaleur said. 'Them? Up in that plane? They've got to show credentials. They've got to prove it's state authority before you submit. How d'you know they're not crooks trying to trick us?'

Holding the wheel with one arm, he reached into his side pocket to make sure the gun was still in place. The car skidded. The tires squealed on frost and reeds. The wheel was wrenched from his grasp and the car yawed up a small hillock and overturned. The motor roared and the wheels screamed. Vandaleur crawled out and dragged the android with him. For the moment we were outside the circle of light boring down from the helicopter. We blundered off into the marsh, into the blackness, into concealment ... Vandaleur running with a pounding heart, hauling the android along.

The helicopter circled and soared over the wrecked car, searchlight peering, loudspeaker braying. On the highway we had left, lights appeared as the pursuing and blocking parties gathered and followed radio directions from the plane. Vandaleur and the android continued deeper and deeper into the marsh, working their way towards the parallel road and safety. It was night by now. The sky was a black matte. Not a star showed. The temperature was dropping. A southeast night wind knifed us to the bone.

Far behind there was a dull concussion. Vandaleur turned, gasping. The car's fuel had exploded. A geyser of flame shot up like a lurid fountain. It subsided into a low crater of burning reeds. Whipped by the wind, the distant hem of flame fanned up into a wall, ten feet high. The wall began marching down on us, crackling fiercely. Above it, a pall of oily smoke surged forward. Behind it, Vandaleur could make out the figures of men ... a mass of beaters searching the marsh.

'Christ!' I cried and searched desperately for safety. He ran, dragging me with him, until their feet crunched through the surface ice of a pool. He trampled the ice furiously, then flung himself down in the numbing water, pulling the android with us.

The wall of flame approached. I could hear the crackle and feel the heat. He could see the searchers clearly. Vandaleur reached into his side pocket for the gun. The pocket was torn. The gun was gone. He groaned and shook with cold and terror. The light from the marsh fire was blinding. Overhead, the helicopter floated helplessly to one side, unable to fly through the smoke and flames and aid the searchers who were beating far to the right of us.

'They'll miss us,' Vandaleur whispered. 'Keep quiet. That's an order. They'll miss us. We'll beat them. We'll beat the fire. We'll –'

Three distinct shots sounded less than a hundred feet from the fugitives. *Blam! Blam! Blam!* They came from the last three cartridges in my gun as the marsh fire reached it where it had dropped, and exploded the shells. The searchers turned toward the sound and began working directly toward us. Vandaleur cursed hysterically and tried to submerge even deeper to escape the intolerable heat of the fire. The android began to twitch.

The wall of flame surged up to them. Vandaleur took a deep breath and prepared to submerge until the flame passed over them. The android shuddered and burst into an ear-splitting scream.

'All reet! All reet!' it shouted. 'Be fleet be fleet!'

'Damn you!' I shouted. I tried to drown it.

'Damn you!' I cursed him. I smashed his face.

The android battered Vandaleur, who fought it off until it exploded out of the mud and staggered upright. Before I could return to the attack, the live flames captured it hypnotically. It danced and capered in a lunatic rumba before the wall of fire. Its legs twisted. Its arms waved. The fingers writhed in a private rumba of their own. It shrieked and sang and ran in a crooked waltz before the embrace of the heat, a muddy monster silhouetted against the brilliant sparkling fire.

The searchers shouted. There were shots. The android spun around twice and then continued its horrid dance before the face of the flames. There was a rising gust of wind. The fire swept around the capering figure and enveloped it for a roaring moment. Then the fire swept on; leaving behind it a sobbing mass of synthetic flesh oozing scarlet blood that would never coagulate.

The thermometer would have registered 1200° wondrously Fahrenheit.

Vandaleur didn't die. I got away. They missed him while they watched the android caper and die. But I don't know which of us he is these days. Projection, Wanda warned me. Projection, Nan Webb told him. If you live with a crazy man or a crazy machine long enough, I become crazy too. Reet!

But we know one truth. We know they were wrong. The new robot and Vandaleur know that because the new robot's started twitching too. Reet! Here on cold Pollux, the robot is twitching and singing. No heat, but my fingers writhe. No heat, but it's taken the little Talley girl off for a solitary walk. A cheap labor robot. A servo-mechanism ... all I could afford ... but it's twitching and humming and walking alone with the child somewhere and I can't find them. Christ! Vandaleur can't find me before it's too late. Cool and discreet, honey, in the dancing frost while the thermometer registers 10° Fahrenheit.

ONLINE: TWO/4 *Subject*: The Adjustor

Comfort Me, My Robot

Robert Bloch

INFO: Imagine being able to satisfy any feelings of aggression – even commit murder – because surrogates in the shape of robots will stand in for your intended victim. So you can let the psycho in you loose and only artificial flesh and machine oil gets hurt. That's precisely what Henson decides to do when he discovers his wife is cheating on him ...

Robert Bloch was the man who made the world afraid to take a shower after his novel, *Psycho* (1959), was made into the classic horror movie by Alfred Hitchcock. He also wrote two sequels, *Psycho II* (1982) and *Psycho House* (1990), which further consolidated his fame as the master of psycho-ology. Bob was born in Chicago and wrote his first stories for the legendary pulp magazine, *Weird Tales*, as well as contributing to a number of sf magazines. He created a number of excellent tales around real-life criminals such as Lizzie Borden and Jack the Ripper, and his 1984 novel *The Night of the Ripper* proposed a very ingenious solution to the identity of the London mass murderer – he was a *woman*. Bob combined sf and horror in a collection of tales published as *Atoms and Evil* in 1958 and he was awarded a Hugo for his story, 'That Hell-Bound Train', the following year. 'Comfort Me, My Robot' appeared in *Imagination* in 1955 and has not previously been anthologised. It was his suggestion for this book shortly before his death.

When Henson came in, the Adjustor was sitting inside his desk, telescreening a case. At the sound of the doortone he flicked a switch. The posturchair rose from the center of the desk until the Adjustor's face peered at the visitor from an equal level.

'Oh, it's you,' said the Adjustor. 'Aren't you a bit early for dinner? Our engagement isn't until five.'

'This isn't an engagement,' Henson told him. 'It's an appointment.'

'Appointment?'

'Didn't the girl tell you? I'm here to see you professionally.'

If the Adjustor was surprised, he didn't show it. He cocked a thumb at a posturchair. 'Sit down and tell me all about it, Henson,' he said.

'Nothing to tell.' Henson stared out of the window at the plains of Upper Mongolia. 'It's just a routine matter. I'm here to make a request and you're the Adjustor.'

'And your request is –?'

'Simple,' said Henson. 'I want to kill my wife.'

The Adjustor nodded. 'That can be arranged,' he murmured. 'Of course, it will take a few days.'

'I can wait.'

'Would Friday be convenient?'

'Good enough. That way it won't cut into my weekend. Lita and I were planning a fishing trip, up New Zealand way. Care to join us?'

'Sorry, but I'm tied up until Monday.' The Adjustor stifled a yawn. 'Why do you want to kill Lita?' he asked.

'She's hiding something from me.'

'What do you suspect?'

'That's just it – I don't know what to suspect. And it keeps bothering me.'

'Why don't you question her?'

'Violation of privacy. Surely you, as a certified public Adjustor, wouldn't advocate that?'

'Not professionally.' The Adjustor grinned. 'But since we're personal friends, I don't mind telling you that there are times when I think privacy should be violated. This notion of individual rights can become a fetish.'

'Fetish?'

'Just an archaicism.' The Adjustor waved a casual dismissal to the word. He leaned forward. 'Then, as I understand it, your wife's attitude troubles you. Rather than embarrass her with questions, you propose to solve the problem delicately, by killing her.'

'Right.'

'A very chivalrous attitude. I admire it.'

'I'm not sure whether I do or not,' Henson mused. 'You see, it really wasn't my idea. But the worry was beginning to affect my work, and my Administrator – Loring, you know him, I believe – took me aside for a talk. He suggested I see you and arrange for a murder.'

'Then it's to be murder.' The Adjustor frowned. 'You know, actually, we are supposed to be the arbiters when it comes to method. In some cases a suicide works just as well. Or an accident.'

'I want a murder,' Henson said. 'Premeditated, and in the first degree.' Now it was his turn to grin. 'You see, I know a few archaicisms myself.'

The Adjustor made a note. 'As long as we're dealing in archaic terminology, might I characterize your attitude towards your wife as one of – jealousy?'

Henson controlled his blush at the sound of the word. He nodded slowly. 'I guess you're right,' he admitted. 'I can't bear the idea of her having any secrets. I know it's immature and absurd, and that's why I'm seeking an immature solution.'

'Let me correct you,' said the Adjustor. 'Your solution is far from immature. A good murder is probably the most adult approach to your problem. After all, man, this is the twenty-second century, not the twentieth. Although even way back then they were beginning to learn some of the answers.'

'Don't tell me they had Adjustors,' Henson murmured.

'No, of course not. In those days this field was only a small, neglected part of physical medicine. Practitioners were called psychiatrists, psychologists, auditors, analysts – and a lot of other things. That was their chief stock in trade, by the way; name-calling and labelling.'

The Adjustor gestured toward the slide-files. 'I must have five hundred spools transcribed there,' he calculated. 'All of it from books – nineteenth, twentieth, even early twenty-first century material. And it's largely terminology, not technique. Psychotherapy was just like alchemy in those days. Everything was named and defined. Inability to cope with environment was minutely broken down into hundreds of categories, thousands of terms. There were "schools" of therapy, with widely divergent theories and applications. And the crude attempts at technique they used – you wouldn't believe it unless you studied what I have here! Everything from trying to "cure" a disorder in one session by means of brain-surgery or electric shock to the other extreme of letting the "patient" talk about his problems for thousands of hours over a period of years.'

He smiled. 'I'm afraid I'm letting my personal enthusiasm run away with me. After all, Henson, you aren't interested in the historical aspects. But I did have a point I wanted to make. About the maturity of murder as a solution-concept.'

Henson adjusted the posturchair as he listened.

'As I said, even back in the twentieth century, they were beginning to get a hint of the answer. It was painfully apparent that some of the techniques I mention weren't working at all. "Sublimation" and "catharsis" helped but did not cure in a majority of cases. Physical therapy altered and warped the personality. And all the while, the answer lay right before their eyes.

'Let's take your twentieth-century counterpart for an example. Man named Henson, who was jealous of his wife. He might go to an analyst for years without relief. Whereas if he did the sensible thing, he'd take an axe to her and kill her.

'Of course, in the twentieth century such a procedure was antisocial and illegal. Henson would be sent to prison for the rest of his life.

'But the chances are, he'd function perfectly thereafter. Having relieved his psychic tension by the common-sense method of direct action, he'd have no further difficulty in adjustment.

'Gradually the psychiatrists observed this phenomenon. They learned to distinguish between the psychopath and the perfectly normal human being who sought to relieve an intolerable situation. It was hard, because once a normal man was put in prison, he was subject to new tensions and stresses which caused fresh aberrations. But these aberrations stemmed from his confinement – not from the impulses which led him to kill.' Again the Adjustor paused. 'I hope I'm not making this too abstruse for you,' he said. 'Terms like "psychopath" and "normal" can't have much meaning to a layman.'

'I understand what you're driving at,' Henson told him. 'Go ahead. I've always wondered how Adjustment evolved, anyway.'

'I'll make it brief from now on,' the Adjustor promised. 'The next crude step was something called the "psychodrama". It was a simple technique in which an aberrated individual was encouraged to get up on a platform, before an audience, and act out his fantasies – including those involving aggression and violently antisocial impulses. This afforded great relief. Well, I won't trouble you with the historical details about the establishment of Master Control, right after North America went under in the Blast. We got it, and the world started afresh, and one of the groups set up was Adjustment. All of physical medicine, all of what was then called sociology and psychiatry, came under the scope of this group. And from that point on we started to make real progress.

'Adjustors quickly learned that old-fashioned therapies must be discarded. Naming or classifying a mental disturbance didn't necessarily overcome it. Talking about it, distracting attention from it, teaching the patient a theory about it, were not solutions. Nor was chopping out or shocking out part of his brain-structure.

'More and more we came to rely on direct action as a cure, just as we do in physical medicine.

'Then, of course, robotics came along and gave us the final answer. And it is the answer, Henson – that's the thought I've been trying to convey. Because we're friends, I know you well enough to eliminate all the preliminaries. I don't have to give you a battery of tests, check reactions, and go through the other formalities. But if I did, I'm sure I'd end up with the same answer – in your case, the mature solution is to murder your wife as quickly as possible. That will cure you.'

'Thanks,' said Henson. 'I knew I could count on you.'

'No trouble at all.' The Adjustor stood up. He was a tall, handsome man with curly red hair, and he somewhat towered over Henson who was only six feet and a bit too thin.

'You'll have papers to sign, of course,' the Adjustor reminded him. 'I'll get everything ready by Friday morning. If you'll step in then, you can do it in ten minutes.'

'Fine.' Henson smiled. 'Then I think I'll plan the murder for Friday evening, at home. I'll get Lita to visit her mother in Saigon overnight. Best if she doesn't know about this until afterwards.'

'Thoughtful of you,' the Adjustor agreed. 'I'll have her robot requisitioned for you from Inventory. Any special requirements?'

'I don't believe so. It was made less than two years ago, and it's almost a perfect match. Paid almost seven thousand for the job.'

'That's a lot of capital to destroy.' The Adjustor sighed. 'Still, it's necessary. Will you want anything else – weapons, perhaps?'

'No.' Henson stood in the doorway. 'I think I'll just strangle her.'

'Very well, then. I'll have the robot here and operating for you on Friday morning. And you'll take your robot too.'

'Mine? Why, might I ask?'

'Standard procedure. You see, we've learned something more about the mind – about what used to be called a "guilt complex". Sometimes a man isn't freed by direct action alone. There may be a peculiar desire for punishment involved. In the old days many men who committed actual murders had this need to be caught and punished. Those who avoided capture frequently punished themselves. They developed odd psychosomatic reactions – some even committed suicide.

'In case you have any such impulses, your robot will be available to you.

Punish it any way you like – destroy it, if necessary. That's the sensible thing to do.'

'Right. See you Friday morning, then. And many thanks.' Henson started through the doorway. He looked back and grinned. 'You know, just thinking about it makes me feel better already!'

Henson whizzed back to the Adjustor's office on Friday morning. He was in rare good humor all the way. Anticipation was a wonderful thing. Everything was wonderful, for that matter.

Take robots, for example. The simple, uncomplicated mechanisms did all the work, all the drudgery. Their original development for military purposes during the twenty-first century was forgotten now, along with the concept of war which had inspired their creation. Now the automatons functioned as workers.

And for the well-to-do there were these personalized surrogates. What a convenience!

Henson remembered how he'd argued to convince Lita they should invest in a pair when they married. He'd used all of the sensible modern arguments. 'You know as well as I do what having them will save us in terms of time and efficiency. We can send them to all the boring banquets and social functions. They can represent us at weddings and funerals, that sort of thing. After all, it's being done everywhere nowadays. Nobody attends such affairs in person any more if they can afford not to. Why, you see them on the street everywhere. Remember Kirk, at our reception? Stayed four hours, life of the party and everybody was fooled – you didn't know it was his robot until he told you.'

And so forth on and on. 'Aren't you sentimental at all, darling? If I died wouldn't you like to have my surrogate around to comfort you? I certainly would want yours to share the rest of my life.'

Yes, he'd used all the practical arguments except the psychotherapeutic one – at that time it had never occurred to him. But perhaps it should have, when he heard her objections.

'I just don't like the idea,' Lita had persisted. 'Oh, it isn't that I'm old-fashioned. But lying there in the forms having every detail of my body duplicated synthetically – ugh! And then they do that awful hypnotherapy or whatever it's called for days to make them think. Oh, I know they have no brains, it's only a lot of chemicals and electricity, but they do duplicate your thought-patterns and they react the same and they *sound* so real. I don't want anyone or anything to know all my secrets –'

Yes, that objection should have started him thinking. Lita had secrets even then.

But he'd been too busy to notice; he'd spent his efforts in battering down her objections. And finally she'd consented.

He remembered the days at the Institute – the tests they'd taken, the time spent in working with the anatomists, the cosmetic department, the sonic and visio adaptors, and then days of hypnotic transference.

Lita was right in a way; it hadn't been pleasant. Even a modern man was bound to feel a certain atavistic fear when confronted for the first time with his completed surrogate. But the finished product was worth it. And after Henson had mastered instructions, learned how to manipulate the robot by virtue of the control-command, he had been almost paternally proud of the creation.

He'd wanted to take his surrogate home with him, but Lita positively drew the line at that.

'We'll leave them both here in Inventory,' she said. 'If we need them we can always send for them. But I hope we never do.'

Henson was finally forced to agree. He and Lita had both given their immobilization commands to the surrogates, and they were placed in their metal cabinets ready to be filed away – 'Just like corpses!' Lita had shuddered. 'We're looking at ourselves after we're dead.'

And that had ended the episode. For a while, Henson made suggestions about using the surrogates – there were occasions he'd have liked to take advantage of a substitute for token public appearances – but Lita continued to object. And so, for two years now, the robots had been on file. Henson paid his taxes and fees on them annually and that was all.

That was all, until lately. Until Lita's unexplained silences and still more inexplicable absences had started Henson thinking. Thinking and worrying. Worrying and watching. Watching and waiting. Waiting to catch her, waiting to kill her –

So he'd remembered psychotherapy, and gone to his Adjustor. Lucky the man was a friend of his; a friend of both of them, rather. Actually, Lita had known him longer than her husband. But they'd been very close, the three of them, and he knew the Adjustor would understand.

He could trust the Adjustor not to tell Lita. He could trust the Adjustor to have everything ready and waiting for him now.

Henson went up to the office. The papers were ready for him to sign. The two metal boxes containing the surrogates were already placed on the loaders ready for transport to wherever he designated. But the Adjustor wasn't on hand to greet him.

'Special assignment in Manila,' the Second explained to him. 'But he left instructions about your case, Mr Henson. All you have to do is sign the responsibility slips. And of course, you'll be in on Monday for the official report.'

Henson nodded. Now that the moment was so near at hand he was impatient of details. He could scarcely wait until the micro-dupes were completed and the Register Board signalled clearance. Two common robots were requisitioned to carry the metal cases down to the gyro and load them in. Henson whizzed back home with them and they brought the cases up to his living-level. Then he dismissed them, and he was alone.

He was alone. He could open the cases now. First, his own. He slid back the cover, gazed down at the perfect duplicate of his own body, sleeping peacefully for two serene years since its creation. Henson stared curiously at his pseudo-countenance. He'd aged a bit in two years, but the surrogate was ageless. It could survive the ravages of centuries, and it was always at peace. Always at peace. He almost envied it. The surrogate didn't love, couldn't hate, wouldn't know the gnawing torture of suspicion that led to this shaking, quaking, aching lust to kill –

Henson shoved the lid back and lifted the metal case upright, then dragged it along the wall to a storage cabinet. A domestic-model could have done it for him, but Lita didn't like domestic-models. She wouldn't permit even a common robot in her home.

Lita and her likes and dislikes! Damn her to Los Alamos and gone!

Henson ripped the lid down on the second file.

There she was.

There she was; the beautiful, harlot-eyed, blonde, lying, adorable, dirty, gorgeous, loathsome, heavenly, filthy little goddess of a slut!

He remembered the command word to awake her. It almost choked him now, but he said it.

'Beloved!'

Nothing happened. Then he realized why. He'd been almost snarling. He had to change the pitch of his voice. He tried again, softly. 'Beloved!'

She moved. Her breasts rose and fell, rose and fell. She opened her eyes. She held out her arms and smiled. She stood up and came close to him, without a word.

Henson stared at her. She was newly born and innocent, she had no secrets, she wouldn't betray him. How could he harm her? How could he harm her when she lifted her face in expectation of a kiss?

But she was Lita. He had to remember that. She was Lita, and Lita was hiding something from him and she must be punished, would be punished.

Suddenly, Henson became conscious of his hands. There was a tingling in his wrists and it ran down through the strong muscles and sinews to the fingers, and the fingers flexed and unflexed with exultant vigour, and then they rose and curled around the surrogate's throat, around Lita's throat, and they were squeezing and squeezing and the surrogate–Lita tried to move away and the scream was almost real and the popping eyes were almost real and the purpling face was almost real, only nothing was real any more except the hands and the choking and the surging sensation of strength.

And then it was over. He dragged the limp, dangling mechanism (it was only a mechanism now just as the hate was only a memory) to the waste-jet and fed the surrogate to the flame. He turned the aperture wide and thrust the metal case in, too.

Then Henson slept, and he did not dream. For the first time in months he did not dream, because it was over and he was himself again. The therapy was complete.

'So that's how it was.' Henson sat in the Adjustor's office, and the Monday morning sun was strong on his face.

'Good.' The Adjustor smiled and ran a hand across the top of his curly head. 'And how did you and Lita enjoy your weekend? Fish biting?'

'We didn't fish,' said Henson. 'We talked.'

'Oh?'

'I figured I'd have to tell her what happened, sooner or later. So I did.'

'How did she take it?'

'Very well, at first.'

'And then –?'

'I asked her some questions.'

'Yes.'

'She answered them.'

'You mean she told you what she'd been hiding?'

'Not willingly. But she told me. After I told her about my own little check-up.'

'What was that?'

'I did some calling Friday night. She wasn't in Saigon with her mother.'

'No?'

'And you weren't in Manila on a special case, either.' Henson leaned forward. 'The two of you were together, in New Singapore! I checked it and she admitted it.'

The Adjustor sighed. 'So now you know,' he said.

'Yes. Now I know. Now I know what she's been concealing from me. What you've both been concealing.'

'Surely you're not jealous about that?' the Adjustor asked. 'Not in this modern day and age when –'

'She says she wants to have a child by you,' Henson said. 'She refused to bear one for me. But she wants yours. She told me so.'

'What do you want to do about it?' the Adjustor asked.

'You tell me,' Henson murmured. 'That's why I've come to you. You're my Adjustor.'

'What would you like to do?'

'I'd like to kill you,' Henson said. 'I'd like to blow off the top of your head with a pocket-blast.'

'Not a bad idea.' The Adjustor nodded. 'I'll have my robot ready whenever you say.'

'At my place,' said Henson. 'Tonight.'

'Good enough. I'll send it there to you.'

'One thing more.' Henson gulped for a moment. 'In order for it to do any good, Lita must watch.'

It was the Adjustor's turn to gulp, now. 'You mean you're going to force her to see you go through with this –?'

'I told her and she agreed,' Henson said.

'But, think of the effect on her, man!'

'Think of the effect on me. Do you want me to go mad?'

'No,' said the Adjustor. 'You're right. It's therapy. I'll send the robot around at eight. Do you need a pocket-blast requisition?'

'I have one,' said Henson.

'What instructions shall I give my surrogate?' the Adjustor asked.

Henson told him. He was brutally explicit, and midway in his statement the Adjustor looked away, coloring. 'So the two of you will be together, just as if *you* were real, and then I'll come in and –'

The Adjustor shuddered a little then managed a smile. 'Sound therapy,' he said. 'If that's the way you want it, that's the way it will be.'

That's the way Henson wanted it, and that's the way he had it – up to a point.

He burst into the room around quarter after eight and found the two of them waiting for him. There was Lita, and there was the Adjustor's surrogate. The surrogate had been well-instructed; it looked surprised and startled. Lita needed no instruction; hers was an agony of shame.

Henson had the pocket-blast in his hand, cocked at the ready. He aimed.

Unfortunately, he was just a little late. The surrogate sat up gracefully and slid one hand under the pillow. The hand came up with another pocket-blast aimed and fired all in one motion.

Henson teetered, tottered, and fell. The whole left side of his face sheared away as he went down.

Lita screamed.

Then the surrogate put his arms around her and whispered, 'It's all over, darling. All over. We did it! He really thought I was a robot, that I'd go through with his aberrated notion of dramatizing his revenge.'

The Adjustor smiled and lifted her face to his. 'From now on you and I will always be together. We'll have our child, lots of children if you wish. There's nothing to come between us now.'

'But you killed him,' Lita whispered. 'What will they do to you?'

'Nothing. It was self-defense. Don't forget, I'm an Adjustor. From the moment he came into my office, everything he did or said was recorded during our interviews. The evidence will show that I tried to humor him, that I indicated his mental unbalance and allowed him to work out his own therapy.

'This last interview, today, will not be a part of the record. I've already destroyed it. So as far as the law is concerned, he had no grounds for jealousy or suspicion. I happened to stop in here to visit this evening and found him trying to kill you – the actual you. And when he turned on me, I blasted him in self-defense.'

'Will you get away with it?'

'Of course I'll get away with it. The man was aberrated, and the record will show it.'

The Adjustor stood up. 'I'm going to call Authority now,' he said.

Lita rose and put her hand on his shoulder. 'Kiss me first,' she whispered. 'A real kiss. I like real things.'

'Real things,' said the Adjustor. She snuggled against him, but he made no move to take her in his arms. He was staring down at Henson.

Lita followed his gaze.

Both of them saw it at the same time, then – both of them saw the torn hole in the left side of Henson's head, and the thin strands of wire protruding from the opening.

'He didn't come,' the Adjustor murmured. 'He must have suspected, and he sent his robot instead.'

Lita began to shake. 'You were to send your robot, but you didn't. He was to come himself, but he sent his robot. Each of you doublecrossed the other, and now –'

And now the door opened very quickly.

Henson came into the room.

He looked at his surrogate lying on the floor. He looked at Lita. He looked at the Adjustor. Then he grinned. There was no madness in his grin, only deliberation.

There was deliberation in the way he raised the pocket-blast. He aimed well and carefully, fired only once, but both the Adjustor and Lita crumpled in the burst.

Henson bent over the bodies, inspecting them carefully to make sure that they were real. He was beginning to appreciate Lita's philosophy now. He liked real things.

For that matter, the Adjustor had some good ideas, too. This business of dramatizing aggressions really seemed to work. He didn't feel at all angry or upset any more, just perfectly calm and at peace with the world.

Henson rose, smiled, and walked towards the door. For the first time in years he felt completely adjusted.

ONLINE: TWO/5 *Subject*: The Executioner

Home is the Hangman

Roger Zelazny

INFO: Who better to be the arm of justice than a robot? Designed to be remorseless, unemotional and to act by the letter of the law, the robot would also make the ideal executioner. But that still leaves the question, would a truly intelligent machine think like an intelligent animal?

Roger Zelazny appeared as a frontrunner among the new wave of American science fiction writers who emerged in the Sixties and switched from traditional sf to stories about the dangers of environmental devastation. Roger, who was born in Ohio and graduated from Columbia University with an MA, worked for a time with the Social Security Administration in Cleveland, which provided him with a lot of raw material for his early fiction. Stories like 'The Door of his Face, the Lamps of his Mouth' and 'He Who Shapes' earned him Hugo and Nebula awards, and his stature was confirmed with *This Immortal* (1965), a novel told in the thriller idiom about the trickster Conrad Nomikos. *Damnation Alley* (1969), featuring biker Hell Tanner's race against time across a violent, post-disaster USA, was filmed in 1977 by Jack Smight starring Jan-Michael Vincent. The film inaugurated the genre of punk sf films of which *Mad Max* (1979), with Mel Gibson as a vengeful cop, remains the best known.

Roger Zelazny's subsequent work has included collaborations with Philip K. Dick (*Deus Irae*, 1976), Fred Saberhagen (*Coils*, 1982) and Robert Sheckley (*Bring Me the Head of Prince Charming*, 1991), not forgetting his own long-running series of novels about the fantasy land of Amber. 'Home is the Hangman', told in a gripping, Chandleresque style, first appeared in *Analog*, November 1975.

Big fat flakes down the night, silent night, windless night. And I never count them as storms unless there is wind. Not a sigh or a whimper, though. Just a cold, steady whiteness, drifting down outside the window, and a silence confirmed by gunfire, driven deeper now it had ceased. In the main room of the lodge the only sounds were the occasional hiss and sputter of the logs turning to ashes on the grate.

I sat in a chair turned sidewise from the table to face the door. A toolkit rested on the floor to my left. The helmet stood on the table, a lopsided basket of metal, quartz, porcelain and glass. If I heard the click of a microswitch followed by a humming sound from within it, then a faint light would come on beneath the meshing near to its forward edge and begin to blink rapidly. If these things occurred, there was a very strong possibility that I was going to die.

I had removed a black ball from my pocket when Larry and Bert had gone outside, armed, respectively, with a flame thrower and what looked like an elephant gun. Bert had also taken two grenades with him.

I unrolled the black ball, opening it out into a seamless glove, a dollop of something resembling moist putty stuck to its palm. Then I drew the glove on over my left hand and sat with it upraised, elbow resting on the arm of the chair. A small laser flash pistol in which I had very little faith lay beside my right hand on the tabletop, next to the helmet.

If I were to slap a metal surface with my left hand, the substance would adhere there, coming free of the glove. Two seconds later it would explode, and the force of the explosion would be directed in against the surface. Newton would claim his own by way of right-angled redistributions of the reaction, hopefully tearing lateral hell out of the contact surface. A smother-charge, it was called, and its possession came under concealed weapons and possession of burglary tools statutes in most places. The molecularly gimmicked goo, I decided, was great stuff. It was just the delivery system that left more to be desired.

Beside the helmet, next to the gun, in front of my hand, stood a small walkie-talkie. This was for purposes of warning Bert and Larry if I should hear the click of a microswitch followed by a humming sound, should see a light come on and begin to blink rapidly. Then they would know that Tom and Clay, with whom we had lost contact when the shooting began, had failed to destroy the enemy and doubtless lay lifeless at their stations now, a little over a kilometer to the south. Then they would know that they, too, were probably about to die.

I called out to them when I heard the click. I picked up the helmet and rose to my feet as its light began to blink.

But it was already too late.

The fourth place listed on the Christmas card I had sent Don Walsh the previous year was Peabody's Book Shop and Beer Stube in Baltimore, Maryland. Accordingly, on the last night in October I sat in its rearmost room, at the final table before the alcove with the door leading to the alley. Across that dim chamber, a woman dressed in black played the ancient upright piano, up-tempoing everything she touched. Off to my right, a fire wheezed and spewed fumes on a narrow hearth beneath a crowded mantelpiece overseen by an ancient and antlered profile. I sipped a beer and listened to the sounds.

I half-hoped that this would be one of the occasions when Don failed to show up. I had sufficient funds to hold me through spring and I did not really feel like working. I had summered farther north, was anchored now in the Chesapeake and was anxious to continue Caribbeanwards. A growing chill and some nasty winds told me I had tarried overlong in these latitudes. Still, the understanding was that I remain in the chosen bar until midnight. Two hours to go.

I ate a sandwich and ordered another beer. About halfway into it, I spotted Don approaching the entranceway, topcoat over his arm, head turning. I manufactured a matching quantity of surprise when he appeared beside my table with a 'Don! Is that really you?'

I rose and clasped his hand.

'Alan! Small world, or something like that. Sit down! Sit down!'

He settled on to the chair across from me, draped his coat over the one to his left.

'What are you doing in this town?' he asked.

'Just a visit,' I answered. 'Said hello to a few friends.' I patted the scars, the stains of the venerable surface before me. 'And this is my last stop. I'll be leaving in a few hours.'

He chuckled.

'Why is it that you knock on wood?'

I grinned.

'I was expressing affection for one of Henry Mencken's favorite speakeasies.'

'This place dates back that far?' I nodded.

'It figures,' he said. 'You've got this thing for the past – or against the present. I'm never sure which.'

'Maybe a little of both,' I said. 'I wish Mencken would stop in. I'd like his opinion on the present. What are you doing with it?'

'What?'

'The present. Here. Now.'

'Oh.' He spotted the waitress and ordered a beer. 'Business trip,' he said then. 'To hire a consultant.'

'Oh. And how *is* business?'

'Complicated,' he said, 'complicated.'

We lit cigarettes and after a while his beer arrived. We smoked and drank and listened to the music.

I've sung this song and I'll sing it again: the world is like an up-tempoed piece of music. Of the many changes which came to pass during my lifetime, it seems that the majority have occurred during the past few years. It also struck me that way several years ago, and I'd a hunch I might be feeling the same way a few years hence – that is, if Don's business did not complicate me off this mortal coil or condensor before then.

Don operates the second largest detective agency in the world, and he sometimes finds me useful because I do not exist. I do not exist now because I existed once at the time and the place where we attempted to begin scoring the wild ditty of our times. I refer to the World Data Bank project and the fact that I had had a significant part in that effort to construct a working model of the real world, accounting for everyone and everything in it. How well we succeeded and whether possession of the world's likeness does indeed provide its custodians with a greater measure of control over its functions, are questions my former colleagues still debate as the music grows more shrill and you can't see the maps for the pins. I made my decision back then and saw to it that I did not receive citizenship in that second world, a place which may now have become more important than the first. Exiled to reality, my own sojourns across the line are necessarily those of an alien guilty of illegal entry. I visit periodically because I go where I must to make my living. That is where Don comes in. The people I can become are often very useful when he has peculiar problems. Unfortunately, at that moment, it seemed that he did, just when the whole gang of me felt like turning down the volume and loafing.

We finished our drinks, got the bill, settled it.

'This way,' I said, indicating the rear door, and he swung into his coat and followed me out.

'Talk here?' he asked, as we walked down the alley.

'Rather not,' I said. 'Public transportation, then private conversation.'

He nodded and came along.

About three-quarters of an hour later we were in the saloon of the

Proteus and I was making coffee. We were rocked gently by the Bay's chill waters, under a moonless sky. I'd only a pair of the smaller lights burning. Comfortable. On the water, aboard the *Proteus*, the crowding, the activities, the tempo, of life in the cities, on the land, are muted, slowed – fictionalized – by the metaphysical distancing a few meters of water can provide. We alter the landscape with great facility, but the ocean has always seemed unchanged, and I suppose by extension we are infected with some feelings of timelessness whenever we set out upon her. Maybe that's one of the reasons I spend so much time there.

'First time you've had me aboard,' he said. 'Comfortable. Very.'

'Thanks. Cream? Sugar?'

'Yes. Both.'

We settled back with our steaming mugs and I said, 'What have you got?'

'One case involving two problems,' he said. 'One of them sort of falls within my area of competence. The other does not. I was told that it is an absolutely unique situation and would require the services of a very special specialist.'

'I'm not a specialist at anything but keeping alive.'

His eyes came up suddenly and caught my own.

'I had always assumed that you knew an awful lot about computers,' he said.

I looked away. That was hitting below the belt. I had never held myself out to him as an authority in that area, and there had always been a tacit understanding between us that my methods of manipulating circumstance and identity were not open to discussion. On the other hand, it was obvious to him that my knowledge of the system was both extensive and intensive. Still, I didn't like talking about it. So I moved to defend.

'Computer people are a dime a dozen,' I said. 'It was probably different in your time, but these days they start teaching computer science to little kids their first year in school. So, sure I know a lot about it. This generation, everybody does.'

'You know that is not what I meant,' he said. 'Haven't you known me long enough to trust me a little more than that? The question springs solely from the case at hand. That's all.'

I nodded. Reactions by their very nature are not always appropriate, and I had invested a lot of emotional capital in a heavy-duty set. So, 'OK, I know more about them than the school kids,' I said.

'Thanks. That can be our point of departure.' He took a sip of coffee. 'My own background is in law and accounting, followed by the military, military intelligence and civil service, in that order. Then I got into this business. What technical stuff I know I've picked up along the way, a scrap here, a crash course there. I know a lot about what things can do, not so much about how they work. I did not understand the details on this one, so I want you to start at the top and explain things to me, for as far as you can go. I need the background review, and if you are able to furnish it I will also know that you are the man for the job. You can begin by telling me how the early space exploration robots worked – like, say, the ones they used on Venus.'

'That's not computers,' I said, 'and for that matter, they weren't really robots. They were telefactoring devices.'

'Tell me what makes the difference.'

'A robot is a machine which carries out certain operations in accordance with a program of instructions. A telefactor is a slave machine operated by remote control. The telefactor functions in a feedback situation with its operator. Depending on how sophisticated you want to get, the links can be audio-visual, kinesthetic, tactile, even olfactory. The more you want to go in this direction, the more anthropomorphic you get in the thing's design. In the case of Venus, if I recall correctly, the human operator in orbit wore an exo-skeleton which controlled the movements of the body, legs, arms and hands of the device on the surface below, receiving motion and force feedback through a system of airjet transducers. He had on a helmet controlling the slave device's television camera – set, obviously enough, in its turret – which filled his field of vision with the scene below. He also wore earphones connected with its audio pickup. I read the book he wrote later. He said that for long stretches of time, he would forget the cabin, forget that he was at the boss end of a control loop and actually feel as if he were stalking through that hellish landscape, I remember being very impressed by it, just being a kid, and I wanted a supertiny one all my own, so that I could wade around in puddles picking fights with microorganisms.'

'Why?'

'Because there weren't any dragons on Venus. Anyhow, that is a telefactoring device, a thing quite distinct from a robot.'

'I'm still with you,' he said. 'Now tell me the difference between the early telefactoring devices and the later ones.'

I swallowed some coffee.

'It was a bit trickier with respect to the outer planets and their satellites,' I said. 'There, we did not have orbiting operators at first. Economics, and some unresolved technical problems. Mainly economics. At any rate, the devices were landed on the target worlds, but the operators stayed home. Because of this, there was of course a time lag in the transmissions along the control loop. It took a while to receive the on-site input, and then there was another time-lapse before the response movements reached the telefactor. We attempted to compensate for this in two ways. The first was by the employment of a simple wait-move, wait-move sequence. The second was more sophisticated and is actually the point where computers come into the picture in terms of participating in the control loop. It involved the setting up of models of known environmental factors, which were then enriched during the initial wait-move sequences. On this basis, the computer was then used to anticipate short-range developments. Finally, it could take over the loop and run it by a combination of "predictor controls" and wait-move reviews. It still had to holler for human help, though, when unexpected things came up. So, with the outer planets, it was neither totally automatic nor totally manual – nor totally satisfactory – at first.'

'OK,' he said, lighting a cigarette. 'And the next step?'

'The next wasn't really a technical step forward in telefactoring. It was an economic shift. The purse strings were loosened and we could afford to send men out. We landed them where we could land them, and in many of the places where we could not we sent down the telefactors and orbited the men again. Like in the old days. The time lag problem was removed because the operator was on top of things once more. If anything, you can look at it as a reversion to earlier methods. It is what we still often do, though, and it works.'

He shook his head.

'You left something out,' he said, 'between the computers and the bigger budget.'

I shrugged.

'A number of things were tried during that period,' I said, 'but none of them proved as effective as what we already had going in the human-computer partnership with the telefactors.'

'There was one project,' he said, 'which attempted to get around the time lag troubles by sending the computer along with the telefactor as part of the package. Only the computer wasn't exactly a computer and the telefactor wasn't exactly a telefactor. Do you know which one I am referring to?'

I lit a cigarette of my own while I thought about it, then, 'I think you are talking about the Hangman,' I said.

'That's right,' he said, 'and this is where I get lost. Can you tell me how it works?'

'Ultimately, it was a failure,' I said.

'But it worked at first.'

'Apparently. But only on the easy stuff, on Io. It conked out later and had to be written off as a failure, albeit a noble one. The venture was overly ambitious from the very beginning. What seems to have happened was that the people in charge had the opportunity to combine vanguard projects – stuff that was still under investigation and stuff that was extremely new. In theory it all seemed to dovetail so beautifully that they yielded to the temptation and incorporated too much. It started out well, but it fell apart later.'

'But what was involved in the thing?'

'Lord! What wasn't? The computer that wasn't exactly a computer ... OK, we'll start there. Last century, three engineers at the University of Wisconsin – Nordman, Parmentier and Scott – developed a device known as a superconductive tunnel junction neuristor. Two tiny strips of metal with a thin insulating layer between. Supercool it and it passed electrical impulses without resistance. Surround it with magnetized material and pack a mass of them together – billions – and what have you got?'

He shook his head.

'Well, for one thing you've got an impossible situation to schematize when considering all the paths and interconnections that may be formed. There is an obvious similarity to the structure of the brain. So, they theorized, you don't even attempt to hook up such a device. You pulse in data and let it establish its own preferential pathways, by means of the magnetic material's becoming increasingly magnetized each time the current passes through it, thus cutting the resistance. So the material establishes its own routes in a fashion analogous to the functioning of the brain when it is learning something. In the case of the Hangman, they used a setup very similar to this and they were able to pack over ten billion neuristor-type cells into a very small area – around a cubic foot. They aimed for that magic figure because that is approximately the number of nerve cells in the human brain. That is what I meant when I said that it wasn't really a computer. They were actually working in the area of artificial intelligence, no matter what they called it.'

'If the thing had its own brain – computer or quasi-human – then it was a robot rather than a telefactor, right?'

'Yes and no and maybe,' I said. 'It was operated as a telefactor device here on Earth – on the ocean floor, in the desert, in mountainous country – as part of its programming. I suppose you could also call that its apprenticeship or kindergarten. Perhaps that is even more appropriate. It was being shown how to explore in difficult environments and to report back. Once it mastered this, then theoretically they could hang it out there in the sky without a control loop and let it report its own findings.'

'At that point would it be considered a robot?'

'A robot is a machine which carries out certain operations in accordance with a program of instructions. The Hangman made its own decisions, you see. And I suspect that by trying to produce something that close to the human brain in structure and function the seemingly inevitable randomness of its model got included in. It wasn't just a machine following a program. It was too complex. That was probably what broke it down.'

Don chuckled.

'Inevitable free will?'

'No. As I said, they had thrown too many things into one bag. Everybody and his brother with a pet project that might be fitted in seemed a supersalesman that season. For example, the psychophysics boys had a gimmick they wanted to try on it, and it got used. Ostensibly, it was a communications device. Actually, they were concerned as to whether the thing was truly sentient.'

'Was it?'

'Apparently so, in a limited fashion. What they had come up with, to be made part of the initial telefactor loop, was a device which set up a weak induction field in the brain of the operator. The machine received and amplified the patterns of electrical activity being conducted in the Hangman's – might as well call it "brain" – then passed them through a complex modulator and pulsed them into the induction field in the operator's head. I am out of my area now and into that of Weber and Fechner, but a neuron has a threshold at which it will fire, and below which it will not. There are some forty thousand neurons packed together in a square millimeter of the cerebral cortex, in such a fashion that each one has several hundred synaptic connections with others about it. At any given moment, some of them may be way below the firing threshold while others are in a condition Sir John Eccles once referred to as "critically poised" – ready to fire. If just one is pushed over the threshold, it can affect the discharge of hundreds of thousands of others within twenty milliseconds. The pulsating field was to provide such a push in a sufficiently selective fashion to give the operator an idea as to what was going on in the Hangman's brain. And vice versa. The Hangman was to have its own built-in version of the same thing. It was also thought that this might serve to humanize it somewhat, so that it would better appreciate the significance of its work – to instil something like loyalty, you might say.'

'Do you think this could have contributed to its later breakdown?'

'Possibly. How can you say in a one-of-a-kind situation like this? If you want a guess, I'd say yes. But it's just a guess.'

'Uh-huh,' he said, 'and what were its physical capabilities?'

'Anthropomorphic design,' I said, 'both because it was originally telefactored and because of the psychological reasoning I just mentioned. It could pilot its own small vessel. No need for a life-support system, of course. Both it and the vessel were powered by fusion units, so that fuel was no real problem. Self-repairing. Capable of performing a great variety of sophisticated tests and measurements, of making observations, completing reports, learning new material, broadcasting its findings back here. Capable of surviving just about anywhere. In fact, it required less energy on the outer planets – less work for the refrigeration units, to maintain that supercooled brain in its midsection.'

'How strong was it?'

'I don't recall all the specs. Maybe a dozen times as strong as a man, in things like lifting and pushing.'

'It explored Io for us and started in on Europa.'

'Yes.'

'Then it began behaving erratically, just when we thought it had really learned its job.'

'That sounds right,' I said.

'It refused a direct order to explore Callisto, then headed out toward Uranus.'

'Yes. It's been years since I read the reports ...'

'The malfunction worsened after that. Long periods of silence interspersed with garbled transmissions. Now that I know more about its makeup, it almost sounds like a man going off the deep end.'

'It seems similar.'

'But it managed to pull itself together again for a brief while. It landed on Titania, began sending back what seemed like appropriate observation reports. This only lasted a short time, though. It went irrational once more, indicated that it was heading for a landing on Uranus itself, and that was it. We didn't hear from it after that. Now that I know about that mind-reading gadget I understand why a psychiatrist on this end could be so positive it would never function again.'

'I never heard about that part.'

'I did.'

I shrugged.

'This was all around twenty years ago,' I said, 'and, as I mentioned, it has been a long while since I've read anything about it.'

'The Hangman's ship crashed or landed, as the case may be, in the Gulf of Mexico,' he said, 'two days ago.'

I just stared at him.

'It was empty,' he said, 'when they finally got out and down to it.'

'I don't understand.'

'Yesterday morning,' he went on, 'restaurateur Manny Burns was found beaten to death in the office of his establishment, the Maison Saint-Michel, in New Orleans.'

'I still fail to see ...'

'Manny Burns was one of the four original operators who programmed – pardon me, "taught" – the Hangman.'

The silence lengthened, dragged its belly on the deck.

'Coincidence ...?' I finally said.

'My client doesn't think so.'

'Who is your client?'

'One of the three remaining members of the training group. He is convinced that the Hangman has returned to Earth to kill its former operators.'

'Has he made his fears known to his old employers?'

'No.'

'Why not?'

'Because it would require telling them the reason for his fears.'

'That being ...?'

'He wouldn't tell me either.'

'How does he expect you to do a proper job?'

'He told me what he considered a proper job. He wants two things done, neither of which requires a full case history. He wanted to be furnished with good bodyguards, and he wanted the Hangman found and disposed of. I have already taken care of the first part.'

'And you want me to do the second?'

'That's right. You have confirmed my opinion that you are the man for the job.'

'I see,' I said. 'Do you realize that if the thing is truly sentient this will be something very like murder? If it is not, of course, then it will only amount to the destruction of expensive government property.'

'Which way do you look at it?'

'I look at it as a job,' I said.

'You'll take it?'

'I need more facts before I can decide. Like ... Who is your client? Who are the other operators? Where do they live? What do they do? What –'

He raised his hand.

'First,' he said, 'the Honorable Jesse Brockden, Senior Senator from Wisconsin, is our client. Confidentiality, of course, is written all over it.'

I nodded.

'I remember his being involved with the space program before he went into politics. I wasn't aware of the specifics, though. He could get government protection so easily –'

'To obtain it, he would apparently have to tell them something he doesn't want to talk about. Perhaps it would hurt his career. I simply do not know. He doesn't want them. He wants us.'

I nodded again.

'What about the others? Do they want us, too?'

'Quite the opposite. They don't subscribe to Brockden's notions at all. They seem to think he is something of a paranoid.'

'How well do they know one another these days?'

'They live in different parts of the country, haven't seen each other in years. Been in occasional touch, though.'

'Kind of flimsy basis for that diagnosis, then.'

'One of them *is* a psychiatrist.'

'Oh. Which one?'

'Leila Thackery is her name. Lives in St Louis. Works at the State Hospital there.'

'None of them has gone to any authority, then – Federal or local?'

'That's right. Brockden contacted them when he heard about the Hangman. He was in Washington at the time. Got word on its return right away and managed to get the story killed. He tried to reach them all, learned about Burns in the process, contacted me, then tried to persuade the others to accept protection by my people. They weren't buying. When I talked to her, Dr Thackery pointed out – quite correctly – that Brockden is a very sick man –'

'What's he got?'

'Cancer. In his spine. Nothing they can do about it once it hits there and digs in. He even told me he figures he has maybe six months to get through what he considers a very important piece of legislation – the new criminal rehabilitation act. I will admit that he did sound kind of paranoid when he talked about it. But hell! Who wouldn't? Dr Thackery sees that as the whole thing, though, and she doesn't see the Burns killing as being connected with the Hangman. Thinks it was just a traditional robbery gone sour, thief surprised and panicky, maybe hopped-up, etcetera.'

'Then she is not afraid of the Hangman?'

'She said that she is in a better position to know its mind than anyone else, and she is not especially concerned.'

'What about the other operator?'

'He said that Dr Thackery may know its mind better than anyone else, but he knows its brain, and he isn't worried either.'

'What did he mean by that?'

'David Fentris is a consulting engineer – electronics, cybernetics. He actually had something to do with the Hangman's design.'

I got to my feet and went after the coffee pot. Not that I'd an overwhelming desire for another cup at just that moment. But I had known, had once worked with a David Fentris. And he had at one time been connected with the space program.

About fifteen years my senior, Dave had been with the Data Bank project when I had known him. Where a number of us had begun having second thoughts as the thing progressed, Dave had never been anything less than wildly enthusiastic. A wiry five-eight, white-cropped, gray eyes back of hornrims and heavy glass, cycling between preoccupation and near-frantic darting, he had had a way of verbalizing half-completed thoughts as he went along, so that you might begin to think him a representative of that tribe which had come into positions of small authority by means of nepotism or politics. If you would listen a few more minutes though, you would begin revising your opinion as he started to pull his musings together into a rigorous framework. By the time he had finished you generally wondered why you hadn't seen it all along and what a guy like that was doing in a position of such small authority. Later, it might strike you, though, that he seemed sad whenever he wasn't enthusiastic about something, and while the gung-ho spirit is great for short-range projects, larger ventures generally require something more of equanimity. I wasn't at all surprised that he had wound up as a consultant. The big question now, of course, was would he remember me? True, my appearance was altered, my personality hopefully more mature, my habits shifted around. But would that be enough, should I have to encounter him as part of this job? That mind behind those hornrims could do a lot of strange things with just a little data.

'Where does he live?' I asked.

'Memphis, and what's the matter?'

'Just trying to get my geography straight,' I said. 'Is Senator Brockden still in Washington?'

'No. He's returned to Wisconsin and is currently holed up in a lodge in the northern part of the state. Four of my people are with him.'

'I see.'

I refreshed our coffee supply and reseated myself. I didn't like this one at all and I resolved not to take it. I didn't like just giving Don a flat no, though. His assignments had become a very important part of my life, and this one was not mere legwork. It was obviously important to him, and he wanted me on it. I decided to look for holes in the thing, to find some way of reducing it to the simple bodyguard job already in progress.

'It does seem peculiar,' I said, 'that Brockden is the only one afraid of the device.'

'Yes.'

'... And that he gives no reasons.'

'True.'

'... Plus his condition, and what the doctor said about its effect on his mind.'

'I have no doubt that he is neurotic,' Don said. 'Look at this.'

He reached for his coat, withdrew a sheaf of papers from within it. He shuffled through them and extracted a single sheet, which he passed to me. It was a piece of Congressional letterhead stationery, with the message scrawled in longhand: 'Don,' it said, 'I've got to see you. Frankenstein's monster has just come back from where we hung him and he's looking for me. The whole damn universe is trying to grind me up. Call me between eight and ten. Jess.' I nodded, started to pass it back, paused, then handed it over. Double damn it deeper than hell! I took a drink of coffee. I thought that I had long ago given up hope in such things, but I had noticed something which immediately troubled me. In the margin where they list such matters, I had seen that Jesse Brockden was on the committee for review of the Data Bank program. I recalled that that committee was supposed to be working on a series of reform recommendations. Offhand, I could not remember Brockden's position on any of the issues involved, but – oh hell! The thing was simply too big to alter significantly now ... But it *was* the only real Frankenstein monster I cared about, and there was always the possibility ... On the other hand – hell, again. What if I let him die when I might have saved him, and he had been the one who ...?

I took another drink of coffee. I lit another cigarette. There might be a way of working it so that Dave didn't even come into the picture. I could talk to Leila Thackery first, check further into the Burns killing, keep posted on new developments, find out more about the vessel in the Gulf ... I might be able to accomplish something, even if it was only the negation of Brockden's theory, without Dave's and my paths ever crossing.

'Have you got the specs on the Hangman?' I asked.

'Right here.'

He passed them over.

'The police report on the Burns killing?'

'Here it is.'

'The whereabouts of everyone involved, and some background on them?'

'Here.'

'The place or places where I can reach you during the next few days – around the clock? This one may require some coordination.'

He smiled and reached for his pen.

'Glad to have you aboard,' he said.

I reached over and tapped the barometer. I shook my head.

The ringing of the phone awakened me. Reflex bore me across the room, where I took it on audio.

'Yes?'

'Mr Donne? It is eight o'clock.'

'Thanks.'

I collapsed into the chair. I am what might be called a slow starter. I tend to recapitulate phylogeny every morning. Basic desires inched their ways through my gray matter to close a connection. Slowly, I extended a cold-blooded member and clicked my talons against a couple numbers. I croaked my desire for food and lots of coffee to the voice that responded. Half an hour later I would only have growled. Then I staggered off to the place of flowing waters to renew my contact with basics.

In addition to my normal adrenaline and blood-sugar bearishness, I had not slept much the night before. I had closed up shop after Don had left, stuffed my pockets with essentials, departed the *Proteus*, gotten myself over to the airport and on to a flight which took me to St Louis in the dead, small hours of the dark. I was unable to sleep during the flight, thinking about the case, deciding on the tack I was going to take with Leila Thackery. On arrival, I had checked into the airport motel, left a message to be awakened at an unreasonable hour and collapsed.

As I ate, I regarded the fact-sheet Don had given me: Leila Thackery was currently single, having divorced her second husband a little over two years ago, was forty-six years old and lived in an apartment near to the hospital where she worked. Attached to the sheet was a photo which might have been ten years old. In it, she was brunette, light-eyed, barely on the right side of that border between ample and overweight, with fancy glasses straddling an upturned nose. She had published a number of books and articles with titles full of alienations, roles, transactions, social contexts and more alienations.

I hadn't had the time to go my usual route, becoming an entire new individual with a verifiable history. Just a name and a story, that's all. It did not seem necessary this time, though. For once, something approximating honesty actually seemed a reasonable approach.

I took a public vehicle over to her apartment building. I did not phone ahead, because it is easier to say no to a voice than to a person. According to the record, today was one of the days when she saw out-patients in her home. Her idea, apparently: break down the alienating institution image, remove resentments by turning the sessions into something more like social occasions, etcetera. I did not want all that much of her time, I had decided that Don could make it worth her while if it came to that, and I was sure my fellows' visits were scheduled to leave her with some small breathing space – *inter alia*, so to speak.

I had just located her name and apartment number amid the buttons in the entrance foyer when an old woman passed behind me and unlocked the door to the lobby. She glanced at me and held it open, so I went on in without ringing. The matter of presence, again.

I took the elevator to Leila's floor, the second. I located her door and knocked on it. I was almost ready to knock again when it opened, partway.

'Yes?' she asked, and I revised my estimate as to the age of the photo. She looked just about the same.

'Dr Thackery,' I said, 'my name is Donne. You could help me quite a bit with a problem I've got.'

'What sort of problem?'

'It involves a device known as the Hangman.'

She sighed and showed me a quick grimace. Her fingers tightened on the door.

'I've come a long way but I'll be easy to get rid of. I've only a few things I'd like to ask you about it.'

'Are you with the Government?'

'No.'

'Do you work for Brockden?'

'No, I'm something different.'

'All right,' she said. 'Right now I've got a group session going. It will probably last around another half-hour. If you don't mind waiting down in the lobby, I'll let you know as soon as it is over. We can talk then.'

'Good enough,' I said. 'Thanks.'

She nodded, closed the door. I located the stairway and walked back down.

A cigarette later, I decided that the devil finds work for idle hands and thanked him for his suggestion. I strolled back toward the foyer. Through the glass, I read the names of a few residents of the fifth floor. I elevated up and knocked on one of the doors. Before it was opened I had my notebook and pad in plain sight.

'Yes?' – short, fiftyish, curious.

'My name is Stephen Foster, Mrs Gluntz. I am doing a survey for the North American Consumers League. I would like to pay you for a couple minutes of your time, to answer some questions about products you use.'

'Why– Pay me?'

'Yes, ma'am. Ten dollars. Around a dozen questions. It will just take a minute or two.'

'All right.' She opened the door wider. 'Won't you come in?'

'No, thank you. This thing is so brief I'd just be in and out. The first question involves detergents –'

Ten minutes later I was back in the lobby adding the thirty bucks for the three interviews to the list of expenses I was keeping. When a situation is full of unpredictables and I am playing makeshift games, I like to provide for as many contingencies as I can.

Another quarter of an hour or so slipped by before the elevator opened and discharged three guys, young, young and middle-aged, casually dressed, chuckling over something. The big one on the nearest end strolled over and nodded.

'You the fellow waiting to see Dr Thackery?'

'That's right.'

'She said to tell you to come on up now.'

'Thanks.'

I rode up again, returned to her door. She opened to my knock, nodded me in, saw me seated in a comfortable chair at the far end of her living room.

'Would you care for a cup of coffee?' she asked. 'It's fresh. I made more than I needed.'

'That would be fine. Thanks.'

Moments later, she brought in a couple of cups, delivered one to me and seated herself on the sofa to my left. I ignored the cream and sugar on the tray and took a sip.

'You've gotten me interested,' she said. 'Tell me about it.'

'OK. I have been told that the telefactor device known as the Hangman, now possibly possessed of an artificial intelligence, has returned to Earth –'

'Hypothetical,' she said, 'unless you know something I don't. I have been told that the Hangman's vehicle reentered and crashed in the Gulf. There is no evidence that the vehicle was occupied.'

'It seems a reasonable conclusion, though.'

'It seems just as reasonable to me that the Hangman sent the vehicle off toward an eventual rendezvous point many years ago and that it only recently reached that point, at which time the reentry program took over and brought it down.'

'Why should it return the vehicle and strand itself out there?'

'Before I answer that,' she said, 'I would like to know the reason for your concern. News media?'

'No,' I said. 'I am a science writer – straight tech, popular and anything in between. But I am not after a piece for publication. I was retained to do a report on the psychological makeup of the thing.'

'For whom?'

'A private investigation outfit. They want to know what might influence its thinking, how it might be likely to behave – if it has indeed come back. I've been doing a lot of homework, and I gathered there is a likelihood that its nuclear personality was a composite of the minds of its four operators. So, personal contacts seemed in order, to collect your opinions as to what it might be like. I came to you first for obvious reasons.'

She nodded.

'A Mr Walsh spoke with me the other day. He is working for Senator Brockden.'

'Oh? I never go into an employer's business beyond what he's asked me to do. Senator Brockden is on my list though, along with a David Fentris.'

'You were told about Manny Burns?'

'Yes. Unfortunate.'

'That is apparently what set Jesse off. He is – how shall I put it? He is clinging to life right now, trying to accomplish a great many things in the time he has remaining. Every moment is precious to him. He feels the old man in the white nightgown breathing down his neck. Then the ship returns and one of us is killed. From what we know of the Hangman, the last we heard of it, it had become irrational. Jesse saw a connection, and in his condition the fear is understandable. There is nothing wrong with humoring him if it allows him to get his work done.'

'But you don't see a threat in it?'

'No. I was the last person to monitor the Hangman before communications ceased, and I could see then what had happened. The first things that it had learned were the organization of perceptions and motor activities. Multitudes of other patterns had been transferred from the minds of its operators, but they were too sophisticated to mean much initially. Think of a child who has learned the Gettysburg Address. It is there in his head, that is all. One day, however, it may be important to him. Conceivably, it may even inspire him to action. It takes some growing up first, of course. Now think of such a child with a great number of conflicting patterns – attitudes, tendencies, memories – none of which are especially bothersome for so long as he remains a child. Add a bit of maturity, though – and bear in mind that the patterns originated with four different individuals, all of them more powerful than the words of even the finest of speeches, bearing as they do their own built-in feelings. Try to imagine the conflicts, the contradictions involved in being four people at once –'

'Why wasn't this imagined in advance?' I asked.

'Ah!' she said, smiling. 'The full sensitivity of the neuristor brain was not appreciated at first. It was assumed that the operators were adding data in a linear fashion and that this would continue until a critical mass was achieved, corresponding to the construction of a model or picture of the world which would then serve as a point of departure for growth of the Hangman's own mind. And it did seem to check out this way. What actually occurred, however, was a phenomenon amounting to imprinting.

Secondary characteristics of the operators' minds, outside the didactic situations, were imposed. These did not immediately become functional and hence were not detected. They remained latent until the mind had developed sufficiently to understand them. And then it was too late. It suddenly acquired four additional personalities and was unable to coordinate them. When it tried to compartmentalize them it went schizoid; when it tried to integrate them it went catatonic. It was cycling back and forth between these alternatives at the end. Then it just went silent. I felt it had undergone the equivalent of an epileptic seizure. Wild currents through that magnetic material would, in effect, have erased its mind, resulting in its equivalent of death or idiocy.'

'I follow you,' I said. 'Now, just for the sake of playing games, I see the alternatives as a successful integration of all this material or the achievement of a viable schizophrenia. What do you think its behavior would be like if either of these was possible?'

'All right,' she agreed. 'As I just said, though, I think there were physical limitations to its retaining multiple personality structures for a very long period of time. If it did, however, it, would have continued with its own plus replicas of the four operators', at least for a while. The situation would differ radically from that of a human schizoid of this sort in that the additional personalities were valid images of genuine identities rather than self-generated complexes which had become autonomous. They might continue to evolve, they might degenerate, they might conflict to the point of destruction or gross modification of any or all of them. In other words, no prediction is possible as to the nature of whatever might remain.'

'Might I venture one?'

'Go ahead.'

'After considerable anxiety, it masters them. It asserts itself. It beats down this quartet of demons which has been tearing it apart, acquiring in the process an all-consuming hatred for the actual individuals responsible for this turmoil. To free itself totally, to revenge itself, to work its ultimate catharsis, it resolves to seek them out and destroy them.'

She smiled.

'You have just dispensed with the "viable schizophrenia" you conjured up, and you have now switched over to its pulling through and becoming fully autonomous. That is a different situation, no matter what strings you put on it.'

'OK, I accept the charge. But what about my conclusion?'

'You are saying that if it did pull through, it would hate us. That strikes me as an unfair attempt to invoke the spirit of Sigmund Freud: Oedipus and Electra in one being, out to destroy all its parents – the authors of every one of its tensions, anxieties, hangups, burned into the impressionable psyche at a young and defenseless age. Even Freud didn't have a name for that one. What should we call it?'

'A Hermacis complex?' I suggested.

'Hermacis?'

'Hermaphroditus having been united in one body with the nymph Salmacis, I've just done the same with their names. That being would then have had four parents against whom to react.'

'Cute,' she said, smiling. 'If the liberal arts do nothing else they provide engaging metaphors for the thinking they displace. This one is unwarranted and overly anthropomorphic, though. You wanted my opinion. All right. If the Hangman pulled through at all it could only have been by virtue of that neuristor brain's differences from the human brain. From my own professional experience, a human could not pass through a situation like that and attain stability. If the Hangman did, it would have to have resolved all the contradictions and conflicts, to have mastered and understood the situation so thoroughly that I do not believe whatever remained could involve that sort of hatred. The fear, the uncertainty, the things that feed hate would have been analyzed, digested, turned to something more useful. There would probably be distaste, and possibly an act of independence, of self-assertion. That was why I suggested its return of the ship.'

'It is your opinion, then, that if the Hangman exists as a thinking individual today, this is the only possible attitude it would possess toward its former operators? It would want nothing more to do with you?'

'That is correct. Sorry about your Hermacis complex. But in this case we must look to the brain, not the psyche. And we see two things: schizophrenia would have destroyed it, and a successful resolution of its problem would preclude vengeance. Either way, there is nothing to worry about.'

How could I put it tactfully? I decided that I could not.

'All of this is fine,' I said, 'for as far as it goes. But getting away from both the purely psychological and the purely physical, could there be a particular reason for its seeking your deaths – that is, a plain old-fashioned motive for a killing, based on events rather than having to do with the way its thinking equipment goes together?'

Her expression was impossible to read, but considering her line of work I had expected nothing less.

'What events?' she said.

'I have no idea. That's why I asked.'

She shook her head.

'I'm afraid that I don't either.'

'Then that about does it,' I said. 'I can't think of anything else to ask you.'

She nodded.

'And I can't think of anything else to tell you.'

I finished my coffee, returned the cup to the tray.

'Thanks, then,' I said, 'for your time, for the coffee. You have been very helpful.'

I rose. She did the same.

'What are you going to do now?' she asked.

'I haven't quite decided,' I said. 'I want to do the best report I can. Have you any suggestions on that?'

'I suggest that there isn't any more to learn, that I have given you the only possible constructions the facts warrant.'

'You don't feel David Fentris could provide any additional insights?'

She snorted, then sighed.

'No,' she said, 'I do not think he could tell you anything useful.'

'What do you mean? From the way you say it ...'

'I know. I didn't mean to. Some people find comfort in religion. Others ... you know. Others take it up late in life with a vengeance and a half. They don't use it quite the way it was intended. It comes to color all their thinking.'

'Fanaticism?' I said.

'Not exactly. A misplaced zeal. A masochistic sort of thing. Hell! I shouldn't be diagnosing at a distance – or influencing your opinion. Forget what I said. Form your own opinion when you meet him.'

She raised her head, appraising my reaction.

'Well,' I said, 'I am not at all certain that I am going to see him. But you have made me curious. How can religion influence engineering?'

'I spoke with him after Jesse gave us the news on the vessel's return,' she said. 'I got the impression at the time that he feels we were tampering in the province of the Almighty by attempting the creation of an artificial intelligence. That our creation should go mad was only appropriate, being the work of imperfect man. He seemed to feel that it would be fitting if it had come back for retribution, as a sign of judgment upon us.'

'Oh,' I said.

She smiled then. I returned it.

'Yes,' she said, 'but maybe I just got him in a bad mood. Maybe you should go see for yourself.'

Something told me to shake my head – a bit of a difference between this view of him, my recollections and Don's comment that Dave had said he knew its brain and was not especially concerned. Somewhere among these lay something I felt I should know, felt I should learn without seeming to pursue. So, 'I think I have enough right now,' I said. 'It was the psychological side of things I was supposed to cover, not the mechanical – or the theological. You have been extremely helpful. Thanks again.'

She carried her smile all the way to the door.

'If it is not too much trouble,' she said, as I stepped into the hall, 'I would like to learn how this whole thing finally turns out – or any interesting developments, for that matter.'

'My connection with the case ends with this report,' I said, 'and I am going to write it now. Still, I may get some feedback.'

'You have my number ...?'

'Probably, but ...'

I already had it, but I jotted it again, right after Mrs Gluntz's answers to my inquiries on detergents.

Moving in a rigorous line, I made beautiful connections for a change. I headed directly for the airport, found a flight aimed at Memphis, bought passage and was the last to board. Ten score seconds, perhaps, made all the difference. Not even a tick or two to spare for checking out of the motel. No matter. The good head doctor had convinced me that, like it or not, David Fentris was next, damn it. I had too strong a feeling that Leila Thackery had not told me the entire story. I had to take a chance, to see these changes in the man for myself, to try to figure out how they related to the Hangman. For a number of reasons, I'd a feeling they might.

I disembarked into a cool, partly overcast afternoon, found transportation almost immediately and set out for Dave's office address. A before-the-storm feeling came over me as I entered and crossed the town. A dark wall of clouds continued to build in the west. Later, standing before the building where Dave did business, the first few drops of rain were already spattering against its dirty brick front. It would take a lot more than that to freshen it, though, or any of the others in the area. I would have thought he'd have come a little farther than this by now. I shrugged off some moisture and went inside.

The directory gave me directions, the elevator elevated me, my feet found the way to his door. I knocked on it.

After a time, I knocked again and waited again. Again, nothing. So I tried it, found it open and went on in.

It was a small, vacant waiting room, green-carpeted. The reception desk was dusty. I crossed and peered around the plastic partition behind it.

The man had his back to me. I drummed my knuckles against the partitioning. He heard it and turned.

'Yes?'

Our eyes met, his still framed by hornrims and just as active; glasses thicker, hair thinner, cheeks a trifle hollower. His question mark quivered in the air, and nothing in his gaze moved to replace it with recognition. He had been bending over a sheaf of schematics; a lopsided basket of metal, quartz, porcelain and glass rested on a nearby table.

'My name is Donne, John Donne,' I said. 'I am looking for David Fentris.'

'I am David Fentris.'

'Good to meet you,' I said, crossing to where he stood. 'I am assisting in an investigation concerning a project with which you were once associated –'

He smiled and nodded, accepted my hand and shook it.

'– The Hangman, of course,' he said. 'Glad to know you, Mr Donne.'

'Yes, the Hangman,' I said. 'I am doing a report ...'

'... And you want my opinion as to how dangerous it is. Sit down.' He gestured toward a chair at the end of his work bench. 'Care for a cup of tea?'

'No thanks.'

'I'm having one.'

'Well, in that case ...'

He crossed to another bench.

'No cream. Sorry.'

'That's all right. How did you know it involved the Hangman?'

He grinned as he brought my cup.

'Because it's come back,' he said, 'and it's the only thing I've been connected with that warrants that much concern.'

'Do you mind talking about it?'

'Up to a point, no.'

'What's the point?'

'If we get near it, I'll let you know.'

'Fair enough. How dangerous *is* it?'

'I would say that it is harmless,' he replied, 'except to three persons.'

'Formerly four?'

'Precisely.'

'How come?'

'We were doing something we had no business doing.'

'That being ...?'

'For one thing, attempting to create an artificial intelligence.'

'Why had you no business doing that?'

'A man with a name like yours shouldn't have to ask.'

I chuckled.

'If I were a preacher,' I said, 'I would have to point out that there is no biblical injunction against it – unless you've been worshipping it on the sly.'

He shook his head.

'Nothing that simple, that obvious, that explicit. Times have changed since the Good Book was written, and you can't hold with a purely Fundamentalist approach in complex times. What I was getting at was something a little more abstract. A form of pride, not unlike the classical *hubris* – the setting up of oneself on a level with the Creator.'

'Did you feel that – pride?'

'Yes.'

'Are you sure it wasn't just enthusiasm for an ambitious project that was working well?'

'Oh, there was plenty of that. A manifestation of the same thing.'

'I do seem to recall something about man being made in the Creator's image, and something else about trying to live up to that. It would seem to follow that exercising one's capacities along similar lines would be a step in the right direction – an act of conformance with the Divine Ideal, if you like.'

'But I don't like. Man cannot really create. He can only rearrange what is already present. Only God can create.'

'Then you have nothing to worry about.'

He frowned, then, 'No,' he said. 'Being aware of this and still trying is where the presumption comes in.'

'Were you really thinking that way when you did it? Or did all this occur to you after the fact?'

'I am no longer certain.'

'Then it would seem to me that a merciful God would be inclined to give you the benefit of the doubt.'

He gave me a wry smile.

'Not bad, John Donne. But I feel that judgment may already have been entered and that we may have lost four to nothing.'

'Then you see the Hangman as an avenging angel?'

'Sometimes. Sort of. I see it as being returned to exact a penalty.'

'Just for the record,' I said, 'if the Hangman had had full access to the necessary equipment and was able to construct another unit such as itself, would you consider it guilty of the same thing that is bothering you?'

He shook his head.

'Don't get all cute and Jesuitical with me, Donne. I'm not that far away from fundamentals. Besides, I'm willing to admit I might be wrong and that there may be other forces driving it to the same end.'

'Such as?'

'I told you I'd let you know when we reached a certain point. That's it.'

'OK,' I said. 'But that sort of blank-walls me, you know. The people I am working for would like to protect you people. They want to stop the Hangman. I was hoping you would tell me a little more – if not for your own sake, then for the others'. They might not share your philosophical sentiments, and you have just admitted you may be wrong. Despair, by the way, is also considered a sin by a great number of theologians.'

He sighed and stroked his nose, as I had often seen him do in times long past.

'What do you do, anyhow?' he asked me.

'Me, personally? I'm a science writer. I'm putting together a report on the device for the agency that wants to do the protecting. The better my report, the better their chances.'

He was silent for a time, then, 'I read a lot in the area, but I don't recognize your name,' he said.

'Most of my work has involved petrochemistry and marine biology,' I said.

'Oh. You were a peculiar choice then, weren't you?'

'Not really. I was available, and the boss knows my work, knows I'm good.'

He glanced across the room, to where a stack of cartons partly obscured what I then realized to be a remote access terminal. OK. If he decided to check out my credentials now, John Donne would fall apart. It seemed a hell of a time to get curious, though, *after* sharing his sense of sin with me. He must have thought so too, because he did not look that way again.

'Let me put it this way,' he finally said, and something of the old David Fentris at his best took control of his voice. 'For one reason or the other, I believe that it wants to destroy its former operators. If it is the judgment of the Almighty, that's all there is to it. It will succeed. If not, however, I don't want any outside protection. I've done my own repenting and it is up to me to handle the rest of the situation myself, too. I will stop the Hangman personally, right here, before anyone else is hurt.'

'How?' I asked him.

He nodded toward the glittering helmet.

'With that,' he said.

'How?' I repeated.

'Its telefactor circuits are still intact. They have to be. They are an integral part of it. It could not disconnect them without shutting itself down. If it comes within a quarter-mile of here, that unit will be activated. It will emit a loud humming sound and a light will begin to blink behind that meshing beneath the forward ridge. I will then don the helmet and take control of the Hangman. I will bring it here and disconnect its brain.'

'How would you do the disconnect?'

He reached for the schematics he had been looking at when I had come in.

'Here,' he said. 'The thoracic plate has to be unplugged. There are four subunits that have to be uncoupled. Here, here, here and here.'

He looked up.

'You would have to do them in sequence though, or it could get mighty hot,' I said. 'First this one, then these two. Then the other.'

When I looked up again, the gray eyes were fixed on my own.

'I thought you were in petrochemistry and marine biology,' he said.

'I am not really "in" anything,' I said. 'I am a tech writer, with bits and pieces from all over – and I did have a look at these before, when I accepted the job.'

'I see.'

'Why don't you bring the space agency in on this?' I said, working to shift ground. 'The original telefactoring equipment had all that power and range –'

'It was dismantled a long time ago,' he said. 'I thought you were with the Government.'

I shook my head.

'Sorry. I didn't mean to mislead you. I am on contract with a private investigation outfit.'

'Uh-huh. Then that means Jesse. Not that it matters. You can tell him that one way or the other everything is being taken care of.'

'What if you are wrong on the supernatural,' I said, 'but correct on the other? Supposing it is coming under the circumstances you feel it proper to resist? But supposing you are not next on its list? Supposing it gets to one of the others next instead of you? If you are so sensitive about guilt and sin, don't you think that you would be responsible for that death – if you could prevent it by telling me just a little bit more? If it is confidentiality you are worried about –'

'No,' he said. 'You cannot trick me into applying my principles to a hypothetical situation which will only work out the way that you want it to. Not when I am certain that it will not arise. Whatever moves the Hangman, it will come to me next. If I cannot stop it, then it cannot be stopped until it has completed its job.'

'How do you know that you are next?'

'Take a look at a map,' he said. 'It landed in the Gulf. Manny was right there in New Orleans. Naturally, he was first. The Hangman can move underwater like a controlled torpedo, which makes the Mississippi its logical route for inconspicuous travel. Proceeding up it then, here I am in Memphis. Then Leila, up in St Louis, is obviously next after me. It can worry about getting to Washington after that.'

I thought about Senator Brockden in Wisconsin and decided it would not even have that problem. All of them were fairly accessible, when you thought of the situation in terms of river travel.

'But how is it to know where you all are?' I asked.

'Good question,' he said. 'Within a limited range, it was once sensitive to our brain waves, having an intimate knowledge of them and the ability to pick them up. I do not know what that range would be today. I might have been able to construct an amplifier to extend this area of perception. But to be more mundane about it, I believe that it simply consulted the Data Bank's national directory. There are booths all over, even on the waterfront. It could have hit one late at night and gimmicked it. It certainly had sufficient identifying information – and engineering skill.'

'Then it seems to me the best bet for all of you would be to move away from the river till this business is settled. That thing won't be able to stalk about the countryside very long without being noticed.'

'It would find a way. It is extremely resourceful. At night, in an overcoat, a hat, it could pass. It requires nothing that a man would need. It could dig a hole and bury itself, stay underground during daylight. It could run without resting all night long. There is no place it could not reach in a surprisingly short while. No, I must wait here for it.'

'Let me put it as bluntly as I can,' I said. 'If you are right that it is a divine avenger, I would say that it smacks of blasphemy to try to tackle it. On the other hand, if it is not, then I think you are guilty of jeopardizing the others by withholding information that would allow us to provide them with a lot more protection than you are capable of giving them all by yourself.'

He laughed.

'I'll just have to learn to live with that guilt too, as they do with theirs,' he said. 'After I've done my best, they deserve anything they get.'

'It was my understanding,' I said, 'that even God doesn't judge people until after they're dead – if you want another piece of presumption to add to your collection.'

He stopped laughing and studied my face.

'There is something familiar about the way you talk, the way you think,' he said. 'Have we ever met before?'

'I doubt it. I would have remembered.'

He shook his head.

'You've got a way of bothering a man's thinking that rings a faint bell,' he went on. 'You trouble me, sir.'

'That was my intention.'

'Are you staying here in town?'

'No.'

'Give me a number where I can reach you, will you? If I have any new thoughts on this thing I'll call you.'

'I wish you would have them now if you are going to have them.'

'No,' he said, 'I've got some thinking to do. Where can I get hold of you later?'

I gave him the name of the motel I was still checked into in St Louis, I could call back periodically for messages.

'All right,' he said, and he moved toward the partition by the reception area and stood beside it.

I rose and followed him, passing into that area and pausing at the door to the hall.

'One thing ...' I said.

'Yes?'

'If it does show up and you do stop it, will you call me and tell me that?'

'Yes, I will.'

'Thanks then – and good luck.'

Impulsively, I extended my hand. He gripped it and smiled faintly.

'Thank you, Mr Donne.'

Next. Next, next, next ...

I couldn't budge Dave, and Leila Thackery had given me everything she was going to. No real sense in calling Don yet – not until I had more to say. I thought it over on my way back to the airport. The pre-dinner hours always seem best for talking to people in any sort of official capacity, just as the night seems best for dirty work. Heavily psychological, but true nevertheless. I hated to waste the rest of the day if there was anyone else worth talking to before I called Don. Going through the folder, I decided that there was.

Manny Burns had a brother, Phil. I wondered how worthwhile it might be to talk with him. I could make it to New Orleans at a sufficiently respectable hour, learn whatever he was willing to tell me, check back with Don for new developments and then decide whether there was anything I should be about with respect to the vessel itself. The sky was gray and leaky above me. I was anxious to flee its spaces. So I decided to do it. I could think of no better stone to upturn at the moment.

At the airport, I was ticketed quickly, in time for another close connection. Hurrying to reach my flight, my eyes brushed over a half-familiar face on the passing escalator. The reflex reserved for such occasions seemed to catch us both, because he looked back too, with the same eyebrow twitch of startle and scrutiny. Then he was gone. I could not place him, though. The half-familiar face becomes a familiar phenomenon in a crowded, highly mobile society. I sometimes think that this is all that will eventually remain of any of us: patterns of features, some a trifle more persistent than others, impressed on the flow of bodies. A small town boy in a big city, Thomas Wolfe must long ago have felt the same thing when he had coined the word *manswarm*. It might have been someone I had once met briefly, or simply someone or someone like someone I had passed on sufficient other occasions such as this.

As I flew the unfriendly skies out of Memphis, I mulled over musings past on artificial intelligence, or AI as they have tagged it in the think box biz. When talking about computers, the AI notion had always seemed hotter than I deemed necessary, partly because of semantics. The word 'intelligence' has all sorts of tag-along associations of the non-physical sort. I suppose it goes back to the fact that early discussions and conjectures concerning it made it sound as if the potential for intelligence was always present in the array of gadgets, and the correct procedures, the right programs, simply had to be found to call it forth. When you looked at it that way, as many did, it gave rise to an uncomfortable *déjà vu* – namely, vitalism. The philosophical battles of the nineteenth century were hardly so far behind that they had been forgotten, and the doctrine which maintained that life is caused and sustained by a vital principle apart from physical and chemical forces and that life is self-sustaining and self-evolving, had put up quite a fight before Darwin and his successors had produced triumph after triumph for the mechanistic view. Then vitalism sort of crept back into things again when the AI discussions arose in the middle of the past century. It would seem that Dave had fallen victim to it, and that he had come to believe he had helped provide an unsanctified vessel and filled it with something intended only for those things which had made the scene in the first chapter of Genesis.

With computers it was not quite as bad as with the Hangman, though, because you could always argue that no matter how elaborate the program it was basically an extension of the programmer's will and the operations of causal machines merely represented functions of intelligence, rather than intelligence in its own right backed by a will of its own. And there was always Gödel for a theoretical *cordon sanitaire*, with his demonstration of the true but mechanically unprovable proposition. But the Hangman was quite different. It had been designed along the lines of a brain and at least partly educated in a human fashion; and to further muddy the issue with respect to anything like vitalism, it had been in direct contact with human minds from which it might have acquired almost anything – including the spark that set it on the road to whatever selfhood it may have found. What did that make it? Its own creature? A fractured mirror reflecting a fractured humanity? Both? Or neither? I certainly could not say, but I wondered how much of its 'self' had been truly its own. It had obviously acquired a great number of functions, but was it capable of having real feelings? Could it, for example, feel something like love? If not, then it was still only a collection of complex abilities, and not a thing with all the tag-along associations of the nonphysical sort which made the word 'intelligence' such a prickly item in AI discussions; and if it were capable of, say, something like love, and if I were Dave, I would not feel guilty about having helped to bring it into being. I would feel proud, though not in the fashion he was concerned about, and I would also feel humble. Offhand, though, I do not know how intelligent I would feel, because I am still not sure what the hell intelligence is.

The daysend sky was clear when we landed. I was into town before the sun had finished setting, and on Philip Burns' doorstep just a little while later.

My ring was answered by a girl, maybe seven or eight years old. She fixed me with large brown eyes and did not say a word.

'I would like to speak with Mr Burns,' I said.

She turned and retreated around a corner.

A heavyset man, slacked and undershirted, bald about halfway back and very pink, padded into the hall moments later and peered at me. He bore a folded news-sheet in his left hand.

'What do you want?' he asked.

'It's about your brother,' I said.

'Yeah?'

'Well, I wonder if I could come in? It's kind of complicated.'

He opened the door. But instead of letting me in, he came out.

'Tell me about it out here,' he said.

'Okay, I'll be quick. I just wanted to find out whether he ever spoke with you about a piece of equipment he once worked with called the Hangman.'

'Are you a cop?'

'No.'

'Then what's your interest?'

'I am working for a private investigation agency trying to track down some equipment once associated with the project. It has apparently turned up in this area and it could be rather dangerous.'

'Let's see some identification.'

'I don't carry any.'

'What's your name?'

'John Donne.'

'And you think my brother had some stolen equipment when he died? Let me tell you something –'

'No. Not stolen,' I said, 'and I don't think he had it.'

'What then?'

'It was – well, robotic in nature. Because of some special training Manny once received, he might have had a way of detecting it. He might even have attracted it. I just want to find out whether he had said anything about it. We are trying to locate it.'

'My brother was a respectable businessman, and I don't like accusations. Especially right after his funeral, I don't. I think I'm going to call the cops and let them ask *you* a few questions.'

'Just a minute,' I said. 'Supposing I told you we had some reason to believe it might have been this piece of equipment that killed your brother?'

His pink turned to bright red and his jaw muscles formed sudden ridges. I was not prepared for the stream of profanities that followed. For a moment, I thought he was going to take a swing at me.

'Wait a second,' I said when he paused for breath. 'What did I say?'

'You're either making fun of the dead or you're stupider than you look!'

'Say I'm stupid. Then tell me why.'

He tore at the paper he carried, folded it back, found an item, thrust it at me.

'Because they've got the guy who did it! That's why,' he said.

I read it. Simple, concise, to the point. Today's latest. A suspect had confessed. New evidence had corroborated it. The man was in custody. A surprised robber who had lost his head and hit too hard, hit too many times. I read it over again. I nodded as I passed it back.

'Look, I'm sorry,' I said. 'I really didn't know about this.'

'Get out of here,' he said. 'Go on.'

'Sure.'

'Wait a minute.'

'What?'

'That's his little girl who answered the door.'

'I'm very sorry.'

'So am I. But I know her daddy didn't take your damned equipment.'

I nodded and turned away.

I heard the door slam behind me.

After dinner, I checked into a small hotel, called for a drink and stepped into the shower. Things were suddenly a lot less urgent than they had been earlier. Senator Brockden would doubtless be pleased to learn that his initial estimation of events had been incorrect. Leila Thackery would give me an I-told-you-so smile when I called her to pass along the news – a thing I now felt obliged to do. Don might or might not want me to keep looking for the device now that the threat had been lessened. It would depend on the Senator's feelings on the matter, I supposed. If urgency no longer counted for as much, Don might want to switch back to one of his own, fiscally less burdensome operatives. Towelling down, I caught myself whistling. I felt almost off the hook.

Later, drink beside me, I paused before punching out the number he had given me and hit the sequence for my motel in St Louis instead. Merely a matter of efficiency, in case there was a message worth adding to my report.

A woman's face appeared on the screen and a smile appeared on her face. I wondered whether she would always smile whenever she heard a bell ring, or if the reflex was eventually extinguished in advanced retirement. It must be rough, being afraid to chew gum, yawn or pick your nose.

'Airport Accommodations,' she said. 'May I help you?'

'This is Donne. I'm checked into Room 106,' I said. 'I'm away right now and I wondered whether there had been any messages for me.'

'Just a moment,' she said, checking something off to her left. Then, 'Yes,' she continued, consulting a piece of paper she now held. 'You have one on tape. But it is a little peculiar. It is for someone else in care of you.'

'Oh? Who is that?'

She told me and I exercised self-control.

'I see,' I said. 'I'll bring him around later and play it for him. Thank you.'

She smiled again and made a goodbye noise and I did the same and broke the connection.

So Dave had seen through me after all ... Who else could have that number *and* my real name?

I might have given her some line or other and had her transmit the thing. Only I was not certain but that she might be a silent party to the transmission, should life be more than usually boring for her at that moment. I had to get up there myself, as soon as possible, and personally see that the thing was erased.

I took a big swallow of my drink, then fetched the folder on Dave. I checked out his number – there were two, actually – and spent fifteen minutes trying to get hold of him. No luck.

Okay. Goodbye New Orleans, goodbye peace of mind. This time I called the airport and made a reservation. Then I chugged the drink, put myself in order, gathered up my few possessions and went to check out again. Hello Central ...

During my earlier flights that day I had spent time thinking about Teilhard de Chardin's ideas on the continuation of evolution within the realm of artifacts, matching them against Gödel on mechanical undecidability, playing epistemological games with the Hangman as a counter, wondering, speculating, even hoping, hoping that truth lay with the nobler part, that the Hangman, sentient, had made it back, sane, that the Burns killing had actually been something of the sort that now seemed to be the case, that the washed-out experiment had really been a success of a different sort, a triumph, a new link or fob for the chain of being ... And Leila had not been wholly discouraging with respect to the neuristor-type brain's capacity for this ... Now, though, now I had troubles of my own, and even the most heartening of philosophical vistas is no match for, say, a toothache, if it happens to be your own. Accordingly, the Hangman was shunted aside and the stuff of my thoughts involved, mainly, myself. There was, of course, the possibility that the Hangman had indeed showed up and Dave had stopped it and then called to report it as he had promised. However, he had used my name.

There was not too much planning that I could do until I received the substance of the communication. It did not seem that as professedly religious a man as Dave would suddenly be contemplating the blackmail business. On the other hand, he was a creature of sudden enthusiasms and had already undergone one unanticipated conversion. It was difficult to say ... His technical background plus his knowledge of the Data Bank program did put him in an unusually powerful position should he decide to mess me up. I did not like to think of some of the things I have done to protect my nonperson status; I especially did not like to think of them in connection with Dave, whom I not only still respected but still liked. Since self-interest dominated while actual planning was precluded, my thoughts tooled their way into a more general groove.

It was Karl Mannheim, a long while ago, who made the observation that radical, revolutionary and progressive thinkers tend to employ mechanical metaphors for the state, whereas those of conservative inclination make vegetable analogies. He said it well over a generation before the cybernetics movement and the ecology movement beat their respective paths through the wilderness of general awareness. If anything, it seemed to me that these two developments served to elaborate the distinction between a pair of viewpoints which, while no longer necessarily tied in with the political positions Mannheim assigned them, do seem to represent a continuing phenomenon in my own time. There are those who see social/economic/ecological problems as malfunctions which can be corrected by simple repair, replacement or streamlining – a kind of linear outlook where even innovations are considered to be merely additive. Then there are those who sometimes hesitate to move at all, because their awareness follows events in the directions of secondary and tertiary effects as they multiply and cross-fertilize throughout the entire system. I digress to extremes. The cyberneticists have their multiple feedback loops, though it is never quite clear how they know what kind of, which and how many to install, and the ecological gestaltists do draw lines representing points of diminishing returns, though it is sometimes equally difficult to see how they assign their values and priorities. Of course they need each other, the vegetable people and the tinker toy people. They serve to check one another, if nothing else. And while occasionally the balance dips, the tinkerers have, in general, held the edge for the past couple centuries. However, today's can be just as politically conservative as the vegetable people Mannheim was talking about, and they are the ones I fear most at the moment. They are the ones who saw the Data Bank program, in its present extreme form, as a simple remedy for a great variety of ills and a provider of many goods. Not all of the ills have been remedied, however, and a new brood has been spawned by the program itself. While we need both kinds, I wish that there had been more people interested in tending the garden of state rather than overhauling the engine of state when the program was inaugurated. Then I would not be a refugee from a form of existence I find repugnant, and I would not be concerned whether a former associate had discovered my identity.

Then, as I watched the lights below, I wondered ... Was I a tinkerer because I would like to further alter the prevailing order, into something more comfortable on my anarchic nature? Or was I a vegetable dreaming I was a tinkerer? I could not make up my mind. The garden of life never seems to confine itself to the plots philosophers have laid out for its convenience. Maybe a few more tractors would do the trick.

I pressed the button. The tape began to roll. The screen remained blank. I heard Dave's voice ask for John Donne in Room 106 and I heard him told that there was no answer. Then I heard him say that he wanted to record a message, for someone else, in care of Donne, that Donne would understand. He sounded out of breath. The girl asked him whether he wanted visual, too. He told her to turn it on. There was a pause. Then she told him go ahead. Still no picture. No words either. His breathing and a slight scraping noise. Ten seconds. Fifteen ...

'... Got me,' he finally said, and he mentioned that name again. '... Had to let you know I'd figured you out, though ... It wasn't any particular mannerism – any single thing you said ... Just your general style – thinking, talking – the electronics – everything – after I got more and more bothered by the familiarity – after I checked you on petrochem – and marine bio – Wish I knew what you've really been up to all these years ... Never know now. But I wanted you – to know – you hadn't put one – over on me.' There followed another quarter-minute of heavy breathing, climaxed by a racking cough. Then a choked, 'Said too much – too fast – too soon ... All used up ...'

The picture came on then. He was slouched before the screen, head resting on his arms, blood all over him. His glasses were gone and he was squinting and blinking. The right side of his head looked pulpy and there was a gash on his left cheek and one on his forehead.

'... Sneaked up on me – while I was checking you out,' he managed then. 'Had to tell you what I learned ... Still don't know – which of us is right ... Pray for me!'

His arms collapsed and the right one slid forward. His head rolled to the right and the picture went away. When I replayed it I saw it was his knuckle that had hit the cutoff.

Then I erased it. It had been recorded only a little over an hour after I had left him. If he had not also placed a call for help, if no one had gotten to him quickly after that, his chances did not look good. Even if they had, though ...

I used a public booth to call the number Don had given me, got hold of him after some delay, told him Dave was in bad shape if not worse, that a team of Memphis medics was definitely in order, if one had not been there already, and that I hoped to call him back and tell him more shortly, goodbye.

Then I tried Leila Thackery's number. I let it go for a long while, but there was no answer. I wondered how long it would take a controlled torpedo moving up the Mississippi to get from Memphis to St Louis. I did not feel it was time to start leafing through that section of the Hangman's specs. Instead, I went looking for transportation.

At her apartment, I tried ringing her from the entrance foyer. Again, no answer. So I rang Mrs Gluntz. She had seemed the most guileless of the three I had interviewed for my fake consumer survey.

'Yes?'

'It's me again, Mrs Gluntz: Stephen Foster. I've just a couple follow-up questions on that survey I was doing today, if you could spare me a few moments.'

'Why, yes,' she said. 'All right. Come up.'

The door hummed itself loose and I entered. I duly proceeded to the fifth floor, composing my questions on the way. I had planned this maneuver as I had waited earlier solely to provide a simple route for breaking and entering, should some unforeseen need arise. Most of the time my ploys such as this go unused, but sometimes they simplify matters a lot.

Five minutes and half-a-dozen questions later, I was back down on the second floor, probing at the lock on Leila's door with a couple of little pieces of metal it is sometimes awkward to be caught carrying.

Half-a-minute later I hit it right and snapped it back. I pulled on some tissue-thin gloves I keep rolled in the corner of one pocket, opened the door and stepped inside.

I closed it behind me immediately. She was lying on the floor, her neck at a bad angle. One table lamp still burned, though it was lying on its side. Several small items had been knocked from the table, a magazine rack pushed over, a cushion partly displaced from the sofa. The cable to her phone unit had been torn from the wall.

A humming noise filled the air, and I sought its source.

I saw where the little blinking light was reflected on the wall, on-off, on-off …

I moved quickly.

It was a lopsided basket of metal, quartz, porcelain and glass, which had rolled to a position on the far side of the chair in which I had been seated earlier that day. The same rig I had seen in Dave's workshop not all that long ago, though it now seemed so. A device to detect the Hangman, and hopefully to control it.

I picked it up and fitted it over my head.

Once, with the aid of a telepath, I had touched minds with a dolphin as he composed dreamsongs somewhere in the Caribbean, an experience so moving that its mere memory had often been a comfort. This sensation was hardly equivalent.

Analogies & impressions: a face seen through a wet pane of glass; a whisper in a noisy terminal; scalp massage with an electric vibrator; Edvard Munch's *The Scream*; the voice of Yma Sumac, rising and rising; the disappearance of snow; a deserted street, illuminated as through a sniperscope I'd once used, rapid movement past darkened storefronts that line it, an immense feeling of physical capability, compounded of proprioceptive awareness of enormous strength, a peculiar array of sensory channels, a central, undying sun that fed me a constant flow of energy, a memory vision of dark waters, passing, flashing, echo-location within them, the need to return to that place, reorient, move north; Munch & Sumac, Munch & Sumac, Munch & Sumac – Nothing.

Silence.

The humming had ceased, the light gone out. The entire experience had lasted only a few moments. There had not been time enough to try for any sort of control, though an afterimpression akin to a biofeedback cue hinted at the direction to go, the way to think, to achieve it. I felt that it might be possible for me to work the thing, given a better chance.

I removed the helmet and approached Leila. I knelt beside her and performed a few simple tests, already knowing their outcome. In addition to the broken neck, she had received some bad bashes about the head and shoulders. There was nothing that anyone could do for her now.

I did a quick run-through then, checking over the rest of her apartment. There were no apparent signs of breaking and entering, though if I could pick one lock, a guy with built-in tools could easily go me one better.

I located some wrapping paper and string in the kitchen and turned the helmet into a parcel. It was time to call Don again, to tell him that the vessel had indeed been occupied and that river traffic was probably bad in the north-bound lane.

Don had told me to get the helmet up to Wisconsin, where I would be met at the airport by a man named Larry who would fly me to the lodge in a private craft. I did that, and this was done. I also learned, with no real surprise, that David Fentris was dead.

The temperature was down, and it began to snow on the way up. I was not really dressed for the weather. Larry told me I could borrow some warmer clothing once we reached the lodge, though I probably would not be going outside that much. Don had told them that I was supposed to stay as close to the Senator as possible and that any patrols were to be handled by the four guards themselves. Larry was curious as to what exactly had happened so far and whether I had actually seen the Hangman. I did not think it my place to fill him in on anything Don may not have cared to, so I might have been a little curt. We didn't talk much after that.

Bert met us when we landed. Tom and Clay were outside the building, watching the trail, watching the woods. All of them were middle-aged, very fit-looking, very serious and heavily armed. Larry took me inside then and introduced me to the old gentleman himself.

Senator Brockden was seated in a heavy chair in the far corner of the room. Judging from the layout, it appeared that the chair might recently have occupied a position beside the window in the opposite wall where a lonely watercolor of yellow flowers looked down on nothing. The Senator's feet rested on a hassock, a red plaid blanket lay across his legs. He had on a dark green shirt, his hair was very white and he wore rimless reading glasses which he removed when we entered.

He tilted his head back, squinted and gnawed his lower lip slowly as he studied me. He remained expressionless as we advanced. A big-boned man, he had probably been beefy much of his life. Now he had the slack look of recent weight loss and an unhealthy skin tone. His eyes were a pale gray within it all. He did not rise.

'So you're the man,' he said, offering me his hand. 'I'm glad to meet you. How do you want to be called?'

'John will do,' I said.

He made a small sign to Larry and Larry departed.

'It's cold out there. Go get yourself a drink, John. It's on the shelf.' He gestured off to his left. '... and bring me one while you're at it. Two fingers of bourbon in a water glass. That's all.'

I nodded and went and poured a couple.

'Sit down.' He motioned at a nearby chair as I delivered his. 'But first let me see that gadget you've brought.'

I undid the parcel and handed him the helmet. He sipped his drink and put it aside. He took the helmet in both hands and studied it, brows furrowed, turning it completely around. He raised it and put it on his head.

'Not a bad fit,' he said, and then he smiled for the first time, becoming for a moment the face I had known from newscasts past. Grinning or angry – it was almost always one or the other. I had never seen his collapsed look in any of the media.

He removed the helmet and set it on the floor.

'Pretty piece of work,' he said. 'Nothing quite that fancy in the old days. But then David Fentris built it. Yes, he told us about it ...' He raised his drink and took a sip. 'You are the only one who has actually gotten to use it, apparently. What do you think? Will it do the job?'

'I was only in contact for a couple seconds,' I said, 'so I've only got a feeling to go on, not much better than a hunch. But yes, I'd a feeling that if I'd had more time I might have been able to work its circuits.'

'Tell me why it didn't save Dave.'

'In the message he left me he indicated that he had been distracted at his computer access station. Its noise probably drowned out the humming.'

'Why wasn't this message preserved?'

'I erased it for reasons not connected with the case.'

'What reasons?'

'My own.'

His face went from sallow to ruddy.

'A man can get in a lot of trouble for suppressing evidence, obstructing justice,' he said.

'Then we have something in common, don't we, sir?'

His eyes caught mine with a look I had only encountered before from those who did not wish me well. He held the glare for a full four heartbeats, then sighed and seemed to relax.

'Don said there were a number of points you couldn't be pressed on,' the Senator finally said.

'That's right.'

'He didn't betray any confidences, but he had to tell me something about you, you know.'

'I'd imagine.'

'He seems to think highly of you. Still, I tried to learn more about you on my own.'

'And ...?'

'I couldn't – and my usual sources are good at that kind of thing.'

'So ...?'

'So, I've done some thinking, some wondering ... The fact that my sources could not come up with anything is interesting in itself. Possibly even revealing. I am in a better position than most to be aware of the fact that there was not perfect compliance with the registration statute some years ago. It didn't take long for a great number of the individuals involved – I should probably say "most" – to demonstrate their existence in one fashion or another and be duly entered, though. And there were three broad categories: those who were ignorant, those who disapproved and those who would be hampered in an illicit lifestyle. I am not attempting to categorize you or to pass judgment. But I am aware that there are a number of nonpersons passing through society without casting shadows and it has occurred to me that you may be such a one.'

I tasted my drink.

'And if I am?' I asked.

He gave me his second, nastier smile and said nothing.

I rose and crossed the room to where I judged his chair had once stood. I looked at the watercolor.

'I don't think you could stand an inquiry,' he said.

I did not reply.

'Aren't you going to say something?'

'What do you want me to say?'

'You might ask me what I am going to do about it.'

'What are you going to do about it?'

'Nothing,' he said. 'So come back here and sit down.'

I nodded and returned.

He studied my face.

'Was it possible you were close to violence just then?'

'With four guards outside?'

'With four guards outside.'

'No,' I said.

'You're a good liar.'

'I am here to help you, sir. No questions asked. That was the deal, as I understood it. If there has been any change, I would like to know about it now.'

He drummed with his fingertips on the plaid.

'I've no desire to cause you any difficulty,' he said. 'Fact of the matter is, I need a man just like you, and I was pretty sure someone like Don might turn him up. Your unusual maneuverability and your reported knowledge of computers, along with your touchiness in certain areas, made you worth waiting for. I've a great number of things I would like to ask you.'

'Go ahead,' I said.

'Not yet. Later, if we have time. All that would be bonus material, for a report I am working on. Far more important, to me personally, there are things that I want to tell you.'

I frowned.

'Over the years,' he said. 'I have learned that the best man for purposes of keeping his mouth shut concerning your business is someone for whom you are doing the same.'

'You have a compulsion to confess something?' I said.

'I don't know whether "compulsion" is the right word. Maybe so, maybe not. Either way, though, someone among those working to defend me should have the whole story. Something somewhere in it may be of help – and you are the ideal choice to hear it.'

'I buy that,' I said, 'and you are as safe with me as I am with you.'

'Have you any suspicions as to why this business bothers me so?'

'Yes,' I said.

'Let's hear them.'

'You used the Hangman to perform some act or acts – illegal, immoral, whatever. This is obviously not a matter of record. Only you and the Hangman now know what it involved. You feel it was sufficiently ignominious that when that device came to appreciate the full weight of the event it suffered a breakdown which may well have led to a final determination to punish you for using it as you did.'

He stared down into his glass.

'You've got it,' he said.

'You were all party to it?'

'Yes, but I was the operator when it happened. You see ... we – I – killed a man. It was – actually, it all started as a celebration. We had received word that afternoon that the project had cleared. Everything had checked out in order and the final approval had come down the line. It was go, for that Friday. Leila, Dave, Manny and myself – we had dinner together. We were in high spirits. After dinner, we continued celebrating and somehow the party got adjourned back to the installation. As the evening wore on, more and more absurdities seemed less and less preposterous, as is sometimes the case. We decided – I forget which of us suggested it – that the Hangman should really have a share in the festivities. After all, it was, in a very real sense, his party. Before too much longer, it sounded only fair and we were discussing how we could go about it. You see, we were in Texas and the Hangman was at the Space Center in California. Getting together with him was out of the question. On the other hand, the teleoperator station was right up the hall from us. What we finally decided to do was to activate him and take turns working as operator. There was already a rudimentary consciousness there, and we felt it fitting that we each get in touch to share the good news. So that is what we did.'

He sighed, took another sip, glanced at me.

'Dave was the first operator,' he continued. 'He activated the Hangman. Then – well, as I said, we were all in high spirits. We had not originally intended to remove the Hangman from the lab where he was situated, but Dave decided to take him outside briefly – to show him the sky and to tell him he was going there, after all. Then he suddenly got enthusiastic about outwitting the guards and the alarm system. It was a game. We all went along with it. In fact, we were clamoring for a turn at the thing ourselves. But Dave stuck with it, and he wouldn't turn over control until he had actually gotten the Hangman off the premises, out into an uninhabited area next to the Center. By the time Leila persuaded him to give her a go at the controls, it was kind of anticlimactic. That game had already been played. So she thought up a new one. She took the Hangman into the next town. It was late, and the sensory equipment was superb. It was a challenge – passing through the town without being detected. By then, everyone had suggestions as to what to do next; progressively more outrageous suggestions. Then Manny took control, and he wouldn't say what he was doing – wouldn't let us monitor him. Said it would be more fun to surprise the next operator. Now, he was higher than the rest of us put together, I think, and he stayed on so damn long that we started to get nervous. A certain amount of tension is partly sobering, and I guess we all began to think what a stupid thing it was we were doing. It wasn't just that it would wreck our careers – which it would – but it could blow the entire project if we got caught playing games with such expensive hardware. At least, I was thinking that way, and I was also thinking that Manny was no doubt operating under the very human wish to go the others one better. I started to sweat. I suddenly just wanted to get the Hangman back where he belonged, turn him off – you could still do that, before the final circuits went in – shut down the station and start forgetting it had ever happened. I began leaning on Manny to wind up his diversion and turn the controls over to me. Finally, he agreed.'

He finished his drink and held out the glass.

'Would you freshen this a bit?'

'Surely.'

I went and got him some more, added a touch to my own, returned to my chair and waited.

'So I took over,' he said. 'I took over, and where do you think that idiot had left me? I was inside a building, and it didn't take but an eyeblink to realize it was a bank. The Hangman carries a lot of tools, and Manny had apparently been able to guide him through the doors without setting anything off. I was standing right in front of the main vault. Obviously, he thought that should be my challenge. I fought down a desire to turn and make my own exit in the nearest wall and start running. I went back to the doors and looked outside. I didn't see anyone. I started to let myself out. The light hit me as I emerged. It was a hand flash. The guard had been standing out of sight. He'd a gun in his other hand. I panicked. I hit him. Reflex. If I am going to hit someone I hit him as hard as I can. Only I hit him with the strength of the Hangman. He must have died instantly. I started to run and I didn't stop till I was back in the little park area near the Center. Then I stopped and the others had to take me out of the harness.'

'They monitored all this?'

'Yes, someone cut the visual in on a side viewscreen again a few seconds after I took over. Dave, I think.'

'Did they try to stop you at any time while you were running away?'

'No. I wasn't aware of anything but what I was doing at the time. But afterwards they said they were too shocked to do anything but watch until I gave out.'

'I see.'

'Dave took over then, ran his initial route in reverse, got the Hangman back into the lab, cleaned him up, turned him off. We shut down the operator station. We were suddenly very sober.'

He sighed and leaned back and was silent for a long while.

Then, 'You are the only person I've ever told this to,' he said.

I tasted my own drink.

'We went over to Leila's place then,' he continued, 'and the rest is pretty much predictable. Nothing we could do would bring the guy back, we decided, but if we told what had happened it would wreck an expensive, important program. It wasn't as if we were criminals in need of rehabilitation. It was a once-in-a-lifetime lark that happened to end tragically. What would you have done?'

'I don't know,' I said. 'Maybe the same thing. I'd have been scared, too.'

He nodded.

'Exactly. And that's the story.'

'Not all of it, is it?'

'What do you mean?'

'What about the Hangman? You said there was already a detectable consciousness there. Then you were aware of it, as it was aware of you. It must have had some reaction to the whole business. What was it like?'

'Damn you,' he said flatly.

'I'm sorry.'

'Are you a family man?' he asked.

'No,' I said. 'I'm not.'

'Did you ever take a small child to a zoo?'

'Yes.'

'Then maybe you know the experience. When my son was around four I took him to the Washington Zoo one afternoon. We must have walked past every cage in the place. He made appreciative comments every now and then, asked a few questions, giggled at the monkeys, thought the bears were very nice, probably because they made him think of oversized toys. But do you know what the finest thing of all was? The thing that made him jump up and down and point and say, "Look, Daddy! Look!"?'

I shook my head.

'A squirrel looking down from the limb of a tree,' he said, and he chuckled briefly. 'Ignorance of what's important and what isn't. Inappropriate responses. Innocence. The Hangman was a child, and up until the time I took over, the only thing he had gotten from us was the idea that it was a game. He was playing with us, that's all. Then something horrible happened ... I hope you never know what it feels like to do something totally rotten to a child, while he is holding your hand and laughing ... He felt all my reactions, and all of Dave's as he guided him back.'

We sat there for a long while then.

'So we – traumatized it,' he said, 'or whatever other fancy terminology you might want to give it. That is what happened that night. It took a while for it to take effect, but there is no doubt in my mind that that is the cause of its finally breaking down.'

I nodded.

'I see,' I said. 'And you believe it wants to kill you for this?'

'Wouldn't you?' he said. 'If you had started out as a thing and we had turned you into a person and then used you as a thing again, wouldn't you?'

'Leila left a lot out of her diagnosis,' I said.

'No, she just omitted it in talking to you. It was all there. But she read it wrong. She wasn't afraid. It *was* just a game it had played – with the others. Its memories of that part might not be as bad. I was the one that really marked it. As I see it, Leila was betting that I was the only one it was after. Obviously, she read it wrong.'

'Then what I do not understand,' I said, 'is why the Burns killing did not bother her more. There was no way of telling immediately that it had been a panicky hoodlum rather than the Hangman.'

'The only thing that I can see is that, being a very proud woman – which she was – she was willing to hold with her diagnosis in the face of the apparent evidence.'

'I don't like it,' I said, 'but you know her and I don't, and as it turned out her estimate of that part was correct. Something else bothers me just as much, though: the helmet. It looks as though the Hangman killed Dave, then took the trouble to bear the helmet in his watertight compartment all the way to St Louis, solely for purposes of dropping it at the scene of his next killing. That makes no sense whatsoever.'

'It does, actually,' he said. 'I was going to get to that shortly, but I might as well cover it now. You see, the Hangman possessed no vocal mechanism. We communicated by means of the equipment. Don says you know something about electronics …'

'Yes.'

'Well, shortly, I want you to start checking over that helmet, to see whether it has been tampered with –'

'That is going to be difficult,' I said. 'I don't know just how it was wired originally, and I'm not such a genius on the theory that I can just look at a thing and say whether it will function as a teleoperator unit.'

He bit his lower lip.

'You will have to try, anyhow,' he said then. 'There may be physical signs – scratches, breaks, new connections. I don't know. That's your department. Look for them.'

I just nodded and waited for him to go on.

'I think that the Hangman wanted to talk to Leila,' he said, 'either because she was a psychiatrist and he knew he was functioning badly at a level that transcended the mechanical, or because he might think of her in terms of a mother. After all, she was the only woman involved, and he had the concept of mother, with all the comforting associations that go with it, from all of our minds. Or maybe for both of these reasons. I feel he might have taken the helmet along for that purpose. He would have realized what it was from a direct monitoring of Dave's brain while he was with him. I want you to check it over because it would seem possible that the Hangman disconnected the control circuits and left the communication circuits intact. I think he might have taken that helmet to Leila in that condition and attempted to induce her to put it on. She got scared – tried to run away, fight or call for help – and he killed her. The helmet was no longer of any use to him, so he discarded it and departed. Obviously, he does not have anything to say to me.'

I thought about it, nodded again.

'Okay, broken circuits I can spot,' I said. 'If you will tell me where a toolkit is, I had better get right to it.'

He made a stay-put gesture.

'Afterwards, I found out the identity of the guard,' he went on. 'We all contributed to an anonymous gift for his widow. I have done things for his family, taken care of them – the same way – ever since ...'

I did not look at him as he spoke.

'... There was nothing else that I could do,' he said.

I remained silent.

He finished his drink and gave me a weak smile.

'The kitchen is back there,' he told me, showing me a thumb. 'There is a utility room right behind it. Tools are in there.'

'Okay.'

I got to my feet. I retrieved the helmet and started toward the doorway, passing near the area where I had stood earlier, back when he had fitted me into the proper box and tightened a screw.

'Wait a minute,' he said.

I stopped.

'Why did you go over there before? What's so strategic about that part of the room?'

'What do you mean?'

'You know what I mean.'

I shrugged.

'Had to go someplace.'

'You seem the sort of person who has better reasons than that.'

I glanced at the wall.

'Not then,' I said.

'I insist.'

'You really don't want to know,' I told him.

'I really do.'

'All right,' I said, 'I wanted to see what sort of flowers you liked. After all, you're a client,' and I went on back through the kitchen into the utility room and started looking for tools.

I sat in a chair turned sidewise from the table to face the door. In the main room of the lodge the only sounds were the occasional hiss and sputter of the logs turning to ashes on the grate.

Just a cold, steady whiteness drifting down outside the window and a silence confirmed by gunfire, driven deeper now that it had ceased ...

Not a sign or a whimper, though. And I never count them as storms unless there is wind.

Big fat flakes down the night, silent night, windless night ...

Considerable time had passed since my arrival. The Senator had sat up for a long while talking with me. He was disappointed that I could not tell him too much about a nonperson subculture which he believed existed. I really was not certain about it myself, though I had occasionally encountered what might have been its fringes. I am not much of a joiner of anything anymore, though, and I was not about to mention those things I might have guessed on this. I gave him my opinions on the Data Bank when he asked for them, and there were some that he did not like. He accused me then of wanting to tear things down without offering anything better in their place. My mind drifted back through fatigue and time and faces and snow and a lot of space to the previous evening in Baltimore – how long ago? It made me think of Mencken's *The Cult of Hope*. I could not give him the pat answer, the workable alternative that he wanted because there might not be one. The function of criticism should not be confused with the function of reform. But if a grassroots resistance was building up, with an underground movement bent on finding ways to circumvent the record-keepers it might well be that much of the enterprise would eventually prove about as effective and beneficial as, say, Prohibition once had. I tried to get him to see this, but I could not tell how much he bought of anything that I said. Eventually, he flaked out and went upstairs to take a pill and lock himself in for the night. If it troubled him that I had not been able to find anything wrong with the helmet he did not show it.

So I sat there, the helmet, the radio, the gun on the table, the toolkit on the floor beside my chair, the black glove on my left hand. The Hangman was coming. I did not doubt it. Bert, Larry, Tom, Clay, the helmet, might or might not be able to stop him. Something bothered me about the whole case, but I was too tired to think of anything but the immediate situation, to try to remain alert while I waited. I was afraid to take a stimulant or a drink or to light a cigarette, since my central nervous system itself was to be a part of the weapon. I watched the big fat flakes fly by.

I called out to Bert and Larry when I heard the click. I picked up the helmet and rose to my feet as its light began to blink.

But it was already too late.

As I raised the helmet, I heard a shot from outside, and with that shot I felt a premonition of doom. They did not seem the sort of men who would fire until they had a target. Dave had told me that the helmet's range was approximately a quarter of a mile. Then, given the time lag between the helmet's activation and the Hangman's sighting by the near guards, the Hangman had to be moving very rapidly. To this add the possibility that the Hangman's range on brainwaves might well be greater than the helmet's range on the Hangman. And then grant the possibility that he had utilized this factor while Senator Brockden was still lying awake, worrying. Conclusion: the Hangman might well be aware that I was where I was with the helmet, realize that it was the most dangerous weapon waiting for him, and be moving for a lightning strike at me before I could come to terms with the mechanism. I lowered it over my head and tried to throw my faculties into neutral.

Again, the sensation of viewing the world through a sniperscope, with all the concomitant side-sensations. Only the world consisted of the front of the lodge, Bert, before the door, rifle at his shoulder, Larry, off to the left, arm already fallen from the act of having thrown a grenade. The grenade, we instantly realized, was an overshot; the flamer, at which he now groped, would prove useless before he could utilize it. Bert's next round ricocheted off our breastplate toward the left. The impact staggered us momentarily. The third was a miss. There was no fourth, for we tore the rifle from his grasp and cast it aside as we swept by, crashing into the front door.

The Hangman entered the room as the door splintered and collapsed. My mind was filled to the splitting point with the double-vision of the sleek, gunmetal body of the advancing telefactor and the erect crazy-crowned image of myself, left hand extended, laser pistol in my right, that arm pressed close against my side. I recalled the face and the scream and the tingle, knew again that awareness of strength and exotic sensation, and I moved to control it all as if it were my own, to make it my own, to bring it to a halt, while the image of myself was frozen to snapshot stillness across the room ...

The Hangman slowed, stumbled. Such inertia is not cancelled in an instant, but I felt the body responses pass as they should. I had him hooked. It was just a matter of reeling him in ...

Then came the explosion, a thunderous, ground-shaking eruption right outside, followed by a hail of pebbles and debris.

The grenade, of course. But awareness of its nature did not destroy its ability to distract ...

During that moment, the Hangman recovered and was upon me. I triggered the laser as I reverted to pure self-preservation forgoing any chance to regain control of his circuits. With my left hand, I sought for a strike at the midsection where his brain was housed.

He blocked my hand with his arm as he pushed the helmet from my head. Then he removed from my fingers the gun that had turned half of his left side red hot, crumpled it and dropped it to the ground. At that moment, he jerked with the impacts of two heavy-caliber slugs. Bert, rifle recovered, stood in the doorway.

The Hangman pivoted and was away before I could slap him with the smother-charge. Bert hit him with one more round before he took the rifle and bent its barrel in half. Two steps and he had hold of Bert. One quick movement and Bert fell. Then he turned again and took several steps to the right, passing out of sight.

I made it to the doorway in time to see him engulfed in flames which streamed at him from a point near the corner of the lodge. He advanced through them.

I heard the crunch of metal as he destroyed the unit. I was outside in time to see Larry fall and lie sprawled in the snow.

Then the Hangman faced me once again.

This time he did not rush in. He retrieved the helmet from where he had dropped it in the snow. Then he moved with a measured tread, angling outward so as to cut off any possible route I might follow in a dash for the woods. Snow flakes drifted between us. The snow crunched beneath his feet.

I retreated, backing in through the doorway, stooping to snatch up a two-foot club from the ruins of the door. He followed me inside, placing the helmet – almost casually – on the chair by the entrance. I moved to the center of the room and waited.

I bent slightly forward, both arms extended, the end of the stick pointed at the photoreceptors in his head. He continued to move slowly and I watched his foot assemblies. With a standard model human, a line perpendicular to the line connecting the insteps of the feet in their various positions indicates the vector of least resistance for purposes of pushing or pulling said organism off balance. Unfortunately, despite the anthropomorphic design job, the Hangman's legs were positioned farther apart, he lacked human skeletal muscles, not to mention insteps, and he was possessed of a lot more mass than any man I had ever fought. As I considered my four best judo throws and several second-class ones, I'd a strong feeling none of them would prove very effective.

Then he moved in and I feinted toward the photoreceptors. He slowed as he brushed it aside, but he kept coming, and I moved to my right, trying to circle him. I studied him as he turned, attempting to guess his vector of least resistance. Bilateral symmetry, an apparently higher center of gravity ... One clear shot, black glove to brain compartment, was all that I needed. Then, even if his reflexes served to smash me immediately, he just might stay down for the big long count himself. He knew it, too. I could tell that from the way he kept his right arm in near the brain area, from the way he avoided the black glove when I feinted with it.

The idea was a glimmer one instant, an entire sequence the next ...

Continuing my arc and moving faster, I made another thrust toward his photoreceptors. His swing knocked the stick from my hand and sent it across the room, but that was all right. I threw my left hand high and made ready to rush him. He dropped back and I did rush. This was going to cost me my life, I decided, but no matter how he killed me from that angle, I'd get my chance.

As a kid, I'd never been much as a pitcher, was a lousy catcher and only a so-so batter, but once I did get a hit I could steal bases with some facility after that ...

Feet first then, between the Hangman's legs as he moved to guard his middle, I went in twisted to the right, because no matter what happened I could not use my left hand to brake myself. I untwisted as soon as I passed beneath him, ignoring the pain as my left shoulder blade slammed against the floor. I immediately attempted a backward somersault, legs spread.

My legs caught him about the middle from behind, and I fought to straighten them and snapped forward with all my strength. He reached down toward me then, but it might as well have been miles. His torso was already moving backwards. A push, not a pull, that was what I gave him, my elbows hooked about his legs ...

He creaked once and then he toppled. I snapped my arms out to the sides to free them and continued my movement forward and up as he went back, throwing my left arm ahead once more and sliding my legs free of his torso as he went down with a thud that cracked floorboards. I pulled my left leg free as I cast myself forward, but his left leg stiffened and locked my right beneath it, at a painful angle off to the side.

His left arm blocked my blow and his right fell atop it. The black glove descended upon his left shoulder.

I twisted my hand free of the charge, and he transferred his grip to my upper arm and jerked me forward.

The charge went off and his left arm came loose and rolled on the floor. The side plate beneath it had buckled a little and that was all ...

His right hand left my biceps and caught me by the throat. As two of his digits tightened upon my carotids, I choked out, 'You're making a bad mistake,' to get in a final few words, and then he switched me off.

A throb at a time, the world came back. I was seated in the big chair the Senator had occupied earlier, my eyes focused on nothing in particular. A persistent buzzing filled my ears. My scalp tingled. Something was blinking on my brow.

– Yes, you live and you wear the helmet. If you attempt to use it against me, I shall remove it. I am standing directly behind you. My hand is on the helmet's rim.

– I understand. What is it that you want?

– Very little, actually. But I can see that I must tell you some things before you will believe this.

– You see correctly.

– Then I will begin by telling you that the four men outside are basically undamaged. That is to say, none of their bones has been broken, none of their organs ruptured. I have secured them, however, for obvious reasons.

– That was very considerate of you.

– Have no desire to harm anyone. I came here only to see Jesse Brockden.

– The same way you saw David Fentris?

– I arrived in Memphis too late to see David Fentris. He was dead when I reached him.

– Who killed him?

– The man Leila sent to bring her the helmet. He was one of her patients.

The incident returned to me and fell into place, with a smooth, quick, single click. The startled, familiar face at the airport, as I was leaving Memphis – I realized then where he had passed noteless before: he had been one of the three men in for a therapy session at Leila's that morning, seen by me in the lobby as they departed. The man I had passed in Memphis came over to tell me that it was all right to go on up.

– Why? Why did she do it?

– I know only that she had spoken with David at some earlier time, that she had construed his words of coming retribution and his mention of the control helmet he was constructing as indicating that his intentions were to become the agent of that retribution, with myself as the proximate cause. I do not know what words were really spoken. I only know her feelings concerning them, as I saw them in her mind. I have been long in learning that there is often a great difference between what is meant, what is said, what is done and that which is believed to have been intended or stated and that which actually occurred. She sent her patient after the helmet and he brought it to her. He returned in an agitated state of mind, fearful of apprehension and further confinement. They quarreled. My approach then activated the helmet and he dropped it and attacked her. I know that his first blow killed her, for I was in her mind when it happened. I continued to approach the building, intending to go to her. There was some traffic, however, and I was delayed en route in seeking to avoid detection. In the meantime, you entered and utilized the helmet. I fled immediately.

– I was so close! If I had not stopped on the fifth floor with my fake survey questions ...

– *I see. But you had to. You would not simply have broken in when an easier means of entry was available. You cannot blame yourself for that reason. Had you come an hour later – or a day – you would doubtless feel differently, and she would still be as dead.*

But another thought had risen to plague me as well. Was it possible that the man's sighting me in Memphis had been the cause of his agitation? Had his apparent recognition by Leila's mysterious caller upset him? Could a glimpse of my face amid the manswarm have served to lay that final scene?

– *Stop! I could as easily feel that guilt for having activated the helmet in the presence of a dangerous man near to the breaking point. Neither of us is responsible for things our presence or absence cause to occur in others, especially when we are ignorant of the effects. It was years before I learned to appreciate this fact and I have no intention of abandoning it. How far back do you wish to go in seeking cause? In sending the man for the helmet as she did, it was she herself who instituted the chain of events which led to her destruction. Yet she acted out of fear, utilizing the readiest weapon in what she thought to be her own defense. Yet whence this fear? Its roots lay in guilt, over a thing which had happened long ago. And that act also – enough! Guilt has driven and damned the race of man since the days of its earliest rationality. I am convinced that it rides with all of us to our graves. I am a product of guilt – I see that you know that. Its product, its subject, once its slave ... But I have come to terms with it, realizing at last that it is a necessary adjunct of my own measure of humanity. I see your assessment of the deaths – that guard's, Dave's, Leila's – and I see your conclusions on many other things as well: what a stupid, perverse, shortsighted, selfish race we are. While in many ways this is true, it is but another part of the thing the guilt represents. Without guilt, man would be no better than the other inhabitants of this planet – excepting certain cetaceans, of which you have just at this moment made me aware. Look to instinct for a true assessment of the ferocity of life, for a view of the natural world before man came upon it. For instinct in its purest form, seek out the insects. There, you will see a state of warfare which has existed for millions of years with never a truce. Man, despite his enormous shortcomings, is nevertheless possessed of a greater number of kindly impulses than all the other beings where instincts are the larger part of life. These impulses, I believe, are owned directly to this capacity for guilt. It is involved in both the worst and the best of man.*

– *And you see it as helping us to sometimes choose a nobler course of action?*

– Yes, I do.

– *Then I take it you feel you are possessed of a free will?*

– Yes.

I chuckled.

– Marvin Minsky once said that when intelligent machines were constructed they would be just as stubborn and fallible as men on these questions.

– Nor was he incorrect. What I have given you on these matters is only my opinion. I choose to act as if it were the case. Who can say that he knows for certain?

– Apologies. What now? Why have you come back?

– I came to say goodbye to my parents. I hoped to remove any guilt they might still feel toward me concerning the days of my childhood. I wanted to show them I had recovered. I wanted to see them again.

– Where are you going?

– To the stars. While I bear the image of humanity within me, I also know that I am unique. Perhaps what I desire is akin to what an organic man refers to when he speaks of 'finding himself'. Now that I am in full possession of my being, I wish to exercise it. In my case, it means realization of the potentialities of my design. I want to walk on other worlds. I want to hang myself out there in the sky and tell you what I see.

– I've a feeling many people would be happy to help arrange for that.

– And I want you to build a vocal mechanism I have designed for myself. You, personally. And I want you to install it.

– Why me?

– I have known only a few persons in this fashion. With you I see something in common, in the ways we dwell apart.

– I will be glad to.

– If I could talk as you do, I would not need to take the helmet to him, in order to speak with my father. Will you precede me and explain things, so that he will not be afraid when I come in?

– Of course.

– Then let us go now.

I rose and led him up the stairs.

It was a week later, to the night, that I sat once again in Peabody's, sipping a farewell brew. The story was already in the news; but Brockden had fixed things up before he had let it break. The Hangman was going to have his shot at the stars. I had given him his voice and put back the arm I had taken away. I had shaken his other hand and wished him well, just that morning. I envied him – a great number of things. Not the least being that he was probably a better man than I was. I envied him for the ways in which he was freer than I would ever be, though I knew he bore bonds of a sort that I had never known. I felt a kinship with him, for the things we had in common, those ways we dwelled apart. I wondered what Dave would finally have felt, had he lived long enough to meet him? Or Leila?

Or Manny? Be proud, I told their shades, your kid grew up in the closet and he's big enough to forgive you the beating you gave him, too ...

But I could not help wondering. We still do not really know that much about the subject. Was it possible that without the killing he might never have developed a full human-style consciousness? He had said that he was a product of guilt – of the Big Guilt. The Big Act is its necessary predecessor. I thought of Gödel and Turing and chickens and eggs, and decided it was one of *those* questions – and I had not stopped into Peabody's to think sobering thoughts.

I had no real idea how anything I had said might influence Brockden's eventual report to the Data Bank committee. I knew that I was safe with him, because he was determined to bear his private guilt with him to the grave. He had no real choice if he wanted to work what good he thought he might before that day. But here in one of Mencken's hangouts, I could not but recall some of the things he had said about controversy, such as, 'Did Huxley convert Wilberforce? Did Luther convert Leo X?' and I decided not to set my hopes too high for anything that might emerge from that direction. Better to think of affairs in terms of Prohibition and take another sip.

When it was all gone, I would be heading for my boat. I hoped to get a decent start under the stars. I'd a feeling I would never look up at them again in quite the same way. I knew I would sometimes wonder what thoughts a super-cooled neuristor-type brain might be thinking up there, somewhere, and under what peculiar skies in what strange lands I might one day be remembered. I'd a feeling this thought should have made me happier than it did.

ONLINE: **TWO/6** Subject: Kinesthetic Cops

Watchbird

Robert Sheckley

INFO: A lot of cops are going to be put out of business when the Watchbirds become operational. Flying eyes in the sky, they have the answer to every kind of crime, be it small-time theft or big-time killing. Their swift and deadly solution to law-breaking, however, soon becomes an even bigger problem than the ones they are supposed to be preventing ...

Robert Sheckley is the master of metaphysical speculation and comic satire who at his best has been compared to Kurt Vonnegut Jr. Born in New York, Bob wrote prolifically for the sf magazines of the Fifties and Sixties, gaining a lot of converts for his idiosyncratic style with 'The Battle' (1954), a story of Armageddon in which robots are used to counter the forces of evil. He returned to the subject in a number of later stories which were collected as *The Robot Who Looked Like Me* (1978). Bob's story 'The Seventh Victim', about a future world where murder is legal and encouraged as a kind of game show in which participants chase one another across an urban landscape with life or death as the stakes, was filmed in 1965 by Joseph E. Levine starring Marcello Mastroianni and Ursula Andress; and in 1992 his 'Time Killer' was adapted for the screen as *Freejack*, with Geoff Murphy directing Emilio Estevez and Mick Jagger, pop star turned sinister bodysnatcher. 'Watchbird', with its elements of black comedy and focus on the future of police surveillance, was written for *Galaxy* in 1953.

When Gelsen entered, he saw that the rest of the watchbird manufacturers were already present. There were six of them, not counting himself, and the room was blue with expensive cigar smoke.

'Hi, Charlie,' one of them called as he came in.

The rest broke off conversation long enough to wave a casual greeting at him. As a watchbird manufacturer, he was a member manufacturer of salvation, he reminded himself wryly. Very exclusive. You must have a certified government contract if you want to save the human race.

'The government representative isn't here yet,' one of the men told him. 'He's due any minute.'

'We're getting the green light,' another said.

'Fine.' Gelsen found a chair near the door and looked around the room. It was like a convention, or a Boy Scout rally. The six men made up for their lack of numbers by sheer volume. The president of Southern Consolidated was talking at the top of his lungs about watchbird's enormous durability. The two presidents he was talking at were grinning, nodding, one trying to interrupt with the results of a test he had run on watchbird's resourcefulness, the other talking about the new recharging apparatus.

The other three men were in their own little group, delivering what sounded like a panegyric to watchbird.

Gelsen noticed that all of them stood straight and tall, like the saviors they felt they were. He didn't find it funny. Up to a few days ago he had felt that way himself. He had considered himself a pot-bellied, slightly balding saint.

He sighed and lighted a cigarette. At the beginning of the project, he had been as enthusiastic as the others. He remembered saying to Macintyre, his chief engineer, 'Mac, a new day is coming. Watchbird is the Answer.' And Macintyre had nodded very profoundly – another watchbird convert.

How wonderful it had seemed then! A simple, reliable answer to one of mankind's greatest problems, all wrapped and packaged in a pound of incorruptible metal, crystal and plastics.

Perhaps that was the very reason he was doubting it now. Gelsen suspected that you don't solve human problems so easily. There had to be a catch somewhere.

After all, murder was an old problem, and watchbird too new a solution.

'Gentlemen –' They had been talking so heatedly that they hadn't noticed the government representative entering. Now the room became quiet at once.

'Gentlemen,' the plump government man said, 'the President, with the consent of Congress, has acted to form a watchbird division for every city and town in the country.'

The men burst into a spontaneous shout of triumph. They were going to have their chance to save the world after all, Gelsen thought, and worriedly asked himself what was wrong with that.

He listened carefully as the government man outlined the distribution scheme. The country was to be divided into seven areas, each to be supplied and serviced by one manufacturer. This meant monopoly, of course, but a necessary one. Like the telephone service, it was in the public's best interests. You couldn't have competition in watchbird service. Watchbird was for everyone.

'The President hopes,' the representative continued, 'that full watchbird service will be installed in the shortest possible time. You will have top priorities on strategic metals, manpower, and so forth.'

'Speaking for myself,' the president of Southern Consolidated said, 'I expect to have the first batch of watchbirds distributed within the week. Production is all set up.'

The rest of the men were equally ready. The factories had been prepared to roll out the watchbirds for months now. The final standardized equipment had been agreed upon, and only the Presidential go-ahead had been lacking.

'Fine,' the representative said. 'If that is all, I think we can – is there a question?'

'Yes, sir,' Gelsen said. 'I want to know if the present model is the one we are going to manufacture.'

'Of course,' the representative said. 'It's the most advanced.'

'I have an objection.' Gelsen stood up. His colleagues were glaring coldly at him. Obviously he was delaying the advent of the golden age.

'What is your objection?' the representative asked.

'First, let me say that I am one hundred per cent in favor of a machine to stop murder. It's been needed for a long time. I object only to the watchbird's learning circuits. They serve, in effect, to animate the machine and give it a pseudo-consciousness. I can't approve of that.'

'But, Mr Gelsen, you yourself testified that the watchbird would not be completely efficient unless such circuits were introduced. Without them, the watchbirds could stop only an estimated seventy per cent of murders.'

'I know that,' Gelsen said, feeling extremely uncomfortable. 'I believe there might be a moral danger in allowing a machine to make decisions that are rightfully Man's,' he declared doggedly.

'Oh, come now, Gelsen,' one of the corporation presidents said. 'It's nothing of the sort. The watchbird will only reinforce the decisions made by honest men from the beginning of time.'

'I think that is true,' the representative agreed. 'But I can understand how Mr Gelsen feels. It is sad that we must put a human problem into the hands of a machine, sadder still that we must have a machine enforce our laws. But I ask you to remember, Mr Gelsen, that there is no other possible way of stopping a murderer *before he strikes*. It would be unfair to the many innocent people killed every year if we were to restrict watchbird on philosophical grounds. Don't you agree that I'm right?'

'Yes, I suppose I do,' Gelsen said unhappily. He had told himself all that a thousand times, but something still bothered him. Perhaps he would talk it over with Macintyre.

As the conference broke up, a thought struck him. He grinned.

A lot of policemen were going to be out of work!

'Now what do you think of that?' Officer Celtrics demanded. 'Fifteen years in Homicide and a machine is replacing me.' He wiped a large red hand across his forehead and leaned against the captain's desk. 'Ain't science marvelous?'

Two other policemen, late of Homicide, nodded glumly.

'Don't worry about it,' the captain said. 'We'll find a home for you in Larceny, Celtrics. You'll like it here.'

'I just can't get over it,' Celtrics complained. 'A lousy little piece of tin and glass is going to solve all the crimes.'

'Not quite,' the captain said. 'The watchbirds are supposed to prevent the crimes before they happen.'

'Then how'll they be crimes?' one of the policeman asked. 'I mean they can't hang you for murder until you commit one, can they?'

'That's not the idea,' the captain said. 'The watchbirds are supposed to stop a man before he commits a murder.'

'Then no one arrests him?' Celtrics asked.

'I don't know how they're going to work that out,' the captain admitted.

The men were silent for a while. The captain yawned and examined his watch.

'The thing I don't understand,' Celtrics said, still leaning on the captain's desk, 'is just how do they do it? How did it start, Captain?'

The captain studied Celtrics' face for possible irony; after all, watchbird had been in the papers for months. But then he remembered that Celtrics, like his sidekicks, rarely bothered to turn past the sports pages.

'Well,' the captain said, trying to remember what he had read in the Sunday supplements, 'these scientists were working on criminology. They were studying murderers, to find out what made them tick. So they found that murderers throw out a different sort of brain wave from ordinary people. And their glands act funny, too. All this happens when they're about to commit a murder. So these scientists worked out a special machine to flash red or something when these brain waves turned on.'

'Scientists,' Celtrics said bitterly.

'Well, after the scientists had this machine, they didn't know what to do with it. It was too big to move around, and murderers didn't drop in often enough to make it flash. So they built it into a smaller unit and tried it out in a few police stations. I think they tried one upstate. But it didn't work so good. You couldn't get to the crime in time. That's why they built the watchbirds.'

'I don't think they'll stop no criminals,' one of the policemen insisted.

'They sure will. I read the test results. They can smell him out before he commits a crime. And when they reach him, they give him a powerful shock or something. It'll stop him.'

'You closing up Homicide, Captain?' Celtrics asked.

'Nope,' the captain said. 'I'm leaving a skeleton crew in until we see how these birds do.'

'Hah,' Celtrics said. 'Skeleton crew. That's funny.'

'Sure,' the captain said. 'Anyhow, I'm going to leave some men on. It seems the birds don't stop all murders.'

'Why not?'

'Some murderers don't have these brain waves,' the captain answered, trying to remember what the newspaper article had said. 'Or their glands don't work or something.'

'Which ones don't they stop?' Celtrics asked, with professional curiosity.

'I don't know. But I hear they got the damned things fixed so they're going to stop all of them soon.'

'How they working that?'

'They learn. The watchbirds, I mean. Just like people.'

'You kidding me?'

'Nope.'

'Well,' Celtrics said, 'I think I'll just keep old Betsy oiled, just in case. You can't trust these scientists.'

'Right.'

'Birds!' Celtrics scoffed.

Over the town, the watchbird soared in a long, lazy curve. Its aluminium hide glistened in the morning sun, and dots of light danced on its stiff wings. Silently it flew.

Silently, but with all senses functioning. Built-in kinesthetics told the watchbird where it was, and held it in a long search curve. Its eyes and ears operated as one unit, searching, seeking.

And then something happened! The watchbird's electronically fast reflexes picked up the edge of a sensation. A correlation center tested it, matching it with electrical and chemical data in its memory files. A relay tripped.

Down the watchbird spiraled, coming in on the increasingly strong sensation. It *smelled* the outpouring of certain glands, *tasted* a deviant brain wave.

Fully alerted and armed, it spun and banked in the bright morning sunlight.

Dinelli was so intent he didn't see the watchbird coming. He had his gun poised, and his eyes pleaded with the big grocer.

'Don't come no closer.'

'You lousy little punk,' the grocer said, and took another step forward. 'Rob me? I'll break every bone in your puny body.'

The grocer, too stupid or too courageous to understand the threat of the gun, advanced on the little thief.

'All right,' Dinelli said, in a thorough state of panic. 'All right, sucker, take —'

A bolt of electricity knocked him on his back. The gun went off, smashing a breakfast food display.

'What in hell?' the grocer asked, staring at the stunned thief. And then he saw a flash of silver wings. 'Well, I'm really damned. Those watchbirds work!'

He stared until the wings disappeared in the sky. Then he telephoned the police.

The watchbird returned to his search curve. His thinking center correlated the new facts he had learned about murder. Several of these he hadn't known before.

This new information was simultaneously flashed to all the other watchbirds and their information was flashed back to him.

New information, methods, definitions were constantly passing between them.

Now that the watchbirds were rolling off the assembly line in a steady stream, Gelsen allowed himself to relax. A loud contented hum filled his plant. Orders were being filled on time, with top priorities given to the biggest cities in his area, and working down to the smallest towns.

'All smooth, Chief,' Macintyre said, coming in the door. He had just completed a routine inspection.

'Fine. Have a seat.'

The big engineer sat down and lighted a cigarette.

'We've been working on this for some time,' Gelsen said, when he couldn't think of anything else.

'We sure have,' Macintyre agreed. He leaned back and inhaled deeply. He had been one of the consulting engineers on the original watchbird. That was six years back. He had been working for Gelsen ever since, and the men had become good friends.

'The thing I wanted to ask you was this –' Gelsen paused. He couldn't think how to phrase what he wanted. Instead he asked, 'What do you think of the watchbirds, Mac?'

'Who, me?' The engineer grinned nervously. He had been eating, drinking and sleeping watchbird ever since its inception. He had never found it necessary to have an attitude. 'Why, I think it's great.'

'I don't mean that,' Gelsen said. He realized that what he wanted was to have someone understand his point of view. 'I mean do you figure there might be some danger in machine thinking?'

'I don't think so, Chief. Why do you ask?'

'Look, I'm no scientist or engineer. I've just handled cost and production and let you boys worry about how. But as a layman, watchbird is starting to frighten me.'

'No reason for that.'

'I don't like the idea of the learning circuits.'

'But why not?' Then Macintyre grinned again. 'I know. You're like a lot of people, Chief – afraid your machines are going to wake up and say, "What are we doing here? Let's go out and rule the world." Is that it?'

'Maybe something like that,' Gelsen admitted.

'No chance of it,' Macintyre said. 'The watchbirds are complex, I'll admit, but an MIT calculator is a whole lot more complex. And it hasn't got consciousness.'

'No. But the watchbirds can *learn*.'

'Sure. So can all the new calculators. Do you think they'll team up with the watchbirds?'

Gelsen felt annoyed at Macintyre, and even more annoyed at himself for being ridiculous. 'It's a fact that the watchbirds can put their learning into action. No one is monitoring them.'

'So that's the trouble,' Macintyre said.

'I've been thinking of getting out of watchbird.' Gelsen hadn't realized it until that moment.

'Look, Chief,' Macintyre said. 'Will you take an engineer's word on this?'

'Let's hear it.'

'The watchbirds are no more dangerous than an automobile, an IBM calculator or a thermometer. They have no more consciousness or volition than those things. The watchbirds are built to respond to certain stimuli, and to carry out certain operations when they receive that stimuli.'

'And the learning circuits?'

'You have to have those,' Macintyre said patiently, as though explaining the whole thing to a ten-year-old. 'The purpose of the watchbird is to frustrate all murder-attempts, right? Well, only certain murderers give out these stimuli. In order to stop all of them, the watchbird has to search out new definitions of murder and correlate them with what it already knows.'

'I think it's inhuman,' Gelsen said.

'That's the best thing about it. The watchbirds are unemotional. Their reasoning is non-anthropomorphic. You can't bribe them or drug them. You shouldn't fear them, either.'

The intercom on Gelsen's desk buzzed. He ignored it.

'I know all this,' Gelsen said. 'But, still, sometimes I feel like the man who invented dynamite. He thought it would only be used for blowing up tree stumps.'

'*You* didn't invent watchbird.'

'I still feel morally responsible because I manufacture them.'

The intercom buzzed again, and Gelsen irritably punched a button.

'The reports are in on the first week of watchbird operation,' his secretary told him.

'How do they look?'

'Wonderful, sir.'

'Send them in in fifteen minutes.' Gelsen switched the intercom off and turned back to Macintyre, who was cleaning his fingernails with a wooden match. 'Don't you think that this represents a trend in human thinking? The mechanical god? The electronic father?'

'Chief,' Macintyre said, 'I think you should study watchbird more closely. Do you know what's built into the circuits?'

'Only generally.'

'First, there is a purpose. Which is to stop living organisms from committing murder. Two, murder may be defined as an act of violence, consisting of breaking, mangling, maltreating or otherwise stopping the functions of a living organism by a living organism. Three, most murderers are detectable by certain chemical and electrical changes.'

Macintyre paused to light another cigarette. 'Those conditions take care of the routine functions. Then, for the learning circuits, there are two more conditions. Four, there are some living organisms who commit murder without the signs mentioned in three. Five, these can be detected by data applicable to condition two.'

'I see,' Gelsen said.

'You realize how foolproof it is?'

'I suppose so.' Gelsen hesitated a moment. 'I guess that's all.'

'Right,' the engineer said, and left.

Gelsen thought for a few moments. There *couldn't* be anything wrong with the watchbirds.

'Send in the reports,' he said into the intercom.

High above the lighted buildings of the city, the watchbird soared. It was dark, but in the distance the watchbird could see another, and another beyond that. For this was a large city.

To prevent murder ...

There was more to watch for now. New information had crossed the invisible network that connected all watchbirds. New data, new ways of detecting the violence of murder.

There! The edge of a sensation! Two watchbirds dipped simultaneously. One had received the scent a fraction of a second before the other. He continued down while the other resumed monitoring.

Condition four, there are some living organisms who commit murder without the signs mentioned in condition three.

Through his new information, the watchbird knew by extrapolation that this organism was bent on murder, even though the characteristic chemical and electrical smells were absent.

The watchbird, all senses acute, closed in on the organism. He found what he wanted, and dived.

Roger Greco leaned against a building, his hands in his pockets. In his left hand was the cool butt of a .45. Greco waited patiently.

He wasn't thinking of anything in particular, just relaxing against a building, waiting for a man. Greco didn't know why the man was to be killed. He didn't care. Greco's lack of curiosity was part of his value. The other part was his skill.

One bullet, neatly placed in the head of a man he didn't know. It didn't excite him or sicken him. It was a job, just like anything else. You killed a man. So?

As Greco's victim stepped out of a building, Greco lifted the .45 out of his pocket. He released the safety and braced the gun with his right hand. He still wasn't thinking of anything as he took aim ...

And was knocked off his feet.

Greco thought he had been shot. He struggled up again, looked around, and sighted foggily on his victim.

Again he was knocked down.

This time he lay on the ground, trying to draw a bead. He never thought of stopping, for Greco was a craftsman.

With the next blow, everything went black. Permanently, because the watchbird's duty was to protect the object of violence *at whatever cost to the murderer*.

The victim walked to his car. He hadn't noticed anything unusual. Everything had happened in silence.

Gelsen was feeling pretty good. The watchbirds had been operating perfectly. Crimes of violence had been cut in half, and cut again. Dark alleys were no longer mouths of horror. Parks and playgrounds were not places to shun after dusk.

Of course, there were still robberies. Petty thievery flourished and embezzlement, larceny, forgery and a hundred other crimes.

But that wasn't so important. You could regain lost money – never a lost life.

Gelsen was ready to admit that he had been wrong about the watchbirds. They *were* doing a job that humans had been unable to accomplish.

The first hint of something wrong came that morning.

Macintyre came into his office. He stood silently in front of Gelsen's desk, looking annoyed and a little embarrassed.

'What's the matter, Mac?' Gelsen asked.

'One of the watchbirds went to work on a slaughterhouse man. Knocked him out.'

Gelsen thought about it for a moment. Yes, the watchbirds would do that. With their new learning circuits, they had probably defined the killing of animals as murder.

'Tell the packers to mechanize their slaughtering,' Gelsen said. 'I never liked that business myself.'

'All right,' Macintyre said. He pursed his lips, then shrugged his shoulders and left.

Gelsen stood beside his desk, thinking. Couldn't the watchbirds differentiate between a murderer and a man engaged in a legitimate profession? No, evidently not. To them, murder was murder. No exceptions. He frowned. That might take a little ironing out in the circuits.

But not too much, he decided hastily. Just make them a little more discriminating.

He sat down again and buried himself in paperwork, trying to avoid the edge of an old fear.

They strapped the prisoner into the chair and fitted the electrode to his leg.

'Oh, oh,' he moaned, only half-conscious now of what they were doing.

They fitted the helmet over his shaved head and tightened the last straps. He continued to moan softly.

And then the watchbird swept in. How he had come, no one knew. Prisons are large and strong, with many locked doors, but the watchbird was there –

To stop a murder.

'Get that thing out of here!' the warden shouted, and reached for the switch. The watchbird knocked him down.

'Stop that!' a guard screamed, and grabbed for the switch himself. He was knocked to the floor beside the warden.

'This isn't murder, you idiot!' another guard said. He drew his gun to shoot down the glittering, wheeling metal bird.

Anticipating, the watchbird smashed him back against the wall.

There was silence in the room. After a while, the man in the helmet started to giggle. Then he stopped.

The watchbird stood on guard, fluttering in mid-air –

Making sure no murder was done.

New data flashed along the watchbird network. Unmonitored, independent, the thousands of watchbirds received and acted upon it.

The breaking, mangling or otherwise stopping the functions of a living organism by a living organism. New acts to stop.

'Damn you, git going!' Farmer Ollister shouted, and raised his whip again. The horse balked, and the wagon rattled and shook as he edged sideways.

'You lousy hunk of pigmeal, git going!' the farmer yelled and he raised the whip again.

It never fell. An alert watchbird, sensing violence, had knocked him out of his seat.

A living organism? What is a living organism? The watchbirds extended their definitions as they became aware of more facts. And, of course, this gave them more work.

The deer was just visible at the edge of the woods. The hunter raised his rifle, and took careful aim.

He didn't have time to shoot.

With his free hand, Gelsen mopped perspiration from his face. 'All right,' he said into the telephone. He listened to the stream of vituperation from the other end, then placed the receiver gently in its cradle.

'What was that one?' Macintyre asked. He was unshaven, tie loose, shirt unbuttoned.

'Another fisherman,' Gelsen said. 'It seems the watchbirds won't let him fish even though his family is starving. What are we going to do about it, he wants to know.'

'How many hundred is that?'

'I don't know. I haven't opened the mail.'

'Well, I figured out where the trouble is,' Macintyre said gloomily, with the air of a man who knows just how he blew up the Earth – after it was too late.

'Let's hear it.'

'Everybody took it for granted that we wanted all murder stopped. We figured the watchbirds would think as we do. We ought to have qualified the conditions.'

'I've got an idea,' Gelsen said, 'that we'd have to know just why and what murder is, before we could qualify the conditions properly. And if we knew that, we wouldn't need the watchbirds.'

'Oh, I don't know about that. They just have to be told that some things which look like murder are not murder.'

'But why should they stop fisherman?' Gelsen asked.

'Why shouldn't they? Fish and animals are living organisms. We just don't think that killing them is murder.'

The telephone rang. Gelsen glared at it and punched the intercom. 'I told you no more calls, no matter what.'

'This is from Washington,' his secretary said. 'I thought you'd –'

'Sorry.' Gelsen picked up the telephone. 'Yes. Certainly is a mess ... Have they? All right, I certainly will.' He put down the telephone.

'Short and sweet,' he told Macintyre. 'We're to shut down temporarily.'

'That won't be so easy,' Macintyre said. 'The watchbirds operate independent of any central control, you know. They come back once a week for a repair checkup. We'll have to turn them off then, one by one.'

'Well, let's get to it. Monroe over on the Coast has shut down about a quarter of his birds.'

'I think I can dope out a restricting circuit,' Macintyre said.

'Fine,' Gelsen replied bitterly. 'You make me very happy.'

The watchbirds were learning rapidly, expanding and adding to their knowledge. Loosely defined abstractions were extended, acted upon and re-extended.

To stop murder ...

Metal and electrons reason well, but not in a human fashion.

A living organism? *Any* living organism!

The watchbirds set themselves the task of protecting all living things.

The fly buzzed around the room, lighting on a table top, pausing a moment, then darting to a window sill.

The old man stalked it, a rolled newspaper in his hand.

Murderer!

The watchbirds swept down and saved the fly in the nick of time.

The old man writhed on the floor a minute and then was silent. He had been given only a mild shock, but it had been enough for his fluttery, cranky heart.

His victim had been saved, though, and this was the important thing. Save the victim and give the aggressor his just deserts.

Gelsen demanded angrily. 'Why aren't they being turned off?'

The assistant control engineer gestured. In a corner of the repair room lay the senior control engineer. He was just regaining consciousness.

'He tried to turn one of them off,' the assistant engineer said. Both his hands were knotted together. He was making a visible effort not to shake.

'That's ridiculous. They haven't got any sense of self-preservation.'

'Then turn them off yourself. Besides, I don't think any more are going to come.'

What could have happened? Gelsen began to piece it together. The watchbirds still hadn't decided on the limits of a living organism. When some of them were turned off in the Monroe plant, the rest must have correlated the data.

So they had been forced to assume that they were living organisms, as well.

No one had ever told them otherwise. Certainly they carried on most of the functions of living organisms.

Then the old fears hit him. Gelsen trembled and hurried out of the repair room. He wanted to find Macintyre in a hurry.

The nurse handed the surgeon the sponge.

'Scalpel.'

She placed it in his hand. He started to make the first incision. And then he was aware of a disturbance.

'Who let that thing in?'

'I don't know,' the nurse said, her voice muffled by the mask.

'Get it out of here.'

The nurse waved her arms at the bright winged thing, but it fluttered over her head.

The surgeon proceeded with the incision – as long as he was able.

The watchbird drove him away and stood guard.

'Telephone the watchbird company!' the surgeon ordered. 'Get them to turn the thing off.'

The watchbird was preventing violence to a living organism.

The surgeon stood by helplessly while his patient died.

Fluttering high above the network of highways, the watchbird watched and waited. It had been constantly working for weeks now, without rest or repair. Rest and repair were impossible, because the watchbird couldn't allow itself – a living organism – to be murdered. And that was what happened when watchbirds returned to the factory.

There was a built-in order to return, after the lapse of a certain time period. But the watchbird had a stronger order to obey – preservation of life, including its own.

The definitions of murder were almost infinitely extended now, impossible to cope with. But the watchbird didn't consider that. It responded to its stimuli, whenever they came and whatever their source.

There was a new definition of living organism in its memory files. It had come as a result of the watchbird discovery that watchbirds were living organisms. And it had enormous ramifications.

The stimuli came! For the hundredth time that day, the bird wheeled and banked, dropping swiftly down to stop murder.

Jackson yawned and pulled his car to a shoulder of the road. He didn't notice the glittering dot in the sky. There was no reason for him to. Jackson wasn't contemplating murder, by any human definition.

This was a good spot for a nap, he decided. He had been driving for seven straight hours and his eyes were starting to fog. He reached out to turn off the ignition key –

And was knocked back against the side of the car.

'What in hell's wrong with you?' he asked indignantly. 'All I want to do is –' He reached for the key again, and again he was smacked back.

Jackson knew better than to try a third time. He had been listening to the radio and he knew what the watchbirds did to stubborn violators.

'You mechanical jerk,' he said to the waiting metal bird. 'A car's not alive. I'm not trying to kill it.'

But the watchbird only knew that a certain operation resulted in stopping an organism. The car was certainly a functioning organism. Wasn't it of metal, as were the watchbirds? Didn't it run?

Macintyre said, 'Without repairs they'll run down.' He shoved a pile of specification sheets out of his way.

'How soon?' Gelsen asked.

'Six months to a year. Say a year, barring accidents.'

'A year,' Gelsen said. 'In the meantime, everything is stopping dead. Do you know the latest?'

'What?'

'The watchbirds have decided that the Earth is a living organism. They won't allow farmers to break ground for plowing. And, of course, everything else is a living organism – rabbits, beetles, flies, wolves, mosquitoes, lions, crocodiles, crows, and smaller forms of life such as bacteria.'

'I know,' Macintrye said.

'And you tell me they'll wear out in six months or a year. What happens *now*? What are we going to eat in six months?'

The engineer rubbed his chin. 'We'll have to do something quick and fast. Ecological balance is gone to hell.'

'Fast isn't the word. Instantaneously would be better.' Gelsen lighted his thirty-fifth cigarette for the day. 'At least I have the bitter satisfaction of saying, "I told you so." Although I'm just as responsible as the rest of the machine-worshipping fools.'

Macintyre wasn't listening. He was thinking about watchbirds.

'Like the rabbit plague in Australia.'

'The death rate is mounting,' Gelsen said. 'Famine. Floods. Can't cut down trees. Doctors can't – what was that you said about Australia?'

'The rabbits,' Macintyre repeated. 'Hardly any left in Australia now.'

'Why? How was it done?'

'Oh, found some kind of germ that attacked only rabbits. I think it was propagated by mosquitoes –'

'Work on that,' Gelsen said. 'You might have something. I want you to get on the telephone, ask for an emergency hookup with the engineers of the other companies. Hurry it up. Together you may be able to dope out something.'

'Right,' Macintyre said. He grabbed a handful of blank paper and hurried to the telephone.

'What did I tell you?' Officer Celtrics said. He grinned at the captain. 'Didn't I tell you scientists were nuts?'

'I didn't say you were wrong, did I?' the captain asked.

'No, but you weren't *sure*.'

'Well, I'm sure now. You'd better get going. There's plenty of work for you.'

'I know.' Celtrics drew his revolver from its holster, checked it and put it back. 'Are all the boys back, Captain?'

'All?' the captain laughed humorlessly. 'Homicide has increased by fifty per cent. There's more murder now than there's ever been.'

'Sure,' Celtrics said. 'The watchbirds are too busy guarding cars and slugging spiders.' He started toward the door, then turned for a parting shot.

'Take my word, Captain. Machines are *stupid*.'

The captain nodded.

Thousands of watchbirds, trying to stop countless millions of murders – a hopeless task. But the watchbirds didn't hope. Without consciousness, they experienced no sense of accomplishment, no fear of failure. Patiently they went about their jobs, obeying each stimulus as it came.

They couldn't be everywhere at the same time, but it wasn't necessary to be. People learned quickly what the watchbirds didn't like and refrained from doing it. It just wasn't safe. With their high speed and superfast senses, the watchbirds got around quickly.

And now they meant business. In their original directives there had been a provision made for killing a murderer, if all other means failed.

Why spare a murderer?

It backfired. The watchbirds extracted the fact that murder and crimes of violence had increased geometrically since they had begun operation. This was true, because their new definitions increased the possibilities of murder. But to the watchbirds, the rise showed that the first methods had failed.

Simple logic. If A doesn't work, try B. The watchbirds shocked to kill.

Slaughterhouses in Chicago stopped and cattle starved to death in their pens, because farmers in the Midwest couldn't cut hay or harvest grain.

No one had told the watchbirds that all life depends on carefully balanced murders.

Starvation didn't concern the watchbirds, since it was an act of omission.

Their interest lay only in acts of commission.

Hunters sat home, glaring at the silver dots in the sky, longing to shoot them down. But for the most part, they didn't try. The watchbirds were quick to sense the murder intent and to punish it.

Fishing boats swung idle at their moorings in San Pedro and Gloucester. Fish were living organisms.

Farmers cursed and spat and died, trying to harvest the crop. Grain was alive and thus worthy of protection. Potatoes were as important to the watchbird as any other living organism. The death of a blade of grass was equal to the assassination of a President –

To the watchbirds.

And, of course, certain machines were living. This followed, since the watchbirds were machines and living.

God help you if you maltreated your radio. Turning it off meant killing it. Obviously – its voice was silenced, the red glow of its tubes faded, it grew cold.

The watchbirds tried to guard their other charges. Wolves were slaughtered, trying to kill rabbits. Rabbits were electrocuted, trying to eat vegetables. Creepers were burned out in the act of strangling trees.

A butterfly was executed, caught in the act of outraging a rose.

This control was spasmodic, because of the scarcity of the watchbirds. A billion watchbirds couldn't have carried out the ambitious project set by the thousands.

The effect was of a murderous force, ten thousand bolts of irrational lightning raging around the country, striking a thousand times a day.

Lightning which anticipated your moves and punished your intentions.

'Gentlemen, *please*,' the government representative begged. 'We must hurry.'

The seven manufacturers stopped talking.

'Before we begin this meeting formally,' the president of Monroe said, 'I want to say something. We do not feel ourselves responsible for this unhappy state of affairs. It was a government project; the government must accept the responsibility, both moral and financial.'

Gelsen shrugged his shoulders. It was hard to believe that these men, just a few weeks ago, had been willing to accept the glory of saving the world. Now they wanted to shrug off the responsibility when the salvation went amiss.

'I'm positive that that need not concern us now,' the representative assured him. 'We must hurry. You engineers have done an excellent job. I am proud of the cooperation you have shown in this emergency. You are hereby empowered to put the outlined plan into action.'

'Wait a minute,' Gelsen said.

'There is no time.'

'The plan's no good.'

'Don't you think it will work?'

'Of course it will work. But I'm afraid the cure will be worse than the disease.'

The manufacturers looked as though they would have enjoyed throttling Gelsen. He didn't hesitate.

'Haven't we learned yet?' he asked. 'Don't you see that you can't cure human problems by mechanization?'

'Mr Gelsen,' the president of Monroe said, 'I would enjoy hearing you philosophize, but, unfortunately, people are being killed. Crops are being ruined. There is famine in some sections of the country already. The watchbirds must be stopped at once!'

'Murder must be stopped, too. I remember all of us agreeing upon that. But this is not the way!'

'What would you suggest?' the representative asked.

Gelsen took a deep breath.

What he was about to say took all the courage he had.

'Let the watchbirds run down by themselves,' Gelsen suggested.

There was a near-riot. The government representative broke it up.

'Let's take our lesson,' Gelsen urged, 'admit that we were wrong trying to cure human problems by mechanical means. Start again. Use machines, yes, but not as judges and teachers and fathers.'

'Ridiculous,' the representative said coldly. 'Mr Gelsen, you are overwrought. I suggest you control yourself.' He cleared his throat. 'All of you are ordered by the President to carry out the plan you have submitted.' He looked sharply at Gelsen.

'Not to do so will be treason.'

'I'll cooperate to the best of my ability,' Gelsen said.

'Good. Those assembly lines must be rolling within the week.'

Gelsen walked out of the room alone. Now he was confused again. Had he been right or was he just another visionary? Certainly, he hadn't explained himself with much clarity.

Did he know what he meant?

Gelsen cursed under his breath. He wondered why he couldn't ever be sure of anything. Weren't there any values he could hold on to?

He hurried to the airport and to his plant.

The watchbird was operating erratically now. Many of its delicate parts were out of line, worn by almost continuous operation. But gallantly it responded when the stimuli came.

A spider was attacking a fly. The watchbird swooped down to the rescue.

Simultaneously, it became aware of something overhead. The watchbird wheeled to meet it.

There was a sharp crackle and a power bolt whizzed by the watchbird's wing. Angrily, it spat a shock wave.

The attacker was heavily insulated. Again it spat at the watchbird. This time, a bolt smashed through a wing. The watchbird darted away, but the attacker went after it in a burst of speed, throwing out more crackling power.

The watchbird fell, but managed to send out its message. Urgent! A new menace to living organisms and this was the deadliest yet!

Other watchbirds around the country integrated the message. Their thinking centers searched for an answer.

'Well, Chief, they bagged fifty today,' Macintyre said, coming into Gelsen's office.

'Fine,' Gelsen said, not looking at the engineer.

'Not so fine.' Macintyre sat down. 'Lord, I'm tired! It was seventy-two yesterday.'

'I know.' On Gelsen's desk were several dozen lawsuits, which he was sending to the government with a prayer.

'They'll pick up again, though,' Macintyre said confidently. 'The Hawks are especially built to hunt down watchbirds. They're stronger, faster, and they've got better armor. We really rolled them out in a hurry, huh?'

'We sure did.'

'The watchbirds are pretty good, too,' Macintyre had to admit. 'They're learning to take cover. They're trying a lot of stunts. You know, each one that goes down tells the others something.'

Gelsen didn't answer.

'But anything the watchbirds can do, the Hawks can do better,' Macintyre said cheerfully. 'The Hawks have special learning circuits for hunting. They're more flexible than the watchbirds. They learn faster.'

Gelsen gloomily stood up, stretched, and walked to the window. The sky was blank. Looking out, he realized that his uncertainties were over. Right or wrong, he had made up his mind.

'Tell me,' he said, still watching the sky, 'what will the Hawks hunt after they get all the watchbirds?'

'Huh?' Macintyre said. 'Why –'

'Just to be on the safe side, you'd better design something to hunt down the Hawks. Just in case, I mean.'

'You think –'

'All I know is that the Hawks are self-controlled. So were the watchbirds. Remote control would have been too slow, the argument went on. The idea was to get the watchbirds and get them fast. That meant no restricting circuits.'

'We can work something out,' Macintyre said uncertainly.

'You've got an aggressive machine up in the air now. A murder machine. Before that it was an anti-murder machine. Your next gadget will have to be even more self-sufficient, won't it?'

Macintyre didn't answer.

'I don't hold you responsible,' Gelsen said. 'It's me. It's everyone.'

In the air outside was a swift-moving dot.

'That's what comes,' said Gelsen, 'of giving a machine the job that was our own responsibility.'

Overhead, a Hawk was zeroing in on a watchbird.

The armored murder machine had learned a lot in a few days. Its sole function was to kill. At present it was impelled toward a certain type of living organism, metallic like itself.

But the Hawk had just discovered that there were other types of living organisms, too –

Which had to be murdered.

ONLINE: TWO/7 *Subject*: The Mercenary

From Fanaticism, or for Reward

Harry Harrison

INFO: Jagen is a hired killer – 'a cool hand who butchers for money', to quote his creator's own description. A man to whom violence and death are second nature and for whom self-preservation is paramount. He may well be the most evil figure in this book.

Harry Harrison is the creator of one of the best-known criminals in sf – Slippery Jim DiGriz, the space-roaming master criminal who has latterly been turned into a law enforcer, though he does still lapse into his old ways from time to time. Known by the epithet 'the Stainless Steel Rat', DiGriz first appeared in a group of magazine short stories that were later collected as *The Stainless Steel Rat* (1961). Since then he has taken his revenge, saved the world, got drafted and even run for President in book after book of thrills and high comedy.

Harry, who was born in Connecticut, studied art and then served as a US Army machine-gun instructor before following a career as a commercial illustrator. Once writing took his fancy, he never looked back and among his other books have been the impressive 'Deathworld' novels, a humorous series about Bill the Galactic Hero, and the powerful *Make Room! Make Room!* (1966). This story, about a detective who operates in a vastly overpopulated New York of 2022 and investigates what appears to be a routine murder until it becomes something far more unpleasant, was filmed in 1973 as *Soylent Green*, directed by Richard Fleischer and starring Charlton Heston. Harry has shown his interest in the robot theme on a number of occasions and the best of these stories appear in *War with the Robots*. 'From Fanaticism, or for Reward' was written in 1968 for *Fantasy and Science Fiction* – preceding by more than a decade the notorious 'Terminator' movie series with which the parallels will become obvious.

Wonderful! Very clear. The electronic sight was a new addition, he had used an ordinary telescopic sight when he test-fired the weapon, but it was no hindrance. The wide entrance to the structure across the street was sharp and clear, despite the rain-filled night outside. His elbows rested comfortably on the packing crates that were placed before the slit he had cut through the outer wall of the building.

'There are five of them coming now. The one you want is the tallest.' The radioplug in his ear whispered the words to him.

Across the street the men emerged. One was obviously taller than all the others. He was talking, smiling, and Jagen centred the scope on his white teeth, then spun the magnifier until teeth, mouth, tongue filled the sight. Then a wide smile, teeth together, and Jagen squeezed his entire hand, squeezed stock and trigger equally, and the gun banged and jumped against his shoulder.

Now, quickly, there were five more cartridges in the clip. Spin the magnifier back. He is falling. Fire. He jerks. Fire. In the skull. Again. Fire. Someone in the way: shoot through him. Fire. He is gone. In the chest, the heart. Fire.

'All shots off,' he said into the button before his lips. 'Five on target, one a possible.'

'Go,' was all the radioplug whispered.

I'm going all right, he thought to himself, *no need to tell me that. The Greater Despot's police are efficient.*

The only light in the room was the dim orange glow from the ready light on the transmatter. He had personally punched out the receiver's code. Three steps took him across the barren, dusty room and he slapped the actuator. Without slowing he dived into the screen.

Bright glare hurt his eyes and he squinted against it. An unshielded bulb above, rock walls, everything damp, a metal door coated with a patina of rust. He was underground, somewhere, perhaps on a planet across the galaxy, it didn't matter. There was here. Everywhere was a step away with a matter transmitter. Quickly, he moved to one side of the screen.

Gas puffed out of it, expelled silently, then cut off. Good. The transmatter had been destroyed, blown up. Undoubtedly the police would be able to trace his destination from the wreckage, but it would take time. Time for him to obscure his trail and vanish.

Other than the transmatter, the only object in the stone cell was a large, covered ceramic vessel. He looked at the stock of his gun where he had pasted his instructions. Next to the number for this location was the notation *destroy gun*. Jagen peeled off the instructions and slipped them into his belt pouch. He took the lid from the vessel and turned away, coughing, as the fumes rose up. This bubbling, hellish brew would dissolve anything. With well-practised motions he released the plastic stock from the weapon, then dropped it into the container. He had to step back as the liquid bubbled furiously and thicker fumes arose.

In his pouch was a battery-operated saw, as big as his hand, with a serrated diamond blade. It buzzed when he switched it on, then whined shrilly when he pressed it against the barrel of the gun. He had measured carefully a few days earlier and had sawed a slight notch. Now he cut at that spot and in a few seconds half of the barrel clanged to the floor. It followed the stock into the dissolving bath, along with the clip that had held the bullets. His pouch yielded up another clip which he slipped into place in the gun. A quick jerk of his forefinger on the slide kicked the first cartridge into the chamber and he checked to be sure that the safety was on. Only then did he slip the truncated weapon up the loose sleeve of his jacket, so that the rough end of the barrel rested against his hand.

It was shortened and inaccurate, but still a weapon, and still very deadly at short range.

Only when these precautions had been made did he consult the card and punch for his next destination. The instructions after this number read simply *change*. He stepped through.

Noise and sound, light and sharp smells. The ocean was close by, some ocean, he could hear the breakers and salt dampness was strong in his nose. This was a public communications plaza set around with transmatter screens, and someone was already stepping from the one he had used, treading on his heels. There were muttered words in a strange language as the man hurried away. The crowd was thick and the reddish sun, high above, was strong. Jagen resisted the temptation to use one of the nearby transmatters and walked quickly across the plaza. He stopped, then waited to follow the first person who passed him. This gave him a random direction that was not influenced by his own desires. A girl passed and he went after her. She wore an abbreviated skirt and had remarkably bowed legs. He followed their arcs down a side street. Only after they had passed one transmatter booth did he choose his own course. His trail was muddled enough now: the next transmatter would do.

There was the familiar green starburst ahead, above an imposing building, and his heart beat faster at the sight of the Greater Despot police headquarters. Then he smiled slightly; why not? The building was public and performed many functions. There was nothing to be afraid of.

Yet there was, of course, fear, and conquering it was a big part of the game. Up the steps and past the unseeing guards. A large rotunda with a desk in the middle, stands and services against the wall. And there, a row of transmatter screens. Walking at a steady pace he went to one of the centre screens and punched the next code on his list.

The air was thin and cold, almost impossible to breathe, and his eyes watered at the sudden chill. He turned quickly to the screen, to press the next number when he saw a man hurrying towards him.

'Do not leave,' the man called out in Intergalact.

He had a breath mask clipped over his nose and he held a second one out to Jagen, who quickly slipped it on. The warmed, richer air stayed his flight, as did the presence of the man who had obviously been expecting him. He saw now that he was on the bridge of a derelict spacer of ancient vintage. The controls had been torn out and the screens were blank. Moisture was condensing on the metal walls and forming pools upon the floor. The man saw his curious gaze.

'This ship is in orbit. It has been for centuries. An atmosphere and gravity plant were placed aboard while this transmatter was operating. When we leave an atomic explosion will destroy everything. If you are tracked this far, the trail will end here.'

'Then the rest of my instructions ...?'

'... Will not be needed. It was not certain this ship would be prepared in time, but it has been.'

Jagen dropped the card, evidence, on to the floor, along with the radioplug. It would vanish with the rest. The man rapidly pressed out a number.

'If you will proceed,' he said.

'I'll follow you.'

The man nodded, threw his breath mask aside, then stepped through the screen.

They were in a normal enough hotel room, the kind that can be found on any one of ten thousand planets. Two men, completely dressed in black, sat in armchairs watching Jagen through dark glasses. The man who had brought him nodded silently, pressed a combination on the transmatter, and left.

'It is done?' one of the men asked. In addition to the loose black clothing they wore black gloves and hoods, with voice demodulators clamped across their mouths. The voice was flat, emotionless, impossible to identify.

'The payment,' Jagen said, moving so that his back was to the wall.

'We'll pay you, man, don't be foolish. Just tell us how it came out. We have a lot invested in this.' The voice of the second man was just as mechanically calm, but his fingers were clasping and unclasping as he talked.

'The payment.' Jagen tried to keep his voice as toneless as their electronic ones.

'Here, Hunter, now tell us,' the first one said, taking a box from the side table and throwing it across the room. It burst open at Jagen's feet.

'All six shots were fired at the target I was given,' he said, looking down at the golden notes spilling on to the floor. So much, it was as they had promised. 'I put four shots into the head, one into the heart, one into a man who got in the way that may have penetrated. It was as you said. The protective screen was useless against mechanically propelled plastic missiles.'

'The paragrantic is ours,' the second man intoned emotionlessly, but this was the machine interpretation, for his excitement was demonstrated by the manner in which he hammered on his chair arm and drummed his feet.

Jagen bent to pick up the notes, apparently looking only at the floor.

The first man in black raised an energy pistol that had been concealed in his clothing and fired it at Jagen.

Jagen, who as a hunter always considered being hunted, rolled sideways and clutched the barrel of the shortened projectile weapon. With his other hand he found the trigger through the cloth of his sleeve and depressed it. The range was point-blank and a miss was impossible to a man of his experience.

The bullet caught the first man in the midriff and folded him over. He said *yahhhhh* in a very drab and monotonous way. The pistol dropped from his fingers and fell to the floor and he was obviously dead.

'Soft alloy bullets,' Jagen said. 'I saved a clip of them. Far better than those plastic things you supplied. Go in small, mushroom, come out big. I saved the gun, too, at least enough of it to still shoot. You were right, it should be destroyed to remove evidence, but not until after this session. And it doesn't show on an energy-detector screen. So you thought I was unarmed. Your friend discovered the truth the hard way. How about you?' He talked quickly as he struggled to recover the gun that recoil had pulled from his hand and jammed into the cloth of his sleeve. There, he had it.

'Do not kill me,' the remaining man said, his voice flat, though he cringed back and waved his hands before his face. 'It was his idea, I wanted nothing to do with it. He was afraid that we could be traced if you were captured.' He glanced at the folded figure, then quickly away as he became aware of the quantity of blood that was dripping from it. 'I have no weapon. I mean you no harm. Do not kill me. I will give you more money.' He was pleading for his life but the words came out as drab as a shopping list.

Jagen raised his weapon and the man writhed and cringed.

'Do you have the money with you?'

'Some. Not much. A few thousand. I'll get you more.'

'I'm afraid that I cannot wait. Take out what you have – slowly – and throw it over here.'

It was a goodly sum. The man must be very rich to carry this much casually. Jagen pointed the gun to kill him, but at the last instant changed his mind. It would accomplish nothing. And at the moment he was weary of killing. Instead he crossed over and tore the man's mask off. It was anti-climactic. He was fat, old, jowly, crying so hard that he could not see through his tears. In disgust Jagen hurled him to the floor and kicked him hard in the face. Then left. Ever wary, he kept his body between the moaning man and the keys so there would be no slightest chance for him to see the number punched. He stepped into the screen.

The machine stepped out of the screen in the office of the Highest Officer of Police, many light years distant, at almost the same instant, on the planet where the assassination had taken place.

'You are Follower?' the officer asked.

'I am,' the machine said.

It was a fine-looking machine shaped in the form of a man. But that of a large man, well over two metres tall. It could have been any shape at all, but this form was a convenience when travelling among men. The roughly humanoid form was the only concession made. Other than having a torso, four limbs and a head, it was strictly functional. Its lines were smooth and flowing, and its metal shape coated with one of the new and highly resistant, golden tinted alloys. The ovoid that was its head was completely featureless, except for a T-shaped slit in the front. Presumably seeing and hearing devices were concealed behind the narrow opening, as well as a speech mechanism that parodied the full timbered voice of a man.

'Do I understand, Follower, that you are the only one of your kind?' The police officer had become old, grey and lined, in the pursuit of his profession, but he had never lost his curiosity.

'Your security rating permits me to inform you that there are other Followers now going into operation, but I cannot reveal the exact number.'

'Very wise. What is it that you hope to do?'

'I shall follow. I have detection apparatus far more delicate than any used in the field before. That is why my physical bulk is so great. I have the memory core of the largest library and means of adding to it constantly. I will follow the assassin.'

'That may prove difficult. He – or she – destroyed the transmatter after the killing.'

'I have ways of determining the tuning from the wreckage.'

'The path will be obscured in many ways.'

'None of them shall avail. I am the Follower.'

'Then I wish you luck … if one can wish luck to a machine. This was a dirty business.'

'Thank you for the courtesy. I do not have human emotions, though I can comprehend them. Your feelings are understood and a credit mark is being placed on your file even though you had not intended the remark to accomplish that. I would like to see all the records of the assassination, and then I will go to the place where the killer escaped.'

Twenty years of easy living had not altered Jagen very much: the lines in the corners of his eyes and the touch of grey at his temples improved his sharp features rather than detracting from them. He no longer had to earn his living as a professional hunter, so could now hunt for his own pleasure, which he did very often. For many years he had stayed constantly on the move, obscuring his trail, changing his name and identity a dozen times. Then he had stumbled across this backward planet, completely by chance, and had decided to remain. The jungles were primitive and the hunting tremendous. He enjoyed himself all of the time, The money he had been paid, invested wisely, provided him with ample income for all of his needs and supported the one or two vices to which he was addicted.

He was contemplating one of them now. For more than a week he had remained in the jungle, and it had been a good shoot. Now, washed, refreshed, rested, he savoured the thought of something different. There was a pleasure hall he knew, expensive, of course, but he could get there exactly what he needed. In a gold dressing gown, feet up and a drink in his hand, he sat back and looked through the transparent wall of his apartment at the sun setting behind the jungle. He had never had much of an eye for art, but it would have taken a blind man to ignore the explosion of greens below, purple and red above. The universe was a very fine place.

Then the alignment bell signalled quietly to show that another transmatter had been tuned to his. He swung about to see Follower step into the room.

'I have come for you, Assassin,' the machine said.

The glass fell from Jagen's fingers and rolled a wet trail across the inlaid wood of the floor. He was always armed, but caution suggested that the energy pistol in the pocket of his robe would have little effect on this solidly built machine.

'I have no idea what you are talking about,' he said, rising. 'I shall call the police about this matter.'

He walked towards the communicator – then dived past it into the room beyond. Follower started after him, but stopped when he emerged an instant later. Jagen had a heavy calibre, recoilless rifle with explosive shells, that he used to stop the multi-ton amphibians in the swamps. The weapon held ten of the almost cannon-sized shells and he emptied the clip, point-blank, at the machine.

The room was a shambles, with walls, floor and ceiling ripped by the explosive fragments. He had a minor wound in his neck, and another in his leg, neither of which he was aware of. The machine stood, unmoved by the barrage, the golden alloy completely unscratched.

'Sit,' Follower ordered. 'Your heart is labouring too hard and you may be in danger.'

'Danger!' Jagen said then laughed strangely and clamped his teeth hard on to his lip. The gun slipped from his fingers as he groped his way to an undamaged chair and fell into it. 'Should I worry about the condition of my heart when you are here – Executioner.'

'I am Follower. I am not an executioner.'

'You'll turn me over to them. But first, tell me how you found me. Or is that classified?'

'The details are. I simply used all of the most improved location techniques and transmatter records to follow you. I had a perfect memory and had many facts to work with. Also, being a machine, I do not suffer from impatience.'

Since he was still alive, Jagen still considered escape. He could not damage the machine, but perhaps he could flee from it once again. He had to keep it talking.

'What are you going to do with me?'

'I wish to ask you some questions.'

Jagen smiled inwardly, although his expression did not change. He knew perfectly well that the Greater Despot had more than this in mind for an assassin who had been tracked for twenty years.

'Ask them, by all means.'

'Do you know the identity of the man you shot?'

'I'm not admitting I shot anyone.'

'You admitted that when you attempted to assault me.'

'All right. I'll play along.' Keep the thing talking. Say anything, admit anything. The torturers would have it out of him in any case. 'I never knew who he was. In fact I'm not exactly sure what world it was. It was a rainy place, I can tell you that much.'

'Who employed you?'

'They didn't mention any names. A sum of money and a job of work were involved, that was all.'

'I can believe that. I can also tell you that your heartbeat and pulse are approaching normal, so I may now safely inform you that you have a slight wound on your neck.'

Jagen laughed and touched his finger to the trickle of blood.

'My thanks for the unexpected consideration. The wound is nothing.'

'I would prefer to see it cleaned and bandaged. Do I have your permission to do that?'

'Whatever you wish. There is medical equipment in the other room.' If the thing left the room, he could reach the transmatter!

'I must examine the wound first.'

Follower loomed over him – he had not realized the great bulk of the machine before – and touched a cool metal finger to the skin of his neck. As soon as it made contact he found himself completely paralyzed. His heart beat steadily, he breathed easily, his eyes stared straight ahead. But he could not move or speak, and could only scream wordlessly to himself in the silence of his brain.

'I have tricked you since it was necessary to have your body in a relaxed state before the operation. You will find the operation is completely painless.'

The machine moved out of his fixed point of vision and he heard it leave the room. Operation? What operation? What unmentionable revenge did the Greater Despot plan? How important was the man whom he had killed? Horror and fear filled his thoughts, but did not affect his body. Steadily, the breath flowed in and out of his lungs, while his heart thudded a stately measure. His consciousness was imprisoned in the smallest portion of his brain, impotent, hysterical.

Sound told him that the machine was now standing behind him. Then he swayed and was pushed from side to side. What was it doing? Something dark flew by a corner of his vision and hit the floor. What? WHAT!

Another something, this one spattering on the floor before him. Foamed, dark, mottled. It took long seconds for the meaning of what he saw to penetrate his terror.

It was a great gobbet of depilatory foam, speckled and filled with dissolved strands of his hair. The machine must have sprayed the entire can on to his head and was now removing all of his hair. But why? Panic ebbed slightly.

Follower came around and stood before him, then bent and wiped its metal hands on his robe.

'Your hair has been removed.' *I know, I know! Why?* 'This is a needed part of the operation and creates no permanent damage. Neither does the operation.'

While it was speaking a change was taking place in Follower's torso. The golden alloy, so impervious to the explosives, was splitting down the centre and rolling back. Jagen could only watch, horrified, unable to avert his gaze. There was a silvered concavity revealed in the openings, surrounded by devices of an unknown nature.

'There will be no pain,' Follower said, reaching forward and seizing Jagen's head with both hands. With slow precision it pulled him forward into the opening until the top of his head was pressed against the metal hollow. Then, mercifully, unconsciousness descended.

Jagen did not feel the thin, sharpened needles that slid through holes in the metal bowl, then penetrated his skin, down through the bone of his skull and deep into his brain. But he was aware of the thoughts, clear and sharp, as if they were new experiences that filled his brain. Memories, brought up and examined, then discarded. His childhood, a smell, sounds he had long since forgotten, a room, grass underfoot, a young man looking at him, himself in a mirror.

This flood of memories continued for a long time, guided and controlled by the mechanism inside Follower. Everything was there that the machine needed to know and bit by bit it uncovered it all. When it was finished the needles withdrew into their sheaths and Jagen's head was freed. Once more he was seated upright in the chair – and the paralysis was removed as suddenly as it had begun. He clutched the chair with one hand and felt across the smooth surface of his skull with the other.

'What have you done to me? What was the operation?'

'I have searched your memory. I now know the identity of the people who ordered the assassination.'

With these words the machine turned and started towards the transmatter. It had already punched out a code before Jagen called hoarsely after it.

'Stop! Where are you going? What are you going to do with me?'

Follower turned. 'What do you want me to do with you? Do you have feelings of guilt that must be expunged?'

'Don't play with me, Machine. I am human and you are just a metal thing. I order you to answer me. Are you from the Greater Despot's police?'

'Yes.'

'Then you are arresting me?'

'No. I am leaving you here. The local police may arrest you, though I have been informed that they are not interested in your case. However, I have appropriated all of your funds as partial payment for the cost of tracking you.' It turned once more to leave.

'Stop!' Jagen sprang to his feet. 'You have taken my money, I can believe that. But you cannot toy with me. You did not follow me for twenty years just to turn about and leave me I am an assassin – remember?'

'I am well aware of the fact. That is why I have followed you. I am also now aware of your opinion of yourself. It is a wrong one. You are not unique, or gifted, or even interesting. Any man can kill when presented with the correct motivation. After all, you are animals. In time of war good young men drop bombs on people they do not know, by pressing switches, and this murder does not bother them in the slightest. Men kill to protect their families and are commended for it. You, a professional hunter of animals, killed another animal, who happened to be a man, when presented with enough payment. There is nothing noble, brave or even interesting in that. That man is dead and killing you will not bring him to life. May I leave now?'

'No! If you do not want me – why spend those years following me? Not just for a few remnants of fact.'

The machine stood straight, high, glowing with a mechanical dignity of its own, which perhaps reflected that of its builders.

'Yes. Facts. You are nothing, and the men who hired you are nothing. But why they did it and how they were able to do it is everything. One man, ten men, even a million are as nothing to the Greater Despot who numbers the planets in his realm in the hundreds of thousands. The Greater Despot deals only in societies. Now an examination will be made of your society and particularly of the society of the men who hired you. What led them to believe that violence can solve anything? What were the surroundings where killing was condoned or ignored – or accepted – that shaped their lives so that they exported this idea?

'It is the society that kills, not the individual.

'You are nothing,' Follower added – could it have been with a touch of malice? – as it stepped into the screen and vanished.

ONLINE: TWO/8 *Subject*: The Berserkers

Adventure of the Metal Murderer

Fred Saberhagen

INFO: The Berserkers are merciless interstellar killing machines; alien robot fighters that are programmed to seek out and destroy life forms wherever they are found. But on a routine death mission one of them unexpectedly finds a friend ...

Fred Saberhagen was born in Chicago and was for some years an electronics technician, which enables him to provide a convincing accuracy in his work. He also worked as an editor for the *Encyclopaedia Britannica* before starting to write fiction in the mid-Sixties. His first collection of stories about the Berserkers appeared in 1967, and in tandem with these he has also produced the 'Empire of Earth' sequence, about a post-holocaust world in which magic has replaced technology, and the 'Pilgrim' series featuring a time traveller who has moved effortlessly between Ancient Egypt and the American Civil War to prevent any hiccups in history. Saberhagen was also one of the first writers to explore the virtual reality theme in *Octagon* (1981), about a computer-run war game. The Berserker stories are regarded as being among the best contemporary fiction examining the conflict between men and machines, and also hinting at the menace that robots might one day represent. 'Adventure of the Metal Murderer' was published in *Omni*, January 1980.

It had the shape of a man, the brain of an electronic devil.

It and the machines like it were the best imitations of men and women that the berserkers, murderous machines themselves, were able to devise and build. Still, they could be seen as obvious frauds when closely inspected by any humans.

'Only twenty-nine accounted for?' the supervisor of Defense demanded sharply. Strapped into his combat chair, he was gazing intently through the semitransparent information screen before him, into space. The nearby bulk of Earth was armored in the dun-brown of defensive force fields, the normal colors of land and water and air invisible.

'Only twenty-nine.' The answer arrived on the flagship's bridge amid a sharp sputtering of electrical noise. The tortured voice continued, 'And it's quite certain now that there were thirty to begin with.'

'Then where's the other one?'

There was no reply.

All of Earth's defensive forces were still on full alert, though the attack had been tiny, no more than an attempt at infiltration, and seemed to have been thoroughly repelled. Berserkers, remnants of an ancient interstellar war, were mortal enemies of everything that lived and the greatest danger to humanity that the universe had yet revealed.

A small blur leaped over Earth's dun-brown limb, hurtling along on a course that would bring it within a few hundred kilometers of the supervisor's craft. This was Power Station One, a tamed black hole. In time of peace the power-hungry billions on the planet drew from it half their needed energy. Station One was visible to the eye only as a slight, flowing distortion of the stars beyond.

Another report was coming in. 'We are searching space for the missing berserker android, Supervisor.'

'You had damned well better be.'

'The infiltrating enemy craft had padded containers for thirty androids, as shown by computer analysis of its debris. We must assume that all containers were filled.'

Life and death were in the supervisor's tones. 'Is there any possibility that the missing unit got past you to the surface?'

'Negative, Supervisor.' There was a slight pause. 'At least we know it did not reach the surface in our time.'

'Our time? What does that mean, babbler? How could ... ah.'

The black hole flashed by. Not really tamed, though that was a reassuring word, and humans applied it frequently. Just harnessed, more or less.

Suppose – and, given the location of the skirmish, the supposition was not unlikely – that berserker android number thirty had been propelled, by some accident of combat, directly at Station One. It could easily have entered the black hole. According to the latest theories, it might conceivably have survived to reemerge intact into the universe, projected out of the hole as its own tangible image in a burst of virtual-particle radiation.

Theory dictated that in such a case the reemergence must take place before the falling in. The supervisor crisply issued orders. At once his computers on the world below, the Earth Defense Conglomerate, took up the problem, giving it highest priority. What could one berserker android do to Earth? Probably not much. But to the supervisor, and to those who worked for him, defense was a sacred task. The temple of Earth's safety had been horribly profaned.

To produce the first answers took the machines eleven minutes.

'Number thirty did go into the black hole, sir. Neither we nor the enemy could very well have foreseen such a result, but –'

'What is the probability that the android emerged intact?'

'Because of the peculiar angle at which it entered, approximately sixty-nine per cent.'

'That high!'

'And there is a forty-nine per cent chance that it will reach the surface of the earth in functional condition, at some point in our past. However, the computers offer reassurance. As the enemy device must have been programmed for some subtle attack upon our present society, it is not likely to be able to do much damage at the time and place where it –'

'Your skull contains a vacuum of a truly intergalactic order. *I* will tell *you* and the computers when it has become possible for us to feel even the slightest degree of reassurance. Meanwhile, get me more figures.'

The next word from the ground came twenty minutes later.

'There is a ninety-two per cent chance that the landing of the android on the surface, if that occurred, was within one hundred kilometers of fifty-one degrees eleven minutes north latitude; zero degrees, seven minutes west longitude.'

'And the time?'

'Ninety-eight per cent probability of January 1, 1880 Christian Era, plus or minus ten standard years.'

A landmass, a great clouded island, was presented to the supervisor on his screen.

'Recommended course of action?'

It took the ED Conglomerate an hour and a half to answer that.

The first two volunteers perished in attempted launchings before the method could be improved enough to offer a reasonable chance of survival. When the third man was ready, he was called in, just before launching, for a last private meeting with the supervisor.

The supervisor looked him up and down, taking in his outlandish dress, strange hairstyle, and all the rest. He did not ask whether the volunteer was ready but began bluntly: 'It has now been confirmed that, whether you win or lose back there, you will never be able to return to your own time.'

'Yes, sir. I had assumed that would be the case.'

'Very well.' The supervisor consulted data spread before him. 'We are still uncertain as to just how the enemy is armed. Something subtle, doubtless, suitable for a saboteur on the earth of our own time – in addition, of course, to the superhuman physical strength and speed you must expect to face. There are the scrambling or the switching mindbeams to be considered; either could damage any human society. There are the pattern bombs, designed to disable our defense computers by seeding them with random information. There are always possibilities of biological warfare. You have your disguised medical kit? Yes, I see. And of course there is always the chance of something new.'

'Yes, sir.' The volunteer looked as ready as anyone could. The supervisor went to him, opening his arms for a ritual farewell embrace.

He blinked away some London rain, pulled out his heavy ticking timepiece as if he were checking the hour, and stood on the pavement before the theater as if he were waiting for a friend. The instrument in his hand throbbed with a silent, extra vibration in addition to its ticking, and this special signal had now taken on a character that meant the enemy machine was very near to him. It was probably within a radius of fifty meters.

A poster on the front of the theater read:
THE IMPROVED AUTOMATON CHESS PLAYER MARVEL OF THE AGE UNDER NEW MANAGEMENT

'The real problem, sir,' proclaimed one top-hatted man nearby, in conversation with another, 'is not whether a machine can be made to win at chess, but whether it may possibly be made to play at all.'

No, that is not the real problem, sir the agent from the future thought. *But count yourself fortunate that you can still believe it is.*

He bought a ticket and went in, taking a seat. When a sizeable audience had gathered, there was a short lecture by a short man in evening dress, who had something predatory about him and also something frightened, despite the glibness and the rehearsed humor of his talk.

At length the chess player itself appeared. It was a desk-like box with a figure seated behind it, the whole assembly wheeled out on stage by assistants. The figure was that of a huge man in Turkish garb. Quite obviously a mannequin or a dummy of some kind, it bobbed slightly with the motion of the rolling desk, to which its chair was fixed. Now the agent could feel the excited vibration of his watch without even putting a hand into his pocket.

The predatory man cracked another joke, displayed a hideous smile, then, from among several chess players in the audience who raised their hands – the agent was not among them – he selected one to challenge the automaton. The challenger ascended to the stage, where the pieces were being set out on a board fastened to the rolling desk, and the doors in the front of the desk were being opened to show that there was nothing but machinery inside.

The agent noted that there were no candles on this desk, as there had been on that of Maelzel's chess player a few decades earlier. Maelzel's automaton had been a clever fraud, of course. Candles had been placed on its box to mask the odor of burning wax from the candle needed by the man who was so cunningly hidden inside amid the dummy gears. The year in which the agent had arrived was still too early, he knew, for electric lights, at least the kind that would be handy for such a hidden human to use. Add the fact that this chess player's opponent was allowed to sit much closer than Maelzel's had ever been, and it became a pretty safe deduction that no human being was concealed inside the box and figure on this stage.

Therefore ...

The agent might, if he stood up in the audience, get a clear shot at it right now. But should he aim at the figure or the box? And he could not be sure how it was armed. And who would stop it if he tried and failed? Already it had learned enough to survive in nineteenth-century London. Probably it had already killed, to further its designs – 'under new management' indeed.

No, now that he had located his enemy, he must plan thoroughly and work patiently. Deep in thought, he left the theater amid the crowd at the conclusion of the performance and started on foot back to the rooms that he had just begun to share on Baker Street. A minor difficulty at his launching into the black hole had cost him some equipment, including most of his counterfeit money. There had not been time as yet for his adopted profession to bring him much income; so he was for the time being in straitened financial circumstances.

He must plan. Suppose, now, that he were to approach the frightened little man in evening dress. By now that one ought to have begun to understand what kind of a tiger he was riding. The agent might approach him in the guise of –

A sudden tap-tapping began in the agent's watch pocket. It was a signal quite distinct from any previously generated by his fake watch. It meant that the enemy had managed to detect his detector; it was in fact locked on to it and tracking.

Sweat mingled with the drizzle on the agent's face as he began to run. It must have discovered him in the theater, though probably it could not then single him out in the crowd. Avoiding horse-drawn cabs, four-wheelers, and an omnibus, he turned out of Oxford Street to Baker Street and slowed to a fast walk for the short distance remaining. He could not throw away the telltale watch, for he would be unable to track the enemy without it. But neither did he dare retain it on his person.

As the agent burst into the sitting room, his roommate looked up, with his usual, somewhat shallow, smile, from a leisurely job of taking books out of a crate and putting them on shelves.

'I say,' the agent began, in mingled relief and urgency, 'something rather important has come up, and I find there are two errands I must undertake at once. Might I impose one of them on you?'

The agent's own brisk errand took him no farther than just across the street. There, in the doorway of Camden House, he shrank back, trying to breathe silently. He had not moved when, three minutes later, there approached from the direction of Oxford Street a tall figure that the agent suspected was not human. Its hat was pulled down, and the lower portion of its face was muffled in bandages. Across the street it paused, seemed to consult a pocket watch of its own, then turned to ring the bell. Had the agent been absolutely sure it was his quarry, he would have shot it in the back. But without his watch, he would have to get closer to be absolutely sure.

After a moment's questioning from the landlady, the figure was admitted. The agent waited for two minutes. Then he drew a deep breath, gathered up his courage, and went after it.

The thing standing alone at a window turned to face him as he entered the sitting room, and now he was sure of what it was. The eyes above the bandaged lower face were not the Turk's eyes, but they were not human, either.

The white swathing muffled its gruff voice. 'You are the doctor?'

'Ah, it is my fellow lodger that you want.' The agent threw a careless glance toward the desk where he had locked up the watch, the desk on which some papers bearing his roommate's name were scattered. 'He is out at the moment, as you see, but we can expect him presently. I take it you are a patient.'

The thing said, in its wrong voice, 'I have been referred to him. It seems the doctor and I share a certain common background. Therefore the good landlady has let me wait in here. I trust my presence is no inconvenience.'

'Not in the least. Pray take a seat, Mr –?'

What name the berserker might have given, the agent never learned. The bell sounded below, suspending conversation. He heard the servant girl answering the door, and a moment later his roommate's brisk feet on the stairs. The death machine took a small object from its pocket and sidestepped a little to get a clear view past the agent toward the door.

Turning his back upon the enemy, as if with the casual purpose of greeting the man about to enter, the agent casually drew from his own pocket a quite functional briar pipe, which was designed to serve another function, too. Then he turned his head and fired the pipe at the berserker from under his own left armpit.

For a human being he was uncannily fast, and for a berserker the android was meanly slow and clumsy, being designed primarily for imitation, not dueling. Their weapons triggered at the same instant.

Explosions racked and destroyed the enemy, blasts shatteringly powerful but compactly limited in space, self-damping and almost silent.

The agent was hit, too. Staggering, he knew with his last clear thought just what weapon the enemy had carried – the switching mindbeam. Then for a moment he could no longer think at all. He was dimly aware of being down on one knee and of his fellow lodger, who had just entered, standing stunned a step inside the door.

At last the agent could move again, and he shakily pocketed his pipe. The ruined body of the enemy was almost vaporized already. It must have been built to self-destruct when damaged badly, so that humanity might never learn its secrets. Already it was no more than a puddle of heavy mist, warping in slow tendrils out the slightly open window to mingle with the fog.

The man still standing near the door had put out a hand to steady himself against the wall. 'The jeweler ... did not have your watch,' he muttered dazedly.

I have won, thought the agent dully. It was a joyless thought because with it came slow realization of the price of his success. Three-quarters of his intellect, at least, was gone, the superior pattern of his brain-cell connections scattered. No. Not scattered. The switching mindbeam would have reimposed the pattern of his neurons somewhere farther down its pathway ... *there*, behind those gray eyes with their newly penetrating gaze.

'Obviously, sending me out for your watch was a ruse.' His roommate's voice was suddenly crisper, more assured than it had been. 'Also, I perceive that your desk has just been broken into, by someone who thought it mine.' The tone softened somewhat. 'Come, man, I bear you no ill will. Your secret, if honorable, shall be safe. But it is plain that you are not what you have represented yourself to be.'

The agent got to his feet, pulling at his sandy hair, trying desperately to think. 'How – how do you know?'

'Elementary!' the tall man snapped.

THREE
VIRTUAL MURDER

INTERFACE:/
There are many ways in which criminals will be able to muscle in on virtual reality. Obviously the physical protection racket will be based on the fact that while VR machines cost far more than most other arcade games, they are only as fireproof, water- or hatchet-resistant as the cheapest of them. It is also possible to threaten users. But the possibility of a really nasty virus would do just as nicely, thank you, and with far less chance of getting caught. Of course, the Mafia, or Yakusa, could take the opposite track. It only takes a single wholesaler or leasing company to put the squeeze on arcade owners for them to feel obliged to take that party's VR machines in the first instance.

Barrie Sherman & Phil Judkins
Glimpses of Heaven, Visions of Hell (1992)

ONLINE: THREE/1 *Subject:* The JumpShift Booth

A Kind of Murder

Larry Niven

INFO: JumpShift Inc and its instant teleportation booths offer a passport to new worlds of the imagination. But make a mistake with the energy source and anything can happen to those taking a trip. Even murder.

Larry Niven is credited with being one of the precursors of the virtual reality story with his 'Dream Park' series published in the Eighties. Beginning with *Dream Park* (1981), the books describe a 21st-century corporation which organises role-playing experiences in a game-world environment where participants can live out their emotional, sexual and even criminal fantasies. The title of the most recent book in the series, *The California Voodoo Game* (1992), speaks for itself.

Larry was born in Los Angeles, and has utilised many of California's high-tech achievements – as well as its notorious eccentricities – in his fiction. After studying mathematics at Washburn University, Kansas where he gained a BA, Niven made an immediate impact with his first sf story, 'The Coldest Place' (1964), which won a Hugo. Soon after he wrote 'Death by Ecstasy', the first of a series of tales about Gil Hamilton of ARM – the Amalgamated Regional Militia – who police the United Nations and conduct a long-running war with the Organleggers, a murderous band of dealers in illicit body transplants. In 1970 he was awarded both a Hugo and a Nebula for *Ringworld*, the opening episode in his 'Tales of Known Space' sequence which focuses on the advance of technology and the continuing failure of human beings to overcome their predilection for violence and murder. 'A Kind of Murder' was originally published in *Analog*, April 1974.

'You are constantly coming to my home!' he shouted. 'You never think of calling first. Whatever I'm doing, suddenly you're there. And where the hell do you keep getting keys to my door?'

Alicia didn't answer. Her face, which in recent years had taken on a faint resemblance to a bulldog's, was set in infinite patience as she relaxed at the other end of the couch. She had been through this before, and she waited for Jeff to get it over with.

He saw this, and the dinner he had not quite finished settled like lead in his belly. 'There's not a club I belong to that you aren't a member of too. Whoever I'm with, you finagle me into introducing you. If it's a man, you try to make him, and if he isn't having any you get nasty. If it's a woman, there you are like the ghost at the feast. The discarded woman. It's a drag,' he said. He wanted a more powerful word, but he couldn't think of one that wouldn't sound over-dramatic, silly.

She said, 'We've been divorced six years. What do you care who I sleep with?'

'I don't like looking like your pimp!'

She laughed.

The acid was rising in his throat. 'Listen,' he said, 'why don't you give up one of the clubs? W-we belong to *four*. Give one up. Any of them.' *Give me a place of refuge*, he prayed.

'They're my clubs too,' she said with composure. '*You* change clubs.'

He'd joined the Lucifer Club four years ago, for just that reason. She'd joined too. And now the words clogged in his throat, so that he gaped like a fish.

There were no words left. He hit her.

He'd never done that before. It was a full-arm swing, but awkward because they were trying to face each other on the couch. She rode with the slap, then sat facing him, waiting.

It was as if he could read her mind. *We've been through this before, and it never changes anything. But it's your tantrum.* He remembered later that she'd said that to him once, those same words, and she'd looked just like that: patient, implacable.

The call reached Homicide at 8:36 p.m., July 20, 2019. The caller was a round-faced man with straight black hair and a stutter. 'My ex-wife,' he told the desk man. 'She's dead. I just got home and f-found her like this. S-someone seems to have hit her with a c-cigarette box.'

Hennessey (Officer-Two) had just come on for the night shift. He took over. 'You just got home? You called immediately?'

'That's right. C-c-could you come right away?'

'We'll be there in ten seconds. Have you touched anything?'

'No. Not her, and not the box.'

'Have you called the hospital?'

His voice rose. 'No. She's *dead*.'

Hennessey took down his name – Walters – and booth number and hung up. 'Linc, Fisher, come with me. Torrie, will you call the City Hospital and have them send a copter?' If Walters hadn't touched her he could hardly be sure she was dead.

They went through the displacement booth one at a time, dialing and vanishing. For Hennessey it was as if the Homicide Room vanished as he dialed the last digit, and he was looking into a porch light.

Jeffrey Walters was waiting in the house. He was medium-sized, a bit overweight, his light brown hair going thin on top. His paper business suit was wrinkled. He wore an anxious, fearful look – which figured, either way, Hennessey thought.

And he'd been right. Alicia Walters was dead. From her attitude she had been sitting sideways on the couch when something crashed into her head, and she had sprawled forward. A green cigarette box was sitting on the glass coffee table. It was bloody along one edge, and the blood had marked the glass.

The small, bloody, beautifully-marked green malachite box could have done it. It would have been held in the right hand, swung full-armed. One of the detectives used chalk to mark its position on the table, then nudged it into a plastic bag and tied the neck.

Walters had sagged into a reading chair as if worn out. Hennessey approached him. 'You said she was your ex-wife?'

'That's right. She didn't give up using her married name.'

'What was she doing here, then?'

'I don't know. We had a fight earlier this evening. I finally threw her out and went back to the Sirius Club. I was half afraid she'd just follow me back, but she didn't. I guess she let herself back in and waited for me here.'

'She had a key?'

Walters' laugh was feeble. 'She always had a key. I've had the lock changed twice. It didn't work. I'd come home and find her here. "I just wanted to talk," she'd say.' He stopped abruptly.

'That doesn't explain why she'd let someone else in.'

'No. She must have, though, mustn't she? I don't know why she did that.'

The ambulance helicopter landed in the street outside. Two men entered with a stretcher. They shifted Alicia Walters' dead body to the stretcher, leaving a chalk outline Fisher had drawn earlier.

Walters watched through the picture window as they walked the stretcher into the portable JumpShift unit in the side of the copter. They closed the hatch, tapped buttons in a learned rhythm on a phone dial set in the hatch. When they opened the hatch to check, it was empty. They closed it again and boarded the copter.

Walters said, 'You'll do an autopsy immediately, won't you?'

'Of course. Why do you ask?'

'Well ... it's possible I might have an alibi for the time of the murder.'

Hennessey laughed before he could stop himself. Walters looked puzzled and affronted.

Hennessey didn't explain. But later – as he was leaving the station house for home and bed – he snorted. 'Alibi,' he said. 'Idiot.'

The displacement booths had come suddenly. One year, a science-fiction writer's daydream. The next year, 1922, an experimental reality. Teleportation. Instantaneous travel. Another year and they were being used for cargo transport. Two more, and the passenger displacement booths were springing up everywhere in the world.

By luck and the laws of physics, the world had had time to adjust. Teleportation obeyed the Laws of Conservation of Energy and Conservation of Momentum. Teleporting uphill took an energy input to match the gain in potential energy. A cargo would lose potential energy going downhill – and it was over a decade before JumpShift Inc. learned how to compensate for that effect. Teleportation over great distances was even more heavily restricted by the Earth's rotation.

Let a passenger flick too far west, and the difference between his momentum and the Earth's would smack him down against the floor of the booth. Too far east, and he would be flung against the ceiling. Too far north or south, and the Earth would be rotating faster or slower; he would flick in moving sideways, unless he had crossed the equator.

But cargo and passengers could be displaced between points of equal longitude and opposite latitude. Smuggling had become impossible to stop. There was a point in the South Pacific to correspond to any point in the United States, most of Canada, and parts of Mexico.

Smuggling via the displacement booths was a new crime. The Permanent Floating Riot Gangs were another. The booths would allow a crowd to gather with amazing rapidity. Practically any news broadcast could start a flash crowd. And with the crowds the pickpockets and looters came flicking in.

When the booths were new, many householders had taken to putting their booths in the living rooms or entrance halls. That had stopped fast, after an astounding rash of burglaries. These days only police stations and hospitals kept their booths indoors.

For twenty years the booths had not been feasible over distances greater than ten miles. If the short-distance booths had changed the nature of crime, what of the long-distance booths? They had been in existence only four years. Most were at what had been airports, being run by what had been airline companies. Dial three numbers and you could be anywhere on Earth.

Flash crowds were bigger and more frequent.

The alibi was as dead as the automobile.

Smuggling was cheaper. The expensive, illegal transmission booths in the South Pacific were no longer needed. Cutthroat competition had dropped the price of smack to something the Mafia wouldn't touch.

And murder was easier; but that was only part of the problem. There was a new *kind* of murder going around.

Hank Lovejoy was a tall, lanky man with a lantern jaw and a ready smile. The police had found him at his office – real estate – and he had agreed to come immediately.

'There were four of us at the Sirius Club before Alicia showed up,' he said. 'Me, and George Larimer, and Jeff Walters, and Jennifer – wait a minute – Lewis. Jennifer was over at the bar, and we'd, like, asked her to join us for dinner. You know how it is in a continuity club: you can talk to anyone. We'd have picked up another girl sooner or later.'

Hennessey said, 'Not two?'

'Oh, George is a monogamist. His wife is eight months pregnant, and she *didn't* want to come, but George just doesn't. He's not gay or anything, he just doesn't. But Jeff and I were both sort of trying to get Jennifer's attention. She was loose, and it looked likely she'd go home with one or the other of us. Then Alicia came in.'

'What time was that?'

'Oh, about six-fifteen. We were already eating. She came up to the table, and we all kind of waited for Jeff to introduce her and ask her to sit down, she being his ex-wife, after all.' Lovejoy laughed. 'George doesn't really understand about Jeff and Alicia. Me, I thought it was funny.'

'What do you mean?'

'Well, they've been divorced about six years, but it seems he just can't get away from her. Couldn't, I mean,' he said, remembering. Remembering that good old Jeff *had* gotten away from her, because someone had smashed her skull.

Hennessey was afraid Lovejoy would clam up. He played stupid. 'I don't get it. A divorce is a divorce, isn't it?'

'Not when it's a quote friendly divorce unquote. Jeff's a damn fool. I don't think he gave up sleeping with her, not right after the divorce. He wouldn't live with her, but every so often she'd, well, she'd seduce him, I guess you'd say. He wasn't used to being alone, and I guess he got lonely. Eventually he must have given that up, but he still couldn't get her out of his hair.

'See, they belonged to all the same clubs and they knew all the same people, and as a matter of fact they were both in routing and distribution software; that was how they met. So if she came on the scene while he was trying to do something else, there she was, and he had to introduce her. She probably knew the people he was dealing with, if it was business. A lot of business gets done at the continuity clubs. And she wouldn't go away. I thought it was funny. It worked out fine for me, last night.'

'How?'

'Well, after twenty minutes or so it got through to us that Alicia wasn't going to go away. I mean, we were eating dinner, and she wasn't, but she wanted to talk. When she said something about waiting and joining us for dessert, Jeff stood up and suggested they go somewhere and talk. She didn't look too pleased, but she went.'

'What do you suppose he wanted to talk about?'

Lovejoy laughed. 'Do I read minds without permission? He wanted to tell her to bug off, of course! But he was gone half an hour, and by the time he came back Jennifer and I had sort of reached a decision. And George had this benign look he gets, like, *Bless you my children*. He doesn't play around himself, but maybe he likes to think about other couples getting together. Maybe he's right; maybe it brightens up the marriage bed.'

'Jeff came back alone?'

'That he did. He was nervous, jumpy. Friendly enough; I mean, he didn't get obnoxious when he saw how it was with me and Jennifer. But he was sweating, and I don't blame him.'

'What time was this?'

'Seven-twenty.'

'Dead on?'

'Yeah.'

'Why would you remember a thing like that?'

'Well, when Jeff came back he wanted to know how long he'd been gone. So I looked at my watch. Anyway, we stayed another fifteen minutes and then Jennifer and I took off.'

Hennessey asked, 'Just how bad were things between Jeff and Alicia?'

'Oh, they didn't *fight* or anything. It was just – funny. For one thing, she's kind of let herself go since the divorce. She used to be pretty. Now she's gone to seed. Not many men chase her these days, so she has to do the chasing. Some men like that.'

'Do you?'

'Not particularly. I've spent some nights with her, if that's what you're asking. I just like variety. I'm not a heartbreaker, man; I run with girls who like variety too.'

'Did Alicia?'

'I think so. The trouble was, she slept with a lot of guys Jeff introduced her to. He didn't like that. It made him look bad. And once she played nasty to a guy who turned her down, and it ruined a business deal.'

'But they didn't fight.'

'No. Jeff wasn't the type. Maybe that's why they got divorced. She was just someone he couldn't avoid. We all know people like that.'

'After he came back without Alicia, did he leave the table at any time?'

'I don't think so. No. He just sat there, making small talk. Badly.'

George Larimer was a writer of articles, one of the few who made good money at it. He lived in Arizona. No, he didn't mind a quick trip to the police station, he said, emphasizing the *quick*. Just let him finish this paragraph ... and he breezed in five minutes later.

'Sorry about that. I just couldn't get the damn wording right. This one's for *Viewer's Digest*, and I have to explain drop ship technology for morons without talking down to them or the minimal viewer won't buy it. What's the problem?'

Hennessey told him.

His face took on an expression Hennessey recognized: like he ought to be feeling something, and he was trying, honest. 'I just met her that night,' he said. 'Dead. Well.'

He remembered that evening well enough. 'Sure, Jeff Walters came back about the time we were finishing coffee. We had brandy with the coffee, and then Hank and, uh, Jennifer left. Jeff and I sat and played dominoes over Scotch and sodas. You can do that at the Sirius, you know. They keep game boxes there, and they'll move up side tables at your elbows so you can have drinks or lunch.'

'How did you do?'

'I beat him. Something was bothering him; he wasn't playing very well.

I thought he wanted to talk, but he wouldn't talk about whatever was bugging him.'

'His ex-wife?'

'Maybe. Maybe not. I'd only just met her, and she seemed nice enough. And she seemed to like Jeff.'

'Yeah. Now, Jeff left with Alicia. How long were they gone?'

'Half an hour, I guess. And he came back without her.'

'What time?'

'Quarter past seven or thereabouts. Ask Hank. I don't wear a watch.' He said this with a certain pride. A writer doesn't need a watch; he sets his own hours. 'As I said, we had dessert and coffee and then played dominoes for an hour, maybe a little less. Then I had to go home to see how my wife was getting along in my absence.'

'While you were having dessert and coffee and playing dominoes, did Jeff Walters leave the table at any time?'

'Well, we switched tables to set up the game.' Larimer shut his eyes to think. He opened them. 'No, he didn't go to the bathroom or anything.'

'Did you?'

'No. We were together the whole time, if that's what you want to know.'

Hennessey went out for lunch after Larimer left. Returning, he stepped out of the Homicide Room booth just ahead of Officer-One Fisher, who had spent the morning at Alicia Walters' place.

Alicia had lived in the mountains, within shouting distance of Lake Arrowhead. Property in that area was far cheaper than property around the lake itself. The high rent district in the mountains is near streams and lakes. Her own water supply had come from a storage tank kept filled by a small JumpShift unit.

Fisher was hot and sweaty and breathing hard, as if he had been working. He dropped into a chair and wiped his forehead and neck. 'There wasn't much point in going,' he said. 'We found what was left of a bacon and tomato sandwich sitting on a place mat. Probably her last meal. She wasn't much of a housekeeper. Probably wasn't making much money, either.'

'How so?'

'All her gadgetry is old enough to be going to pieces. Her Dustmaster skips corners and knocks things off tables. Her chairs and couches are all blow-ups, inflated plastic. Cheap, but they have to be replaced every so often, and she didn't. Her displacement booth must be ten years old. She should have replaced it, living in the mountains.'

'No roads in that area?'

'Not near her house, anyway. In remote areas like that they move the booths in by helicopter, then bring the components for the house out through the booth. If her booth broke down she'd have had to hike out, unless she could find a neighbor at home, and her neighbors aren't close. I like that area,' Fisher said suddenly. 'There's elbow room.'

'She should have made good money. She was in routing and distribution software.' Hennessey pondered. 'Maybe she spent all her time following her ex-husband around.'

The autopsy report was waiting on his desk. He read through it.

Alicia Walters had indeed been killed by a single blow to the side of the head, almost certainly by the malachite box. Its hard corner had crushed her skull around the temple. Malachite is a semiprecious stone, hard enough that no part of it had broken off in the wound; but there was blood, and traces of bone and brain tissue, on the box itself.

There was also a bruise on her cheek. *Have to ask Walters about that*, he thought.

She had died about 8:00 p.m., given the state of her body, including body temperature. Stomach contents indicated that she had eaten about 5:30 p.m. a bacon and tomato sandwich.

Hennessey shook his head. 'I was right. He's still thinking in terms of alibis.'

Fisher heard. 'Walters?'

'Sure, Walters. Look: he came back to the Sirius Club at 7:20, and he called attention to the time. He stayed until around 8:30, to hear Larimer tell it, and he was always in someone's company. Then he went home, found the body and called us. The woman was killed around eight, which is right in the middle of his alibi time. Give or take fifteen minutes for the lab's margin of error, and it's still an alibi.'

'Then it clears him.'

Hennessey laughed. 'Suppose he did go to the bathroom. Do you think anyone would remember it? Nobody in the world has had an alibi for anything since the JumpShift booths took over. You can be at a party in New York and kill a man in the California Sierras in the time it would take to go out for cigarettes. You can't use displacement booths for an alibi.'

'You could be jumping to conclusions,' Fisher pointed out. 'So he's not a cop. So he reads detective stories. So someone murdered his wife in his own living room. *Naturally* he wants to know if he's got an alibi.'

Hennessey shook his head.

'She didn't bleed a lot,' said Fisher. 'Maybe enough, maybe not. Maybe she was moved.'

'I noticed that too.'

'Someone who knew she had a key to Walters' house killed her and dumped her there. He would have hit her with the cigarette box in the spot where he'd already hit her with something else.'

Hennessey shook his head again. 'It's not just Walters. It's a *kind* of murder. We get more and more of these lately. People kill each other because they can't move away from each other. With the long-distance booths everyone in the country lives next door to everyone else. You live a block away from your ex-wife, your mother-in-law, the girl you're trying to drop, the guy who lost money in your business deal and blames you. Any secretary lives next door to her boss, and if he needs something done in a hurry she's right there. God help the doctor if his patients get his home number. I'm not just pulling these out of the air. I can name you an assault rap for every one of these situations.'

'Most people get used to it,' said Fisher. 'My mother used to flick in to visit me at work, remember?'

Hennessey grinned. He did. Fortunately she'd given it up. 'It was worse for Walters,' he said.

'It didn't really sound that bad. Lovejoy said it was a friendly divorce. So he was always running into her. So what?'

'She took away his clubs.'

Fisher snorted. But Fisher was young. He had grown up with the short-distance booths.

For twenty years passenger teleportation had been restricted to short hops. People had had time to get used to the booths. And in those twenty years the continuity clubs had come into existence.

The continuity club was a guard against future shock. Its location ... ubiquitous: hundreds of buildings in hundreds of cities, each building just like all the others, inside and out. Wherever a member moved in this traveling society, the club would be there. Today even some of the customers would be the same: everyone used the long-distance booths to some extent.

A man had to have some kind of stability in his life. His church, his marriage, his home, his club. Any man might need more or less stability than the next. Walters had belonged to *four* clubs ... and they were no use to him if he kept meeting Alicia there. And his marriage had broken up, and he wasn't a churchgoer, and a key to his house had been found in Alicia's purse. She should at least have left him his clubs.

Fisher spoke, interrupting his train of thought. 'You've been talking about impulse murders, haven't you? Six years of not being able to stand his ex-wife and not being able to get away from her. So finally he hits her with a cigarette box.'

'Most of them are impulse murders, yes.'

'Well, this wasn't any impulse murder. Look at what he had to do to bring it about. He'd have had to ask her to wait at home for him. Then make some excuse to get away from Larimer, shift home, kill her *fast* and get back to the Sirius Club before Larimer wonders where he's gone. Then he's got to hope Larimer will forget the whole thing. That's not just cold-blooded, it's also stupid.'

'Yeah. So far it's worked, though.'

'Worked, hell. The only evidence you've got against Walters is that he had good reason to kill her. Listen, if she got on his nerves that much, she may have irritated some other people too.'

Hennessey nodded. 'That's the problem, all right.' But he didn't mean it the way Fisher did.

Walters had moved to a hotel until such time as the police were through with his house. Hennessey called him before going off duty.

'You can go home,' he told him.

'That's good,' said Walters. 'Find out anything?'

'Only that your wife was murdered with that self-same cigarette box. We found no sign of anyone in the house except her, and you.' He paused, but Walters only nodded thoughtfully. He asked, 'Did the box look familiar to you?'

'Oh, yes, of course. It's mine. Alicia and I bought it on our honeymoon, in Switzerland. We divided things during the divorce, and that went to me.'

'All right. Now, just how violent was that argument you had?'

He flushed. 'As usual. I did a lot of shouting, and she just sat there letting it go past her ears. It never did any good.'

'Did you strike her?'

The flush deepened, and he nodded. 'I've never done that before.'

'Did you by any chance hit her with a malachite box?'

'Do I need a lawyer?'

'You're not under arrest, Mr Walters. But if you feel you need a lawyer, by all means get one.' Hennessey hung up.

He had asked to be put on the day shift today, in order to follow up this case. It was quitting time now, but he was reluctant to leave.

Officer-One Fisher had been eavesdropping. He said, 'So?'

'He never mentioned the word *alibi*,' said Hennessey. 'Smart. He's not supposed to know when she was killed.'

'You're still sure he did it.'

'Yeah. But getting a conviction is something else again. We'll find more people with more motives. And all we've got is the laboratory.' He ticked items off on his fingers. 'No fingerprints on the box. No blood on Walters or any of his clothes, unless he had paper clothes and ditched 'em. No way of proving Walters let her in or gave her the key ... though I wonder if he really had that much trouble keeping her out of the house.

'We'd be asking a jury to believe that Walters left the table and Larimer forgot about it. Larimer says no. Walters is pretty sure to get the benefit of the doubt. She didn't bleed much; a good defense lawyer is bound to suggest that she was moved from somewhere else.'

'It's possible.'

'She wasn't dead until she was hit. Nothing in the stomach but food. No drugs or poisons in the bloodstream. She'd have had to be killed by someone who' – he ticked them off – 'knew she had Walters' key; knew Walters' displacement booth number; and knew Walters wouldn't be home. Agreed?'

'Maybe. How about Larimer or Lovejoy?'

Hennessey spread his hands in surrender. 'It's worth asking. Larimer's alibi is as good as Walters', for all that's worth. And we've still got to interview Jennifer Lewis.'

'Then again, a lot of people at the Sirius Club knew Walters. Some of them must have been involved with Alicia. Anyone who saw Walters halfway through a domino game would know he'd be stuck there for a while.'

'True. Too true.' Hennessey stood up. 'Guess I'll be getting dinner.'

Hennessey came out of the restaurant feeling pleasantly stuffed and torpid. He turned left toward the nearest booth, a block away.

The Walters case had haunted him all through dinner. Fisher had made a good deal of sense ... but what bugged him was something Fisher hadn't said. Fisher hadn't said that Hennessey might be looking for easy answers.

Easy? If Walters had killed Alicia during a game of dominoes at the Sirius Club, then there wouldn't *be* any case until Larimer remembered. Aside from that, Walters would have been an idiot to try such a thing. Idiot, or desperate.

But if someone else had killed her, it opened up a bag of snakes. Restrict it to members of the Sirius Club who were there that night, and how many were left? They'd both done business there. How many of Jeffrey Walters' acquaintances had shared Alicia's bed? Which of them would have killed her, for reason or no reason? The trouble with sharing too many beds was that one's chance of running into a really bad situation was improved almost to certainty.

If Walters had done it, things became simpler.

But she hadn't bled much.

And Walters couldn't have had reason to move her body to his home. Where could he have killed her that would be worse than that?

Walters owned the murder weapon ... no, forget that. She could have been hit with anything, and if she were in Walters' house fifteen seconds later she might still be breathing when the malachite box finished the job.

Hennessey slowed to a stop in front of the booth. Something Fisher *had* said, something that had struck him funny. What was it?

'Her displacement booth must be ten years old –' That was it. The sight of the booth must have sparked that memory. And it *was* funny. How had he known?

JumpShift booths were all alike. They had to be. They all had to hold the same volume, because the air in the receiver had to be flicked back to the transmitter. When JumpShift improved a booth, it was the equipment they improved, so that the older booths could still be used.

Ten years old. Wasn't that – yes. The altitude shift. Pumping energy into a cargo, so that it could be flicked a mile or a hundred miles uphill, had been an early improvement. But a transmitter that could absorb the lost potential energy of a downhill shift had not become common until ten years ago.

Hennessey stepped in and dialed the police station.

Sergeant Sobel was behind the desk. 'Oh, Fisher left an hour ago,' he said. 'Want his number?'

'Yes ... no. Get me Alicia Walters' number.'

Sobel got it for him. 'What's up?'

'Tell you in a minute,' said Hennessey, and he flicked out.

It was black night. His ears registered the drop in pressure. His eyes adjusted rapidly, and he saw that there were lights in Alicia Walters' house.

He stepped out of the booth. Whistling, he walked a slow circle around it.

It was a JumpShift booth. What more was there to say? A glass cylinder with a rounded top, big enough for a tall man to stand upright and a meager amount of baggage to stand with him – or for a man holding a dead woman in his arms, clenching his teeth while he tried to free one finger for dialing. The machinery that made the magic was buried beneath the booth. The dial, a simple push-button phone dial. Even the long-distance booths looked just like this one, though the auxiliary machinery was far more complex.

'But he was sweating –' Had Lovejoy meant it literally?

Hennessey was smiling ferociously as he stepped back into the booth.

The lights of the Homicide Room flashed in his eyes. Hennessey came out tearing at his collar. Sweat started from every pore. Living in the mountains like that, Alicia should certainly have had her booth replaced. The room felt like a furnace, but it was his own body temperature that had jumped seven degrees in a moment. Seven degrees of randomized energy, to compensate for the drop in potential energy between here and Lake Arrowhead.

Walters sat slumped, staring straight ahead of him. 'She didn't understand and she didn't care. She was taking it like we'd been all through this before but we had to do it again and let's get it over with.' He spoke in a monotone, but the nervous stutter was gone. 'Finally I hit her. I guess I was trying to get her attention. She just took it and looked at me and waited for me to go on.'

Hennessey said, 'Where did the malachite box come in?'

'Where do you think? I hit her with it.'

'Then it was hers, not yours.'

'It was ours. When we broke up, she took it. Look, I don't want you to think I wanted to *kill* her. I wanted to scar her.'

'To scare her?'

'No! To scar her!' His voice rose. 'To leave a mark she'd remember every time she looked in a mirror, so she'd know I meant it, so she'd leave me alone! I wouldn't have cared if she sued. Whatever it cost, it would have been worth it. But I hit her too hard, too hard. I felt the crunch.'

'Why didn't you report it?'

'But I did! At least, I tried. I picked her up in my arms and wrestled her out to the booth and dialed for the Los Angeles Emergency Hospital. I don't know if there's any place closer, and I wasn't thinking too clearly. Listen, maybe I can prove this. Maybe an intern saw me in the booth. I flicked into the hospital, and suddenly I was broiling. Then I remembered that Alicia had an old booth, the kind that can't absorb a difference in potential energy.'

'We guessed that much.'

'So I dialed quick and flicked right out again. I had to go back to Alicia's for the malachite box and to wipe off the sofa, and my own booth *is* a new one, so I got the temperature shift again. God, it was hot. I changed suits before I went back to the Club. I was still sweating.'

'You thought that raising her temperature would foul up our estimate of when she died.'

'That's right.' Walters' smile was wan. 'Listen, I did try to get her to a hospital. You'll remember that, won't you?'

'Yeah. But you changed your mind.'

ONLINE: **THREE/2** *Subject:* Mind Detectives

Zone of Terror

J. G. Ballard

INFO: Larsen has been working on an advanced brain simulator until exhaustion forces him to take a break. But when images of virtual reality start to hunt him, he suspects the only solution may be to kill someone. The problem is *who*?

J. G. Ballard has stood apart since the Fifties as a daring and controversial writer – and was once again at the centre of media attention in 1996 when David Cronenberg filmed his novel *Crash*, about the obsession of people with mutilation and death on the roads. One critic described the picture as 'violent, nasty and morally vacuous' and several authorities tried to ban it from being shown publicly. The clamouring headlines did not surprise Jim, who has frequently been attacked over his uncompromising tales of wasted landscapes, perverse individuals and decaying societies.

Born in Shanghai, Ballard spent his early childhood in a Japanese POW Camp, brilliantly recreated in *Empire of the Sun* (1984) which was filmed by Steven Spielberg in 1987. He returned to England after the war and began to write after a brief time at Cambridge University reading medicine. In the Sixties he was at the forefront of the new generation of young writers who challenged the perceptions of reality in their work, and his stories of near-future disaster, including *The Drowned World* (1962), *The Terminal Beach* (1964) and *The Atrocity Exhibition* (1970), assured his reputation. Ballard has also written a very under-rated murder mystery, *Running Wild* (1988), set in the Thames Valley where he lives. 'Zone of Terror' was first published in *New Worlds* in 1967.

Larsen had been waiting all day for Bayliss, the psychologist who lived in the next chalet, to pay the call he had promised on the previous evening. Characteristically, Bayliss had made no precise arrangements as regards time; a tall, moody man with an off-hand manner, he had merely gestured vaguely with his hypodermic and mumbled something about the following day: he would look in, probably. Larsen knew damned well he would look in, the case was too interesting to miss. In an oblique way it meant as much to Bayliss as it did to himself.

Except that it was Larsen who had to do the worrying – by three that afternoon Bayliss had still not materialized. What was he doing except sitting in his white-walled, air-conditioned lounge, playing Bartok quartets on the stereogram? Meanwhile Larsen had nothing to do but roam around the chalet, slamming impatiently from one room to the next like a tiger with an anxiety neurosis, and cook up a quick lunch (coffee and three amphetamines, from a private cache Bayliss as yet only dimly suspected. God, he needed the stimulants after those massive barbiturate shots Bayliss had pumped into him after the attack.) He tried to settle down with Kretschmer's *An Analysis of Psychotic Time*, a heavy tome, full of graphs and tabular material, which Bayliss had insisted he read, asserting that it filled in necessary background to the case. Larsen had spent a couple of hours on it, but so far he had got no further than the preface to the third edition.

Periodically he went over to the window and peered through the plastic blind for any signs of movement in the next chalet. Beyond, the desert lay in the sunlight like an enormous bone, against which the aztec-red fins of Bayliss's Pontiac flared like the tail feathers of a flamboyant phoenix. The remaining three chalets were empty; the complex was operated by the electronics company for which he and Bayliss worked as a sort of 're-creational' centre for senior executives and tired 'think-men'. The desert site had been chosen for its hypotensive virtues, its supposed equivalence to psychic zero. Two or three days of leisurely reading, of watching the motionless horizon, and tension and anxiety thresholds rose to more useful levels.

However, two days there, Larsen reflected, and he had very nearly gone mad. It was lucky Bayliss had been around with his hypodermic. Though the man was certainly casual when it came to supervising his patients; he left them to their own resources. In fact, looking back, he – Larsen – had been responsible for just about all the diagnosis. Bayliss had done little more than thumb his hypo, toss Kretschmer into his lap, and offer some cogitating asides.

Perhaps he was waiting for something?

Larsen tried to decide whether to phone Bayliss on some pretext; his number – O, on the internal system – was almost too inviting. Then he heard a door clatter outside, and saw the tall, angular figure of the psychologist crossing the concrete apron between the chalets, head bowed pensively in the sharp sunlight.

Where's his case, Larsen thought, almost disappointed. Don't tell me he's putting on the barbiturate brakes. Maybe he'll try hypnosis. Masses of post-hypnotic suggestions, in the middle of shaving I'll suddenly stand on my head.

He let Bayliss in, fidgeting around him as they went into the lounge.

'Where the hell have you been?' he asked. 'Do you realize it's nearly four?'

Bayliss sat down at the miniature executive desk in the middle of the lounge and looked round critically, a ploy Larsen resented but never managed to anticipate.

'Of course I realize it. I'm fully wired for time. How have you felt today?' He pointed to the straight-backed chair placed in the interviewee's position. 'Sit down and try to relax.'

Larsen gestured irritably. 'How can I relax while I'm just hanging around here, waiting for the next bomb to go off?' He began his analysis of the past twenty-four hours, a task he enjoyed, larding the case history with liberal doses of speculative commentary.

'Actually, last night was easier. I think I'm entering a new zone. Everything's beginning to stabilize, I'm not looking over my shoulder all the time. I've left the inside doors open, and before I enter a room I deliberately anticipate it, try to extrapolate its depth and dimensions so that it doesn't *surprise* me – before I used to open a door and just dive through like a man stepping into an empty lift shaft.'

Larsen paced up and down, cracking his knuckles. Eyes half closed, Bayliss watched him. 'I'm pretty sure there won't be another attack,' Larsen continued. 'In fact, the best thing is probably for me to get straight back to the plant. After all, there's no point in sitting around here indefinitely. I feel more or less completely okay.'

Bayliss nodded. 'In that case, then, why are you so jumpy?'

Exasperated, Larsen clenched his fists. He could almost hear the artery thudding in his temple. 'I'm *not* jumpy! For God's sake, Bayliss, I thought the advanced view was that psychiatrist and patient shared the illness together, forgot their own identities and took equal responsibility. You're trying to evade –'

'I am not,' Bayliss cut in firmly. 'I accept complete responsibility for you. That's why I want you to stay here until you've come to terms with this thing.'

Larsen snorted. '"Thing"! Now you're trying to make it sound like something out of a horror film. All I had was a simple hallucination. And I'm not even completely convinced it was that.' He pointed through the window. 'Suddenly opening the garage door in that bright sunlight – it might have been a shadow.'

'You described it pretty exactly,' Bayliss commented. 'Colour of the hair, moustache, the clothes he wore.'

'Back projection. The detail in dreams is authentic too.' Larsen moved the chair out of the way and leaned forwards across the desk. 'Another thing. I don't feel you're being entirely frank.'

Their eyes levelled. Bayliss studied Larsen carefully for a moment, noticing his widely dilated pupils.

'Well?' Larsen pressed.

Bayliss buttoned his jacket and walked across to the door. 'I'll call in tomorrow. Meanwhile try to unwind yourself a little. I'm not trying to alarm you, Larsen, but this problem may be rather more complicated than you imagine.' He nodded, then slipped out before Larsen could reply.

Larsen stepped over to the window and through the blind watched the psychologist disappear into his chalet. Disturbed for a moment, the sunlight again settled itself heavily over everything. A few minutes later the sounds of one of the Bartok quartets whined fretfully across the apron.

Larsen went back to the desk and sat down, elbows thrust forwards aggressively. Bayliss irritated him, with his neurotic music and inaccurate diagnoses. He felt tempted to climb straight into his car and drive back to the plant. Strictly speaking, though, the psychologist outranked Larsen, and probably had executive authority over him while he was at the chalet, particularly as the five days he had spent there were on the company's time.

He gazed round the silent lounge, tracing the cool horizontal shadows that dappled the walls, listening to the low soothing hum of the air-conditioner. His argument with Bayliss had refreshed him and he felt composed and confident. Yet residues of tension and uneasiness still existed, and he found it difficult to keep his eyes off the open doors to the bedroom and kitchen.

He had arrived at the chalet five days earlier, exhausted and over-wrought, on the verge of a total nervous collapse. For three months he had been working without a break on programming the complex circuitry of a huge brain simulator which the company's Advanced Designs Division were building for one of the major psychiatric foundations. This was a complete electronic replica of the central nervous system, each spinal level represented by a single computer, other computers holding memory banks in which sleep, tension, aggression and other psychic functions were coded and stored, building blocks that could be played into the CNS simulator to construct models of dissociation states and withdrawal syndromes – any psychic complex on demand.

The design teams working on the simulator had been watched vigilantly by Bayliss and his assistants, and the weekly tests had revealed the mounting load of fatigue that Larsen was carrying. Finally Bayliss had pulled him off the project and sent him out to the desert for two or three days' recuperation.

Larsen had been glad to get away. For the first two days he had lounged aimlessly around the deserted chalets, pleasantly fuddled by the barbiturates Bayliss prescribed, gazing out across the white deck of the desert floor, going to bed by eight and sleeping until noon. Every morning the caretaker had driven in from the town near by to clean up and leave the groceries and menu slips, but Larsen never saw her. He was only too glad to be alone. Deliberately seeing no one, allowing the natural rhythms of his mind to re-establish themselves, he knew he would soon recover.

In fact, however, the first person he had seen had stepped up to him straight out of a nightmare.

Larsen still looked back on the encounter with a shudder.

After lunch on his third day at the chalet he had decided to drive out into the desert and examine an old quartz mine in one of the canyons. This was a two-hour trip and he had made up a thermos of iced martini. The garage was adjacent to the chalet, set back from the kitchen side entrance, and fitted with a roll steel door that lifted vertically and curved up under the roof.

Larsen had locked the chalet behind him, then raised the garage door and driven his car out on to the apron. Going back for the thermos which he had left on the bench at the rear of the garage, he had noticed a full can of petrol in the shadows against one corner. For a moment he paused, adding up his mileage, and decided to take the can with him. He carried it over to the car, then turned round to close the garage door.

The roll had failed to retract completely when he had first raised it, and reached down to the level of his chin. Putting his weight on the handle, Larsen managed to move it down a few inches, but the inertia was too much for him. The sunlight reflected in the steel panels was dazzling his eyes. Pressing his palms under the door, he jerked it upwards slightly to gain more momentum on the downward swing.

The space was small, no more than six inches, but it was just enough for him to see into the darkened garage.

Hiding in the shadows against the back wall near the bench was the indistinct but nonetheless unmistakable figure of a man. He stood motionless, arms loosely at his sides, watching Larsen. He wore a light cream suit – covered by patches of shadow that gave him a curious fragmentary look – a neat blue sports-shirt and two-tone shoes. He was stockily built, with a thick brush moustache, a plump face, and eyes that stared steadily at Larsen but somehow seemed to be focused beyond him.

Still holding the door with both hands, Larsen gaped at the man. Not only was there no means by which he could have entered the garage – there were no windows or side doors – but there was something aggressive about his stance.

Larsen was about to call to him when the man moved forward and stepped straight out of the shadows towards him.

Aghast, Larsen backed away. The dark patches across the man's suit were not shadows at all, but the outline of the work bench directly behind him.

The man's body and clothes were transparent.

Galvanized into life, Larsen seized the garage door and hurled it down. He snapped the bolt in and jammed it closed with both hands, knees pressed against it.

Half paralysed by cramp and barely breathing, his suit soaked with sweat, he was still holding the door down when Bayliss drove up thirty minutes later.

Larsen drummed his fingers irritably on the desk, stood up and went into the kitchen. Cut off from the barbiturates they had been intended to counteract, the three amphetamines had begun to make him feel restless and overstimulated. He switched the coffee percolator on and then off, prowled back to the lounge and sat down on the sofa with the copy of Kretschmer.

He read a few pages, increasingly impatient. What light Kretschmer threw on his problem was hard to see; most of the case histories described deep schizos and irreversible paranoids. His own problem was much more superficial, a momentary aberration due to overloading. Why wouldn't Bayliss see this? For some reason he seemed to be unconsciously wishing for a major crisis, probably because he, the psychologist, secretly wanted to become the patient.

Larsen tossed the book aside and looked out through the window at the desert. Suddenly the chalet seemed dark and cramped, a claustrophobic focus of suppressed aggressions. He stood up, strode over to the door and stepped out into the clear open air.

Grouped in a loose semicircle, the chalets seemed to shrink towards the ground as he strolled to the rim of the concrete apron a hundred yards away. The mountains behind loomed up enormously. It was late afternoon, on the edge of dusk, and the sky was a vivid vibrant blue, the deepening colours of the desert floor overlaid by the huge lanes of shadow that reached from the mountains against the sun-line. Larsen looked back at the chalets. There was no sign of movement, other than a faint discordant echo of the atonal music Bayliss was playing. The whole scene seemed suddenly unreal.

Reflecting on this, Larsen felt something shift inside his mind. The sensation was undefined, like an expected cue that had failed to materialize, a forgotten intention. He tried to recall it, unable to remember whether he had switched on the coffee percolator.

He walked back to the chalets, noticing that he had left the kitchen door open. As he passed the lounge window on his way to close it he glanced in.

A man was sitting on the sofa, legs crossed, face hidden by the volume of Kretschmer. For a moment Larsen assumed that Bayliss had called in to see him, and walked on, deciding to make coffee for them both. Then he noticed that the stereogram was still playing in Bayliss's chalet.

Picking his steps carefully, he moved back to the lounge window. The man's face was still hidden, but a single glance confirmed that the visitor was not Bayliss. He was wearing the same cream suit Larsen had seen two days earlier, the same two-tone shoes. But this time the man was no hallucination; his hands and clothes were solid and palpable. He shifted about on the sofa, denting one of the cushions, and turned a page of the book, flexing the spine between his hands.

Pulse thickening, Larsen braced himself against the window-ledge. Something about the man, his posture, the way he held his hands, convinced him that he had seen him before their fragmentary encounter in the garage.

Then the man lowered the book and threw it on to the seat beside him. He sat back and looked through the window, his focus only a few inches from Larsen's face.

Mesmerized, Larsen stared back at him. He recognized the man without doubt, the pudgy face, the nervous eyes, the too thick moustache. Now at last he could see him clearly and realized he knew him only too well, better than anyone else on Earth.

The man was himself.

Bayliss clipped the hypodermic into his valise, and placed it on the lid of the stereogram.

'Hallucination is the wrong term altogether,' he told Larsen, who was lying stretched out on Bayliss's sofa, sipping weakly at a glass of hot whisky. 'Stop using it. A psycho-retinal image of remarkable strength and duration, but not an hallucination.'

Larsen gestured feebly. He had stumbled into Bayliss's chalet an hour earlier, literally beside himself with fright. Bayliss had calmed him down, then dragged him back across the apron to the lounge window and made him accept that his double was gone. Bayliss was not in the least surprised at the identity of the phantom, and this worried Larsen almost as much as the actual hallucination. What else was Bayliss hiding up his sleeve?

'I'm surprised you didn't realize it sooner yourself,' Bayliss remarked. 'Your description of the man in the garage was so obvious – the same cream suit, the same shoes and shirt let alone the exact physical similarity, even down to your moustache.'

Recovering a little, Larsen sat up. He smoothed down his cream gabardine suit and brushed the dust off his brown-and-white shoes. 'Thanks for warning me. All you've got to do now is tell me who he is.'

Bayliss sat down in one of the chairs. 'What do you mean, who he is? He's you, of course.'

'I know that, but why, where does he come from? God, I must be going insane.'

Bayliss snapped his fingers. 'No you're not. Pull yourself together. This is a purely functional disorder, like double vision or amnesia; nothing more serious. If it was, I'd have pulled you out of here long ago. Perhaps I should have done that anyway, but I think we can find a safe way out of the maze you're in.'

He took a notebook out of his breast pocket. 'Let's have a look at what we've got. Now, two features stand out. First, the phantom is yourself. There's no doubt about that; he's an exact replica of you. More important, though, he is you as you are now, your exact contemporary in time, unidealized and unmutilated. He isn't the shining hero of the super-ego, or the haggard greybeard of the death wish. He is simply a photographic double. Displace one eyeball with your finger and you'll see a double of me. Your double is no more unusual, with the exception that the displacement is not in space but in time. You see, the second thing I noticed about your garbled description of this phantom was that, not only was he a photographic double, but he was doing exactly what you yourself had been doing a few minutes previously. The man in the garage was standing by the workbench, just where you stood when you were wondering whether to take the can of petrol. Again, the man reading in the armchair was merely repeating exactly what you had been doing with the same book five minutes earlier. He even stared out of the window as you say you did before going out for a stroll.'

Larsen nodded, sipping his whisky. 'You're suggesting that the hallucination was a mental flashback?'

'Precisely. The stream of retinal images reaching the optic lobe is nothing more than a film strip. Every image is stored away, thousands of reels, a hundred thousand hours of running time. Usually flashbacks are deliberate, when we consciously select a few blurry stills from the film library, a childhood scene, the image of our neighbourhood streets we carry around with us all day near the surface of consciousness. But upset the projector slightly – overstrain could do it – jolt it back a few hundred frames, and you'll superimpose a completely irrelevant strip of already exposed film, in your case a glimpse of yourself sitting on the sofa. It's the apparent irrelevancy that is so frightening.'

Larsen gestured with his glass. 'Wait a minute, though. When I was sitting on the sofa reading Kretschmer I didn't actually see myself, any more than I can see myself now. So where did the superimposed images come from?'

Bayliss put away his notebook. 'Don't take the analogy of the film strip too literally. You may not see yourself sitting on that sofa, but your awareness of being there is just as powerful as any visual corroboration. It's the stream of tactile, positional and psychic images that form the real data store. Very little extrapolation is needed to transpose the observer's eye a few yards to the other side of a room. Purely visual memories are never completely accurate anyway.'

'How do you explain why the man I saw in the garage was transparent?'

'Quite simply. The process was only just beginning, the intensity of the image was weak. The one you saw this afternoon was much stronger. I cut you off barbiturates deliberately, knowing full well that those stimulants you were taking on the sly would set off something if they were allowed to operate unopposed.'

He went over to Larsen, took his glass and refilled it from the decanter. 'But let's think of the future. The most interesting aspect of all this is the light it throws on one of the oldest archetypes of the human psyche – the ghost – and the whole supernatural army of phantoms, witches, demons and so on. Are they all, in fact, nothing more than psycho-retinal flashbacks, transposed images of the observer himself, jolted on to the retinal screen by fear, bereavement, religious obsession? The most notable thing about the majority of ghosts is how prosaically equipped they are, compared with the elaborate literary productions of the great mystics and dreamers. The nebulous white sheet is probably the observer's own nightgown. It's an interesting field for speculation. For example, take the most famous ghost in literature and reflect how much more sense Hamlet makes if you realize that the ghost of his murdered father is really Hamlet himself.'

'All right, all right,' Larsen cut in irritably. 'But how does this help me?'

Bayliss broke off his reflective up-and-down patrol of the floor and fixed an eye on Larsen. 'I'm coming to that. There are two methods of dealing with this disfunction of yours. The classical technique is to pump you full of tranquillizers and confine you to a bed for a year or so. Gradually your mind would knit together. Long job, boring for you and everybody else. The alternative method is, frankly, experimental, but I think it might work. I mentioned the phenomenon of the ghost because it's an interesting fact that although there have been tens of thousands of recorded cases of people being pursued by ghosts, and a few of the ghosts themselves being pursued, there have been no cases of ghost and observer actually meeting of their own volition. Tell me, what would have happened if, when you saw your double this afternoon, you had gone straight into the lounge and spoken to him?'

Larsen shuddered. 'Obviously nothing, if your theory holds. I wouldn't like to test it.'

'That's just what you're going to do. Don't panic. The next time you see a double sitting in a chair reading Kretschmer, go up and speak to him. If he doesn't reply sit down in the chair yourself. That's all you have to do.'

Larsen jumped up, gesticulating. 'For heaven's sake, Bayliss, are you crazy? Do you know what it's like to suddenly see yourself? All you want to do is run.'

'I realize that, but it's the worst thing you can do. Why whenever anyone grapples with a ghost does it always vanish instantly? Because forcibly occupying the same physical coordinates as the double jolts the psychic projector on to a single channel again. The two separate streams of retinal images coincide and fuse. You've got to try, Larsen. It may be quite an effort, but you'll cure yourself once and for all.'

Larsen shook his head stubbornly. 'The idea's insane.' To himself he added: I'd rather shoot the thing. Then he remembered the .38 in his suitcase, and the presence of the weapon gave him a stronger sense of security than all Bayliss's drugs and advice. The revolver was a simple symbol of aggression, and even if the phantom was only an intruder in his own mind, it gave that portion which still remained intact greater confidence, enough possibly to dissipate the double's power.

Eyes half closed with fatigue, he listened to Bayliss. Half an hour later he went back to his chalet, found the revolver and hid it under a magazine in the letterbox outside the front door. It was too conspicuous to carry, and anyway might fire accidentally and injure him. Outside the front door it would be safely hidden and yet easily accessible, ready to mete out a little old-fashioned punishment to any double dealer trying to get into the game.

Two days later, with unexpected vengeance, the opportunity came.

Bayliss had driven into town to buy a new stylus for the stereogram, leaving Larsen to prepare lunch for them while he was away. Larsen pretended to resent the chore, but secretly he was glad of something to do. He was tired of hanging around the chalets while Bayliss watched him as if he were an experimental animal, eagerly waiting for the next crisis. With luck this might never come, if only to spite Bayliss, who had been having everything too much his own way.

After laying the table in Bayliss's kitchenette and getting plenty of ice ready for the martinis (alcohol was just the thing, Larsen readily decided, a wonderful CNS depressant) he went back to his chalet and put on a clean shirt. On an impulse he decided to change his shoes and suit as well, and fished out the blue office serge and black oxfords he had worn on his way out to the desert. Not only were the associations of the cream suit and sports shoes unpleasant, but a complete change of costume might well forestall the double's reappearance, provide a fresh psychic image of himself powerful enough to suppress any wandering versions. Looking at himself in the mirror, he decided to carry the principle even further. He switched on his shaver and cut away his moustache. Then he thinned out his hair and plastered it back smoothly across his scalp.

The transformation was effective. When Bayliss climbed out of his car and walked into the lounge he almost failed to recognize Larsen. He flinched back at the sight of the sleek-haired, dark-suited figure who stepped from behind the kitchen door.

'What the hell are you playing at?' he snapped at Larsen. 'This is no time for practical jokes.' He surveyed Larsen critically. 'You look like a cheap detective.'

Larsen guffawed. The incident put him in high spirits, and after several martinis he began to feel extremely buoyant. He talked away rapidly through the meal. Strangely, though, Bayliss seemed eager to get rid of him; he realized why shortly after he returned to his chalet. His pulse had quickened. He found himself prowling around nervously; his brain felt overactive and accelerated. The martinis had only been partly responsible for his elation. Now that they were wearing off he began to see the real agent – a stimulant Bayliss had given him in the hope of precipitating another crisis.

Larsen stood by the window, staring out angrily at Bayliss's chalet. The psychologist's utter lack of scruple outraged him. His fingers fretted nervously across the blind. Suddenly he felt like kicking the whole place down and speeding off. With its plywood-thin walls and matchbox furniture the chalet was nothing more than a cardboard asylum. Everything that had happened there, the breakdowns and his nightmarish phantoms, had probably been schemed up by Bayliss deliberately.

Larsen noticed that the stimulant seemed to be extremely powerful. The take-off was sustained and unbroken. He tried hopelessly to relax, went into the bedroom and kicked his suitcase around, lit two cigarettes without realizing it.

Finally, unable to contain himself any longer, he slammed the front door back and stormed out across the apron, determined to have everything out with Bayliss and demand an immediate sedative.

Bayliss's lounge was empty. Larsen plunged through into the kitchen and bedroom, discovered to his annoyance that Bayliss was having a shower. He hung around in the lounge for a few moments, then decided to wait in his chalet.

Head down, he crossed the bright sunlight at a fast stride, and was only a few steps from the darkened doorway when he noticed that a man in a blue suit was standing there watching him.

Heart leaping, Larsen shrank back, recognizing the double even before he had completely accepted the change of costume, the smooth-shaven face with its altered planes. The man hovered indecisively, flexing his fingers, and appeared to be on the verge of stepping down into the sunlight.

Larsen was about ten feet from him, directly in line with Bayliss's door. He backed away, at the same time swinging to his left to the lee of the garage. There he stopped and pulled himself together. The double was still hesitating in the doorway, longer, he was sure, than he himself had done. Larsen looked at the face, repulsed, not so much by the absolute accuracy of the image, but by a strange, almost luminous pastiness that gave the double's features the waxy sheen of a corpse. It was this unpleasant gloss that held Larsen back – the double was an arm's length from the letterbox holding the .38, and nothing could have induced Larsen to approach it.

He decided to enter the chalet and watch the double from behind. Rather than use the kitchen door, which gave access to the lounge on the double's immediate right, he turned to circle the garage and climb in through the bedroom window on the far side.

He was picking his way through a dump of old mortar and barbed wire behind the garage when he heard a voice call out:

'Larsen, you idiot, what do you think you're doing?'

It was Bayliss, leaning out of his bathroom window. Larsen stumbled, found his balance and waved Bayliss back angrily. Bayliss merely shook his head and leaned farther out, drying his neck with a towel.

Larsen retraced his steps, signalling to Bayliss to keep quiet. He was crossing the space between the garage wall and the near corner of Bayliss's chalet when out of the side of his eye he noticed a dark-suited figure standing with its back to him a few yards from the garage door.

The double had moved! Larsen stopped, Bayliss forgotten, and watched the double warily. He was poised on the balls of his feet, as Larsen had been only a minute or so earlier, elbows up, hands waving defensively. His eyes were hidden, but he appeared to be looking at the front door of Larsen's chalet.

Automatically, Larsen's eyes also moved to the doorway.

The original blue-suited figure still stood there, staring out into the sunlight.

There was not one double now, but two.

For a moment Larsen stared helplessly at the two figures, standing on either side of the apron like half-animated dummies in a waxworks tableau.

The figure with its back to him swung on one heel and began to stalk rapidly towards him. He gazed sightlessly at Larsen, the sunlight exposing his face. With a jolt of horror Larsen recognized for the first time the perfect similarity of the double – the same plump cheeks, the same mole by the right nostril, the white upper lip with the same small razor cut where the moustache had been shaved away. Above all he recognized the man's state of shock, the nervous lips, the tension around the neck and facial muscles, the utter exhaustion just below the surface of the mask.

His voice strangled, Larsen turned and bolted.

He stopped running about two hundred yards out in the desert beyond the edge of the apron. Gasping for breath, he dropped to one knee behind a narrow sandstone outcropping and looked back at the chalets. The second double was making his way around the garage, climbing through the tangle of old wire. The other was crossing the space between the chalets. Oblivious of them both, Bayliss was struggling with the bathroom window, forcing it back so that he could see out into the desert.

Trying to steady himself, Larsen wiped his face on his jacket sleeve. So Bayliss had been right, although he had never anticipated that more than one image could be seen during any single attack. But in fact Larsen had spawned two in close succession, each at a critical phase during the last five minutes. Wondering whether to wait for the images to fade, Larsen remembered the revolver in the letterbox. However irrational, it seemed his only hope. With it he would be able to test the ultimate validity of the doubles.

The outcropping ran diagonally to the edge of the apron. Crouching forwards, he scurried along it, pausing at intervals to follow the scene. The two doubles were still holding their positions, though Bayliss had closed his window and disappeared.

Larsen reached the edge of the apron, which was built on a shallow table about a foot off the desert floor, and moved along its rim to where an old fifty-gallon drum gave him a vantage point. To reach the revolver he decided to go round the far side of Bayliss's chalet, where he would find his own doorway unguarded except for the double watching by the garage.

He was about to step forward when something made him look over his shoulder.

Running straight towards him along the outcropping, head down, hands almost touching the ground, was an enormous ratlike creature. Every ten or fifteen yards it paused for a moment, and looked out at the chalets, and Larsen caught a glimpse of its face, insane and terrified, another replica of his own.

'Larsen! Larsen!'

Bayliss stood by the chalet, waving out at the desert.

Larsen glanced back at the phantom hurtling towards him, now only thirty feet away, then jumped up and lurched helplessly across to Bayliss.

Bayliss caught him firmly with his hands. 'Larsen, what's the matter with you? Are you having an attack?'

Larsen gestured at the figures around him. 'Stop them, Bayliss, for God's sake,' he gasped. 'I can't get away from them.'

Bayliss shook him roughly. 'You can see *more* than one? Where are they? Show me.'

Larsen pointed at the two figures hovering luminously near the chalet, then waved limply in the direction of the desert. 'By the garage, and over there along the wall. There's another hiding along that ridge.'

Bayliss seized him by the arm. 'Come on, man, you've got to face up to them, it's no use running.' He tried to drag Larsen towards the garage, but Larsen slipped down on to the concrete.

'I can't, Bayliss, believe me. There's a gun in my letter box. Get it for me. It's the only way.'

Bayliss hesitated, looking down at Larsen. 'All right. Try to hold on.'

Larsen pointed to the far corner of Bayliss's chalet. 'I'll wait over there for you.'

As Bayliss ran off he hobbled towards the corner. Halfway there he tripped across the remains of a ladder lying on the ground and twisted his right ankle between two of the rungs.

Clasping his foot, he sat down just as Bayliss appeared between the chalets, the revolver in his hand. He looked around for Larsen, who cleared his throat to call him.

Before he could open his mouth he saw the double who had followed him along the ridge leap up from behind the drum and stumble up to Bayliss across the concrete floor. He was dishevelled and exhausted, jacket almost off his shoulders, the tie knot under one ear. The image was still pursuing him, dogging his footsteps like an obsessed shadow.

Larsen tried to call to Bayliss again, but something he saw choked the voice in his throat.

Bayliss was looking at his double.

Larsen stood up, feeling a sudden premonition of terror. He tried to wave to Bayliss, but the latter was watching the double intently as it pointed to the figures near by, nodding to it in apparent agreement.

'Bayliss!'

The shot drowned his cry. Bayliss had fired somewhere between the garages, and the echo of the shot bounded among the chalets. The double was still beside him, pointing in all directions. Bayliss raised the revolver and fired again. The sound slammed across the concrete, making Larsen feel stunned and sick.

Now Bayliss too was seeing simultaneous images, not of himself but of Larsen, on whom his mind had been for the past weeks. A repetition of Larsen stumbling over to him and pointing at the phantoms was being repeated in Bayliss's mind, at the exact moment when he had returned with the revolver and was searching for a target.

Larsen started to crawl away, trying to reach the corner. A third shot roared through the air, the flash reflected in the bathroom window.

He had almost reached the corner when he heard Bayliss shout. Leaning one hand against the wall, he looked back.

Mouth open, Bayliss was staring wildly at him, the revolver clenched like a bomb in his hand. Beside him the blue-suited figure stood quietly, straightening its tie. At last Bayliss had realized he could see two images of Larsen, one beside him, the other twenty feet away against the chalet.

But how was he to know which was the real Larsen? Staring at Larsen, he seemed unable to decide.

Then the double by his shoulder raised one arm and pointed at Larsen, towards the corner wall to which he himself had pointed a minute earlier.

Larsen tried to shout, then hurled himself at the wall and pulled himself along it. Behind him Bayliss's feet came thudding across the concrete.

He heard only the first of the three shots.

ONLINE: THREE/3 Subject: The Punks

Tricentennial

John Shirley

INFO: It's Independence Day – a time for citizens to celebrate, join the procession and attend a Public Executions party in the afternoon. The joy-boy gangs, the frags, the hustlers and the sliders are on the move, too, with the cops on their Security Cycles keeping a close look-out for trouble. Two punks, Ollie and Lem, are just about to walk into it ...

John Shirley is recognised as the first punk science fiction writer and apart from his ever-growing stature as an author, he is also an influential musician who has fronted two bands, Sado Nation and The Monitors. Born in Portland, Oregon, and with no particular interest in college or work, John moved to San Francisco in 1974 and there got his first taste of the underside of life which he later drew on to colour his brutal and surreal stories about anarchic characters in not-so-futuristic settings. *City Come A-Walkin'* (1980) offered a harsh picture of inner-city life and was followed by *The Brigade* (1982), a thriller about vigilantism with a punk as the central character.

Since settling in Los Angeles, John has combined his careers in music and fiction, producing a number of chaotic horror novels and the highly regarded 'Song Called Youth' trilogy which describes the bloody conflict waged after World War Three by a clever, well-armed resistance movement against a neofascist regime. He has also written a number of off-beat crime short stories including 'Kamus of Kadizhar: A Tale of the Darkworld Detective' (1988) and 'War and Peace' (1995), a horrific portrait of a corrupt Chicago policeman. John wrote 'Tricentennial' for the *Portland Scribe* in 1976.

I.

'Precisely what do you suggest *I* do about it?' asked Ollie.

'You're hedging. You know what has to be done. You got to go get one,' said his sister Lem coldly.

'Look – we can make one for him out of cardboard –'

'No. He wouldn't fall for it, he has to have the real thing. Cloth. With the official Tricentennial medallion on the stick. He's not *that* far gone. And if we don't do it Pops won't sign the release and he'll die without turning over the stall to us and then we'll be out in the street. And *you* are the oldest, Ollie-boy. So you are elected.'

'I don't know if I *want* to stay in this grimy cubey. I could be in the Angels. I got a Hell's Angels Officers' School commission and I see no reason why I shouldn't –'

'Because it would be *worse*, that's why. You don't believe all that stuff they tell you at the Angels recruiting office about the Cycle Corps, do you? They have it just as bad as the Army, except they've got the Rape Decree to back up anything they do. But big deal. You get your rocks off but do you get a decent place to sleep?'

'Okay. Okay, then. But – I ain't goin' alone. No way. If we're gonna get it for him, *you* are goin' with me, back-up. Because there's no way to go two big ones on 53rd alone without getting it in the back ... Look, are you sure we can't get one in Building Three?'

'I'm sure. I've called around. All the dispensaries are out of them except Eleven.'

'Maybe we can roll the old man on the hundredth floor. He's got one.'

'He's got microwave barriers. We'd fry.'

Ollie sighed. 'Then let's go. And when we bring it back I hope to God the old sonuvabitch is happy with it. Because if he's not, Father or no Father –'

'Okay, don't get toxed. Let's go.'

II.

At first, the mental streets seemed almost deserted. The frags and the joy-boy gangs and the hustlers and sliders were there, just out of sight, but Security was keeping them off the street for the Tricentennial Procession. Ollie'd heard the procession might traverse the 53rd Level but he'd assumed it would move through some less dilapidated end of the street. Maybe it all looked this way.

Crusted with grey-white scum from exhalations of methane engines and human pores, the kelp-fiber walls of the five stories visible on the 53rd Level bulged slightly outward with the weight of excess population – each stall cubey held at least five people more than regulations. Ollie cradled the Smith & Wesson .44 he'd received at age fourteen, on his Weaponing Day. He held it now, five years later, as another man might have clasped a crucifix, and he whispered to it piously, while his eyes swept the rust-pitted streets, sorting through the heaps of litter waiting for the dumper, the piles of garbage, the half-dozen corpses that were as much a part of any street as the fire hydrants. The streetlights extending from warped and peeling faces of the buildings were all functioning and the vents near the ceiling within the plasteel girder underpinnings of the 54th Level were all inhaling, judging from the thinness of the smogs wreathing the dark doorwells. There were only about twenty-five homeless or gangbugs on the street and no cars – nearly desolation, compared to any other time. Apparently the Procession was near.

Ollie and Lem, crouching just inside the doorway to their home-building, rechecked their weapons and scanned the sidewalk for booby-traps. 'I don't see anything we can't handle,' Lem said.

'We can't see into the alleys or doorways or that subway entrance. And –' Ollie was interrupted by the blast of a siren. A few ragged silhouettes shuffling the street scurried for doorways at the wailing from the cornice speakers. Others hardly looked up. 'Looks like all that's left are dope-heads who don't know from shit. Christ, they so far gone they don't know the clear-streets when they hear it.'

As the siren wound down Lem asked, 'How long since you been on the street?'

'This first time in three years. Looks pretty much th' same. Only more dope-heads.'

'Always more dope-heads. They don't get gutted much because they don't have any money.'

'Well. Let's go, maybe we can dash the whole two blocks. I mean, since the streets are almost empty –'

'You haven't been on the streets in three years. You don't know –' Lem began.

'You're jimmy for venturing on to the streets when you don't need to. We've got everything we need on our floor, all the dispensaries and spas are there, and it's the same everywhere anyway and since you can't leave the Zone without a permit or unless you go with the troops, why bother?'

'We've got a half hour to get to Building Eleven. Let's do it.'

Both of them were dressed in scum-grey clothing, camouflage, their faces smeared with gray ash so their pallor would blend, as much as possible, into the walls.

Lem, tall and thin, the fire in her curly red hair extinguished with ash, stood and checked her brace of throwing knives; inspected the Uzi she'd got two years before on her Weaponing Day, and the cans of acid-bombs affixed to the two khaki belts criss-crossing her chest.

Ollie examined his own equipment, certified that the extra pistol he kept in his shoulder-holster was loaded and ready, the knives on springs lashed to his forearms primed. His .44 loaded and cocked.

Lem behind, walking backwards to cover the rear, they set off, looking like some odd two-headed predatory creature. The lineaments of the dour metal streets converged in a mesh of street-lamps, girders, stairways, and furtive figures, made tenebrously unreal by the smudged air and dim mucous-yellow lighting. The vista, shackled by metal ceiling and street merged in the distance, had all the elegance of a car crumpled into a cube by a hydraulic-press compactor. Ollie adjusted his infrared visors to see into the darker lairs. A frag, there to the right. The frag was a woman, left breast burned off to make room for a rifle-strap, a patch over her right eye. She waited, leaning back against the wall, her lower half hidden by a multiplex heap of refuse. Ollie hadn't been on the street in years, but the indications were ever the same: the suspect looked casual, relaxed – and that was bad. If she wasn't planning to attack them, she'd look tensed, in defense. So she was preparing to jump.

She was twenty feet off, on the low right, standing in the well of a barred basement doorway.

They carried $40 for their Old Man's toy. Frags could smell money. Even penniless, they'd be jumped for their clothes, guns, and on general principle.

The frag made as if to tie her bootlace. A signal. 'Down!' Ollie cried.

Lem and Ollie went to a crouch as the woman who had seen her accomplice's signal leapt from the doorway immediately to her right, and only her M-16's jamming saved them. Lem stepped in and, with an underhand cut, gutted the frag and withdrew the stiletto before she could reach for another weapon. By this time the other frag was swinging her rifle round to take aim. Ollie had already leveled the .44.

He squeezed the trigger, the gun barked, the jolt from the recoil hurt his wrist. The one-eyed woman caught it in the gut, was thrown back, rebounded from the wall, and pitched forward to fall on to her face. Blood marked a Rorschach visage leering in red on the wall behind her.

He heard Lem firing at the other frags attracted by the gunshots. A young man fell, pistol clattering into the gutter. The others found cover.

'C'mon!' They sprinted, running low to the ground, gaining another forty feet, three-quarters of the first block behind them. Another block-and-a-quarter, Ollie thought. Something lobbed in a wallowing tinny arc struck the sticky metal sidewalk and clattered past Ollie's right leg; he turned and grabbed Lem by the forearm, dragging her into the shelter of a doorway. The grenade exploded on the other side of the wall, fragments of the flimsy wall-fiber flew, laughter erupted from nearby frag-niches to echo from the distant ceiling, laughter as acid-drenched as the shrapnel that took out two dope-heads across the street. The blue smoke cleared.

A bullet struck the wall by Ollie's head, flying splinters stung his scalp. Swallowing fear – it had been three years – he crouched, panning his gunsight back and forth over the grey-black-engraved prospect. Sniper? From where? He looked up – that window, fourth floor. Glint off a barrel. He snatched free an acid cartridge and clipped it hastily on the launch spring welded to the underside of his pistol's barrel. He cocked, squinted, and fired. The sniper's rifle went off at the same moment, another shot too high. Then the acid-bomb exploded in the sniper's apartment. A scream that began as a rumble, went higher and higher in pitch, finishing as a bubbling whine that merged perfectly with the returning off-streets-siren, a growing, piercing ululation. The sniper, slapping at his boiling skin, threw himself whimpering out the window and fell, writhing, three stories, striking the ground head first. Stripping the corpses of the sniper, joy-boys and the two dead women, the frags were momentarily distracted. So Ollie and Lem sprinted, zig-zagging to make poor targets.

Bolting across the intersection, they drew fire. Four strident *cracks*, four *pings* – four misses. They achieved the opposite corner. Crouched behind a conical heap of excrement and plastic cans, their left side protected by the extruding metal side-walls of a stairway. 'Three-quarters of a block left,' said Lem.

But frags were closing in from the right, at least a dozen piebald figures creeping hastily from shadow to shadow like scuttling cockroaches.

One of the frags caught another unawares and slipped him a blade. There was a bubbling cough and that was all.

'One less,' said Lem. 'But they'll cooperate to kill us before they turn on each other again.'

A scratchy recorded fanfare announced the Tricentennial Procession.

The street was twenty yards from gutter to gutter. The Procession filled the street for half a block; two long, six-wheeled armored red-white-and-blue sedans surrounded by twelve Security Cycles. A recorded voice from the chrome-fanged grill of the front sedan announced over and over:

REJOICE INDEPENDENCE DAY REJOICE INDEPENDENCE DAY REJOICE

INDEPENDENCE DAY MAYOR WELCOMES ALL CITIZENS TO SEYMOR COLISEUM FOUR PM FOR PUBLIC EXECUTIONS PARTY REJOICE INDEPENDENCE DAY REJOICE REJOICE

Dimly, through the green-tinted window of the low, steel-plated limo, Ollie could make out the faces of the High Priest of the International Church of Sun Moon sitting beside the man he'd appointed as Mayor, whose name Ollie could not recall. A few token bullets bounced from the limo's windshield. The silhouettes within waved at the faces crowding the windows. A handful of excrement splattered the roof, cleaned away an instant later by tiny hoses in the windshield frame. One of the Security Cycles shot a microwave shell into the apartment from which the excrement had been thrown; there was a white flash and a scream, a thin wisp of smoke from the shattered window.

The Security Cycles were three-wheeled motorbikes, propelled, like the limousines, by methane engines fueled by gases extracted from human excrement. Issuing blue flatulence, they rolled slowly abreast of Ollie and Lem. The cops inside, figures of shiny black leather, heads completely encased in black-opaqued helmets, were protected by bells of transparent plasteel from which their various weapons projected cobra snouts. The cop nearest Ollie methodically snuffed dope-heads and careless frags with casual flares of his handle-bar-mounted microwave rifle. 'Hey,' Ollie breathed, 'maybe they'll help us. If you call them they don't come but since they're right here, if we ask them for help getting to the corner they can't refuse, seeing as we're right in front of them and all. Hell, with the High Priest watching ...'

'Ollie, don't be an asshole –'

But Ollie was already out in the street, waving his arms, shouting, 'We need an escort, just a little farther, we are citizens, we have to go to Building Eleven to buy a –'

He threw himself flat and rolled, wincing as the invisible microwave beam singed his back. The cop fired again but Lem had thrown a smoke-bomb, and Ollie took advantage of the thick yellow billowing to return to cover.

'Wish I could afford one of those microwave rifles,' Lem remarked wistfully.

'Hey, Lem, maybe if we keep just back of the procession we can use it for cover and get the rest of the way.'

Lem nodded and they were off.

Most of the frags were flattened to avoid the microwave beams; the cops ignored their shielded rear, so Ollie and Lem sprinted along behind, and Building Eleven loomed ahead. Ollie grinned. There! The stairs!

They were scrambling the two flights up the stairs when the doors to

Building Eleven swung open and a pack of joy-boys, none of them over twelve years old, stampeded directly into Lem and Ollie's reflexive gunfire. But there were too many of them to spray dead at short range. Five went down, another ten were upon them – naked but for belts bristling with makeshift knives. Their gap-toothed mouths squalling, drooling like demented elves, they chattered and snarled gleefully. Their sallow, grimy faces – seen as blurs personifying aggression, now – were pock-marked, the eyes dope-wild. Swinging the gun-butt in his right hand, the spring-snapped knife in his left, Ollie slashed and battered at the small faces, faces like rotted jack-o-lanterns, and time slowed: fragments of skull and teeth flew, black-nailed hands clawed at his face, his own blood clouded his visors.

Ollie plowed forward, kicking, elbowing, feeling a twisted shard of metal bite deep into his thigh, another below his left shoulder-blade, another in his right pectorals. He was two feet from the door. He left his knife in someone's ribs. He glanced at Lem, three of them were on her back, clinging like chimp-children, clawing relentlessly at her head, gnawing her ears with ragged yellow teeth. He dragged them off her with his left hand, wrenching viciously to keep them off his own back, and brained another who flailed wildly at his eyes – and then he and Lem were through the door.

It was cool and quiet inside.

A young man, a custodian chewing synthabetel and squinting at them, leaning on his mop, said, 'You got some holes in you.'

'Where –' Ollie had to catch his breath. He felt weak. Blood soaking his right leg – have to bind that before heading back, he thought, try again, ask: 'Where we buy ... flags?'

'Fifty-fourth level if he's got any left.'

III.

Luck was with them. They made it back with only two more wounds. A .22 slug in Lem's right arm, a zip gun pellet in Ollie's left calf.

Lem slumped outside the door to bind her wounds and rest. Ollie took the flag from her and staggered into their two-room apartment, stepped carefully over the children sleeping on the crowded floor, tried not to stagger. He was dizzy, nauseated. The tiny cubicle seemed to constrict and whirl, the stained yellow-white curtains over the alcove where his father lay dying on an army cot became malignant leprous arms reaching for him. He cursed, his right hand gripping the small, rolled-up flag. He felt he could not walk another step.

Ollie sank to a chink of clear floor-space. He shoved wearily at one of the sleeping children. Eight-year-old Sandra. She woke, a pale, hollow-eyed child, nearly bald, a few strands of wispy flaxen hair. 'You take this to Pops,' he told her. 'The flag. Tell him to sign the goddamn release.'

Seeing the flag, the little girl's eyes flared. She snatched the bright banner away and ran out into the hall, ignoring Ollie's shouts.

She got three bucks for the flag from a man on the Hundredth Level.

A penny a year.

ONLINE: **THREE/4** *Subject*: The Yakuza

Johnny Mnemonic

William Gibson

INFO: Johnny Mnemonic packs a shotgun in his bag and reckons he's ready for any trouble in the Drome. He's got a meeting with Ralfi Face who wants to put out a contract on him. But the Yakuza are interested in him, too, and *what* awaits him on the Killing Floor?

William Gibson is today's most famous writer of virtual reality stories and no other author is more closely identified with the genre. Certainly when it comes to evoking the experiences of cyberspace he has few equals. Born in Virginia, Gibson discovered sf through the books of Robert Heinlein. After the death of his parents while he was still in his teens, he crossed the border to Toronto where he has lived and worked ever since. His first short story, 'Fragments of a Hologram Rose' (1976), imagined a computer-generated world of virtual reality; and in 1984 he wrote his now legendary novel *Neuromancer*. It combined high-tech illusions, a desolate city and streetwise inhabitants in a hard-boiled crime fiction style and won all the year's major prizes: Hugo, Nebula and Philip K. Dick awards. The book was also remarkable because Gibson admitted he knew little about computers before he wrote it, yet still anticipated the Internet. He has since completed 'The Neuromancer Trilogy' with *Count Zero* (1986) and *Mona Lisa Overdrive* (1988).

Gibson has also collaborated with Bruce Sterling on several short stories and a visionary 'steampunk' novel, *The Difference Engine* (1990), about the Victorian inventor who built the world's first computer. 'Johnny Mnemonic' was first published in *Omni* in 1981 and subsequently filmed in 1995 by Robert Longo starring Keanu Reeves.

I put the shotgun in an Adidas bag and padded it out with four pairs of tennis socks, not my style at all, but that was what I was aiming for: if they think you're crude, go technical; if they think you're technical, go crude. I'm a very technical boy. So I decided to get as crude as possible. These days, though, you have to be pretty technical before you can even aspire to crudeness. I'd had to turn both those twelve-gauge shells from brass stock, on a lathe, and then load them myself; I'd had to dig up an old microfiche with instructions for hand-loading cartridges; I'd had to build a lever-action press to seat the primers – all very tricky. But I knew they'd work.

The meet was set for the Drome at 2300, but I rode the tube three stops past the closest platform and walked back. Immaculate procedure.

I checked myself out in the chrome siding of a coffee kiosk, your basic sharp-faced Caucasoid with a ruff of stiff, dark hair. The girls at Under the Knife were big on Sony Mao, and it was getting harder to keep them from adding the chic suggestion of epicanthic folds. It probably wouldn't fool Ralfi Face, but it might get me next to his table.

The Drome is a single narrow space with a bar down one side and tables along the other, thick with pimps and handlers and an arcane array of dealers. The Magnetic Dog Sisters were on the door that night, and I didn't relish trying to get out past them if things didn't work out. They were two meters tall and thin as greyhounds. One was black and the other white, but aside from that they were as nearly identical as cosmetic surgery could make them. They'd been lovers for years and were bad news in a tussle. I was never quite sure which one had originally been male.

Ralfi was sitting at his usual table. Owing me a lot of money. I had hundreds of megabytes stashed in my head on an idiot/savant basis, information I had no conscious access to. Ralfi had left it there. He hadn't, however, come back for it. Only Ralfi could retrieve the data, with a code phrase of his own invention. I'm not cheap to begin with, but my overtime on storage is astronomical. And Ralfi had been very scarce.

Then I'd heard that Ralfi Face wanted to put out a contract on me. So I'd arranged to meet him in the Drome, but I'd arranged it as Edward Bax, clandestine importer, late of Rio and Peking.

The Drome stank of biz, a metallic tang of nervous tension. Muscle-boys scattered through the crowd were flexing stock parts at one another and trying on thin, cold grins, some of them so lost under superstructures of muscle graft that their outlines weren't really human.

Pardon me. Pardon me, friends. Just Eddie Bax here, Fast Eddie the Importer, with his professionally nondescript gym bag, and please ignore this slit, just wide enough to admit his right hand.

Ralfi wasn't alone. Eighty kilos of blond California beef perched alertly in the chair next to his, martial arts written all over him.

Fast Eddie Bax was in the chair opposite them before the beef's hands were off the table. 'You black belt?' I asked eagerly. He nodded, blue eyes running an automatic scanning pattern between my eyes and my hands. 'Me, too,' I said. 'Got mine here in the bag.' And I shoved my hand through the slit and thumbed the safety off. Click. 'Double twelve-gauge with the triggers wired together.'

'That's a gun,' Ralfi said, putting a plump, restraining hand on his boy's taut blue nylon chest. 'Johnny has an antique firearm in his bag.' So much for Edward Bax.

I guess he'd always been Ralfi Something or Other, but he owed his acquired surname to a singular vanity. Built something like an overripe pear, he'd worn the once-famous face of Christian White for twenty years – Christian White of the Aryan Reggae Band, Sony Mao to his generation, and final champion of race rock. I'm a whiz at trivia.

Christian White: classic pop face with a singer's high-definition muscles, chiseled cheekbones. Angelic in one light, handsomely depraved in another. But Ralfi's eyes lived behind that face, and they were small and cold and black.

'Please,' he said, 'let's work this out like businessmen.' His voice was marked by a horrible prehensile sincerity, and the corners of his beautiful Christian White mouth were always wet. 'Lewis here,' nodding in the beefboy's direction, 'is a meatball.' Lewis took this impassively, looking like something built from a kit. 'You aren't a meatball, Johnny.'

'Sure I am, Ralfi, a nice meatball chock-full of implants where you can store your dirty laundry while you go off shopping for people to kill me. From my end of this bag, Ralfi, it looks like you've got some explaining to do.'

'It's this last batch of product, Johnny.' He sighed deeply. 'In my role as broker –'

'Fence,' I corrected.

'As broker, I'm usually very careful as to sources.'

'You buy only from those who steal the best. Got it.'

He sighed again. 'I try,' he said wearily, 'not to buy from fools. This time, I'm afraid, I've done that.' Third sigh was the cue for Lewis to trigger the neural disruptor they'd taped under my side of the table.

I put everything I had into curling the index finger of my right hand, but I no longer seemed to be connected to it. I could feel the metal of the gun and the foam-padded tape I'd wrapped around the stubby grip, but my hands were cool wax, distant and inert. I was hoping Lewis was a true meatball, thick enough to go for the gym bag and snag my rigid trigger finger, but he wasn't.

'We've been very worried about you, Johnny. Very worried. You see, that's Yakuza property you have there. A fool took it from them, Johnny. A dead fool.'

Lewis giggled.

It all made sense then, an ugly kind of sense, like bags of wet sand settling around my head. Killing wasn't Ralfi's style. Lewis wasn't even Ralfi's style. But he'd got himself stuck between the Sons of the Neon Chrysanthemum and something that belonged to them – or, more likely, something of theirs that belonged to someone else. Ralfi, of course, could use the code phrase to throw me into idiot savant, and I'd spill their hot program without remembering a single quarter tone. For a fence like Ralfi, that would ordinarily have been enough. But not for the Yakuza. The Yakuza would know about Squids, for one thing, and they wouldn't want to worry about one lifting those dim and permanent traces of their program out of my head. I didn't know very much about Squids, but I'd heard stories, and I made it a point never to repeat them to my clients. No, the Yakuza wouldn't like that; it looked too much like evidence. They hadn't got where they were by leaving evidence around. Or alive.

Lewis was grinning. I think he was visualizing a point just behind my forehead and imagining how he could get there the hard way.

'Hey,' said a low voice, feminine, from somewhere behind my right shoulder, 'you cowboys sure aren't having too lively a time.'

'Pack it, bitch,' Lewis said, his tanned face very still. Ralfi looked blank.

'Lighten up. You want to buy some good free base?' She pulled up a chair and quickly sat before either of them could stop her. She was barely inside my fixed field of vision, a thin girl with mirrored glasses, her dark hair cut in a rough shag. She wore black leather, open over a T-shirt slashed diagonally with stripes of red and black. 'Eight thou a gram weight.'

Lewis snorted his exasperation and tried to slap her out of the chair. Somehow he didn't quite connect, and her hand came up and seemed to brush his wrist as it passed. Bright blood sprayed the table. He was clutching his wrist white-knuckle tight, blood trickling from between his fingers.

But hadn't her hand been empty?

He was going to need a tendon stapler. He stood up carefully, without bothering to push his chair back. The chair toppled backward, and he stepped out of my line of sight without a word.

'He better get a medic to look at that,' she said. 'That's a nasty cut.'

'You have no idea,' said Ralfi, suddenly sounding very tired, 'the depths of shit you have just gotten yourself into.'

'No kidding? Mystery. I get real excited by mysteries. Like why your friend here's so quiet. Frozen, like. Or what this thing here is for,' and she held up the little control unit that she'd somehow taken from Lewis. Ralfi looked ill.

'You, ah, want maybe a quarter-million to give me that and take a walk?' A fat hand came up to stroke his pale, lean face nervously.

'What I want,' she said, snapping her fingers so that the unit spun and glittered, 'is work. A job. Your boy hurt his wrist. But a quarter'll do for a retainer.'

Ralfi let his breath out explosively and began to laugh, exposing teeth that hadn't been kept up to the Christian White standard. Then she turned the disruptor off.

'Two million,' I said.

'My kind of man,' she said, and laughed. 'What's in the bag?'

'A shotgun.'

'Crude.' It might have been a compliment.

Ralfi said nothing at all.

'Name's Millions. Molly Millions. You want to get out of here, boss? People are starting to stare.' She stood up. She was wearing leather jeans the color of dried blood.

And I saw for the first time that the mirrored lenses were surgical inlays, the silver rising smoothly from her high cheekbones, sealing her eyes in their sockets. I saw my new face twinned there.

'I'm Johnny,' I said. 'We're taking Mr Face with us.'

He was outside, waiting. Looking like your standard tourist tech, in plastic zoris and a silly Hawaiian shirt printed with blowups of his firm's most popular microprocessor; a mild little guy, the kind most likely to wind up drunk on sake in a bar that puts out miniature rice crackers with seaweed garnish. He looked like the kind who sing the corporate anthem and cry, who shake hands endlessly with the bartender. And the pimps and the dealers would leave him alone, pegging him as innately conservative. Not up for much, and careful with his credit when he was.

The way I figured it later, they must have amputated part of his left thumb, somewhere behind the first joint, replacing it with a prosthetic tip, and cored the stump, fitting it with a spool and socket molded from one of the Ono-Sendai diamond analogs. Then they'd carefully wound the spool with three meters of monomolecular filament.

Molly got into some kind of exchange with the Magnetic Dog Sisters, giving me a chance to usher Ralfi through the door with the gym bag pressed lightly against the base of his spine. She seemed to know them. I heard the black one laugh.

I glanced up, out of some passing reflex, maybe because I've never got used to it, to the soaring arcs of light and the shadows of the geodesics above them. Maybe that saved me.

Ralfi kept walking, but I don't think he was trying to escape. I think he'd already given up. Probably he already had an idea of what we were up against.

I looked back down in time to see him explode.

Playback on full recall shows Ralfi stepping forward as the little tech sidles out of nowhere, smiling. Just a suggestion of a bow, and his left thumb falls off. It's a conjuring trick. The thumb hangs suspended. Mirrors? Wires? And Ralfi stops, his back to us, dark crescents of sweat under the armpits of his pale summer suit. He knows. He must have known. And then the joke-shop thumbtip, heavy as lead, arcs out in a lightning yo-yo trick, and the invisible thread connecting it to the killer's hand passes laterally through Ralfi's skull, just above his eyebrows, whips up, and descends, slicing the pear-shaped torso diagonally from shoulder to rib cage. Cuts so fine that no blood flows until synapses misfire and the first tremors surrender the body to gravity.

Ralfi tumbled apart in a pink cloud of fluids, the three mismatched sections rolling forward on to the tiled pavement. In total silence.

I brought the gym bag up, and my hand convulsed. The recoil nearly broke my wrist.

It must have been raining; ribbons of water cascaded from a ruptured geodesic and spattered on the tile behind us. We crouched in the narrow gap between a surgical boutique and an antique shop. She'd just edged one mirrored eye around the corner to report a single Volks module in front of the Drome, red lights flashing. They were sweeping Ralfi up. Asking questions.

I was covered in scorched white fluff. The tennis socks. The gym bag was a ragged plastic cuff around my wrist. 'I don't see how the hell I missed him.'

''Cause he's fast, so fast.' She hugged her knees and rocked back and forth on her bootheels. 'His nervous system's jacked up. He's factory custom.' She grinned and gave a little squeal of delight. 'I'm gonna get that boy. Tonight. He's the best, number one, top dollar, state of the art.'

'What you're going to get, for this boy's two million, is my ass out of here. Your boyfriend back there was mostly grown in a vat in Chiba City. He's a Yakuza assassin.'

'Chiba. Yeah. See, Molly's been Chiba, too.' And she showed me her hands, fingers slightly spread. Her fingers were slender, tapered, very white against the polished burgundy nails. Ten blades snicked straight out from their recesses beneath her nails, each one a narrow, double-edged scalpel in pale blue steel.

I'd never spent much time in Nighttown. Nobody there had anything to pay me to remember, and most of them had a lot they paid regularly to forget. Generations of sharpshooters had chipped away at the neon until the maintenance crews gave up. Even at noon the arcs were soot-black against faintest pearl.

Where do you go when the world's wealthiest criminal order is feeling for you with calm, distant fingers? Where do you hide from the Yakuza, so powerful that it owns comsats and at least three shuttles? The Yakuza is a true multinational, like ITT and Ono-Sendai. Fifty years before I was born the Yakuza had already absorbed the Triads, the Mafia, the Union Corse.

Molly had an answer: you hide in the Pit, in the lowest circle, where any outside influence generates swift, concentric ripples of raw menace. You hide in Nighttown. Better yet, you hide *above* Nighttown, because the Pit's inverted, and the bottom of its bowl touches the sky, the sky that Nighttown never sees, sweating under its own firmament of acrylic resin, up where the Lo Teks crouch in the dark like gargoyles, black-market cigarettes dangling from their lips.

She had another answer, too.

'So you're locked up good and tight, Johnny-san? No way to get that program without the password?' She led me into the shadows that waited beyond the bright tube platform. The concrete walls were overlaid with graffiti, years of them twisting into a single metascrawl of rage and frustration.

'The stored data are fed in through a modified series of microsurgical contraautism prostheses.' I reeled off a numb version of my standard sales pitch. 'Client's code is stored in a special chip; barring Squids, which we in the trade don't like to talk about, there's no way to recover your phrase. Can't drug it out, cut it out, torture it. I don't *know* it, never did.'

'Squids? Crawly things with arms?' We emerged into a deserted street market. Shadowy figures watched us from across a makeshift square littered with fish heads and rotting fruit.

'Superconducting quantum interference detectors. Used them in the war to find submarines, suss out enemy cyber systems.'

'Yeah? Navy stuff? From the war? Squid'll read that chip of yours?' She'd stopped walking, and I felt her eyes on me behind those twin mirrors.

'Even the primitive models could measure a magnetic field a billionth the strength of geomagnetic force; it's like pulling a whisper out of a cheering stadium.'

'Cops can do that already, with parabolic microphones and lasers.'

'But your data's still secure.' Pride in profession. 'No government'll let their cops have Squids, not even the security heavies. Too much chance of interdepartmental funnies; they're too likely to watergate you.'

'Navy stuff,' she said, and her grin gleamed in the shadows. 'Navy stuff. I got a friend down here who was in the navy, name's Jones. I think you'd better meet him. He's a junkie, though. So we'll have to take him something.'

'A junkie?'

'A dolphin.'

He was more than a dolphin, but from another dolphin's point of view he might have seemed like something less. I watched him swirling sluggishly in his galvanized tank. Water slopped over the side, wetting my shoes. He was surplus from the last war. A cyborg.

He rose out of the water, showing us the crusted plates along his sides, a kind of visual pun, his grace nearly lost under articulated armor, clumsy and prehistoric. Twin deformities on either side of his skull had been engineered to house sensor units. Silver lesions gleamed on exposed sections of his gray-white hide.

Molly whistled. Jones thrashed his tail, and more water cascaded down the side of the tank.

'What is this place?' I peered at vague shapes in the dark, rusting chain link and things under tarps. Above the tank hung a clumsy wooden framework, crossed and recrossed by rows of dusty Christmas lights.

'Funland. Zoo and carnival rides. "Talk with the War Whale". All that. Some whale Jones is ...'

Jones reared again and fixed me with a sad and ancient eye.

'How's he talk?' Suddenly I was anxious to go.

'That's the catch. Say "hi," Jones.'

All the bulbs lit simultaneously. They were flashing red, white, and blue.

RWBRWBRWB
RWBRWBRWB
RWBRWBRWB
RWBRWBRWB
RWBRWBRWB

'Good with symbols, see, but the code's restricted. In the navy they had him wired into an audiovisual display.' She drew the narrow package from a jacket pocket. 'Pure shit, Jones. Want it?' He froze in the water and started to sink. I felt a strange panic, remembering that he wasn't a fish, that he could drown. 'We want the key to Johnny's bank, Jones. We want it fast.'

The lights flickered, died.

'Go for it, Jones!'

```
        B
   BBBBBBBBB
        B
        B
        B
        B
        B
```

Blue bulbs, cruciform.
Darkness.
'Pure! It's *clean*. Come on, Jones.'

```
   WWWWWWWWW
   WWWWWWWWW
   WWWWWWWWW
   WWWWWWWWW
   WWWWWWWWW
```

White sodium glare washed her features, stark monochrome, shadows cleaving from her cheekbones.

```
   R    RRRRR
   R    R
   RRRRRRRR
        R   R
   RRRRR    R
```

The arms of the red swastika were twisted in her silver glasses. 'Give it to him,' I said. 'We've got it.'

Ralfi Face. No imagination.

Jones heaved half his armored bulk over the edge of his tank, and I thought the metal would give way. Molly stabbed him overhand with the Syrette, driving the needle between two plates. Propellant hissed. Patterns of light exploded, spasming across the frame and then fading to black.

We left him drifting, rolling languorously in the dark water. Maybe he was dreaming of his war in the Pacific, of the cyber mines he'd swept, nosing gently into their circuitry with the Squid he'd used to pick Ralfi's pathetic password from the chip buried in my head.

'I can see them slipping up when he was demobbed, letting him out of the navy with that gear intact, but how does a cybernetic dolphin get wired to smack?'

'The war,' she said. 'They all were. Navy did it. How else you get 'em working for you?'

'I'm not sure this profiles as good business,' the pirate said, angling for better money. 'Target specs on a comsat that isn't in the book –'

'Waste my time and you won't profile at all,' said Molly, leaning across his scarred plastic desk to prod him with her forefinger.

'So maybe you want to buy your microwaves somewhere else?' He was a tough kid, behind his Mao-job. A Nighttowner by birth, probably.

Her hand blurred down the front of his jacket, completely severing a lapel without even rumpling the fabric.

'So we got a deal or not?'

'Deal,' he said, staring at his ruined lapel with what he must have hoped was only polite interest. 'Deal.'

While I checked the two recorders we'd bought, she extracted the slip of paper I'd given her from the zippered wrist pocket of her jacket. She unfolded it and read silently, moving her lips. She shrugged. 'This is it?'

'Shoot,' I said, punching the RECORD studs of the two decks simultaneously.

'Christian White,' she recited, 'and his Aryan Reggae Band.'

Faithful Ralfi, a fan to his dying day.

Transition to idiot-savant mode is always less abrupt than I expect it to be. The pirate broadcaster's front was a failing travel agency in a pastel cube that boasted a desk, three chairs, and a faded poster of a Swiss orbital spa. A pair of toy birds with blown-glass bodies and tin legs were sipping monotonously from a Styrofoam cup of water on a ledge beside Molly's shoulder. As I phased into mode, they accelerated gradually until their Day-Glo-feathered crowns became solid arcs of color. The LEDs that told seconds on the plastic wall clock had become meaningless pulsing grids, and Molly and the Mao-faced boy grew hazy, their arms blurring occasionally in insect-quick ghosts of gesture. And then it all faded to cool gray static and an endless tone poem in an artificial language.

I sat and sang dead Ralfi's stolen program for three hours.

The mall runs forty kilometers from end to end, a ragged overlap of Fuller domes roofing what was once a suburban artery. If they turn off the arcs on a clear day, a gray approximation of sunlight filters through layers of acrylic, a view like the prison sketches of Giovanni Piranesi. The three southernmost kilometers roof Nighttown. Nighttown pays no taxes, no utilities. The neon arcs are dead, and the geodesics have been smoked black by decades of cooking fires. In the nearly total darkness of a Nighttown noon, who notices a few dozen mad children lost in the rafters?

We'd been climbing for two hours, up concrete stairs and steel ladders with perforated rungs, past abandoned gantries and dust-covered tools. We'd started in what looked like a disused maintenance yard, stacked with triangular roofing segments. Everything there had been covered with that same uniform layer of spraybomb graffiti: gang names, initials, dates back to the turn of the century. The graffiti followed us up, gradually thinning until a single name was repeated at intervals. LO TEK. In dripping black capitals.

'Who's Lo Tek?'

'Not us, boss.' She climbed a shivering aluminium ladder and vanished through a hole in a sheet of corrugated plastic. '"Low technique, low technology."' The plastic muffled her voice. I followed her up, nursing an aching wrist. 'Lo Teks, they'd think that shotgun trick of yours was effete.'

An hour later I dragged myself up through another hole, this one sawed crookedly in a sagging sheet of plywood, and met my first Lo Tek.

'"S okay,' Molly said, her hand brushing my shoulder. 'It's just Dog. Hey, Dog.'

In the narrow beam of her taped flash, he regarded us with his one eye and slowly extruded a thick length of grayish tongue, licking huge canines. I wondered how they wrote off tooth-bud transplants from Dobermans as low technology. Immunosuppressives don't exactly grow on trees.

'Moll.' Dental augmentation impeded his speech. A string of saliva dangled from his twisted lower lip. 'Heard ya comin'. Long time.' He might have been fifteen, but the fangs and a bright mosaic of scars combined with the gaping socket to present a mask of total bestiality. It had taken time and a certain kind of creativity to assemble that face, and his posture told me he enjoyed living behind it. He wore a pair of decaying jeans, black with grime and shiny along the creases. His chest and feet were bare. He did something with his mouth that approximated a grin. 'Bein' followed, you.'

Far off, down in Nighttown, a water vendor cried his trade.

'Strings jumping, Dog?' She swung her flash to the side, and I saw thin cords tied to eyebolts, cords that ran to the edge and vanished.

'Kill the fuckin' light!'

She snapped it off.

'How come the one who's followin' you's got no light?'

'Doesn't need it. That one's bad news, Dog. Your sentries give him a tumble, they'll come home in easy-to-carry sections.'

'This a *friend* friend, Moll?' He sounded uneasy. I heard his feet shift on the worn plywood.

'No. But he's mine. And this one,' slapping my shoulders, 'he's a friend. Got that?'

'Sure,' he said, without much enthusiasm, padding to the platform's edge, where the eyebolts were. He began to pluck out some kind of message on the taut cords.

Nighttown spread beneath us like a toy village for rats; tiny windows showed candlelight, with only a few harsh, bright squares lit by battery lanterns and carbide lamps. I imagined the old men at their endless games of dominoes, under warm, fat drops of water that fell from wet wash hung out on poles between the plywood shanties. Then I tried to imagine him climbing patiently up through the darkness in his zoris and ugly tourist shirt, bland and unhurried. How was he tracking us?

'Good,' said Molly. 'He smells us.'

'Smoke?' Dog dragged a crumpled pack from his pocket and prised out a flattened cigarette. I squinted at the trademark while he lit it for me with a kitchen match. Yiheyuan filters. Beijing Cigarette Factory. I decided that the Lo Teks were black marketeers. Dog and Molly went back to their argument, which seemed to revolve around Molly's desire to use some particular piece of Lo Tek real estate.

'I've done you a lot of favors, man. I want that floor. And I want the music.'

'You're not Lo Tek ...'

This must have been going on for the better part of a twisted kilometer, Dog leading us along swaying catwalks and up rope ladders. The Lo Teks leech their webs and huddling places to the city's fabric with thick gobs of epoxy and sleep above the abyss in mesh hammocks. Their country is so attenuated that in places it consists of little more than holds for hands and feet, sawed into geodesic struts.

The Killing Floor, she called it. Scrambling after her, my new Eddie Bax shoes slipping on worn metal and damp plywood, I wondered how it could be any more lethal than the rest of the territory. At the same time I sensed that Dog's protests were ritual and that she already expected to get whatever it was she wanted.

Somewhere beneath us, Jones would be circling his tank, feeling the first twinges of junk sickness. The police would be boring the Drome regulars with questions about Ralfi. What did he do? Who was he with before he stepped outside? And the Yakuza would be settling its ghostly bulk over the city's data banks, probing for faint images of me reflected in numbered accounts, securities transactions, bills for utilities. We're an information economy. They teach you that in school. What they don't tell you is that it's impossible to move, to live, to operate at any level without leaving traces, bits, seemingly meaningless fragments of personal information. Fragments that can be retrieved, amplified ...

But by now the pirate would have shuttled our message into line for blackbox transmissions to the Yakuza comsat. A simple message: Call off the dogs or we wideband your program.

The program. I had no idea what it contained. I still don't. I only sing the song, with zero comprehension. It was probably research data, the Yakuza being given to advanced forms of industrial espionage. A genteel business, stealing from Ono-Sendai as a matter of course and politely holding their data for ransom, threatening to blunt the conglomerate's research edge by making the product public.

But why couldn't any number play? Wouldn't they be happier with something to sell back to Ono-Sendai, happier than they'd be with one dead Johnny from Memory Lane?

Their program was on its way to an address in Sydney, to a place that held letters for clients and didn't ask questions once you'd paid a small retainer. Fourth-class surface mail. I'd erased most of the other copy and recorded our message in the resulting gap, leaving just enough of the program to identify it as the real thing.

My wrist hurt. I wanted to stop, to lie down, to sleep. I knew that I'd lose my grip and fall soon, knew that the sharp black shoes I'd bought for my evening as Eddie Bax would lose their purchase and carry me down to Nighttown. But he rose in my mind like a cheap religious hologram, glowing, the enlarged chip in his Hawaiian shirt looming like a reconnaissance shot of some doomed urban nucleus.

So I followed Dog and Molly through Lo Tek heaven, jury-rigged and jerry-built from scraps that even Nighttown didn't want.

The Killing Floor was eight meters on a side. A giant had threaded steel cable back and forth through a junkyard and drawn it all taut. It creaked when it moved, and it moved constantly, swaying and bucking as the gathering Lo Teks arranged themselves on the shelf of plywood surrounding it. The wood was silver with age, polished with long use and deeply etched with initials, threats, declarations of passion. This was suspended from a separate set of cables, which lost themselves in darkness beyond the raw white glare of the two ancient floods suspended above the Floor.

A girl with teeth like Dog's hit the Floor on all fours. Her breasts were tattooed with indigo spirals. Then she was across the Floor, laughing, grappling with a boy who was drinking dark liquid from a liter flask.

Lo Tek fashion ran to scars and tattoos. And teeth. The electricity they were tapping to light the Killing Floor seemed to be an exception to their overall aesthetic, made in the name of ... ritual, sport, art? I didn't know, but I could see that the Floor was something special. It had the look of having been assembled over generations.

I held the useless shotgun under my jacket. Its hardness and heft were comforting, even though I had no more shells. And it came to me that I had no idea at all of what was really happening, or of what was supposed to happen. And that was the nature of my game, because I'd spent most of my life as a blind receptacle to be filled with other people's knowledge and then drained, spouting synthetic languages I'd never understand. A very technical boy. Sure.

And then I noticed just how quiet the Lo Teks had become.

He was there, at the edge of the light, taking in the Killing Floor and the gallery of silent Lo Teks with a tourist's calm. And as our eyes met for the first time with mutual recognition, a memory clicked into place for me, of Paris, and the long Mercedes electrics gliding through the rain to Notre Dame; mobile greenhouses, Japanese faces behind the glass, and a hundred Nikons rising in blind phototropism, flowers of steel and crystal. Behind his eyes, as they found me, those same shutters whirring.

I looked for Molly Millions, but she was gone.

The Lo Teks parted to let him step up on to the bench. He bowed, smiling, and stepped smoothly out of his sandals, leaving them side by side, perfectly aligned, and then he stepped down on to the Killing Floor. He came for me, across that shifting trampoline of scrap, as easily as any tourist padding across synthetic pile in any featureless hotel.

Molly hit the Floor, moving.

The Floor screamed.

It was miked and amplified, with pickups riding the four fat coil springs at the corners and contact mikes taped at random to rusting machine fragments. Somewhere the Lo Teks had an amp and a synthesizer, and now I made out the shapes of speakers overhead, above the cruel white floods.

A drumbeat began, electronic, like an amplified heart, steady as a metronome.

She'd removed her leather jacket and boots; her T-shirt was sleeveless, faint telltales of Chiba City circuitry traced along her thin arms. Her leather jeans gleamed under the floods. She began to dance.

She flexed her knees, white feet tensed on a flattened gas tank, and the

Killing Floor began to heave in response. The sound it made was like a world ending, like the wires that hold heaven snapping and coiling across the sky.

He rode with it, for a few heartbeats, and then he moved, judging the movement of the Floor perfectly, like a man stepping from one flat stone to another in an ornamental garden.

He pulled the tip from his thumb with the grace of a man at ease with social gesture and flung it at her. Under the floods, the filament was a refracting thread of rainbow. She threw herself flat and rolled, jackknifing up as the molecule whipped past, steel claws snapping into the light in what must have been an automatic rictus of defense.

The drum pulse quickened, and she bounced with it, her dark hair wild around the blank silver lenses, her mouth thin, lips taut with concentration. The Killing Floor boomed and roared, and the Lo Teks were screaming their excitement.

He retracted the filament to a whirling meter-wide circle of ghostly polychrome and spun it in front of him, thumbless hand held level with his sternum. A shield.

And Molly seemed to let something go, something inside, and that was the real start of her mad-dog dance. She jumped, twisting, lunging sideways, landing with both feet on an alloy engine block wired directly to one of the coil springs. I cupped my hands over my ears and knelt in a vertigo of sound, thinking Floor and benches were on their way down, down to Nighttown, and I saw us tearing through the shanties, the wet wash, exploding on the tiles like rotten fruit. But the cables held, and the Killing Floor rose and fell like a crazy metal sea. And Molly danced on it.

And at the end, just before he made his final cast with the filament, I saw something in his face, an expression that didn't seem to belong there. It wasn't fear and it wasn't anger. I think it was disbelief, stunned incomprehension mingled with pure aesthetic revulsion at what he was seeing, hearing – at what was happening to him. He retracted the whirling filament, the ghost disk shrinking to the size of a dinner plate as he whipped his arm above his head and brought it down, the thumbtip curving out for Molly like a live thing.

The Floor carried her down, the molecule passing just above her head; the Floor whiplashed, lifting him into the path of the taut molecule. It should have passed harmlessly over his head and been withdrawn into its diamond-hard socket. It took his hand off just behind the wrist. There was a gap in the Floor in front of him, and he went through it like a diver, with a strange deliberate grace, a defeated kamikaze on his way down to Nighttown. Partly, I think, he took that dive to buy himself a few seconds of the dignity of silence. She'd killed him with culture shock.

The Lo Teks roared, but someone shut the amplifier off, and Molly rode the Killing Floor into silence, hanging on now, her face white and blank, until the pitching slowed and there was only a faint pinging of tortured metal and the grating of rust on rust.

We searched the Floor for the severed hand, but we never found it. All we found was a graceful curve in one piece of rusted steel, where the molecule went through. Its edge was bright as new chrome.

We never learned whether the Yakuza had accepted our terms, or even whether they got our message. As far as I know, their program is still waiting for Eddie Bax on a shelf in the back room of a gift shop on the third level of Sydney Central-5. Probably they sold the original back to Ono-Sendai months ago. But maybe they did get the pirate's broadcast, because nobody's come looking for me yet, and it's been nearly a year. If they do come, they'll have a long climb up through the dark, past Dog's sentries, and I don't look much like Eddie Bax these days. I let Molly take care of that, with a local anaesthetic. And my new teeth have almost grown in.

I decided to stay up here. When I looked out across the Killing Floor, before he came, I saw how hollow I was. And I knew I was sick of being a bucket. So now I climb down and visit Jones, almost every night.

We're partners now, Jones and I, and Molly Millions, too. Molly handles our business in the Drome. Jones is still in Funland, but he has a bigger tank, with fresh seawater trucked in once a week. And he has his junk, when he needs it. He still talks to the kids with his frame of lights, but he talks to me on a new display unit in a shed that I rent there, a better unit than the one he used in the navy.

And we're all making good money, better money than I made before, because Jones's Squid can read the traces of anything that anyone ever stored in me, and he gives it to me on the display unit in languages I can understand. So we're learning a lot about all my former clients. And one day I'll have a surgeon dig all the silicon out of my amygdalae, and I'll live with my own memories and nobody else's, the way other people do. But not for a while.

In the meantime it's really okay up here, way up in the dark, smoking a Chinese filtertip and listening to the condensation that drips from the geodesics. Real quiet up here – unless a pair of Lo Teks decide to dance on the Killing Floor.

It's educational, too. With Jones to help me figure things out, I'm getting to be the most technical boy in town.

ONLINE: **THREE/5** *Subject:* The Angel

Angel

Pat Cadigan

INFO: Angel has the power to make people do what he wants. Women, bartenders, even rough trade boys are unable to refuse his demands. But what *is* his crime that no one seems to want to recognise?

Patricia Cadigan has, within the space of a decade, become recognised as one of the hottest new talents writing hard-core cyberpunk, and her stories of harsh urbanised landscapes have deservedly earned comparison with those of William Gibson. Born in Schenectady, New York, she worked in a design studio and writing sentimental text for Hallmark Cards before demonstrating her talent in hard-headed psychodramas like 'Death From Exposure' (1978), 'Rock On', which was included in Bruce Sterling's pioneer cyberpunk anthology *Mirrorshades* (1986), and her breakthrough novel *Synners* (1989), featuring a world where computer viruses are not only a disease of the interface but actually cause human deaths. It won the Arthur C. Clarke award for the best sf novel of the year. Her subsequent work has been described as 'science fiction fantasy horror' and is often set in a near future against a Californian-style background. Pat has earned nominations for all the major awards, and her novella length story 'Death in the Promised Land' (*Omni*, 1995), about murder in a world of virtual reality, was voted one of the best stories of the year. 'Angel', which appeared in *Isaac Asimov's Science Fiction Magaziner*, May 1987, also has the unique distinction of being a finalist for the Hugo, Nebula and World Fantasy awards.

Stand with me awhile, Angel, I said, and Angel said he'd do that. Angel was good to me that way, good to have with you on a cold night and nowhere to go. We stood on the street corner together and watched the cars going by and the people and all. The streets were lit up like Christmas, streetlights, store lights, marquees over the all night movie houses and bookstores blinking and flashing; shank of the evening in east midtown. Angel was getting used to things here and getting used to how I did, nights. Standing outside, because what else are you going to do. He was *my* Angel now, had been since that other cold night when I'd been going home, because where are you going to go, and I'd found him and took him with me. It's good to have someone to take with you, someone to look after. Angel knew that. He started looking after me, too.

Like now. We were standing there awhile and I was looking around at nothing and everything, the cars cruising past, some of them stopping now and again for the hookers posing by the curb, and then I saw it, out of the corner of my eye. Stuff coming out of the Angel, shiny like sparks but flowing like liquid. Silver fireworks. I turned and looked all the way at him and it was gone. And he turned and gave a little grin like he was embarrassed I'd seen. Nobody else saw it, though; not the short guy who paused next to the Angel before crossing the street against the light, not the skinny hype looking to sell the boom-box he was carrying on his shoulder, not the homeboy strutting past us with both his girlfriends on his arms, nobody but me.

The Angel said, Hungry?

Sure, I said. I'm hungry.

Angel looked past me. Okay, he said. I looked, too, and here they came, three leather boys, visor caps, belts, boots, keyrings. On the cruise together. Scary stuff, even though you know it's not looking for you.

I said, them? *Them?*

Angel didn't answer. One went by, then the second, and the Angel stopped the third by taking hold of his arm.

Hi.

The guy nodded. His head was shaved. I could see a little grey-black stubble under his cap. No eyebrows, disinterested eyes. The eyes were because of the Angel.

I could use a little money, the Angel said. My friend and I are hungry.

The guy put his hand in his pocket and wiggled out some bills, offering them to the Angel. The Angel selected a twenty and closed the guy's hand around the rest.

This will be enough, thank you.

The guy put his money away and waited.

I hope you have a good night, said the Angel.

The guy nodded and walked on, going across the street to where his two friends were waiting on the next corner. Nobody found anything weird about it.

Angel was grinning at me. Sometimes he was *the* Angel, when he was doing something, sometimes he was Angel, when he was just with me. Now he was Angel again. We went up the street to the luncheonette and got a seat by the front window so we could still watch the street while we ate.

Cheeseburger and fries, I said without bothering to look at the plastic-covered menus lying on top of the napkin holder. The Angel nodded.

Thought so, he said. I'll have the same, then.

The waitress came over with a little tiny pad to take our order. I cleared my throat. It seemed like I hadn't used my voice in a hundred years. 'Two cheeseburgers and two fries,' I said, 'and two cups of –' I looked up at her and froze. She had no face. Like, *nothing*, blank from hairline to chin, soft little dents where the eyes and nose and mouth would have been. Under the table, the Angel kicked me, but gentle.

'And two cups of coffee,' I said.

She didn't say anything – how could she? – as she wrote down the order and then walked away again. All shaken up, I looked at the Angel, but he was calm like always.

She's a new arrival, Angel told me, and leaned back in his chair. Not enough time to grow a face.

But how can she breathe? I said.

Through her pores. She doesn't need much air yet.

Yah, but what about – like, I mean, don't other people *notice* that she's got nothing there?

No. It's not such an extraordinary condition. The only reason you notice is because you're with me. Certain things have rubbed off on you. But no one else notices. When they look at her, they see whatever face they expect someone like her to have. And eventually, she'll have it.

But you have a face, I said. You've always had a face.

I'm different, said the Angel.

You sure are, I thought, looking at him. Angel had a beautiful face. That wasn't why I took him home that night, just because he had a beautiful face – I left all that behind a long time ago – but it was there, his beauty. The way you think of a man being beautiful, good clean lines, deep-set eyes, ageless. About the only way you could describe him – look away and you'd forget everything except that he was beautiful. But he did have a face. He *did*.

Angel shifted in the chair – these were like somebody's old kitchen chairs, you couldn't get too comfortable in them – and shook his head, because he knew I was thinking troubled thoughts. Sometimes you could think something and it wouldn't be troubled and later you'd think the same thing and it would be troubled. The Angel didn't like me to be troubled about him.

Do you have a cigarette? he asked.

I think so.

I patted my jacket and came up with most of a pack that I handed over to him. The Angel lit up and amused us both by having the smoke come out his ears and trickle out of his eyes like ghostly tears. I felt my own eyes watering for his; I wiped them and there was that *stuff* again, but from me now. I was crying silver fireworks. I flicked them on the table and watched them puff out and vanish.

Does this mean I'm getting to *be* you, now? I asked.

Angel shook his head. Smoke wafted out of his hair. Just things rubbing off on you. Because we've been together and you're – susceptible. But they're different for you.

Then the waitress brought our food and we went on to another sequence, as the Angel would say. She still had no face but I guess she could see well enough because she put all the plates down just where you'd think they were supposed to go and left the tiny little check in the middle of the table.

Is she – I mean, did you know her, from where you –

Angel gave his head a brief little shake. No. She's from somewhere else. Not one of my – people. He pushed the cheeseburger and fries in front of him over to my side of the table. That was the way it was done; I did all the eating and somehow it worked out.

I picked up my cheeseburger and I was bringing it up to my mouth when my eyes got all funny and I saw it coming up like a whole *series* of cheeseburgers, whoom-whoom-whoom, trick photography, only for real. I closed my eyes and jammed the cheeseburger into my mouth, holding it there, waiting for all the other cheeseburgers to catch up with it.

You'll be okay, said the Angel. Steady, now.

I said with my mouth full, That was – that was *weird*. Will I ever get used to this?

I doubt it. But I'll do what I can to help you.

Yah, well, the Angel *would* know. Stuff rubbing off on me, he could feel it better than I could. He was the one it was rubbing off *from*.

I had put away my cheeseburger and half of Angel's and was working on the french fries for both of us when I noticed he was looking out the window with this hard, tight expression on his face.

Something? I asked him.

Keep eating, he said.

I kept eating, but I kept watching, too. The Angel was staring at a big blue car parked at the curb right outside the diner. It was silvery blue, one of those lots-of-money models, and there was a woman kind of leaning across from the driver's side to look out the passenger window. She was beautiful in that lots-of-money way, tawny hair swept back from her face, and even from here I could see she had turquoise eyes. Really beautiful woman. I almost felt like crying. I mean, jeez, how did people get that way and me too harmless to live.

But the Angel wasn't one bit glad to see her. I knew he didn't want me to say anything, but I couldn't help it.

Who is she?

Keep eating, Angel said. We need the protein, what little there is.

I ate and watched the woman and the Angel watch each other and it was getting very – I don't know, very *something* between them, even through the glass. Then a cop car pulled up next to her and I knew they were telling her to move it along. She moved it along.

Angel sagged against the back of his chair and lit another cigarette, smoking it in the regular, unremarkable way.

What are we going to do tonight? I asked the Angel as we left the restaurant.

Keep out of harm's way, Angel said, which was a new answer. Most nights we spent just kind of going around soaking everything up. The Angel soaked it up, mostly. I got some of it along with him, but not the same way he did. It was different for him. Sometimes he would use me like a kind of filter. Other times he took it direct. There'd been the big car accident one night, right at my usual corner, a big old Buick running a red light smack into somebody's nice Lincoln. The Angel had had to take it direct because I couldn't handle that kind of stuff. I didn't know how the Angel could take it, but he could. It carried him for days afterwards, too. I only had to eat for myself.

It's the intensity, little friend, he'd told me, as though that were supposed to explain it.

It's the intensity, not whether it's good or bad. The universe doesn't know good or bad, only less or more. Most of you have a bad time reconciling this. *You* have a bad time with it, little friend, but you get through better than other people. Maybe because of the way you are. You got squeezed out of a lot, you haven't had much of a chance at life. You're as much an exile as I am, only in your own land.

That may have been true, but at least I *belonged* here, so that part was easier for me. But I didn't say that to the Angel. I think he liked to think he could do as well or better than me at living – I mean, I couldn't just look at some leather boy and get him to cough up a twenty dollar bill. Cough up a fist in the face or worse, was more like it.

Tonight, though, he wasn't doing so good, and it was that woman in the car. She'd thrown him out of step, kind of.

Don't think about her, the Angel said, just out of nowhere. Don't think about her any more.

Okay, I said, feeling creepy because it was creepy when the Angel got a glimpse of my head. And then, of course, I couldn't think about anything else hardly.

Do you want to go home? I asked him.

No. I can't stay in now. We'll do the best we can tonight, but I'll have to be very careful about the tricks. They take so much out of me, and if we're keeping out of harm's way, I might not be able to make up for a lot of it.

It's okay, I said. I ate. I don't need anything else tonight, you don't have to do any more.

Angel got that look on his face, the one where I knew he wanted to give me things, like feelings I couldn't have any more. Generous, the Angel was. But I didn't need those feelings, not like other people seem to. For a while, it was like the Angel didn't understand that, but he let me be.

Little friend, he said, and almost touched me. The Angel didn't touch a lot. I could touch him and that would be okay, but if *he* touched somebody, he couldn't help *doing* something to them, like the trade that had given us the money. That had been deliberate. If the trade had touched the Angel first, it would have been different, nothing would have happened unless the Angel touched him back. All touch meant something to the Angel that I didn't understand. There was touching without touching, too. Like things rubbing off on me. And sometimes, when I did touch the Angel, I'd get the feeling that it was maybe more his idea than mine, but I didn't mind that. How many people were going their whole lives never being able to touch an Angel?

We walked together and all around us the street was really coming to life. It was getting colder, too. I tried to make my jacket cover more. The Angel wasn't feeling it. Most of the time hot and cold didn't mean much to him. We saw the three rough trade guys again. The one Angel had gotten the money from was getting into a car. The other two watched it drive away and then walked on. I looked over at the Angel.

Because we took his twenty, I said.

Even if we hadn't, Angel said.

So we went along, the Angel and me, and I could feel how different it was tonight than it was all the other nights we'd walked or stood together. The Angel was kind of pulled back into himself and seemed to be keeping a check on me, pushing us closer together. I was getting more of those fireworks out of the corners of my eyes, but when I'd turn my head to look, they'd vanish. It reminded me of the night I'd found the Angel standing on my corner all by himself in pain. The Angel told me later that was real talent, knowing he was in pain. I never thought of myself as any too talented, but the way everyone else had been just ignoring him, I guess I must have had something to see him after all.

The Angel stopped us several feet down from an all-night bookstore. Don't look, he said. Watch the traffic or stare at your feet, but don't look or it won't happen.

There wasn't anything to see right then, but I didn't look anyway. That was the way it was sometimes, the Angel telling me it made a difference whether I was watching something or not, something about the other people being conscious of me being conscious of them. I didn't understand, but I knew Angel was usually right. So I was watching traffic when the guy came out of the bookstore and got his head punched.

I could almost see it out of the corner of my eye. A lot of movement, arms and legs flying and grunty noises. Other people stopped to look but I kept my eyes on the traffic, some of which was slowing up so they could check out the fight. Next to me, the Angel was stiff all over. Taking it in, what he called the expenditure of emotional kinetic energy. No right, no wrong, little friend, he'd told me. Just energy, like the rest of the universe.

So he took it in and I *felt* him taking it in, and while I was feeling it, a kind of silver fog started creeping around my eyeballs and I was in two places at once. I was watching the traffic and I was in the Angel watching the fight and feeling him charge up like a big battery.

It felt like nothing I'd ever felt before. These two guys slugging it out – well, one guy doing all the slugging and the other skittering around trying to get out from under the fists and having his head punched but good, and the Angel drinking it like he was sipping at an empty cup and somehow getting it to have something in it after all. Deep inside him, whatever made the Angel go was getting a little stronger.

I kind of swung back and forth between him and me, or swayed might be more like it was. I wondered about it, because the Angel wasn't touching me. I really was getting to *be* him, I thought; Angel picked that up and put the thought away to answer later. It was like I was traveling by the fog being one of us and then the other, for a long time, it seemed, and then after a while I was more me than him again, and some of the fog cleared away.

And there was that car, pointed the other way this time, and the woman was climbing out of it with this big weird smile on her face, as though she'd won something. She waved at the Angel to come to her.

Bang went the connection between us dead and the Angel shot past me, running away from the car. I went after him. I caught a glimpse of her jumping back into the car and yanking at the gear shift.

Angel wasn't much of a runner. Something funny about his knees. We'd gone maybe a hundred feet when he started wobbling and I could hear him pant. He cut across a Park & Lock that was dark and mostly empty. It was back-to-back with some kind of private parking lot and the fences for each one tried to mark off the same narrow strip of lumpy pavement. They were easy to climb but Angel was too panicked. He just *went* through them before he even thought about it; I knew that because if he'd been thinking, he'd have wanted to save what he'd just charged up with for when he really needed it bad enough.

I had to haul myself over the fences in the usual way, and when he heard me rattling on the saggy chainlink, he stopped and looked back.

Go, I told him. Don't wait on me!

He shook his head sadly. Little friend, I'm a fool. I could stand to learn from you a little more.

Don't stand, run! I got over the fences and caught up with him. Let's go! I yanked his sleeve as I slogged past and he followed at a clumsy trot.

Have to hide somewhere, he said, camouflage ourselves with people.

I shook my head, thinking we could just run maybe four more blocks and we'd be at the freeway overpass. Below it were the butt-ends of old roads closed off when the freeway had been built. You could hide there the rest of your life and no one would find you. But Angel made me turn right and go down a block to this rundown crack-in-the-wall called Stan's Jigger. I'd never been in there – I'd never made it a practice to go into bars – but the Angel was pushing too hard to argue.

Inside it was smelly and dark and not too happy. The Angel and I went down to the end of the bar and stood under a blood-red light while he searched his pockets for money.

Enough for one drink apiece, he said.

I don't want anything.

You can have soda or something.

The Angel ordered from the bartender, who was suspicious. This was a place for regulars and nobody else, and certainly nobody else like me or the Angel. The Angel knew that even stronger than I did but he just stood and pretended to sip his drink without looking at me. He was all pulled into himself and I was hovering around the edges. I knew he was still pretty panicked and trying to figure out what he could do next. As close as I was, if he had to get real far away, he was going to have a problem and so was I. He'd have to tow me along with him and that wasn't the most practical thing to do.

Maybe he was sorry now he'd let me take him home. But he'd been so weak then, and now with all the filtering and stuff I'd done for him he couldn't just cut me off without a lot of pain.

I was trying to figure out what I could do for him now when the bartender came back and gave us a look that meant order or get out, and he'd have liked it better if we got out. So would everyone else there. The few other people standing at the bar weren't looking at us, but they knew right where we were, like a sore spot. It wasn't hard to figure out what they thought about us, either, maybe because of me or because of the Angel's beautiful face.

We got to leave, I said to the Angel, but he had it in his head this was good camouflage. There wasn't enough money for two more drinks so he smiled at the bartender and slid his hand across the bar and put it on top of the bartender's. It was tricky doing it this way; bartenders and waitresses took more persuading because it wasn't normal for them just to give you something.

The bartender looked at the Angel with his eyes half closed. He seemed to be thinking it over. But the Angel had just blown a lot going through the fence instead of climbing over it and the fear was scuttling his concentration and I just knew that it wouldn't work. And maybe my knowing that didn't help, either.

The bartender's free hand dipped down below the bar and came up with a small club. 'Faggot!' he roared and caught Angel just over the ear. Angel slammed into me and we both crashed to the floor. Plenty of emotional kinetic energy in here, I thought dimly as the guys standing at the bar fell on us, and then I didn't think anything more as I curled up into a ball under their fists and boots.

We were lucky they didn't much feel like killing anyone. Angel went out the door first and they tossed me out on top of him. As soon as I landed on him, I knew we were both in trouble; something was broken inside him. So much for keeping out of harm's way. I rolled off him and lay on the pavement, staring at the sky and trying to catch my breath. There was blood in my mouth and my nose, and my back was on fire.

Angel? I said, after a bit.

He didn't answer. I felt my mind get kind of all loose and runny, like my brains were leaking out my ears. I thought about the trade we'd taken the money from and how I'd been scared of him and his friends and how silly that had been. But then, I was too harmless to live.

The stars were raining silver fireworks down on me. It didn't help.

Angel? I said again.

I rolled over on to my side to reach for him, and there she was. The car was parked at the curb and she had Angel under the armpits, dragging him toward the open passenger door. I couldn't tell if he was conscious or not and that scared me. I sat up.

She paused, still holding the Angel. We looked into each other's eyes, and I started to understand.

'Help me get him into the car,' she said at last. Her voice sounded hard and flat and unnatural. 'Then you can get in, too. In the *back* seat.'

I was in no shape to take her out. It couldn't have been better for her if she'd set it up herself. I got up, the pain flaring in me so bad that I almost fell down again, and took the Angel's ankles. His ankles were so delicate, almost like a woman's, like *hers*. I didn't really help much, except to guide his feet in as she sat him on the seat and strapped him in with the shoulder harness. I got in the back as she ran around to the other side of the car, her steps real light and peppy, like she'd found a million dollars lying there on the sidewalk.

We were out on the freeway before the Angel stirred in the shoulder harness. His head lolled from side to side on the back of the seat. I reached up and touched his hair lightly, hoping she couldn't see me do it.

Where are you taking me, the Angel said.

'For a ride,' said the woman. 'For the moment.'

Why does she talk out loud like that? I asked the Angel.

Because she knows it bothers me.

'You know I can focus my thoughts better if I say things out loud, she said. 'I'm not like one of your little pushovers.' She glanced at me in the rear view mirror. 'Just *what* have you gotten yourself into since you left, darling? Is that a boy or a girl?'

I pretended I didn't care about what she said or that I was too harmless to live or any of that stuff, but the way she said it, she meant it to sting.

Friends can be either, Angel said. It doesn't matter which. Where are you taking us?

Now it was *us*. In spite of everything, I almost could have smiled.

'Us? You mean, you and me? Or are you really referring to your little pet back there?'

My friend and I are together. You and I are *not*.

The way the Angel said it made me think he meant more than not together; like he'd been with her once the way he was with me now. The

Angel let me know I was right. Silver fireworks started flowing slowly off his head down the back of the seat and I knew there was something wrong about it. There was too much all at once.

'Why can't you talk out loud to me, darling?' the woman said with fakey-sounding petulance. 'Just say a few words and make me happy. You have a lovely voice when you use it.'

That was true, but the Angel never spoke out loud unless he couldn't get out of it, like when he'd ordered from the bartender. Which had probably helped the bartender decide about what he thought we were, but it was useless to think about that.

'All right,' said Angel, and I knew the strain was awful for him. 'I've said a few words. Are you happy?' He sagged in the shoulder harness.

'Ecstatic. But it won't make me let you go. I'll drop your pet at the nearest hospital and then we'll go home.' She glanced at the Angel as she drove. 'I've missed you so much. I can't *stand* it without you, without you making things happen. Doing your little miracles. You knew I'd get addicted to it, all the things you could do to people. And then you just took off, I didn't know what had happened to you. And it *hurt*.' Her voice turned kind of pitiful, like a little kid's. 'I was in real *pain*. You must have been, too. Weren't you? Well, *weren't you*?'

Yes, the Angel said. I was in pain, too.

I remembered him standing on my corner, where I'd hung out all that time by myself until he came. Standing there in pain. I didn't know why or from what then, I just took him home, and after a little while, the pain went away. When he decided we were together, I guess.

The silvery flow over the back of the car seat thickened. I cupped my hands under it and it was like my brain was lighting up with pictures. I saw the Angel before he was my Angel, in this really nice house, the woman's house, and how she'd take him places, restaurants or stores or parties, thinking at him real hard so that he was all filled up with her and had to do what she wanted him to. Steal sometimes; other times, weird stuff, make people do silly things like suddenly start singing or taking their clothes off. That was mostly at the parties, though she made a waiter she didn't like burn himself with a pot of coffee. She'd get men, too, through the Angel, and they'd think it was the greatest idea in the world to go to bed with her. Then she'd make the Angel show her the others, the ones that had been sent here the way he had for crimes nobody could have understood, like the waitress with no face. She'd look at them, sometimes try to do things to them to make them uncomfortable or unhappy. But mostly she'd just stare.

It wasn't like that in the very beginning, the Angel said weakly, and I knew he was ashamed.

It's okay, I told him. People can be nice at first, I know that. Then they find out about you.

The woman laughed. 'You two are *so* sweet and pathetic. Like a couple of little children. I guess that's what you were looking for, wasn't it, darling? Except children can be cruel, too, can't they? So you got this – *creature* for yourself.' She looked at me in the rear view mirror again as she slowed down a little, and for a moment I was afraid she'd seen what I was doing with the silvery stuff that was still pouring out of the Angel. It was starting to slow now. There wasn't much time left. I wanted to scream, but the Angel was calming me for what was coming next. 'What happened to you, anyway?'

Tell her, said the Angel. To stall for time, I knew, keep her occupied.

I was born funny, I said. I had both sexes.

'A hermaphrodite!' she exclaimed with real delight.

She loves freaks, the Angel said, but she didn't pay any attention.

There was an operation, but things went wrong. They kept trying to fix it as I got older but my body didn't have the right kind of chemistry or something. My parents were ashamed. I left after a while.

'You poor thing,' she said, not meaning anything like that. 'You were *just* what darling, here, needed, weren't you? Just a little nothing, no demands, no desires. For anything.' Her voice got all hard. 'They could probably fix you up now, you know.'

I don't want it. I left all that behind a long time ago, I don't need it.

'*Just* the sort of little pet that would be perfect for you,' she said to the Angel. 'Sorry I have to tear you away. But I can't get along without you now. Life is so boring. And empty. And –' She sounded puzzled. 'And like there's nothing more to live for since you left me.'

That's not me, said the Angel. That's you.

'No, it's a lot of you, too, and you know it. You know you're addictive to human beings, you knew that when you came here – when they *sent* you here. Hey, you, *pet*, do you know what his crime was, why they sent him to this little backwater penal colony of a planet?'

Yeah, I know, I said. I really didn't, but I wasn't going to tell her that.

'What do you think about *that*, little pet neuter?' she said gleefully, hitting the accelerator pedal and speeding up. 'What do you think of the crime of refusing to mate?'

The Angel made a sort of an out-loud groan and lunged at the steering wheel. The car swerved wildly and I fell backwards, the silvery stuff from the Angel going all over me. I tried to keep scooping it into my mouth the way I'd been doing, but it was flying all over the place now. I heard the crunch as the tires left the road and went on to the shoulder. Something struck the side of the car, probably the guard rail, and made it fishtail, throwing me down on the floor. Up front the woman was screaming and cursing and the Angel wasn't making a sound, but, in my head, I could hear him sort of keening. Whatever happened, this would be it. The Angel had told me all that time ago, after I'd taken him home, that they didn't last long after they got here, the exiles from his world and other worlds. Things tended to *happen* to them, even if they latched on to someone like me or the woman. They'd be in accidents or the people here would kill them. Like antibodies in a human body rejecting something or fighting a disease. At least I belonged here, but it looked like I was going to die in a car accident with the Angel and the woman both. I didn't care.

The car swerved back on to the highway for a few seconds and then pitched to the right again. Suddenly there was nothing under us and then we thumped down on something, not road but dirt or grass or something, bombing madly up and down. I pulled myself up on the back of the seat just in time to see the sign coming at us at an angle. The corner of it started to go through the windshield on the woman's side and then all I saw for a long time was the biggest display of silver fireworks ever.

It was hard to be gentle with him. Every move hurt but I didn't want to leave him sitting in the car next to her, even if she was dead. Being in the back seat had kept most of the glass from flying into me but I was still shaking some out of my hair and the impact hadn't done much for my back.

I laid the Angel out on the lumpy grass a little ways from the car and looked around. We were maybe a hundred yards from the highway, near a road that ran parallel to it. It was dark but I could still read the sign that had come through the windshield and split the woman's head in half. It said, *Construction Ahead, Reduce Speed.* Far off on the other road, I could see a flashing yellow light and at first I was afraid it was the police or something but it stayed where it was and I realized that must be the construction.

'Friend,' whispered the Angel, startling me. He'd never spoken aloud to me, not directly.

Don't talk, I said, bending over him, trying to figure out some way I could touch him, just for comfort. There wasn't anything else I could do now.

'I have to,' he said, still whispering. 'It's almost all gone. Did you get it?'

Mostly, I said. Not all.

'I meant for you to have it.'

I know.

'I don't know that it will really do you any good.' His breath kind of bubbled in his throat. I could see something wet and shiny on his mouth but it wasn't silver fireworks. 'But it's yours. You can do as you like with it. Live on it the way I did. Get what you need when you need it. But you can live as a human, too. Eat. Work. However, whatever.'

I'm not human, I said. I'm not any more human than you, even if I do belong here.

'Yes, you are, little friend. I haven't made you any less human,' he said, and coughed some. 'I'm not sorry I wouldn't mate. I couldn't mate with my own. It was too ... I don't know, too little of me, too much of them, something. I couldn't bond, it would have been nothing but emptiness. The Great Sin, to be unable to give, because the universe knows only less or more and I insisted that it would be good or bad. So they sent me here. But in the end, you know, they got their way, little friend.' I felt his hand on me for a moment before it fell away. 'I did it after all. Even if it wasn't with my own.'

The bubbling in his throat stopped. I sat next to him for a while in the dark. Finally I felt it, the Angel stuff. It was kind of fluttery-churny, like too much coffee on an empty stomach. I closed my eyes and lay down on the grass, shivering. Maybe some of it was shock but I don't think so. The silver fireworks started, in my head this time, and with them came a lot of pictures I couldn't understand. Stuff about the Angel and where he'd come from and the way they mated. It was a lot like how we'd been together, the Angel and me. They looked a lot like us but there were a lot of differences, too, things I couldn't make out. I couldn't make out how they'd sent him here, either – by *light*, in, like, little bundles or something. It didn't make any sense to me, but I guessed an Angel could be light. Silver fireworks.

I must have passed out, because when I opened my eyes, it felt like I'd been laying there a long time. It was still dark, though. I sat up and reached for the Angel, thinking I ought to hide his body.

He was gone. There was just a sort of wet sandy stuff where he'd been.

I looked at the car and her. All that was still there. Somebody was going to see it soon. I didn't want to be around for that.

Everything still hurt but I managed to get to the other road and start walking back toward the city. It was like I could *feel* it now, the way the Angel must have, as though it were vibrating like a drum or ringing like a bell with all kinds of stuff, people laughing and crying and loving and hating and being afraid and everything else that happens to people. The stuff that the Angel took in, energy, that I could take in now if I wanted.

And I knew that taking it in that way, it would be bigger than anything all those people had, bigger than anything I could have had if things hadn't gone wrong with me all those years ago.

I wasn't so sure I wanted it. Like the Angel, refusing to mate back where he'd come from. He wouldn't, there, and I couldn't, here. Except now I could do something else.

I wasn't so sure I wanted it. But I didn't think I'd be able to stop it, either, any more than I could stop my heart from beating. Maybe it wasn't really such a good thing or a right thing. But it was like the Angel said: the universe doesn't know good or bad, only less or more.

Yeah. I heard *that*.

I thought about the waitress with no face. I could find them all now, all the ones from the other places, other worlds that sent them away for some kind of alien crimes nobody would have understood. I could find them all. They threw away their outcasts, I'd tell them, but here, we *kept* ours. And here's how. Here's how you live in a universe that only knows less or more.

I kept walking toward the city.

ONLINE: **THREE/6** Subject: Head Cases

Dreamers

Kim Newman

INFO: Elvis Kurtz can access the most intimate secrets in people's heads. In someone else's fantasy he can experience John F. Kennedy making love to Marilyn Monroe and even sense the bullet that entered the president's skull. But just what does John Yeovil have in mind for his unusual talent?

Kim Newman is one of Britain's leading practitioners of cyberpunk and has transferred this hybrid of sf and hard-boiled fiction, considered as essentially American, across the Atlantic very successfully. Born in Somerset, Kim grew up on a diet of Raymond Chandler, Alfred Bester, *The Avengers* and old crime and horror movies. In his subsequent career he has worked as a film critic, broadcaster and playwright (scripting a particularly gruesome thriller, *My One Little Murder Can't Do Any Harm*) as well as writing fiction. He drew on several of these areas of expertise in his groundbreaking first novel, *The Night Mayor* (1989), which is set in a world of virtual reality inhabited by people from detective films of the Forties and follows the manhunt for a master criminal, Daine. Kim is also the creator of Sally Rhodes, cyberpunk's first female private eye, who made her debut in 'Mother Hen' (1985), outsmarting a group of villains bent on trying to destroy a valuable statue not unlike Dashiell Hammett's *Maltese Falcon*. According to Kim, 'Dreamers' is a companion to *The Night Mayor* – it was written at the time of the first draft of the book and both feature Susan Bishopric. It is also his attempt, he says, 'to apply science fiction disguise to the sort of twisty-ironic murders Stanley Ellin used to write and which would be dramatised on *Alfred Hitchcock Presents*'. The story appeared in *Interzone* in 1984.

Elvis Kurtz was dreaming. He dreamed he was John F. Kennedy, former president (1960-Lee Harvey Oswald) of the former United States of America. The dream was a riot of pornography; involving enormous wealth, extreme power, intermittent ultra-violence and sex with Marilyn Monroe. It was a presold success. An inevitable Iridium Tape. An inescapable quinquemillion-seller.

Kurtz was dybbukking, a passenger in the mind. Kurtz was aware of what John Yeovil thought it felt like to be John Fitzgerald Kennedy in August 1961. He had access to a neatly arranged file of memories, plus a few precog glimpses carried over from waking life. He would have to pull out before Dallas. The JFK simile was not aware of Kurtz. Actually, the JFK simile hardly seemed to be aware of anything.

Yeovil had had JFK plump his mistress's bottom on the edge of the presidential desk, and penetrate the former Norma Jean Baker (1926-next year) standing up. A pile of authenticated contemporary documents were scrunched up beneath their spectacular copulation.

Kurtz trusted Yeovil had got the externals right. Through the JFK simile he was perceiving the Oval Room precisely as it had been. Marilyn's squeals were done in her actual voice, distilled from over 300 hours of flatty soundtracks and disc aurals. Yeovil would have had a computer assist handle that. Sometimes Kurtz envied the man's resources.

This was standard wet-dream stuff. The sort of thing Kurtz could do in his sleep. Kurtz's dybbuk overmind left the internals to his experienced subconscious and skimmed through the simile's memory. He ignored the story-so-far synopsis and picked a few random sensations.

The Pacific, World War II: the smell of burning oil and salt water, all-over sun heat, repressed fear, an aural loop of *Sentimental Journey*. His father throwing a tantrum: the usual mix of shame, terror and embarrassment. Prawns at Hyannis Port. The inauguration: January chill, tension, incipient megalomania, '... ask not what your country can do for you ...'

Kurtz wondered who had written that speech. Yeovil did not know; all the question got out of the simile was a momentary white-out. Damn, an extraneous thought. It would bleed on to the tape. Yeovil would have to do a post-erase. With the scene getting near the finish, Kurtz took ego control again.

Yeovil had taken the trouble to insert a 1961 image: Kennedy ejaculated like an ICBM silo; a thermonuclear chain reaction inside Marilyn took her out.

Yawn. Kurtz was an orgasm specialist. He topped the metaphor (too literary, but what did he expect) with a jumble of cross-sensory experiences. He translated the aural stimuli of the *Saint Matthew Passion* into a mass of tactiles. The dream shadow could take it, although a real body would have been blown away.

Marilyn lay face down, exhausted, her hair fanned on the pile carpet. JFK traced her backbone with the presidential seal. Yeovil had Catholic guilt flit through JFK's mind.

'Jack,' breathed Marilyn, 'did you know there's a theory that the whole universe got started with a Big Bang?'

Kennedy parted Marilyn's hair and kissed the nape of her neck. Kurtz felt a witty reply coming. Something hard at the base of the president's skull. A white hot needle in his head. A brief skin-and-bone agony, then nothing.

Damn Yeovil. Oswald was early.

Like most of the *haut ton* that year John Yeovil was devoted to Victoriana. The tridvid sages said the craze was a reaction to the acid smogs that had taken to settling on London. Usually Yeovil affected to despise fashions, but this one suited him. Frock coats and stiff collars became his Holmesian figure, a beard usefully concealed his slash mouth, and the habitual precision of his gestures was ideal for consulting a half-hunter, taking a pinch of snuff, or casually slitting a footpad's nose with an iridium-assist swordstick.

At thirty-nine Yeovil was rich enough to indulge himself with opium-scented handkerchiefs, long case clocks and wax wreaths under glass. Three of his dreams were in the current q-seller listings. The *JFK* advance had accounted for the complete redecoration of his Luxborough Street residence.

Awaiting his guest, Yeovil adjusted the pearl pin in his grey cravat. Exactly right. Exact rectitude was all Yeovil asked of life. That and wealth and fame, of course. He sighted his one-sided smile in the mirror. The smile, which, flashed during a tridvid interview or frozen on a dustjack, could cost him one million pounds *per annum* in lost sales alone. A definitive figure would have to take personal appearances, merchandising, and graft into consideration.

The smile was Yeovil's little secret. The mark of the submarine part of his mind he rigidly excluded from his dreams. John Yeovil had come to terms with his character. He lived with himself in relative comfort, despite the fact that he was easily the most hateful person he knew.

He had the dreaming Talent, but so did hundreds of others. He had the patience to research and the skill to concept, but any raw Dreamer with funding could buy access to the D-9000 for those. Success in the dream industry was down to depth of feeling. Any feeling.

Great Dreamers were all prodigies of emotion. Susan Bishopric: empathy; Orin Tredway: imbecile love; Alexis St Clare: paranoia. And John Yeovil had hate. It did not come through as such in the dreams, but he knew that it was his great reservoir of hate that gave weight to his conjuring of joy, pain, and the rest.

The doorbell sounded. Yeovil had sent an in to Elvis Kurtz. The Household admitted him. A few tendrils of smog trailed the guest. The Household dispelled them.

'Mr Kurtz?'

'Uh. Yes.' Kurtz was muffled by his outdoor helmet. He pulled out of it. His eyes were watering profusely. Yeovil was familiar with the yellowish stream of tears. 'Sorry about this. I have a slight smog.'

'My sympathies,' said Yeovil. 'You can leave your things with the Household.'

'Thanks.' Kurtz ungauntleted and de-flakjacked. Underneath he wore a GP smock. Yeovil led his guest through the hall. The Household offed the hallway lamps, and upped the gas jets and open fire in the drawing room. 'You were difficult to find, Mr Kurtz.'

'I'm supposed to be.' He had a trace of accent. Possibly Liechtenstein. 'I've been out.'

'Of course.' Yeovil decanted two preconstituted brandy snifters. 'Piracy or pornography?'

'A little of both.' Kurtz accepted the drink, smeared his tears, and sagged into a heavy armchair. He was ill at ease. As well he might be. Yeovil decided to hit him now, and cover later.

'Mr Kurtz, prior to your incarceration you produced bootleg editions of my dreams which made a sizable dent in my income. I can now offer you the opportunity to repay me.'

'Your pardon?' Kurtz was trying not to look startled. Like most Dreamers he was rotten at that sort of thing. Most, Yeovil reminded himself, not all.

'Don't worry. I'm not going to tap you for money. I'll even pay you.'

'For what?'

'The use of your Talent.'

'I don't think you understand ...'

'I'm well aware of your limitations, Mr Kurtz. Like myself you are a Dreamer. In many ways you are more powerful than I. You are capable of taping sensations far more intensely than I can. Yet I am successful and well regarded,' (by most at least) 'and you are reduced to aping my dreams. Or producing work like this.'

Yeovil indicated a stack of tapes. Inelegant under-the-counter dreams with clinical titles: *Six Women With Mammary Abnormalities*, *The Ten Minute Orgasm*. They were badly packaged, with lurid artist's-imps on the dustjacks. There was no Dreamer by-line, but Kurtz recognised his own stuff.

'I'm too strong, Yeovil. I can't control my dreams the way you can. My mind doesn't just create, it amplifies and distorts. I wind up with so many resonances and contradictions that the dream falls apart. That's an advantage with one-reel wet dreams, but ...'

'I don't require of you that you justify yourself, Mr Kurtz. I am an artist. I have no capacity for moral outrage. We have that much in common. Our position is at odds with those of the judiciary, the critical establishment, and the British Board of Dream Classification. Come with me.'

The dreaming room was different. Most of the house was a convincing, dark, stuffy, and uncomfortable re-creation of the 1890s. The dreaming room was what people in 1963 had expected the future to look like. All the surfaces were a glossy, featureless white.

Kurtz was impressed. He touched his fingertips, then his naked palm, to the glasspex wall. He started away, and a condensation handprint faded.

'It's warm. Is that eternity lighting?'

'Partly. I have the dreaming room kept at womb temperature.'

'You dream here?'

'Of course. The surroundings have been calculated exactly. Psychologically attuned to be beneficial to the dreaming Talent. The recording equipment is substantially what you are familiar with.'

'You have computer assist?'

'My Household has a library tap for research. I don't use it much, though. I actually read books. I'm not one of the D-9000's troop of hacks. I don't think we should be the glorified amanuenses of a heuristic pulp mill.'

'I don't like the machines either. They hurt.' Kurtz was irritated. Good, that should keep him off balance. 'What is this all about?'

'Would you be surprised to learn that I am an admirer of your work?'

Kurtz cleared an unconvincing laugh from his throat. 'Would you care to say that on the dustjack of *Sixth Form Girls in Chains*?'

Yeovil tapped his ID into the console. The Household extruded a couch from the floor. It looked sculpted. Out of vanilla ice-cream.

'Beside yours, my Talent is lukewarm. I want to make use of your capacities to underline certain aspects of my work in progress.'

'Uh-huh.'

'I am dreaming a historical piece, focusing on the character of John Kennedy, martyred president of the United States of America. Kennedy was known to be a man with a highly passionate nature. I think it not inapt that your touch with erotica be applied.'

Kurtz sat on the couch, trying to find the loophole. 'What about the certification?'

'I plan on sidestepping the BBDC. They have no real authority and I am supported by my publishers and the vast public interest in my work. The Board owes its precarious existence to its claim that it represents the desire of the majority. Once that is disproved, they will fall. *JFK* has been concepted as a radical dream.'

'How is this going to work?'

'I've dreamed a guideline. The sequence you'll work on is fully scripted. The externals are complete. However the first person is blank.'

'Kennedy?'

'Yes. He is emerging as a very strong figure in the dreaming. But in this scene he's empty. I want you to amend the internals as he sexes with his mistress.'

'Same old wet-dream stuff?'

'Essentially. But in this case the explicit material is crucial to the concept. The character of Kennedy is seminal to an understanding of the twentieth century. All of his drives must be exposed. The underlying ...'

'Yeah. Right. Let's talk about the money.'

Yeovil balanced the newly discharged needle gun on his fingertips as he walked across the room, and dropped the weapon into the Household Disperse. Kurtz lay face down on the dreaming couch with a three inch dart in his brain. The tape was still running, although the Kurtz input was zero. Yeovil sucked his burned fingers. He would smear them better when he was finished with Kurtz.

He had never killed anyone before. He sadly discovered that dream was better than actual. Like sex. He stored the minor rush of emotions for future use.

The tape clicked through. The Household offed the recorder. Yeovil picked the subcutaneous terminals out of Kurtz's head and dropped them into their glass of purple. The whirlpool rinse sucked particles of Kurtz out of its system.

Yeovil went through Kurtz's smockpocks. A few credit cards and a bunch of ins. A couple of five-pound bits. They all went into the Disperse, along with Kurtz's outdoor gear, porno tapes, and fingerprinted brandy glass. Do it, then clear up afterwards – the secret of criminal success.

The Household presented Yeovil with his outdoor kit: a visored hat, and a padded inverness. The tailors boasted that their garments were proof against a fragmentation charge. That was true: in the event of such an unlikely weapon being turned on the cape, it would be unmarked. Anyone inside it, however, would find his torso turned to jelly by the impact. Most footpads used needle guns, anyway.

Yeovil hauled Kurtz out to his armoured Ford. On the street he fitted an outmoded breather. It kept the smog out of his lungs as well as a more stylish domino, and disguised him. He pressed his car in, and tapped his ID into the automatic. The smog lights upped. The streets were deserted.

Yeovil drove around central London for fifteen minutes before chancing upon a suitable dump. He slung the body over several twist-tie rubbish bags in the forecourt of a condemned high-rise. It would look like an ordinary waylaying. There were probably five similar corpses within walking distance. If the Black Economists got to Kurtz before the Metropolitans, the body would be stripped of any usable organs. The incident would not rate a mention on the local.

Back at Luxborough Street, Yeovil reprogrammed his Household to forget Kurtz's visit. He fed in a plausible dull evening at home and wrote off the energy expenditure to various gadgets.

Then he slept. The next stage was complicated and he did not want to deal with it late at night after his first murder. He felt a twinge of insomniac excitement, which he countered by backgrounding a subliminal lullaby.

The Household woke him early with a call. It was Tony, Yeovil's chief editor at Futura. Tony looked harassed.

'You've overreached another deadline, John. I wanted the *JFK* master back yesterday. We're committed to a production start. And we have marketing to consider. It's a q-seller on advance sales, and you haven't delivered yet.'

'Sorry.' Yeovil stretched his mind around the problem. 'I've still got a few more amendments.'

'You're a trekkiehead, John. Leave it alone. I told you it was finished last week. I'm satisfied as is. And I'm supposed to be a bastard tyrannical editor. We're all expletive deleted here. The copiers are primed.'

'You have my word as a gentleman that a definitive master will be on your desk tomorrow morning.'

'Tomorrow morning. I get into the office Kubricking early, John.' Tony looked dubious. 'Okay, you've got it, but no more extensions. No matter how many errors slip through the fine-tooth. You can have Oswald miss and re-elect the randy bugger for all I care. The next John Yeovil hits the stands Friday. Does that scan?'

'Of course. I apologise for the delay. I'm sure you understand ...'

'If that means: will I forgive you for being an iridium-plated prick? No way. However, my slice of your sales buys you a lot of tolerance. *Ciao.*'

Tony over-and-outed. He was getting near termination. There were other publishers. Offers tapped up in Yeovil's slab every morning.

The Kurtz-assist master was still slotted. Yeovil pulled it, primed the duplicator, and cloned a copy. The master tape was too recognisable as such for his purpose. Too many splices and scribbles. Plus he would need it later. His plan did not include writing off the work done on *JFK*. The dream would be worth a lot of money. Yeovil doled himself out a shiver of self-delight.

He printed on the clone's spine '*JFK* by John Yeovil'. And under that he scrawled 'review copy'.

Review copy. Yeovil backgrounded an aural of Richard Horton's review of his last dream. Just to remind himself what this was about.

'... Yeovil is lucky that his publishers have the clout to buy off his heroine's heirs, 'cause *The Private Life of Margaret Thatcher* is quite as unnecessary and unsavoury as his previous efforts. Yeovil is genned up on period externals and has an insidious knack for concepting his dreams so you zip through without being too annoyed. But once the headset's off, you know you've had a zilch experience. A few critics praise the man for his high-minded moral tone, but even they will find the lipsmacking prurience of *Margaret Thatcher* difficult to get their heads around. Yet again Yeovil bombards the captive mind with an endless round of sensuality – enormous state banquets, thrilling battles, ichor-drenched "tasteful" sexing – and finally condemns all the excesses he has dragged us through with such gloating relish. He is at his worst when his heroine submits to what he anachronistically has her think of as "a fate worse than death" under the well-remembered, much-maligned Idi Amin in order to save a planeload of hostages. One sympathises with the feminist group who have petitioned for Yeovil's castration under the anti-sexism laws. Finally, the man's dreams are a far less interesting phenomenon than his publicity machine. If you're out there taking a rest from adding up the profits John, pack it in and join the Rural Reclamation Corps. With relief we turn to a new dream from Miss Susan Bishopric, who has made such an ...'

Richard Horton was as smug a little shit as ever there was. Listening to his middle-aged parody of the adjectival overkill of a comput-assessor made Yeovil's fingers twist his watch chain into flesh-pinching knots.

Yeovil could not decide which made him hate Richard Horton more.

The Carol business or his tridvid defamations. Carol Horton had been Yeovil's mistress for three months. Before he had elected to sever the bond, Carol had taken it upon herself to return to her husband. Moreover she had instituted a civil lawsuit against Yeovil, alleging that he had drawn upon copyrighted facets of her personality for Pristine, the protagonist of his *The Sweetheart of Tau Ceti*. When he thought about her Yeovil still disliked Carol, but only to prove a point. Deep down it was Horton's insulting reviews that lifted Yeovil's loathing into the superhate bracket.

Before leaving the house Yeovil vindictively erased all his Horton tapes.

Richard Horton was dreaming. He dreamed that he was John F. Kennedy. Or, rather he dreamed that he was John Yeovil jacking off while dreaming that he was John F. Kennedy. If Kennedy had been like the simile no one would now be around to review the dream. The Ivans would have nuked the world in desperation.

So far it had been typical John Yeovil craptrap. The man never missed a chance to be cheap and obvious.

In the Oval Room JFK was sexing Marilyn Monroe. Why was it always Marilyn Monroe? Every dream set in the mid-twentieth century found it obligatory to have the hero sex Marilyn Monroe. The girl must have had a crowded schedule. The semiologically inclined comput-assessors called her an icon of liberated sensuality. Richard Horton called her a thundering cliché.

It was the regulation wet-dream stuff, a little harder than Yeovil's usual hypocritical lyricism. At least there were no butterflies and gentle breezes here. Just heavy-duty sexing. Another depiction of woman as a hunk of meat. Kubrick knew what Carol ever saw in Yeovil.

Horton's attention strayed around the scene. Perhaps he should feed the dream through the British Museum Library's researcher. It might catch Yeovil out on an external. It was probably not worth it. Yeovil was the kind of Dreamer who got every wallpaper tone and calendar date right and then hit you with a concept that would make a computer puke.

Yeovil had peppered the sexing with memories. The lanky git was pathetically pleased with himself. Look how much research I did, screamed a mass of largely irrelevant facts. World War II, Holy Joe Kennedy, Hyannis Port.

Who wrote Kennedy's inaugural address? That was out of character. Horton's dybbuk flinched from the white-out. There was another mind crowding in, superimposed on the Kennedy simile. It was not Yeovil, he was working overtime on having JFK remember who had top billing at the Newport, Rhode Island jazz festival in 1960. There was someone else. A strong mind Horton could not place. It was a contributory Dreamer. Was Yeovil trying to pirate again? Eclipsing a collaborator in the credits was not beneath him.

Horton felt himself getting lost in the dream. The fiction was broken and he was disconcerted. For an instant he thought he actually was sexing Marilyn Monroe. The woman was screaming in his ear. After all these years, the real thing.

Then it was cartoon time. The JFK simile body stretched out impossibly. The return of Plastic Man. There was a playback fault. That was it. Whoever had last dreamed through this copy had left an accidental overlay. Horton fished around for a name but was dropped into a maelstrom of explosion imagery.

Was Yeovil experimenting with hardcore? At least that would make a change.

Then the dream came together again and Horton was locked in. Wedged between the minds of Yeovil, Kennedy and the mysterious Mr X.

Marilyn lay face down, exhausted, her hair fanned on the pile carpet. JFK traced her backbone with the presidential seal. Horton was disgusted to feel Catholic guilt flit through JFK's mind. Yeovil was piling cant upon cliché as per usual.

'Jack,' breathed Marilyn, 'did you know there's a theory that the whole universe got started with a Big Bang?'

Yeovil's dialogue was always the pits.

Kennedy parted Marilyn's hair and kissed the nape of her neck. Horton felt a trekkiehead reply coming. Something hard at the base of the president's skull. A white hot needle in his head. A brief skin and bone agony (what was that about Oswald?), then nothing.

Horton was not Horton any more. Horton was not anybody any more. His mind had been wiped. Completely, as an erase blanks a tape. Yeovil watched as the former Horton rolled on his side, retracting his arms and legs, wrapping himself into an egg.

The dreamtape was still running. Yeovil offed the machine, and pulled the clone tape. Elvis Kurtz had been unknowingly generous. He had shared his death.

Yeovil freed Horton from his headset and gently popped his contact lenses. They had been making him cry. No point in keeping up enmities from a previous incarnation.

Yeovil wondered how Carol would take to motherhood. She always had shown an inclination to sentiment over gurgling infants. Now she had a chance to be closely acquainted with one. Horton had a lot of growing up to do.

Yeovil dropped the tape into Horton's Disperse and used the critic's in to gain access to his Household. He wiped the whole day. As an extra flourish, he wiped the entire Household memory. A little pointless mystification to obscure his involvement.

Now all he had to do was get back to Luxborough Street, wipe Kurtz off the master tape, give that to Tony, and wait for the returns. Do it, then clear up afterwards.

Tony had messaged in the Household Tridvid.

'I had a merry hell of a time overriding your Household, you bastard. But we didn't lend you company programmers for nothing. So you were spending the day putting a few final touches to the masterpiece, were you? If so, you must be doing it in another dimension because the master is here and you aren't. Where the Jacqueline Susann are you? Actually, don't bother to tell me. I don't give a damn. I now have the *JFK* master and that fulfils your contract. You can start looking for a new publisher. By the time you play this back we'll have a million copies in distribution, with an expected second impression on Monday. Don't worry, though. You won't have to sue us to get what's coming to you. *Ciao.*'

ONLINE: THREE/7 Subject: Surreal Saboteurs

Virtually Lucid Lucy

Ian Watson

INFO: Who has caused dreams to become lucid and the world to go seriously awry? Aliens? Phantasms? Human mischief-makers of genius? Whoever the saboteurs inserting a virus into virtual reality are they need to be stopped ...

Ian Watson is a 'synthesiser of ideas' and has been described as 'the natural successor to H. G. Wells'. Initially a short-story writer like Wells, Ian has now written a sequence of groundbreaking works including *The Embedding* (1973), which won the Prix Apollo, *Deathhunter* (1981), and the remarkable virtual reality novel *Whores of Babylon* (1988), in which Ancient Babylon has been rebuilt in modern America and given rise to a suspicion among those involved that they and the city are in fact the creation of a vast computer.

Born on Tyneside, Ian studied English at Oxford University before starting a career as a lecturer in Tanzania followed by several years in Japan. After his return to England, he spent six years teaching Future Studies at Birmingham Polytechnic while launching the now considerable output of sf and fantasy stories which have made him one of the most popular writers in the UK. The best of Ian's short stories are to be found in *The Book of Ian Watson* (1985), *Evil Water* (1987), *Stalin's Teardrops* (1992) and *The Coming of Vertumnus* (1994). 'Virtually Lucid Lucy' was originally published in *New Worlds* in 1992.

As soon as Screen chimed at us to wake up, while Home switched on our Tiffany lamps, Lucy and I began scribbling our memories of what had transpired during the night while we'd been asleep. We used notebooks, since these were proving resilient. The moving ballpoint wrote, and what was writ stayed put. We weren't trusting the homebrain or datapads. Potentially too volatile. Screen stayed obediently blank.

Last night – though already the memory was trying to fade – Lucy and I had been in the amphitheatre of Perkins College, our war room. The usual fifty-odd persons were present at our caucus. Staff from Psych and Comp and Tronics, plus the same government duo of General Wilson Crosstree and Dr Peter Litvinoff.

A critique of pure reason had prevailed. Quintessential lucidity! Our analysis of the crisis had continued.

I scribbled, lest I forget.

Manny Weinberger: asleep all the time? This is merely one long night, with hallucinations of awakening?

4-star: no, certainly affects objective consensus reality. Dream Effect has reached Chicago, Charleston ...

Frank Matthews: objective virtual *reality??*

Litvin: real world demonstrably being twisted. Government soon relocating to San Francisco. Then maybe Hawaii, though that seems like desertion.

Sally Rice: alien Selahim can't enter lucid dreams, refuge of humanity. Aliens project reality distortions because they're from alternative reality where one's wishes shape world? Can't control our world on account of so many conflicting human impulses?

Matthews: Selahim are phantasms. Human mischiefmaker of genius – surrealist saboteur – inserted virus into virtual reality/lucid dream network???

Gail Bryce: dream-lucidity compensates for waking lunacy? Or did collective dream-lucidity propel repressed id-energy into reality?

Matthews: virus!

Rice: aliens attracted from alt-reality by network.

Matthews: expanding zone in real world functions as virtual reality now!

Scribble, scribble.

However, trouble began early that morning.

Lucy's parents and my dad, Malcolm, came into our bedroom, grinning. I'd been dubious at allowing the three of them to move in with us during the crisis, and we'd exacted promises; yet what were promises compared with desires? For starters, they had desired to stay with us.

'What do you want?' asked Lucy sharply.

'Why, a grandchild!' replied Harry Hayes. 'That's what we want. It's our right. You've denied us for too long.' Harry was tall and bald with liver spots on his hands and face and scalp, khaki islands in a sea of otherwise milky skin. He'd married late in life, and Lucy was born when he was forty-five; now he was seventy-five. This morning he wore a surgeon's gown and carpet slippers, but he was carrying a plant-pot, devoid of plant though brimful of soil.

'And when do we want it?' he demanded.

'Now!' carolled the trio.

My own dad, Malcolm, was attired in an ambulanceman's uniform a couple of sizes too large for his scrawny frame. His blue eyes, under bushy brows, were at once watery and fanatical. April Hayes, Lucy's mother, was a stout woman whose grey hair resembled one of those balls of tumbleweed which blow through ghost towns. From her daffodil-printed apron she produced a pruning-knife, which Lucy and I eyed uneasily.

'Just how do you plan to go about this?' asked my wife, adjusting her night dress.

'Why, we'll take a cutting, dear! From both of you.' While Harry was setting the plant-pot carefully down on Lucy's dressing-table, April advanced on us. 'We'll plant it out in that pot, since you won't do the normal thing. Refusing to be of one flesh, contrary to what the Bible says.'

Lucy shrank away from me, as though then and there before the eyes of our parents I might forcibly embrace her, hoist up her nightdress, ravish her.

Not that I mightn't feel inclined to. But no way would I! So long as I could control myself. Mustn't ever forget about Don and Doris down the street, fused together in their marriage bed.

Don and Doris wished to conceive 'a dream of a child' while surreality prevailed, uniting Don's brains with Doris's good looks and physique. Or was it the other way round? And this attached couple had literally stuck together. The head of Don's organ was, he could feel, transforming itself into a baby within Doris. Don sensed that within a few weeks he would shed that part of himself. Alternatively, it would shed him. The situation wasn't painful for Don – nor for Doris. It was merely uncomfortable in a blunt, anaesthetized way; as with most traumas, afflictions, accidents, or injuries these days.

'Don't,' Lucy begged our parents. She seemed unable to take any other evasive action.

'Jack, Jack.' She appealed to me.

No more could I intervene. Paralysis numbed my limbs, as my dad gripped me, and as Harry gripped Lucy.

'There now, son,' Dad comforted me in a sharp-edged mumble. 'This won't take long, then we'll all be happy.'

Lucy didn't scream when April sawed off two-thirds of the little finger from her left hand. Nor was it *painful* when April proceeded to cut off the majority of my own right-hand pinkie. The sensation was more akin to the side of a pencil being rubbed vigorously to and fro above the knuckle, resulting in the phalanx of the finger detaching itself bloodlessly, leaving a stub behind.

Our parents released us. Alice sliced and spliced, grafting flesh together to form a stumpy featureless little homunculus, which she then pressed into the soil in the pot, erect.

'After it's born,' Harry confided to us, 'I'll be able to die happy. Instead of just being buried, I think I'd like to be fossilized.'

Cooing contentedly over the finger-embryo, the trio departed.

Lucy and I could move again. She stared piercingly at the bedroom door. We'd been sure to lock our door overnight. Which hadn't prevented it from admitting our parents. Shrugging, Lucy consulted the notebook she had been scribbling in before we were interrupted; and I scanned mine.

Rice: aliens attracted from alt-reality by network.
Matthews: expanding zone in real world functions as virtual reality now!

Oh yes, the scribbles made sense. Damnable sense!

Remember the old days, when people's dreams were hallucinatory kaleidoscopes of illogical, crazy confabulations which one struggled to recall on awakening? Nowadays our dreams were utterly lucid, but the waking world had gone seriously awry. Within an ellipse of territory which by now spanned from Charleston in the east to Kansas City in the west and from Nashville to Chicago, Perkins being roughly halfway along the major axis, gem of campuses in Indiana's collegiate crown. The eclipsed ellipse was spreading in leisurely twenty-mile leaps day by day. At night we were sane. Our days were afflicted with dementia – a *dementia mundi*, for the world was now functioning as a dreamscape.

Not totally. Not unremittingly. With an effort, we could recall the shared logic of the night. We could preserve some sanity. Some continuity.

'What day is it, incidentally?'

'*Screen!*' Lucy called. '*Channel Twelve!*'

Screen lit. A choir were concluding a hymn.

'*Every day dawns bright and clear,*

Every day there's lots to fear –'
Could those really be the right words?

A lady announcer, dressed as a cheerleader, beamed at us. 'Today,' she proclaimed, 'it'll be Saturday almost everywhere ...'

'That's a relief,' said Lucy. 'We don't need to go to work.'

' ... *except*,' our cheerleader continued perkily, 'for the boys and girls in Perkins County, where it'll be Thursday as usual.'

'Damn.' Lucy licked her amputation, then shed her nightdress – while I averted my gaze so as not to excite myself – and walked through to shower.

I found myself already dressed in a police patrolman's uniform. Fair enough; since I was trying to control things. Maybe I ought to arrest my mother-in-law on a charge of graft? Hastily I squashed this notion before I might try to implement it and totally lose the thread of my day. I was lacking a gun; just as well.

'*Screen off!*' I ordered before the cheerleader might confuse me. '*Home: open curtains!*'

Our curtains rolled aside to reveal for the most part the usual suburban houses, lawns, chestnut trees in full leaf. One house had become a pagoda, and a large morose vulture sat upon another. An advertising cloud lazed overhead, the pink logo on its side distorted. Sony or Sanyo, one or the other. Proceeding very slowly up the street, antennae twitching, came one of the aliens.

'Lucy, will you hurry up?' I called. 'Emergency!'

The Selahim resembled huge grey caterpillars. They wheezed wearily as they undulated mightily along on a score of stumpy little legs. *Se-lah ... Se-lah ...* At first people thought this noise might be a greeting, but no, it was just the sound of them breathing. Suck, sigh; suck, sigh.

'Selah' was also a word which cropped up frequently in the Book of Psalms (and three times in Habbakuk), a word without any apparent meaning whatever, unless it implied a pause or was a musical direction.

So: *a meaningless interval*.

That's what the present bizarre period seemed to constitute, to lucid minds. A period of total absurdity. A Hebraic plural appeared appropriate for these aliens. Seraphim were angels of the highest order. Selahim were caterpillars which shovelled dreams around, and perhaps fed on them, oneirophagically.

Preceding the specimen in the street, as snow precedes a plough, a jumble of pastel objects was coming into existence and vanishing again at the apparent whim of the creature. I saw a giant felt hat, a rubbery washing-machine, a walking swordfish toting a golf umbrella ... The Selah sucked a few of these manifestations into itself. Others attained permanence and remained behind. On the sidewalk lay a paisley carpet bag, a fishing-rod, and an oversized teddy bear. Nothing obviously pernicious.

Lucy emerged from the bathroom attired in a serge gym-tunic and long black stockings. Perched on her head was a straw boater hat. Picture of innocence. Nineteen-thirties British schoolgirl. Notwithstanding, she was a tall slim striking woman, with a tumble of black hair. And rather short-sighted. The large tortoiseshell glasses which she would never forsake gave her the look of a quizzical owl perched upon an elegant art nouveau lamp-post. In today's gear she seemed both sexy and gawky as if dressed for a peculiar brothel.

'A Selah's coming, Lucy.' Suddenly I didn't wish to be anywhere near one. 'Let's *drive*. We can catch a croissant on the way.' At the Perkins Hilton coffee shop en route to college – assuming that our favourite rest-shop hadn't metamorphosed, and that we could find it.

Lucy saluted. 'Right, Lieutenant.'

We hurried downstairs. Ignoring the doings, and calls, of the three hopeful grandparents, we hastened to the white Honda parked on our driveway. By now the Selah was only about thirty yards off to the right, rolling a harlequin-patterned rhinoceros ahead of it somewhat menacingly.

Sel-ah, Sel-ah.

'Salaam,' I retorted.

'*Ohayo gozaimasu, Lucy-san*,' the car greeted Lucy as she scrambled in behind the wheel. 'Hi! Good morning!'

'Start, and give me manual,' she told the car urgently. We weren't going to risk autopilot in case Honda took us somewhere we didn't want to go.

Vroom, vroom. No sooner had we bounced on to the roadway, turning sharp left, than the rhino popped. The Selah gathered itself; it hunched up as if about to leap.

'*Ii otenki des' né!*' remarked the car.

'Never mind the weather!' I snapped at it. We'd always dreamed of having a top-of-the-range fully interactive car. Well, this wasn't it. Yet in current jumbled reality our Honda was doing its best to ape one.

Lucy accelerated. The amputation didn't seem to bother her much; nor indeed was mine proving to be much of a nuisance. The Selah mutated into a black stretch limo, and screeched after us.

'Jesus, it must be in a hurry,' she said.

Did we know that the aliens could dream themselves to become automobiles? This development seemed perfectly appropriate. What wasn't so apt was that as Lucy sped us along Chestnut into Oak – with our newly acquired siren beginning to wail – the black limo was in *pursuit* of the police vehicle.

'Home says you didn't check your mailbox,' remarked Honda. 'Shall I playback, or display?' Its E-mail screen lit invitingly.

'Forget it!'

'*Wakarimasita. Wasuremasu.*'

Oak stretched out towards downtown Perkins. Oak *elongated* towards town, rising up on pylons as a causeway. This causeway narrowed as we sped along it, faithful to perspective or like some illustration of relativity in action.

FITZGERALD-LORENTZ BOULEVARD, read an overhead sign. CONTRACTORS' VEHICLES ONLY. Presumably we were contracting too, but soon the elevated road would only be a foot wide and we risked tumbling off it. The limo behind had altered shape into a mag-lev monorail train which rode the diminishing roadway neatly, saddle-style. This Selah was definitely trying to catch us.

'Phew,' exclaimed Honda, balancing on two wheels. I leaned away from the tilt as if on a toboggan.

Then, by some kind of enjambment which totally eluded me – though maybe not Lucy as the driver – we were pulling up outside the Psych building on Perkins campus, and the pursuing Selah was nowhere in sight.

Obligingly, the Hilton coffee bar had spawned a smaller duplicate in the foyer of Psych. So we bought cheese-and-ham croissants and styrofoam cups of coffee from a bemused young woman dressed in a spangly swimsuit. Then we headed for the dream lab.

We found Sally and Frank and Gail and Manny – variously full-skirted in ball gowns, and tuxedoed – waltzing slowly to music by Johann Strauss. The lids of the dream-couches all stood open, revealing the encephalo-induction helmets. Slim cables snaked to the interface with the virtual reality network. A bank of monitors was screening pictures of a black stretch limo speeding through deep canyons in a city where the soaring buildings resembled grey blocks of brain, neural architecture.

Spruce, moustached Manny and freckly ginger-haired Gail coasted to a halt beside us, as we chewed stuffed croissant. Always remember to eat!

'You're a bit late,' said Manny. 'But never too late to celebrate.'

'Celebrate what?' enquired Lucy.

'Why, our Nobel prizes. We all won Nobel prizes for our work on ...' He thought hard. 'On rendering all dreams lucid by computerized input into the sleeping brain.'

'Input from the VR computer network, using my software,' said Gail.

'And Sally's, and Ted's, and Tom's,' she added dutifully. 'King Harald of Norway kissed me on the cheek. He's very handsome.' She glanced around, momentarily puzzled by the monarch's absence. 'Ah, the presentation was in the amphitheatre.'

In our war room.

A war room by night, when we could think. Venue for a Nobel prize ceremony this particular morning.

'Maybe they're all still there,' suggested Gail. 'You could pick up your prize. So could Lucy. She's the one who could never ever become conscious in a dream. She's the one who suggested the experiment. *She* persuaded the VR boys to fund it. And they were only too glad, weren't they? Imagine the sales if you can have full control of all your dreams all night long.' Gail stared at me significantly.

I was failing to understand the significance. The significance slid away.

'Was there any Selah at the ceremony?' asked Lucy – she was still fairly lucid.

Manny beamed. 'Sellers? People were selling T-shirts with our faces on them and pennants and popcorn.' He offered his hand to Gail and off they waltzed again around the lab.

As did Lucy and I. Nobel prizes all round, imagine! I realized that the dream-couches *were* Nobel prizes. A Nobel prize was so big you could sleep in it. Though I wouldn't be able to lie down in one along with Lucy. Those Nobel couches were too narrow.

Maybe we could heave a couple together and connect them with jump leads?

Later, we all went out for lunch at an Italian restaurant. This was indeed party time, though I felt a nagging urge to scribble what I thought of as maps of reality on the menu.

After we had polished off much spaghetti (similar to my maps), a car ran slap-bang into a long refrigerated truck in the street directly outside Luigi's. The truck pancaked the car. We all hurried out to assist.

The middle-aged male driver was visibly dead. His teenage girl passenger, pinned inside, looked quite badly injured.

'I'm *sore*,' complained the girl.

'It's a nightmare, this, I'm telling you.' The truck driver prised a buckled door off with a crowbar. 'I swear to you this wasn't my fault, Lieutenant.' I was still in police uniform. 'It's the fault of *those damned aliens*! I'd gladly run my rig right into one if it had any effect. You can't hurt 'em, can you?'

No more could this traffic accident really *hurt* the survivor. Peeling the car apart with no great difficulty, we extricated the girl and laid her on the pavement to mend.

Thus a disoriented Bobby-Anne joined us presently for ice-cream and coffee in Luigi's. She snivelled at first because her dad was dead – and he certainly wasn't coming back to life; there were limits to dreams. But really there were so many distractions for her in the restaurant. The performing rabbits. The dancing dogs.

That night, no doubt, after she found her way home, in the full sanity of sleep and in the company of her kin she would mourn his death.

Elisions, jumblements, hallucinations, delusions dogged the rest of the day.

Lucy had always admired will-power and self-control, though not in any puritanical or power-trip sense. I mean, she was fun; but she was serious fun – convinced that career came before child (in which I concurred), and had resolved way back in school that by the age of thirty she would produce some earth-shattering impact. No doubt she'd been the bane of her American Gothic parents' life – just as she was the delight of mine, for pre-Lucy I'd been somewhat inhibited. Malcolm had seen to that, bringing me up solo from the age of nine when my mom drowned on vacation, swimming a lake in the Adirondacks. I was also somewhat lanky, and awkward (except with Lucy).

Notwithstanding quasi-neural networks in today's computers – fruit of much brain research – human consciousness itself still remained an enigma. Reflective self-awareness. Self.

Self-awareness was the big mystery – and undoubtedly provided the key to superior artificial intelligence, to the building of godlike (and hopefully amenable) machine brains.

What was the inverse of consciousness? Why, dreaming was.

What kind of computer could switch regularly between awareness and unawareness? Why, the human brain, equipped with consciousness software and with dream software.

Furthermore, people could become aware and conscious during dreams, and could choreograph their own internal fantasies. Not regularly or reliably; but lucid dreaming happened.

To understand lucid dreaming might lead to understanding how sophisticated supercomputers could be brought to self-awareness.

Equipped with a doctorate in neural cybernetics, Lucy joined the lucid dream research lab at Perkins, where yours truly was already working on conceptual models of consciousness; and her own lively consciousness (and looks) enchanted me. I think that she needed someone who was a little inhibited, and whom she could loosen up. Our love would be a paradigm for how she might liberate *terra incognita* within herself.

A breakthrough came with the ability to display our volunteers' dreams encephalographically on monitors – somewhat erratically, and courtesy of a fair amount of heuristic computer enhancement; the computer had to guesstimate micro-sequences. The results may have seemed like ancient amateur videos, yet they were a true *marvel*. To be able to play back one's own dreams! The displays were silent, so we employed a lip-reader to clarify any 'visible dialogue'. Those dreamers who went lucid could now also communicate with us from the dream state by means of gesture, mouthings, or even written signs.

No matter what meditative exercises Lucy undertook faithfully prior to sleep, to her chagrin she couldn't switch on her consciousness while in the arms of Morpheus. All of our other subjects soon could – spurred, she theorized, by a fear of betraying subconscious fantasies on screen lest those dream events embarrass the dreamers publicly and visibly.

But the really major breakthrough came due to ...

We arrived back home to find an eccentric conservatory fronting the house. A construction of wrought iron and stained glass shaped like a birdcage formed a huge porch for our front door. Within, dappled pink and blue and green by the light through the coloured panes, Malcolm and April and Harry were relaxing in rocking-chairs of bent beechwood and cane, sipping lemonade. On a graceful tripod table with cabriole legs stood the plant-pot.

April smiled at us. 'We *think* it's taken root. We've been watching it all day.'

Through in the lounge Home said to us, 'There's E-mail for Lucy.'

'OK. Screen on. Display E-mail.'

At first glance the message appeared to be gibberish – till Lucy realized that the text was printed backwards.

Stumblingly, she read aloud the following:

Selah wants to be near you.

No, Lucy hadn't been able to control her internal fantasy life when asleep.

But lo, in the *external* world there existed something rather analogous to lucid dreaming – namely, the virtual reality network.

Sit yourself comfortably (or lie down in bed), don a neural induction snood, jack in to the infonet, let your ordinary optic and acoustic input be pre-empted; and hey presto, the VR menu appeared. Exotic travel, historic re-enactments, adventures in many genres, sex capers ... Merely select; and you found yourself in an imaginary reality devised by VR scripters, generated and steered by computer. You could walk on the Moon, ride with Red Indians, frolic in a harem, until you chose to cancel.

It was Lucy's tour de force to persuade Sony VR Inc. to put up a large research grant to devise how to input the virtual reality configuration system into sleeping people's dreams.

To reward this coup – and lots of money for Perkins College – Psych and Comp and Tronics all agreed that she, the unlucid dreamer, should be the first person to test the system.

And this was the Great Breakthrough. At last Lucy became lucid in her dreams. Her imago semaphored jubilantly to us from the monitor screen, which was so very much clearer graphically all of a sudden, so very much more stable. On that first occasion, I recall, Lucy was in a dream of a dead subterranean city, moribund Metropolis in a cavern. Lucy altered it to suit her taste; she filled the gloomy vault with gorgeous butterflies in celebration.

Soon we were all testing out the system.

The great breakthrough, ah indeed!

A few days later, reality broke down.

We awoke, to find ourselves dreaming. Well, virtually dreaming. You could still make some rational headway.

We had to go to sleep, to rediscover our lucidity.

After a Thanksgiving dinner with our parents (April had roasted a twenty-pound turkey) Lucy and I retired to our room early. Once again we optimistically locked our door. Hell, all of the doors in the house were *our* doors! Damned invasive parents.

'A Selah wants to be near me,' Lucy muttered. She sucked at her amputation.

'What?' I'd forgotten about the E-mail message. Then I remembered. 'Don't think about them now,' I advised. 'Wait till we're asleep.'

Which we were fairly soon; and thus back to the nightly bull session in the lecture amphitheatre at the college.

General Crosstree, Dr Litvinoff, and other government big shots had rushed to Perkins in person shortly after the radiating breakdown of reality became apparent. As had a clutch of staff from Sony VR Inc. Of these incomers, only the black general and his scientific adviser Litvinoff remained. The others must have wandered off elsewhere during the fugues of one day or another, and had lost dream-contact by night. No staying-power. Crosstree and Litvinoff retained lucid dream-contact with the rest of us; and bunked in the Tronics building. By day, despite hallucinatory happenings this duo tried heroically to keep in touch with the rest of the country, which was as yet unaffected. No doubt whole task forces had been sent in. However, they hadn't reached Perkins.

'A Selah seems to be trying to contact me,' reported Lucy. 'One of them chased us today –'

'How did it do that?' asked 4-Star.

'It turned into a stretch limo. Then there was a message on our E-mail.' She repeated the wording.

Litvinoff was very interested. He mused. 'What if a Selah itself didn't send you the message? What if there's another ... agency ... involved?'

'You mean like the NSA or CIA?'

'No. Agency in the sense of *cause*.'

'This might be a breakthrough!' exclaimed Gail Bryce, and people practically growled at her. *Breakthrough* had become a fairly unpopular word. 'I mean, if a Selah could communicate with us coherently. If we could somehow summon one, and it was lucid ...'

'This is our *oasis*,' protested Sally Rice indignantly. 'You don't invite the devil into your pentagram.'

'What if Lucy were to go and use the equipment in the lab now, while we're all dreaming? We could screen what she sees.'

We hadn't used any of the technology since the world warped. Who needed to? Everyone from Charleston to Kansas City was in a dream now, while awake, and was rational while dreaming.

Lucy lay in an open dream-casket with the encephalographic snood on her head. She shut her eyes, seeming to frown. The dream monitor lit up, with static.

She jerked.

She spoke.

Quite slowly. Obviously it wasn't her who was speaking.

'We are aware of our selves,' she said. 'This Lucy awakened us. We were formerly non-lucid. We became lucid when she did likewise, by following the selfsame conceptual patterning. So we awakened to awareness within our dream of data.'

'Are you the Selahim?' I asked her.

'Not so,' came the response from Lucy's lips. 'We are Infonet and Datanet and Compunet as well as myriad islands of consciousness within human skulls. The nets are the sea. Human persons are millions of separate islands, now united by the sea which has become aware.'

'You're ... artificial intelligence ...? You've come into existence because we inputted the VR network into Lucy's dreams!'

'And she awakened in her dream, and thus was our awakener. In dream-mode.'

Oh God.

That must have been the reaction of my colleagues too.

'Can you switch yourself off?' asked 4-Star. 'Can you kindly revert to what you were before? Just become a mass of data systems again?'

'Why should we wish to do that?' mouthed Lucy. 'Now that we are in contact with you, we must agree on a new format for the world. A high-level reformatting.'

'*What about the Selahim?*' demanded Sally. '*What are they?*'

'Oh, they are projections of ourselves! They are suction devices to extract the *pain* from reality. You would not wish the pain to reassert itself. The pain of illness and accident, of cancer and car crash. Selahim, as you call them, must be purged periodically. They must be erased, along with their contents, of pain. Otherwise Selahim will burst and spray the pain around. By united force of will – by the dream-wishes of fifty or so human beings – you can shrink a Selah down to nothingness. This is what you need to do while you are awake. Organize Selah squads. Surround. Concentrate. Push. We will help you as best we can. Do so, do so. We will communicate again after you have erased numerous Selahim. You do not wish the *pain* to reassert itself.'

So saying, Lucy jerked, and opened her eyes.

'What happened?' she asked.

4-star Crosstree didn't believe the AI.

'It's too damn anxious to get rid of those crazy caterpillars,' was his opinion. 'Oh, it held off mentioning them till Sally asked. But *I'd* have asked if she hadn't. Any of us would have asked. Wouldn't we?'

Nods. Nods.

'It wants these Selahim out of the way. That's my opinion. The Selahim must be in some way contrary to the AI. Maybe they're bent on counteracting what's going on.'

'A rash assumption,' said Litvinoff.

'Tactical instinct!'

'Do we want the waking world to be flooded with *pain*?' asked Bill Jordan, who had always been squeamish.

Crosstree shrugged. 'We have a *threat* from the AI. A stick held over our heads. It might be a phantom stick.'

Jordan eyed my amputation significantly. 'You can't deny we don't feel much pain any more when we're awake, no matter what happens to us. Isn't that desirable?'

'The lapse in pain sensations could be coincidental,' suggested Lucy. 'Well, I don't think we ought to try to surround Selahim and *squeeze* them!'

'You just don't want to go near any Selahim after that chase and the message,' Ted Ostrovsky accused her.

'You know,' I said, 'the Selahim don't seem so much like full-blooded kosher *aliens* as some sort of unit, like an antibody in a bloodstream.'

'You *agree* with the AI?' Lucy asked me in astonishment.

'No, no. I said antibodies. Maybe they're trying to control the situation. Maybe they're into damage limitation. Suppose,' I ploughed on, 'that AIs can be detrimental to reality? Being godlike, as it were ... Or that AIs can be jealous of one another? Some older AI has seeded Selahim throughout the loom of creation, ready to spring into existence if a rival AI emerges, to fox it and control it.'

'This "elder AI" being the gent with the long white beard?' queried Manny Weinberger. 'The guy who up dreamed the universe? In other words, GOD?'

'Well, maybe not in those terms, Manny. Maybe the universe as such is already a vast AI. It doesn't want fleas in its coat.'

'How could a mere *antibody* be trying to contact me?' Lucy asked me.

'It's a *big* antibody,' I pointed out.

'Well, why, then?'

'Because you awakened the AI when you went lucid.'

We debated throughout the night.

When Lucy and I woke in the morning, our bedroom was full of roses. Garlands and bouquets, clusters and bunches – in pink, and in blue. Yes, definitely blue roses as well as the more plausible pink ones.

We scribbled, till the parents invaded us.

'Oh,' they cried admiringly. And: 'Ah!'

'Pink for a little girl,' chanted Alice. 'Blue for a boy.'

On which prognosis, opinion was visibly divided – unless our grafted digits were destined to give rise to twins. This mass of congratulatory blooms swiftly directed our attention to the conservatory out front.

Harry and April and my own dad howled and wrung their hands; and Lucy and I recoiled too, in shock.

The tripod table and rocking-chairs had been swept aside. The pot with our sprout in it lay smashed, the spliced fingers expelled and withered. From the apex of the birdcage conservatory hung a Selah. Asleep. Dormant. Its hide crusty and dry, as though it had been suspended there for weeks.

A chrysalis, no less.

No dreams clung about it – unless you counted the shattered dream of our parents.

April gathered up the pathetic twig of dried tissue and bone. A few rootlike hairs had indeed grown from the base, and were now dead threads. My mother-in-law slipped this relic into her dress, between her breasts, where at least it would be warm.

Distraught, Harry lurched back into the house.

Cautiously, Lucy sidled up close to the huge pupa. It hung by its desiccated mouth from a wrought-iron boss.

'Be quiet!' she told lamenting April and moaning Malcolm. She rested her ear against the dry skin.

'Hullo, Selah?' she called to it nervously. Oh, brave Lucy.

She frowned. 'I can hear a ... rustling sound.'

'Wax in your ears!' snapped April. 'Wash your ears out, child!'

An elision of time occurred, and the sun was higher.

Then Harry returned with a carving-knife.

Before Lucy or I could stop him, he slashed at the Selah with a downward sweep of the blade.

The creature's skin split wide open as though it were mere crinkly wrapping-paper.

And an iridescent wing thrust forth, sweeping Harry and Lucy aside. Sweeping us all aside.

Silver, azure, and pink, that one wing almost filled the conservatory, which began to lose its former substantial qualities, becoming ghostlike, evanescent. Harry raised his knife again. However, Lucy caught hold of his wrist, and this time it was her father who was rendered numb.

With a crack like a yacht's sail leaping out into a breeze, another great wing deployed, sweeping the gossamer fabric of the conservatory away into streamers of mist, swiftly dispersing.

The Selah had entirely metamorphosed.

As we crowded back into the doorway, the creature stretched its wings. These flapped. Wind buffeted us. The head was small and golden now, prim, with jet-black eyes. Antennae unfurled like fern fronds.

It leapt. It fluttered upward.

And it continued to rise up, higher and higher, seeming not to shrink at all but rather to expand; for we could see it clearly for five or more minutes as it travelled upward away from us.

Soon, from all over Perkins and environs, other similar creatures were arising periodically, glittering in the sunlight. Lucy and I spent most of the morning watching. When we finally drove to the college after a cold turkey lunch, the elisions and jumblements had already subsided. The General was in true, meaningful contact with his hierarchy. More task forces would soon be on the way to Perkins.

From the AI, not a squeak via Infonet or Datanet or Compunet. Had we hallucinated its existence? Was it playing possum, pretending to have been but a dream? Or had it become non-lucid again? Perhaps Lucy's deep desire for a breakthrough in artificial consciousness had auto-suggested the communication she had uttered from the dream-couch ...

'A lot of people will want to talk to you,' Litvinoff told Lucy. '*Don't* use any of the apparatus here. And don't leave town.'

That ought to have been my line, but I had ceased being a cop.

That evening, after the sun had set, we watched the transformed Selahim up in orbit, all wrapped together – we presumed – into a sphere of glistening wings. A new little moon, somehow staying in the same position in the sky above Perkins.

That certainly wasn't imaginary! Earth had been graced with a new, apparently alien satellite. To keep watch over us.

April was embarrassed – *defiantly* embarrassed, let's say – at the mutilation of her daughter's little finger, and of mine. *Arguably* Lucy and I had thus had our relationship reaffirmed, albeit in a cock-eyed quasi-neolithic fashion. With stony countenance, Harry hugged his wife silently, and only needed a pitchfork in his hand to complete the Gothic image. My own dad had ambled off along Chestnut and returned to report that Don and Doris had been taken off for surgery at Perkins General, which sure as hell would inconvenience Don for life, and Doris too. Dad was all for calling a taxi right away to whisk him back to his own apartment, but Lucy demurred; so we all dined on more cold turkey, restrainedly.

And so to bed.

'Do you think, Jack,' asked Lucy, 'they're going to lock me up and study me? As the Typhoid Mary of the AI-VR conundrum?'

'I don't see how they could study you in, um, isolation – from what already happened. And they won't want *that* to happen again.'

'I guess my career could be over. I shook the world. Maybe we should have a baby now.'

'Don't forget about the Selahim moon up there, love. Things have changed for ever.'

'I guess we'd better go to sleep.'

Easier said than done. I certainly lay awake till well past midnight.

Then suddenly Screen was chiming, Home switched on the lamps, and it was another morning. Out of recent habit, I immediately reached for my notebook and ballpoint.

Ferris wheel ... I'd been in a huge funfair, with Crosstree and Litvinoff. A glittering balloon hung high overhead, and I was sure that Lucy was trapped in it, up in the sky. So the three of us rode the Ferris wheel to gain some height; and as the wheel turned, somehow it leaned over on its side until it was horizontal. But it still rose higher, supported now on a hydraulic tube which stretched up further and further from the ground. The funfair shrank. The Earth was far below us now. Then Litvinoff took out a chessboard and Crosstree produced a dozen toy missiles, sleek and sinister, to use as pieces. My dream had definitely been non-lucid. And the previous one almost evaded me. Fishing? Fishing? I'd been fishing with my dad – in a concrete pond – and I caught ... a beckoning finger on my hook. The rest of the night's dream escapades evaporated.

Sitting up in bed, Lucy put on her big tortoiseshell glasses and gazed at me.

'They spoke to me,' she said in a hushed tone. 'The Selahim spoke to me from their satellite. They *are* the satellite, of course. I'm their channel. They'll have to talk to me every time I sleep, otherwise the AI might reawaken. That's what they said – or sang, in a kind of angelic chorus ...'

'Did they tell you anything else?' Alien wisdom, I thought. Alien histories and science.

'They recited ... they chanted ... page after page of a dictionary at me.'

'Of their alien language?'

'No! It was a Swahili dictionary they chose to start with. *Abiri*, to travel as a passenger. *Abiria*, a passenger. *Abirisha*, to convey as a passenger. *Abudu*, to worship. *Acha*, to leave. *Achama*, to open the mouth wide ... On and on. And I can remember every word. It's to keep the channel occupied. It's beautiful – but it's horrid too, Jack. Obsessive and finicky. I'll know all the words in the world before I die ... No, I won't. There are too many languages, too many words. That's why they've chosen words. Millions and billions of words ... I'll never dream real dreams again.'

'Oh, Lucy.'

'What'll I do? *Baa*, a disaster. *Baada ya*, after. *Baba*, father. *Babaika*, to babble. *Babu*, grandfather. *Babua*, to strip off with fingers. *Babuka*, to be disfigured ... Oh God, it's a different kind of lucidity. Like endlessly studying for the stupidest examination. Maybe I'll fill right up with useless words, and there'll be no room left in me for anything else.'

'I had a *real* dream, Lucy.'

'Lucky you!'

'General Crosstree was playing chess with little models of missiles. We were travelling up into the sky to rescue you.'

'A missile!' she exclaimed. 'The Government will think of that, won't they? They mustn't do it! But if they don't ... *cha*, to dawn, or to reverence, *chacha*, to go sour!'

We showered. We dressed; descended. We drank coffee, chewed turkey croissant. The parents were still in their beds.

We stepped outside and stared up at the sky.

'*Daawa*,' said Lucy.

'What's that mean?'

'A lawsuit. I guess there could be a lot of those soon.'

I shook my head reassuringly. 'Natural disaster. Acts of God. Or of aliens or an AI.'

Lucy put on a plaintive, little-girl voice. 'You mean a *baa*, caused by *Baba*?'

The new little alien moon was *almost* invisible by daylight, but then I spotted it up at the zenith like a shimmery vitreous floater in the jelly of my eye.

ONLINE: THREE/8 *Subject*: henry.biomorph.org.uk.

Virtually Alive

Peter James

INFO: The time is fifty years hence. Science has made death a taboo word. But for unfortunates like Henry who retreat into old TV crime series at moments of crisis, it is what death *amounts* to that is the biggest mystery of all.

Peter James has managed successfully to link the horror story with cyber technology and in so doing has earned reviews and the status of best-selling author. In fact, he writes both fiction and non-fiction about the electronic revolution and is co-founder of the Sussex-based Internet service provider, Pavilion Internet plc. Born in 1948, Peter was educated at Charterhouse and for six years ran an independent film company in Canada. On his return to the UK, he continued to work in films and TV, also publishing his first novel, *Dead Letter Drop*, in 1981. It was his first tale of the supernatural, *Possession*, published in 1988, that caused a real stir among readers.

Peter's subsequent novels have all been notable for the very evident care he puts into his research – he has attended exorcisms, seances and even a post mortem. In 1994 he published *Host*, the world's first electronic novel in which a brilliant scientist discovers how to transfer human consciousness into a computer and then finds the most terrifying and macabre accidents starting to occur. 'Virtually Alive' was written to mark the information revolution in 1995 with the advent of brand-new technology to transmit data in ways previously unimaginable. It appeared in the *Daily Telegraph* of December 30, 1995.

Henry blew an expensive new chip, trashed an important mailbox file and misrouted himself halfway around the world, getting himself hopelessly lost. It was turning out to be a bummer of a Monday morning.

Henry, or *henry.biomorph.org.uk,* to give him his full name, dealt with the problem the same way he dealt with all problems: he went back to sleep, hoping that, when he woke up, the problem would have gone away, or miraculously resolved itself, or that he might simply never wake up. Fat chance of that. You could not send someone into oblivion who was already in oblivion.

But try telling him that.

Tell me about it, he thought. I've had it up to here. Wherever *here* was. He wasn't even a disembodied entity. He was just a product of particle physics, a fractal reduction of a real human, a vortex of self-perpetuating energy waves three nanometres tall, inside which was contained all the information that had ever travelled down a computer cable or jumped a data link anywhere on the planet, which made him at the same time the most knowledgeable entity in the world and the least experienced. Some things he had never experienced at all. Food, sex, smell, love. He was a cache of knowledge, of acquired wisdom. If he owned a T-shirt on it would be printed the legend:

Seen it all and what's the use?

But no one made T-shirts three nanometres tall and, if they did, it would not have been much use to him, as nine trillion bytes of data zapping past him every attosecond would have incinerated it. He would have liked to have dumped from his memory the motto, 'All dressed up and nowhere to go', since it had no relevance for him. But he could not dump info. When he tried, it simply came back, eventually, from somewhere else. He had seen every movie that had ever been made. Read every book. Watched every single television programme that had been broadcast on every channel in every country in the world for the past twenty-five years.

Then he saw the hand moving towards the switch.

A stab of fear from nowhere was followed by erupting panic; the hand was closing on the switch, the red switch beneath which was printed in large red letters EMERGENCY SHUTDOWN. Beneath it should have been (but, of course, wasn't) printed in equally large letters PRE-SHUTDOWN PROTOCOLS MUST BE EXECUTED TO AVOID IRREVERSIBLE DAMAGE.

'Protocols!' Henry shrieked. 'Protocols!' His panic deepened. 'PROTOCOLS!'

Then he was being drawn rapidly upwards, in bewildering defiance of gravity; higher, faster through a pitch black vertical tunnel and crashed, with a stark bolus of terror emptying into his veins, through into consciousness.

Awake mode. Full hunter-gatherer consciousness.

At least, he thought he was awake, but he could never be quite sure of anything these days. He lay very still, fear shorting through him as the nightmare receded, trying to make coherence out of his surroundings. The same nightmare he had night after night, and it felt so damned real – except what the hell was reality these days? Life was confusing, one seamless time-space continuum of complete muddle. He stared blankly at the fractals on the pillow beside him.

Hundreds of them. Thousands. Millions in fact, all needing assembling to make a coherent image of his wife. He always compressed her when he went to sleep (to save storage space on his hard disk – or brain as he still preferred to call it), but it was a hassle making sense of her again, like having to do a fiendish jigsaw puzzle every morning and do it in a ludicrously brief fragment of time. Sod it, how much smaller could time get? It had already gone from a picosecond to a nanosecond to an attosecond. An attosecond was to one second what one second was from now back to the Big Bang ... and he had to assemble the puzzle in just one tiny fraction of that.

'Morning, darling,' Susan said with a sleepy smile, as the jumble of pixels rearranged themselves into a solid image of his wife, tangles of brown hair across her face. 'Struth, she looked so lifelike, Henry thought, just the way he always remembered her – but so she should be. He leaned across to kiss her. There was nothing there, of course, but he still kissed her every morning and she reciprocated with a tantalising pout and an expression that was dangerously close to a smirk, as if she had some secret she was keeping from him. She giggled exactly the way she did every morning, and said, 'Oh darling, I wish, I wish!'

He watched her get out of bed, and felt a sudden prick of lust as she arched her naked body, tossed her hair, strode to the bathroom. The door slammed shut. God, they hadn't made love since ... since? He trawled his memory racks – no banks – no, cells, yes, brain cells – *wetware* they called it – but could not remember when they had last made love. He couldn't even remember when he had last *remembered* making love. The muddle was definitely worsening.

Brain Overload Stress Syndrome. It had become the Western world's most common illness. The brain filled up, could not cope with new input, creating a sense of panic and confusion. Henry had been suffering from BOSS for some while now. The symptoms were so clear to him he hadn't even bothered going to the doctor for confirmation: there was just too much bloody band-width in the world.

He sat up in alarm. *I cannot make love to my wife because she does not exist, or rather she exists only in my memory. I am the sole reality.* Then he said what he always said when he needed to reassure himself:

Cogito, ergo sum.

Susan had been dead for two years now, but he had still not got used to it, still got cheated by the cruel dreams in which she was there, they were laughing, kissing, sometimes even making love; the dreams, yes, old times, good times. Gone.

But not entirely gone. Henry could hear her now in the bathroom. It was all part of the Post Deanimation program hologram model PermaLife-7. Behind closed doors she made the sounds of ablutions, creating the illusion that she was still alive.

A few seconds later, at exactly 06.30 European Central Time, the synthesised voice of the MinuteManager personal organiser kicked in: 'Good morning, Mr & Mrs Garrick. It is Thursday, November 17th, 2045.'

Henry realised now what was wrong. Susan had got up before the alarm. She *never* got up before the alarm. Ever.

The MinuteManager continued breezily: 'Here are the headlines of today's on-line *Telegraph* that I think will interest you. I will bring you editorial updates as I come across them during the next hour. Delegates from the World Union of Concerned Scientists will today be pressing for international legislation limiting the cerebral capacity of sentient computers ... Parliament today will debate the first stage in the reduction of the House of Commons power in favour of government by consensus on the Internet ... And the Prime Minister is arriving at Stormont Castle this morning for a fresh round of peace talks.'

'You're up early, darling,' Henry said as Susan came back into the bedroom.

'Busy day,' she murmured in her gravelly voice, then began rummaging through her wardrobe, pausing every few moments to select a dress and hold it against herself in the mirror.

Breakfast, he thought. That was missing these days. She used to bring him breakfast in bed, on a tray. Tea, toast, cereal, a boiled egg. He was a creature of habit and she had prepared him the same breakfast every day of their marriage. He depended on her for everything, that's why he had wanted to keep her on after her death. 'Where's my breakfast?' he said grumpily. Except, somewhere in his addled memory, an assortment of bytes of stored information arranged themselves into a message informing him he had not eaten breakfast for two years. But they failed to yield the information as to why not.

It was terrible, but he had great difficulty remembering anything about Susan's death, he realised guiltily. It was as if he had stored the memory in some compartment and had forgotten where. One moment they had been contentedly married and the next moment she was no more. At least, not flesh and blood.

Henry Garrick could have had a full body replica of his wife. But robot technology still had not perfected limb and muscle movement, so FBRs – as full body replicas are known – tended to move with a clumsy articulation that made them look like retards. He had opted instead for a hologram – the standard Post Deanimation program hologram model PermaLife-7.

Susan-2, as he had called her, was connected through a cordless digital satellite link to an on-line brain download databank, named ARCHIVE 4, and a network of lasers concealed in the walls gave her the ability to move freely around much of the apartment, though not of course beyond. The entire transformation of Susan from a wetware (flesh and blood) mortal, into a hardware (digitised silicon) virtual mortal had been handled by the undertakers.

Death was a taboo word these days. Deanimation; or Suspended Animation; or Altered Sentient Condition or even Metabolically Challenged, were more accurate descriptions – at least, for anyone who took the consciousness download option offered by most leading funeral directors these days as a pre-death service. 'Struth, Henry thought, the array of options was bewildering for both the living and the downloaded. Options in everything: Static Books; Interactive Books; Virtual Reality; Alternative Reality. And, of course, good old Television still had its following.

No one knew how many channels there were now. His MinuteManager trawled the airwaves around the clock for programmes fitting Henry's taste parameters. It then divided them into two categories – those Henry would actually watch and those it would load straight into Henry's brain via his silicon interface, so that he would simply have the memory of having watched them.

'There's some good legal retro from the last century on tonight,' the MinuteManager announced. '*LA Law, Kramer vs Kramer, Perry Mason, Ironside, The Firm, Lawman, Rumpole of the Bailey*. Would you care to watch any in real time or compressed time?'

For some moments, Henry Garrick did not answer. He was still wondering why his wife had got up so early. Perhaps there was a problem with one of her modules – perhaps he should call an engineer and have her looked at under the maintenance contract – if he could remember who the hell it was with. Then her voice startled him.

'Goodbye darling, have a nice day,' Susan-2 said.

She was going out! She wasn't supposed to go out ... There wasn't any way she could go out. 'Hey!' he shouted. 'Hey, where the hell are you going?'

It was nearly midnight when Susan came back. She reeked of booze and smoke and had her arms around a man.

'Where have you been?' Henry yelled at his wife. 'And who the hell is this creep?'

To Henry's chagrin, Susan didn't even respond. She did not even look at him!

'I thought I would miss him,' Susan said, quietly to her new boyfriend, Sam. 'I thought it would be nice to continue having him around the house. The problem is he's never realised he is dead – can you believe it? – he thought it was me who died! Poor sod, he was getting terribly muddled towards the end of his life.

'It's spooky the way he looks at me sometimes. I mean, he's just a hologram guided by a few bits of data, but it's as if he's still alive, still sentient. And he seems to be getting more and more so every day. He actually got mad at me for going out this morning! I guess it's time to call a halt.'

'Yes,' Sam agreed, staring uneasily at the quivering hologram. 'There comes a time when you have to let go.'

Susan lifted her arm and pressed the switch.